CHEER UP!

LOVE AND POMPOMS

CHEER UP! LOVE AND POMPOMS

WRITTEN BY **CRYSTAL FRASIER**

ART BY **VAL WISE**

LETTERED BY **OSCAR O. JUPITER**

AN ONI PRESS PUBLICATION

Dedicated to Aunty Jen

Your love saved a thousand children.
We will use it to save a hundred thousand more.

—Crystal

Designed by **HILARY THOMPSON**
with **KATE Z. STONE**

Edited by **SHAWNA GORE**
with **ROBIN HERRERA** and **ARI YARWOOD**

PUBLISHED BY ONI-LION FORGE PUBLISHING GROUP, LLC

JAMES LUCAS JONES, president & publisher · **SARAH GAYDOS,** editor in chief · **CHARLIE CHU,** e.v.p. of creative & business development · **BRAD ROOKS,** director of operations · **AMBER O'NEILL,** special projects manager · **MARGOT WOOD,** director of marketing & sales · **KATIE SAINZ,** marketing manager · **TARA LEHMANN,** publicist · **HOLLY AITCHISON,** consumer marketing manager **TROY LOOK,** director of design & production **KATE Z. STONE,** senior graphic designer · **HILARY THOMPSON,** graphic designer · **SARAH ROCKWELL,** graphic designer · **ANGIE KNOWLES,** digital prepress lead · **VINCENT KUKUA,** digital prepress technician · **JASMINE AMIRI,** senior editor · **SHAWNA GORE,** senior editor · **AMANDA MEADOWS,** senior editor · **ROBERT MEYERS,** senior editor, licensing · **DESIREE RODRIGUEZ,** editor **GRACE SCHEIPETER,** editor · **ZACK SOTO,** editor **CHRIS CERASI,** editorial coordinator · **STEVE ELLIS,** vice president of games · **BEN EISNER,** game developer · **MICHELLE NGUYEN,** executive assistant **JUNG LEE,** logistics coordinator

JOE NOZEMACK, publisher emeritus

onipress.com
🔲 f 🐦 @onipress

🐦 @AmazonChique
🐦 🔲 @valkwise

First edition: August 2021

ISBN 978-1-62010-955-7
eISBN 978-1-62010-956-4

PRINTED IN CANADA.

Library of Congress Control Number 2021936125

10 9 8 7 6 5 4 3 2 1

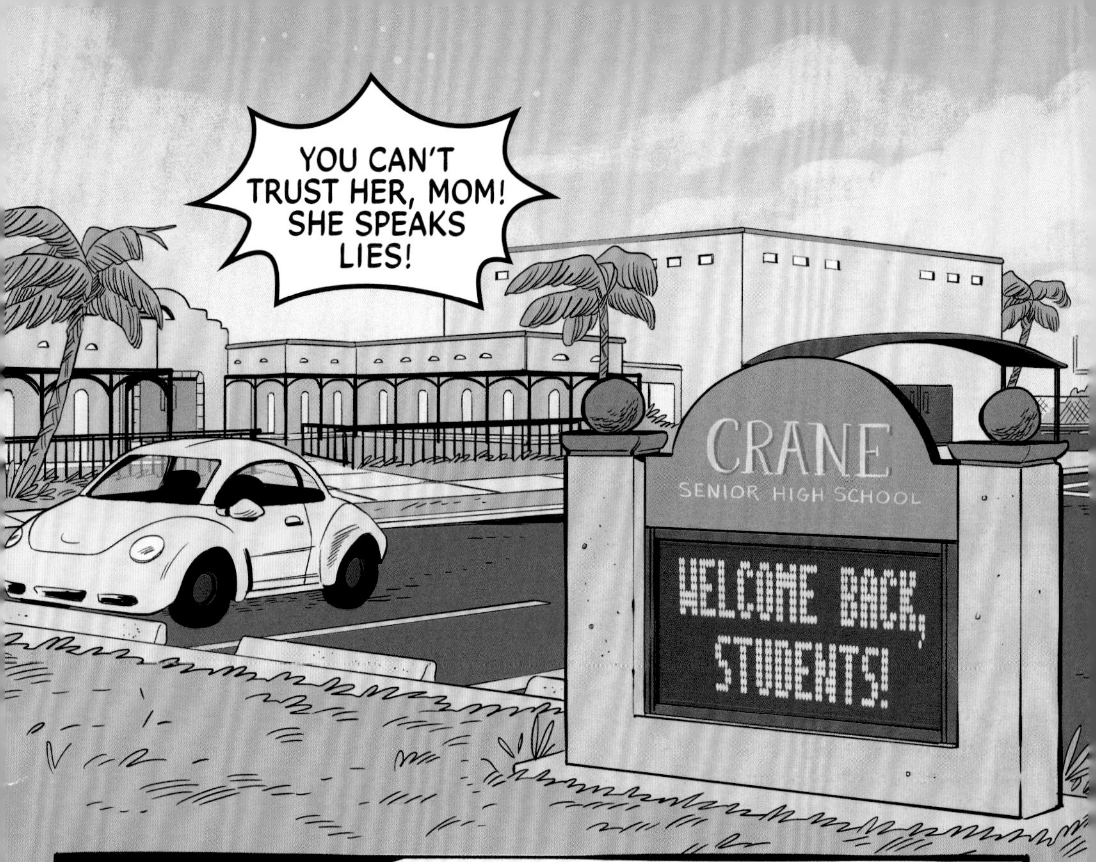
YOU CAN'T TRUST HER, MOM! SHE SPEAKS LIES!
CRANE
SENIOR HIGH SCHOOL
WELCOME BACK, STUDENTS!

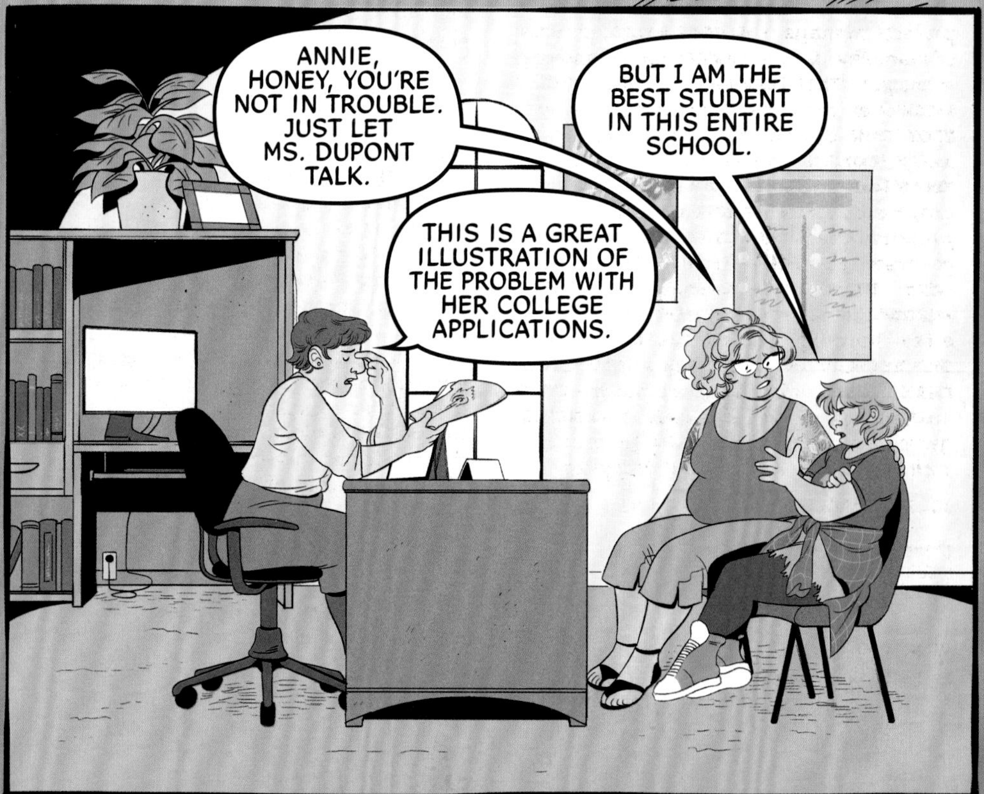
ANNIE, HONEY, YOU'RE NOT IN TROUBLE. JUST LET MS. DUPONT TALK.
BUT I AM THE BEST STUDENT IN THIS ENTIRE SCHOOL.
THIS IS A GREAT ILLUSTRATION OF THE PROBLEM WITH HER COLLEGE APPLICATIONS.

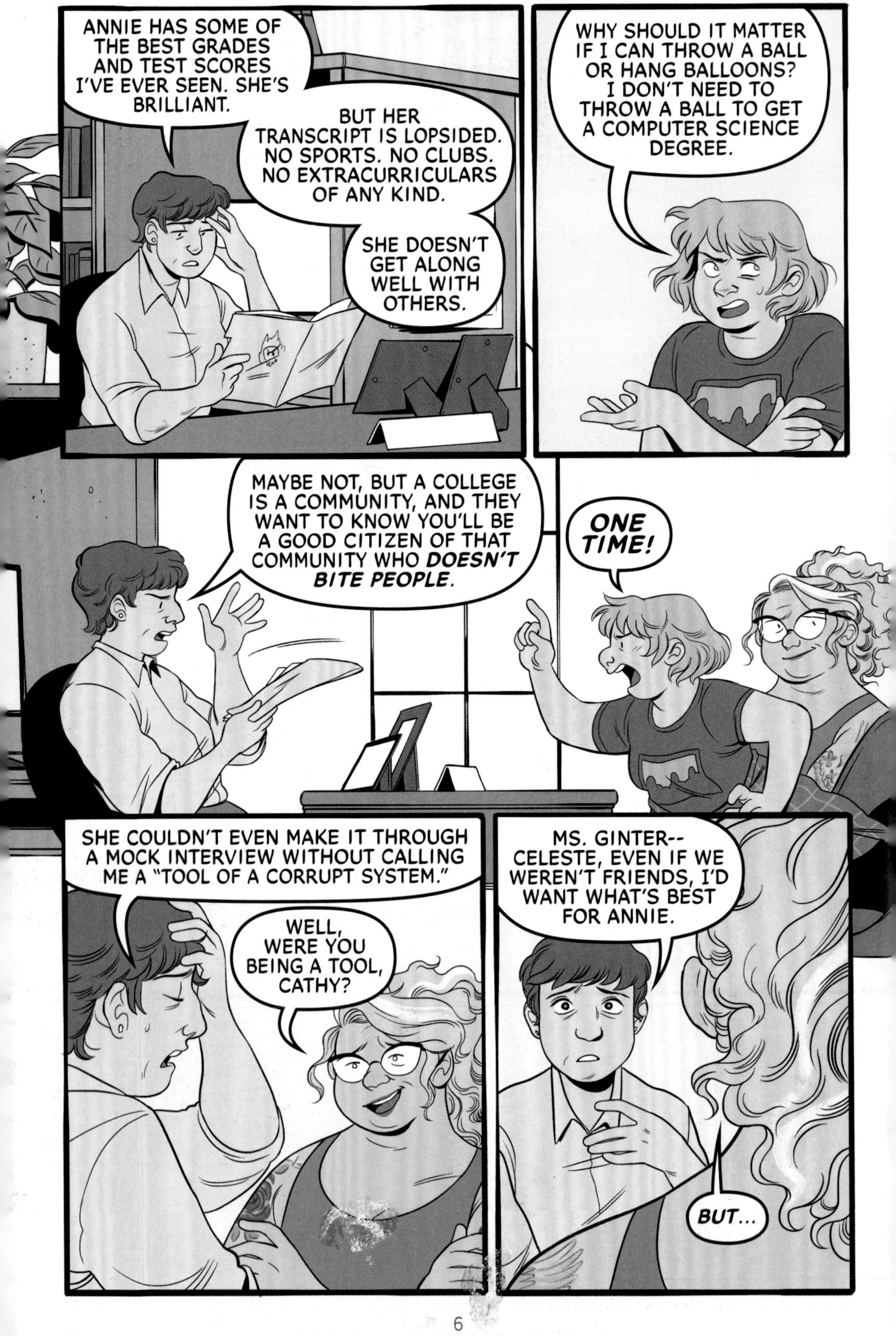
ANNIE HAS SOME OF THE BEST GRADES AND TEST SCORES I'VE EVER SEEN. SHE'S BRILLIANT.
BUT HER TRANSCRIPT IS LOPSIDED. NO SPORTS. NO CLUBS. NO EXTRACURRICULARS OF ANY KIND.
SHE DOESN'T GET ALONG WELL WITH OTHERS.
WHY SHOULD IT MATTER IF I CAN THROW A BALL OR HANG BALLOONS? I DON'T NEED TO THROW A BALL TO GET A COMPUTER SCIENCE DEGREE.
MAYBE NOT, BUT A COLLEGE IS A COMMUNITY, AND THEY WANT TO KNOW YOU'LL BE A GOOD CITIZEN OF THAT COMMUNITY WHO ***DOESN'T BITE PEOPLE***.
ONE TIME!
SHE COULDN'T EVEN MAKE IT THROUGH A MOCK INTERVIEW WITHOUT CALLING ME A "TOOL OF A CORRUPT SYSTEM."
WELL, WERE YOU BEING A TOOL, CATHY?
MS. GINTER-- CELESTE, EVEN IF WE WEREN'T FRIENDS, I'D WANT WHAT'S BEST FOR ANNIE.
BUT...

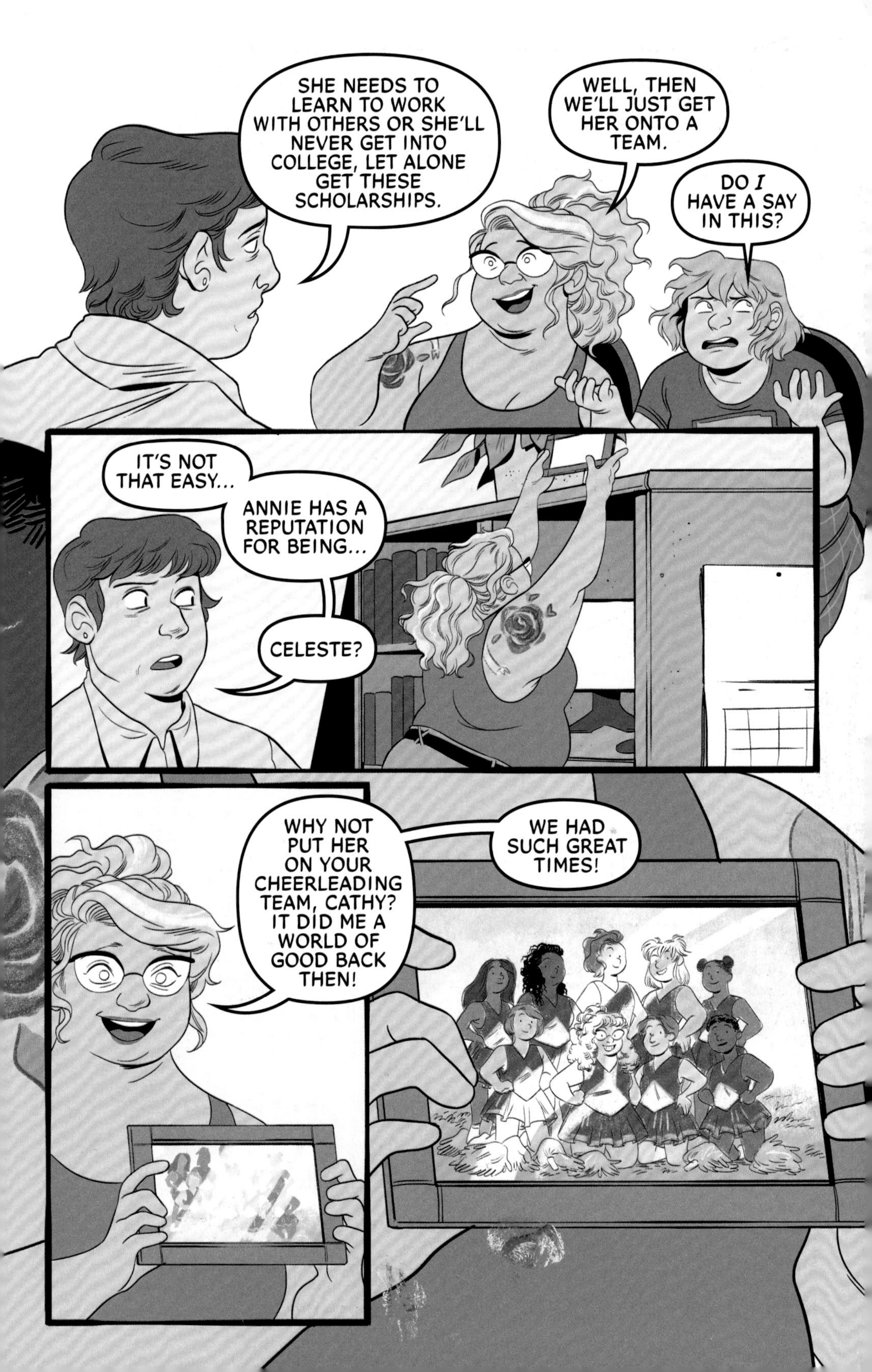
SHE NEEDS TO LEARN TO WORK WITH OTHERS OR SHE'LL NEVER GET INTO COLLEGE, LET ALONE GET THESE SCHOLARSHIPS.
WELL, THEN WE'LL JUST GET HER ONTO A TEAM.
DO *I* HAVE A SAY IN THIS?
IT'S NOT THAT EASY...
ANNIE HAS A REPUTATION FOR BEING...
CELESTE?
WHY NOT PUT HER ON YOUR CHEERLEADING TEAM, CATHY? IT DID ME A WORLD OF GOOD BACK THEN!
WE HAD SUCH GREAT TIMES!

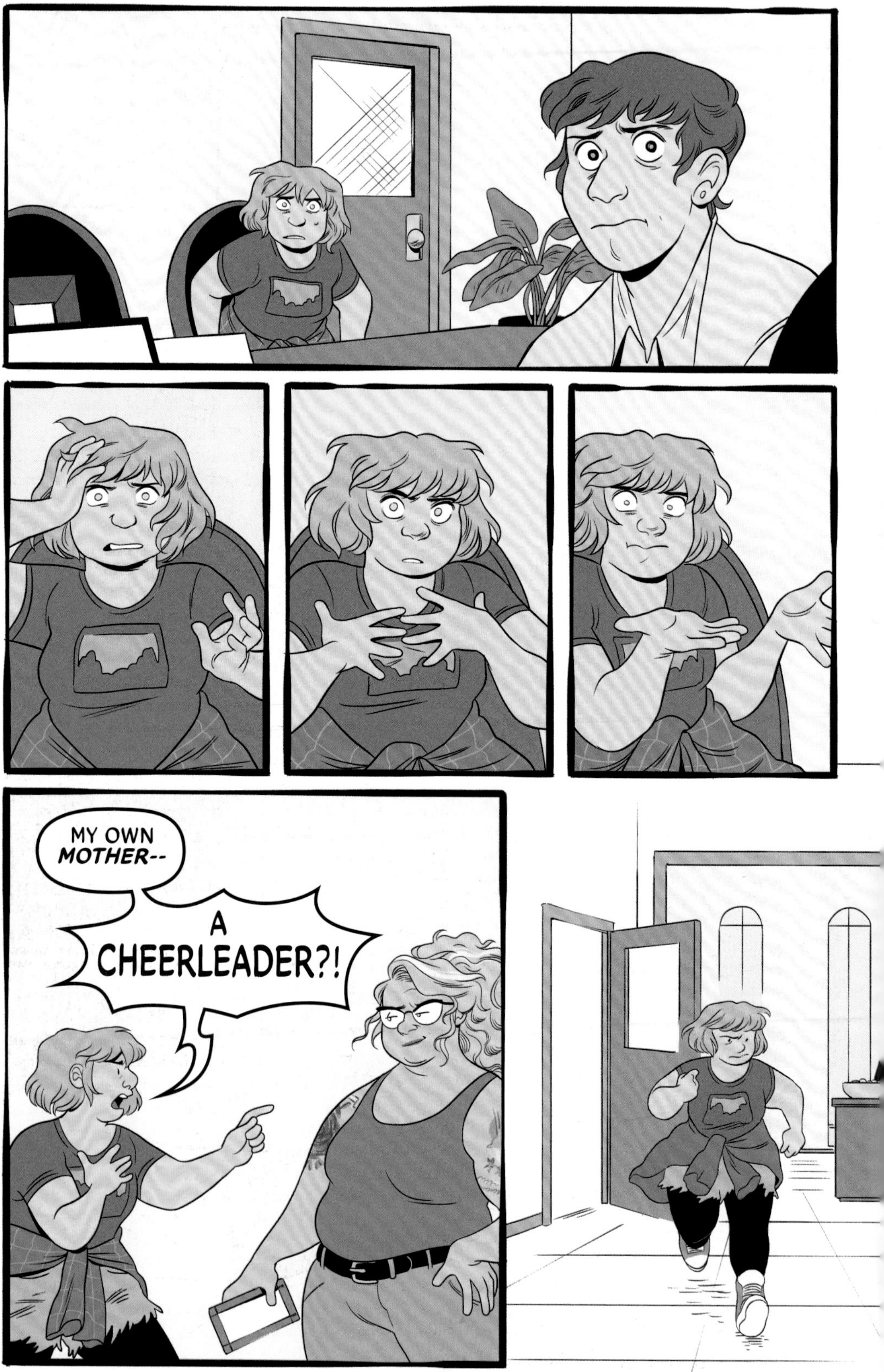
MY OWN MOTHER--
A CHEERLEADER?!

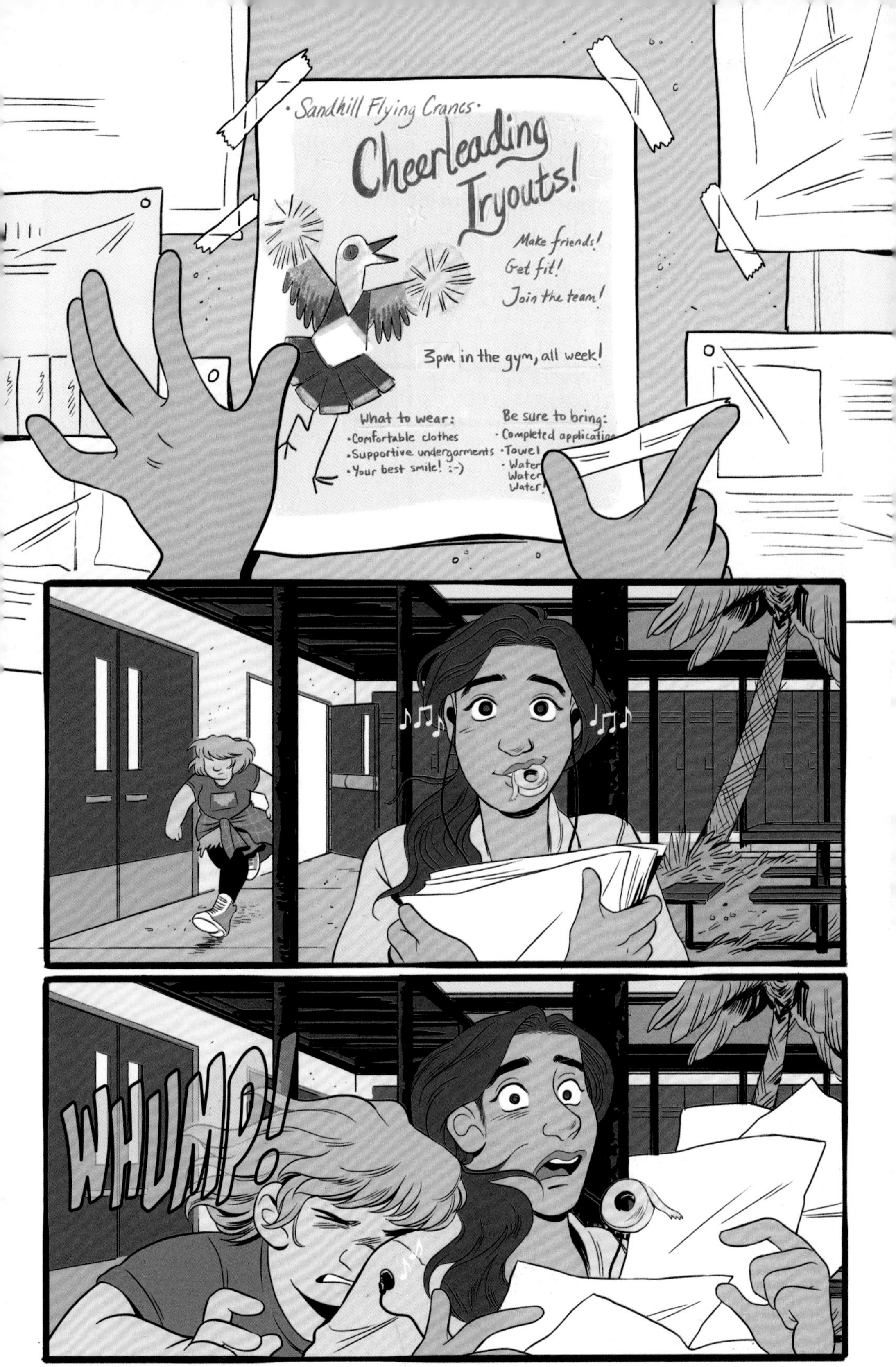

·Sandhill Flying Cranes·
Cheerleading Tryouts!
Make friends!
Get fit!
Join the team!
3pm in the gym, all week!
What to wear:
·Comfortable clothes
·Supportive undergarments
·Your best smile! :-)
Be sure to bring:
·Completed applica
·Towel
·Water
Water
Water
WHUMP!

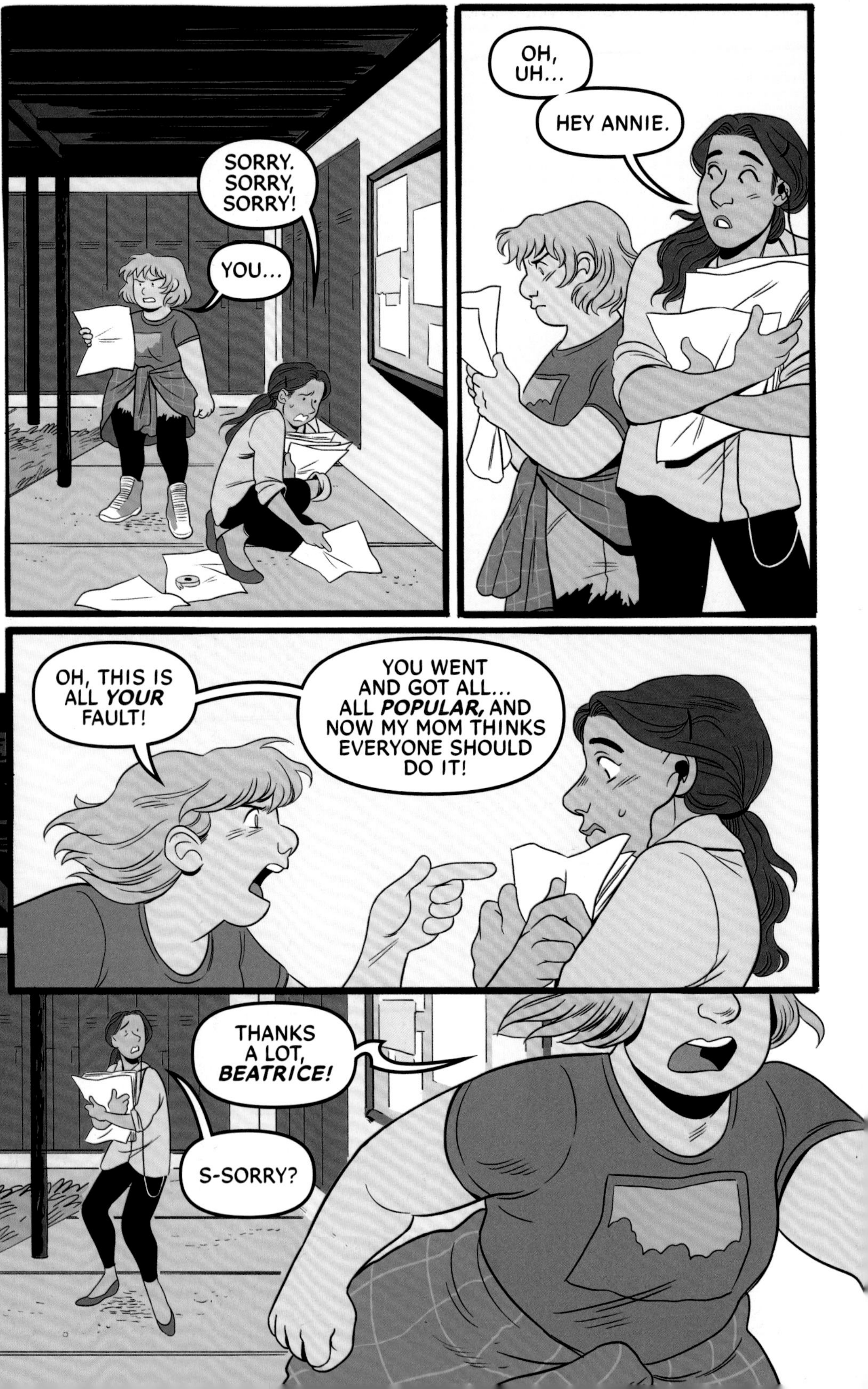
SORRY. SORRY, SORRY!
YOU...
OH, UH...
HEY ANNIE.
OH, THIS IS ALL *YOUR* FAULT!
YOU WENT AND GOT ALL... ALL *POPULAR,* AND NOW MY MOM THINKS EVERYONE SHOULD DO IT!
THANKS A LOT, *BEATRICE!*
S-SORRY?

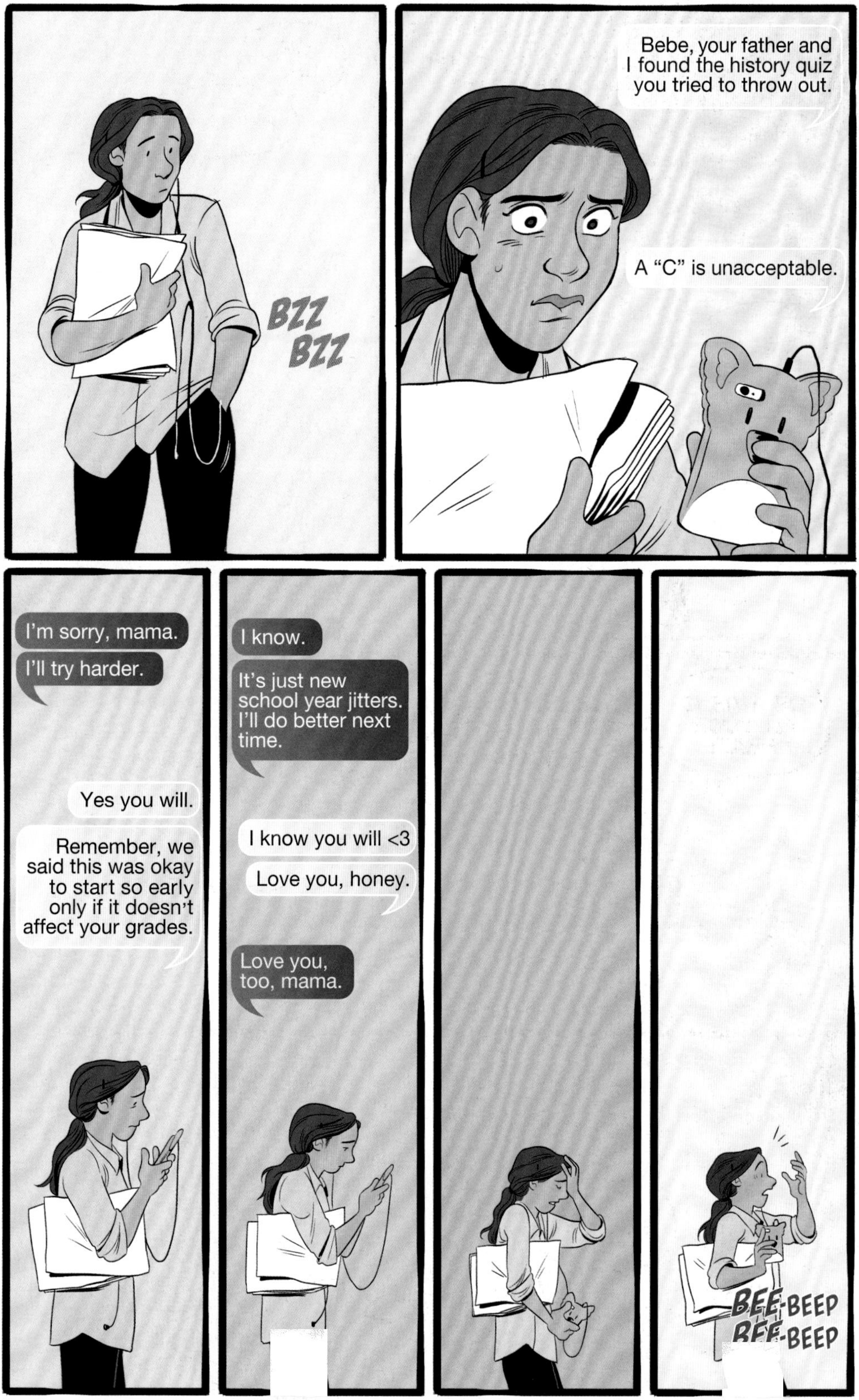
BZZ
BZZ
Bebe, your father and I found the history quiz you tried to throw out.
A "C" is unacceptable.
I'm sorry, mama.
I'll try harder.
Yes you will.
Remember, we said this was okay to start so early only if it doesn't affect your grades.
I know.
It's just new school year jitters. I'll do better next time.
I know you will <3
Love you, honey.
Love you, too, mama.
BEE-BEEP
BEE-BEEP

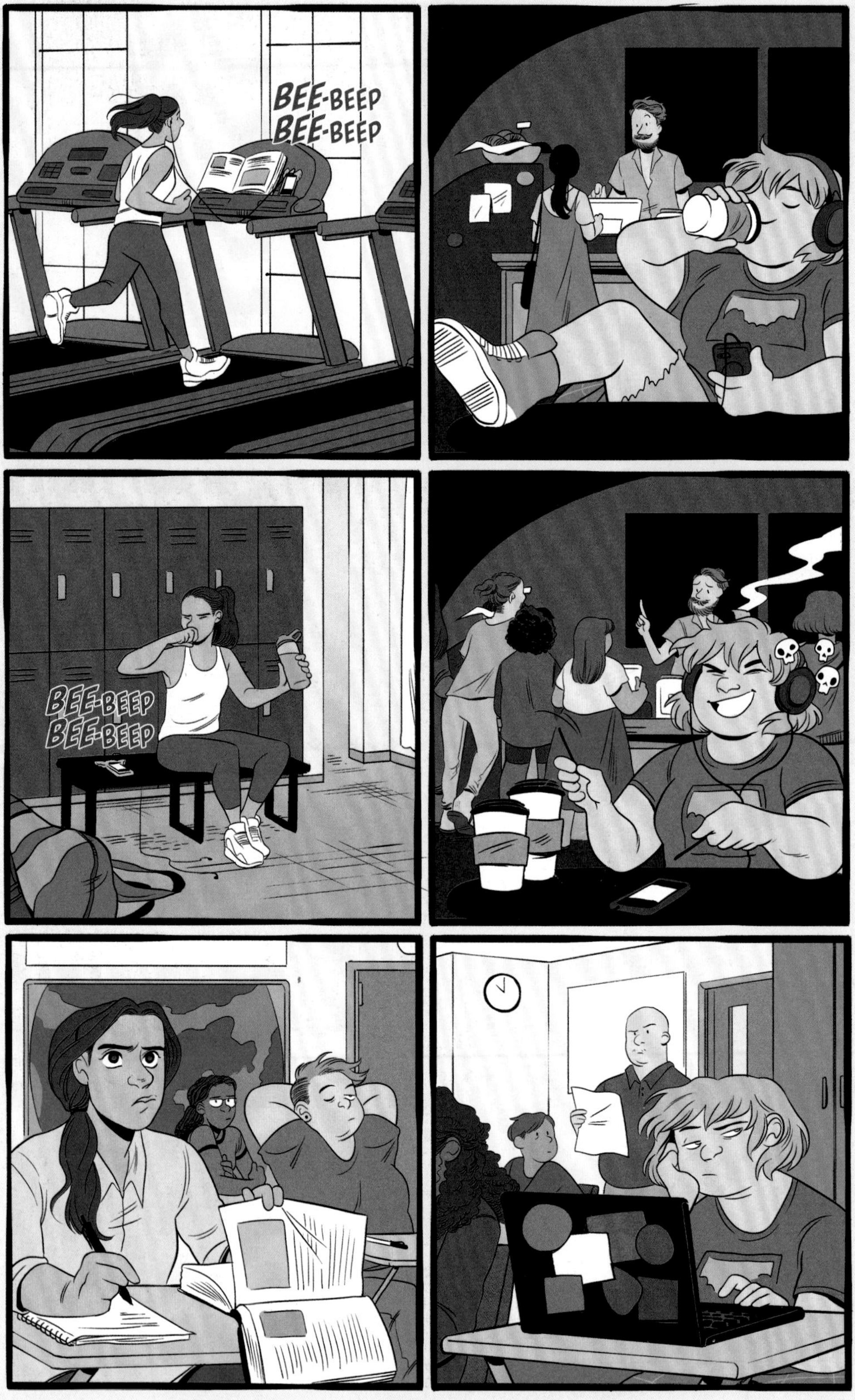
BEE-BEEP
BEE-BEEP
BEE-BEEP
BEE-BEEP

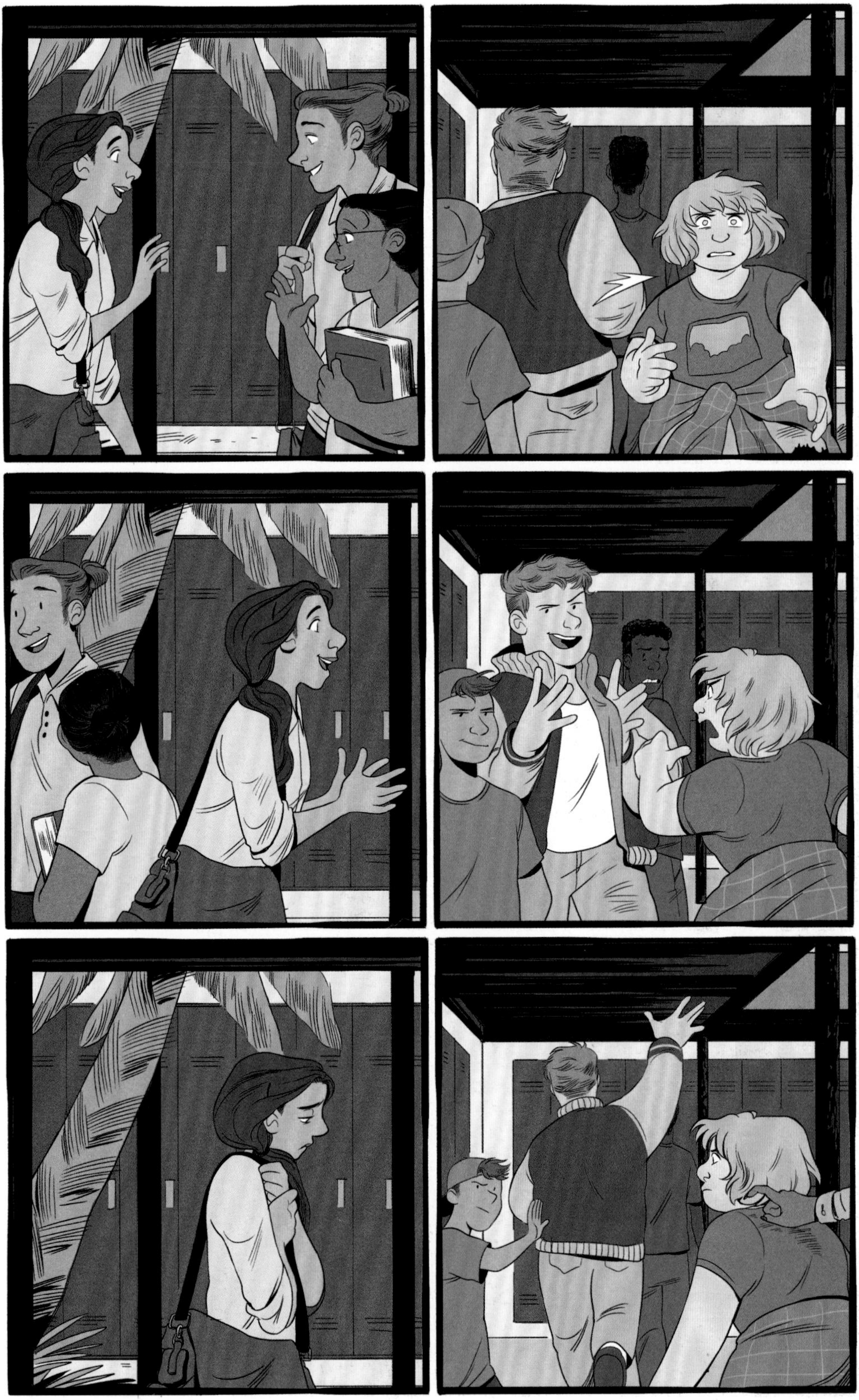

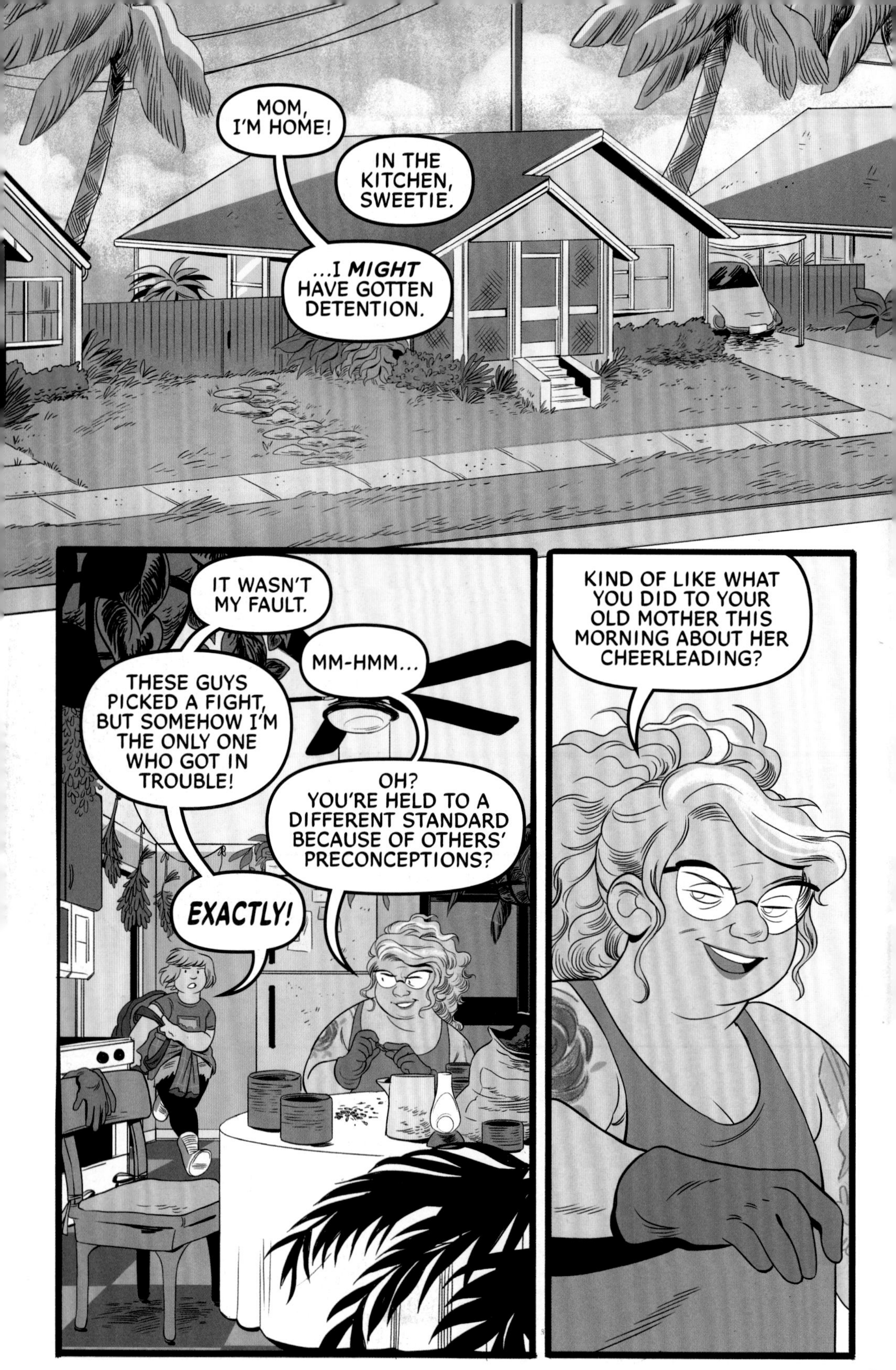
MOM, I'M HOME!
IN THE KITCHEN, SWEETIE.
...I *MIGHT* HAVE GOTTEN DETENTION.
IT WASN'T MY FAULT.
MM-HMM...
THESE GUYS PICKED A FIGHT, BUT SOMEHOW I'M THE ONLY ONE WHO GOT IN TROUBLE!
OH? YOU'RE HELD TO A DIFFERENT STANDARD BECAUSE OF OTHERS' PRECONCEPTIONS?
EXACTLY!
KIND OF LIKE WHAT YOU DID TO YOUR OLD MOTHER THIS MORNING ABOUT HER CHEERLEADING?

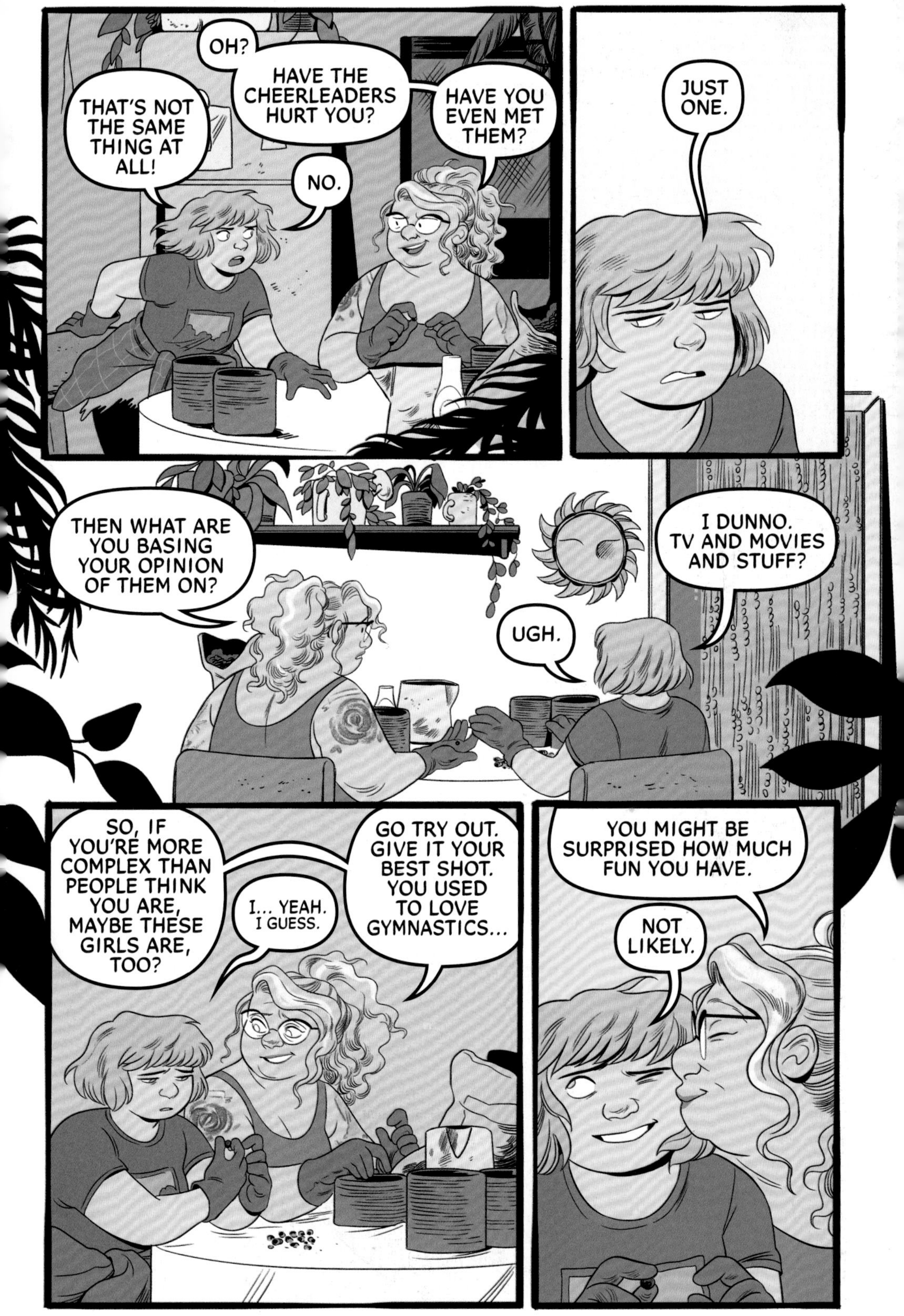
THAT'S NOT THE SAME THING AT ALL!
OH?
HAVE THE CHEERLEADERS HURT YOU?
NO.
HAVE YOU EVEN MET THEM?
JUST ONE.
THEN WHAT ARE YOU BASING YOUR OPINION OF THEM ON?
I DUNNO. TV AND MOVIES AND STUFF?
UGH.
SO, IF YOU'RE MORE COMPLEX THAN PEOPLE THINK YOU ARE, MAYBE THESE GIRLS ARE, TOO?
I... YEAH. I GUESS.
GO TRY OUT. GIVE IT YOUR BEST SHOT. YOU USED TO LOVE GYMNASTICS...
YOU MIGHT BE SURPRISED HOW MUCH FUN YOU HAVE.
NOT LIKELY.

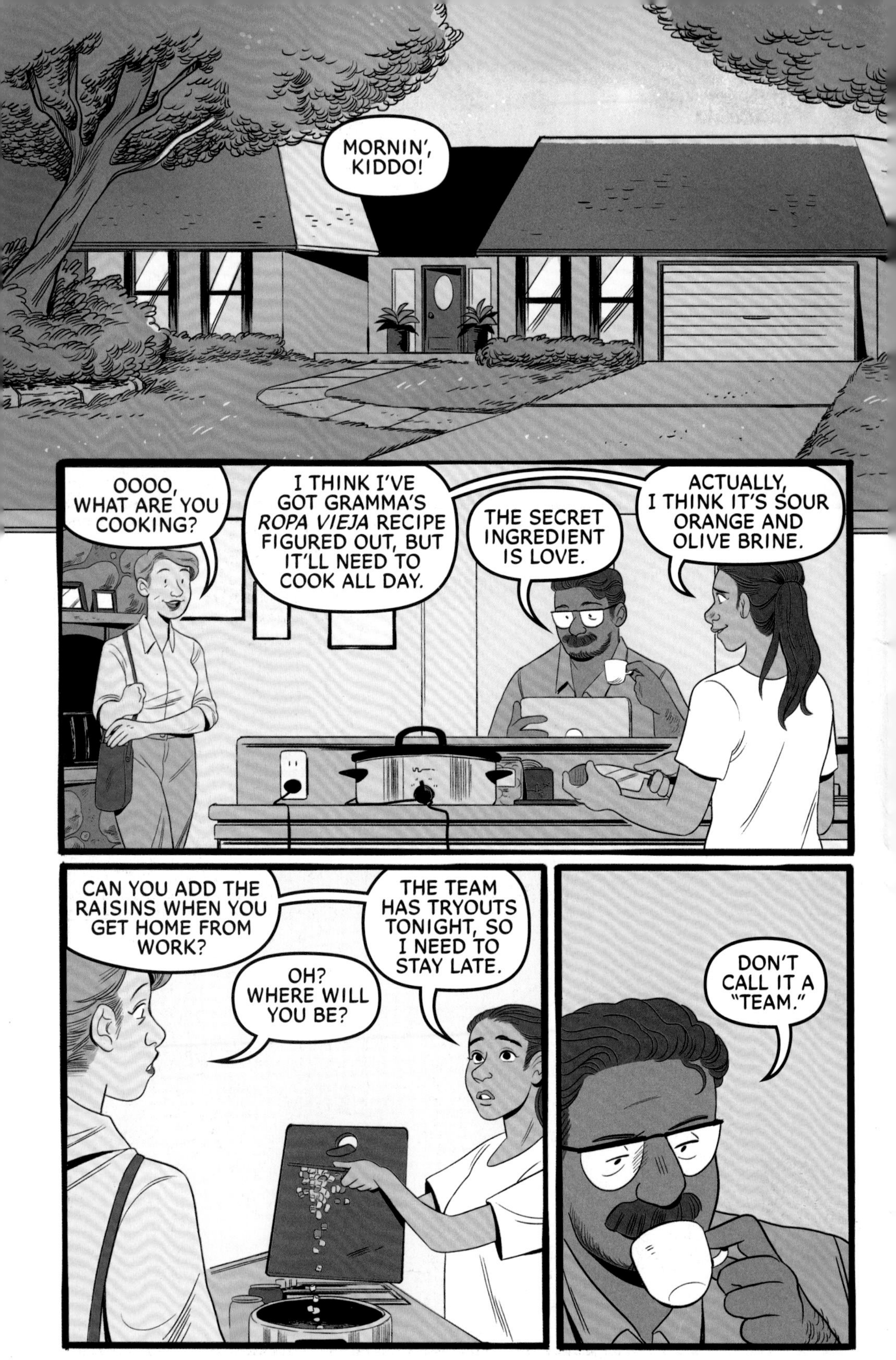
MORNIN', KIDDO!
OOOO, WHAT ARE YOU COOKING?
I THINK I'VE GOT GRAMMA'S *ROPA VIEJA* RECIPE FIGURED OUT, BUT IT'LL NEED TO COOK ALL DAY.
THE SECRET INGREDIENT IS LOVE.
ACTUALLY, I THINK IT'S SOUR ORANGE AND OLIVE BRINE.
CAN YOU ADD THE RAISINS WHEN YOU GET HOME FROM WORK?
THE TEAM HAS TRYOUTS TONIGHT, SO I NEED TO STAY LATE.
OH? WHERE WILL YOU BE?
DON'T CALL IT A "TEAM."

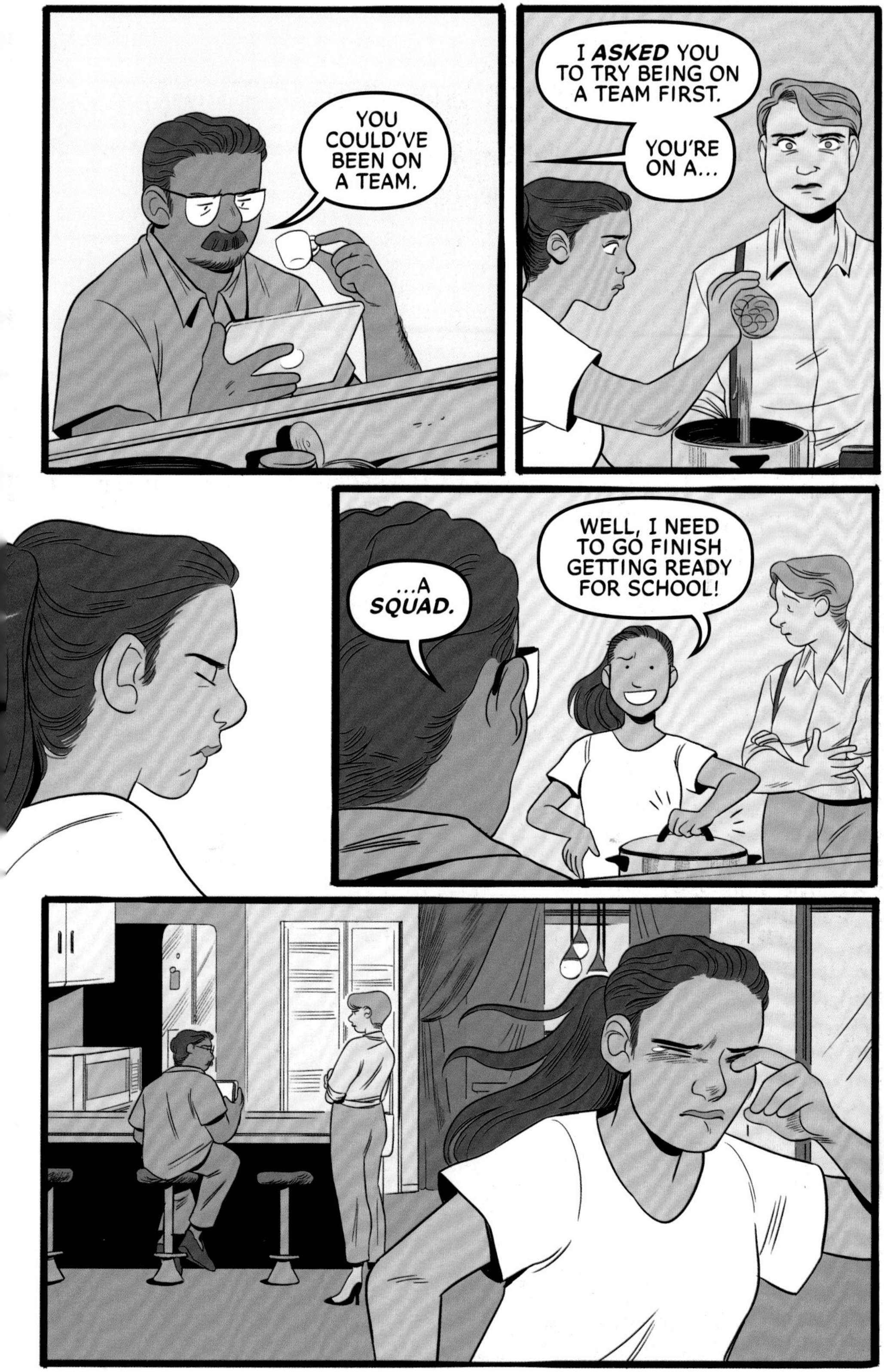
YOU COULD'VE BEEN ON A TEAM.
I ASKED YOU TO TRY BEING ON A TEAM FIRST.
YOU'RE ON A...
...A SQUAD.
WELL, I NEED TO GO FINISH GETTING READY FOR SCHOOL!

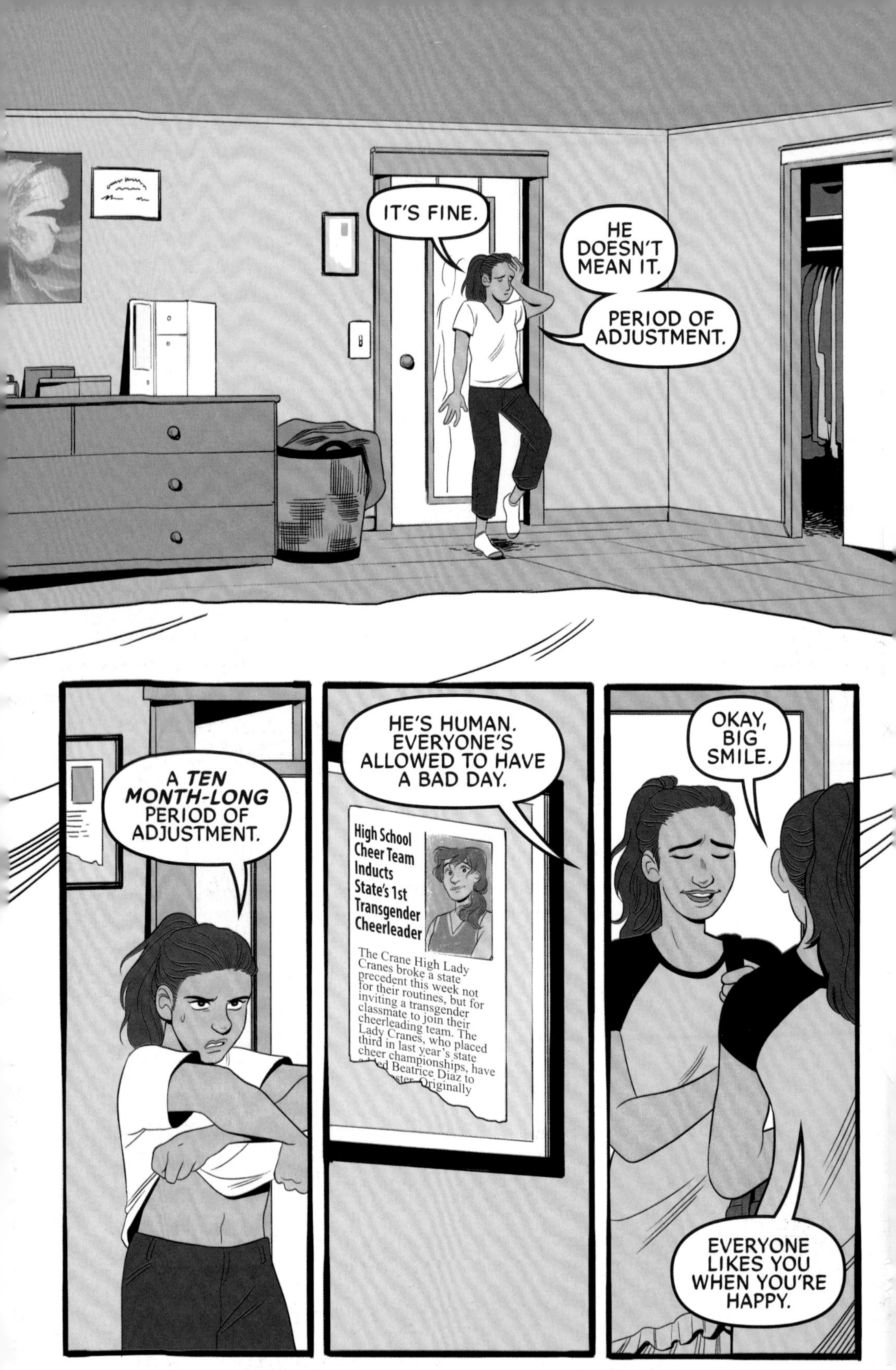
IT'S FINE.
HE DOESN'T MEAN IT.
PERIOD OF ADJUSTMENT.
A *TEN MONTH-LONG* PERIOD OF ADJUSTMENT.
HE'S HUMAN. EVERYONE'S ALLOWED TO HAVE A BAD DAY.
High School Cheer Team Inducts State's 1st Transgender Cheerleader
The Crane High Lady Cranes broke a state precedent this week not for their routines, but for inviting a transgender classmate to join their cheerleading team. The Lady Cranes, who placed third in last year's state cheer championships, have
Beatrice Diaz to
Originally
OKAY, BIG SMILE.
EVERYONE LIKES YOU WHEN YOU'RE HAPPY.

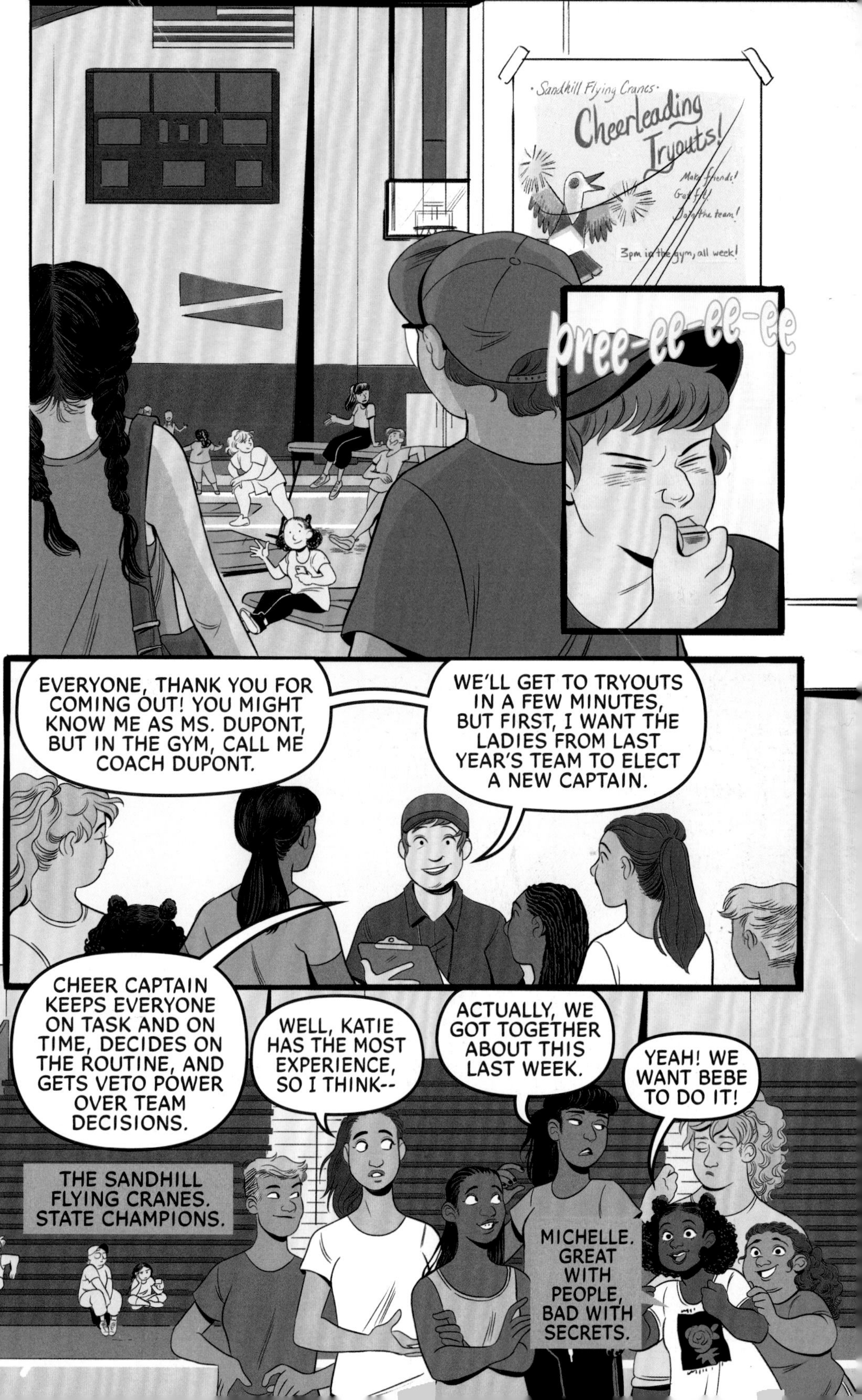
· Sandhill Flying Cranes ·
Cheerleading Tryouts!
3pm in the gym, all week!
pree-ee-ee-ee
EVERYONE, THANK YOU FOR COMING OUT! YOU MIGHT KNOW ME AS MS. DUPONT, BUT IN THE GYM, CALL ME COACH DUPONT.
WE'LL GET TO TRYOUTS IN A FEW MINUTES, BUT FIRST, I WANT THE LADIES FROM LAST YEAR'S TEAM TO ELECT A NEW CAPTAIN.
CHEER CAPTAIN KEEPS EVERYONE ON TASK AND ON TIME, DECIDES ON THE ROUTINE, AND GETS VETO POWER OVER TEAM DECISIONS.
WELL, KATIE HAS THE MOST EXPERIENCE, SO I THINK--
ACTUALLY, WE GOT TOGETHER ABOUT THIS LAST WEEK.
YEAH! WE WANT BEBE TO DO IT!
THE SANDHILL FLYING CRANES. STATE CHAMPIONS.
MICHELLE. GREAT WITH PEOPLE, BAD WITH SECRETS.

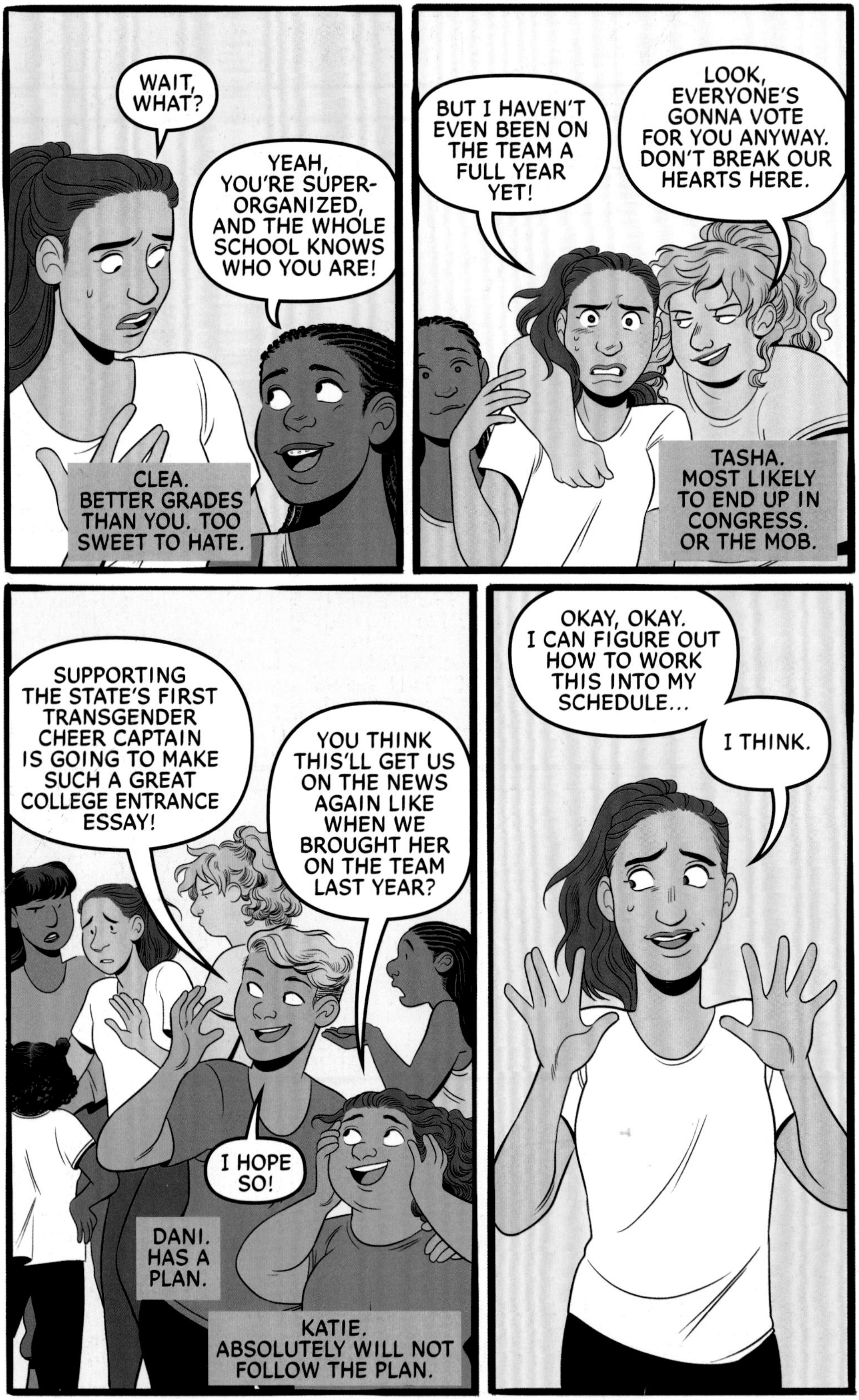
WAIT, WHAT?
YEAH, YOU'RE SUPER-ORGANIZED, AND THE WHOLE SCHOOL KNOWS WHO YOU ARE!
CLEA. BETTER GRADES THAN YOU. TOO SWEET TO HATE.
BUT I HAVEN'T EVEN BEEN ON THE TEAM A FULL YEAR YET!
LOOK, EVERYONE'S GONNA VOTE FOR YOU ANYWAY. DON'T BREAK OUR HEARTS HERE.
TASHA. MOST LIKELY TO END UP IN CONGRESS. OR THE MOB.
SUPPORTING THE STATE'S FIRST TRANSGENDER CHEER CAPTAIN IS GOING TO MAKE SUCH A GREAT COLLEGE ENTRANCE ESSAY!
YOU THINK THIS'LL GET US ON THE NEWS AGAIN LIKE WHEN WE BROUGHT HER ON THE TEAM LAST YEAR?
I HOPE SO!
DANI. HAS A PLAN.
KATIE. ABSOLUTELY WILL NOT FOLLOW THE PLAN.
OKAY, OKAY. I CAN FIGURE OUT HOW TO WORK THIS INTO MY SCHEDULE...
I THINK.

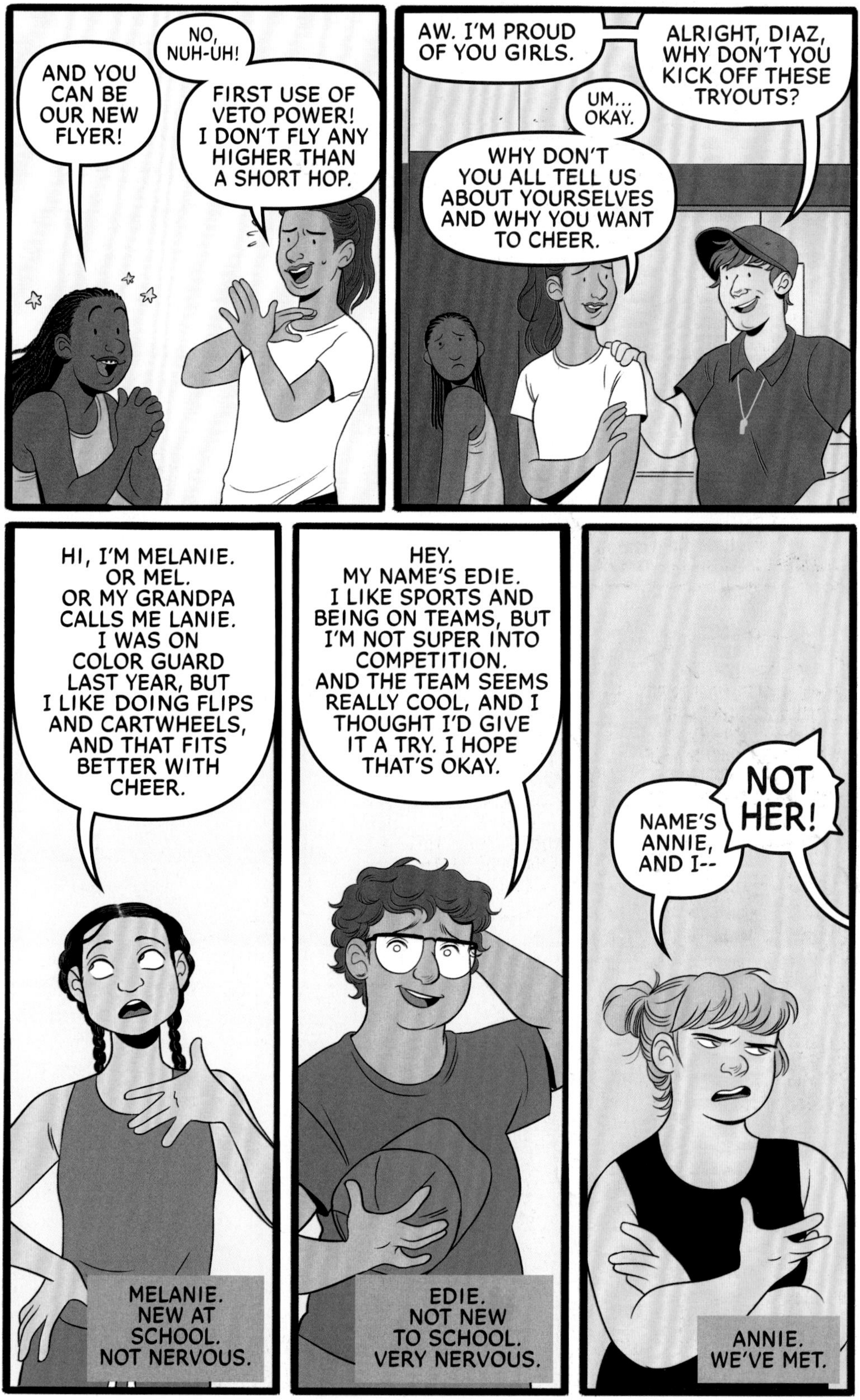
AND YOU CAN BE OUR NEW FLYER!
NO, NUH-UH!
FIRST USE OF VETO POWER! I DON'T FLY ANY HIGHER THAN A SHORT HOP.
AW. I'M PROUD OF YOU GIRLS.
ALRIGHT, DIAZ, WHY DON'T YOU KICK OFF THESE TRYOUTS?
UM... OKAY.
WHY DON'T YOU ALL TELL US ABOUT YOURSELVES AND WHY YOU WANT TO CHEER.
HI, I'M MELANIE. OR MEL. OR MY GRANDPA CALLS ME LANIE. I WAS ON COLOR GUARD LAST YEAR, BUT I LIKE DOING FLIPS AND CARTWHEELS, AND THAT FITS BETTER WITH CHEER.
MELANIE. NEW AT SCHOOL. NOT NERVOUS.
HEY. MY NAME'S EDIE. I LIKE SPORTS AND BEING ON TEAMS, BUT I'M NOT SUPER INTO COMPETITION. AND THE TEAM SEEMS REALLY COOL, AND I THOUGHT I'D GIVE IT A TRY. I HOPE THAT'S OKAY.
EDIE. NOT NEW TO SCHOOL. VERY NERVOUS.
NAME'S ANNIE, AND I--
NOT HER!
ANNIE. WE'VE MET.

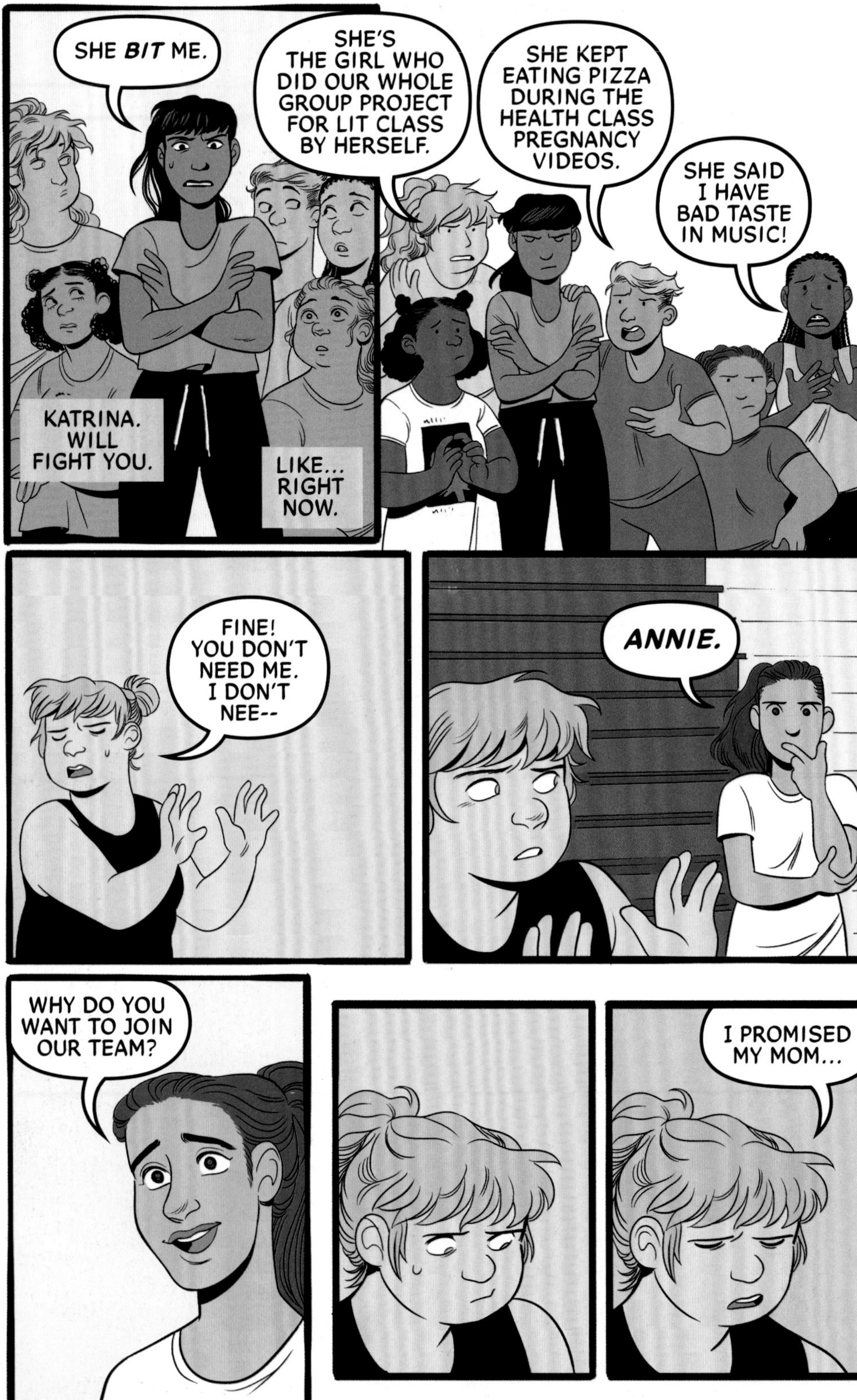
SHE *BIT* ME.
SHE'S THE GIRL WHO DID OUR WHOLE GROUP PROJECT FOR LIT CLASS BY HERSELF.
SHE KEPT EATING PIZZA DURING THE HEALTH CLASS PREGNANCY VIDEOS.
SHE SAID I HAVE BAD TASTE IN MUSIC!
KATRINA. WILL FIGHT YOU.
LIKE... RIGHT NOW.
FINE! YOU DON'T NEED ME. I DON'T NEE--
ANNIE.
WHY DO YOU WANT TO JOIN OUR TEAM?
I PROMISED MY MOM...

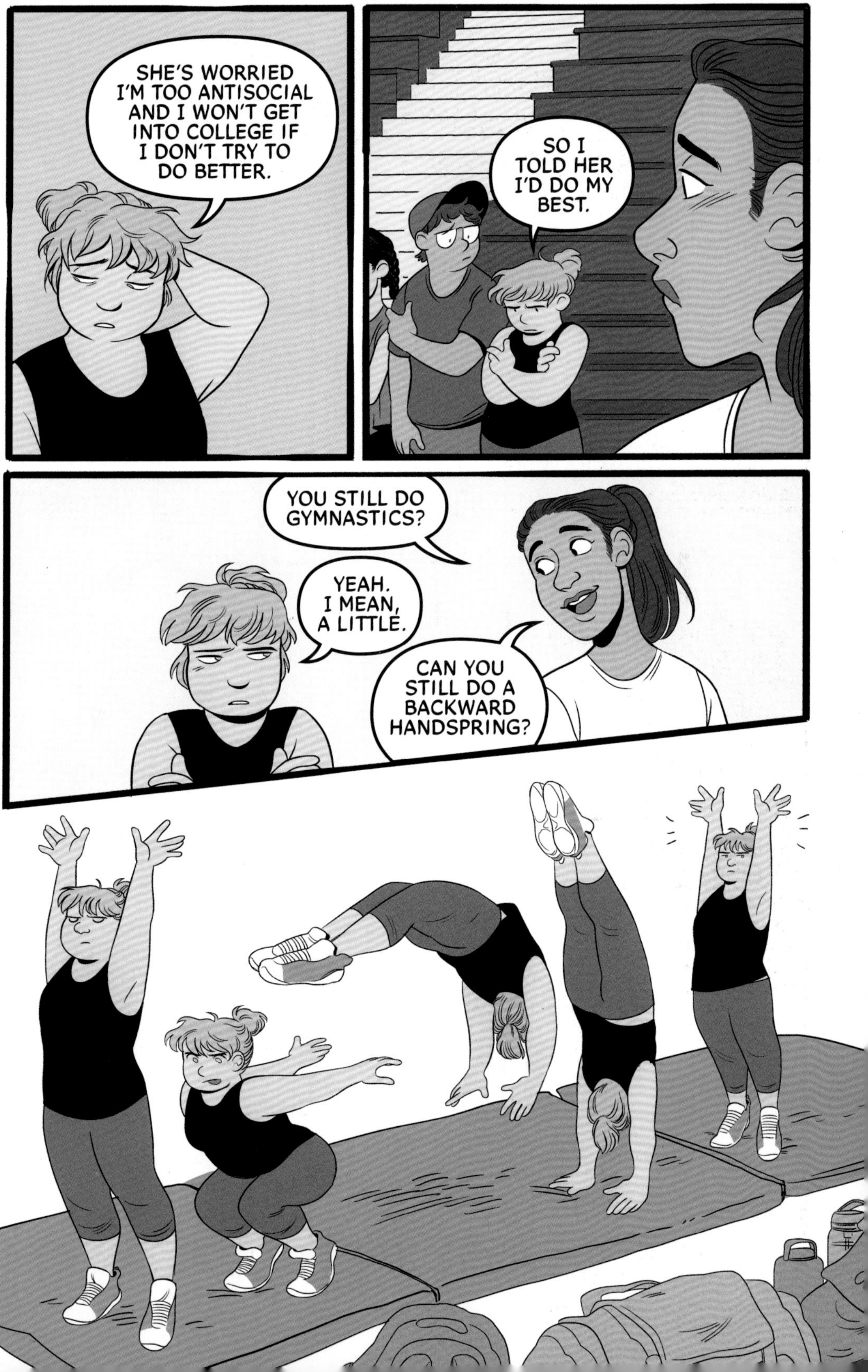
SHE'S WORRIED I'M TOO ANTISOCIAL AND I WON'T GET INTO COLLEGE IF I DON'T TRY TO DO BETTER.
SO I TOLD HER I'D DO MY BEST.
YOU STILL DO GYMNASTICS?
YEAH. I MEAN, A LITTLE.
CAN YOU STILL DO A BACKWARD HANDSPRING?

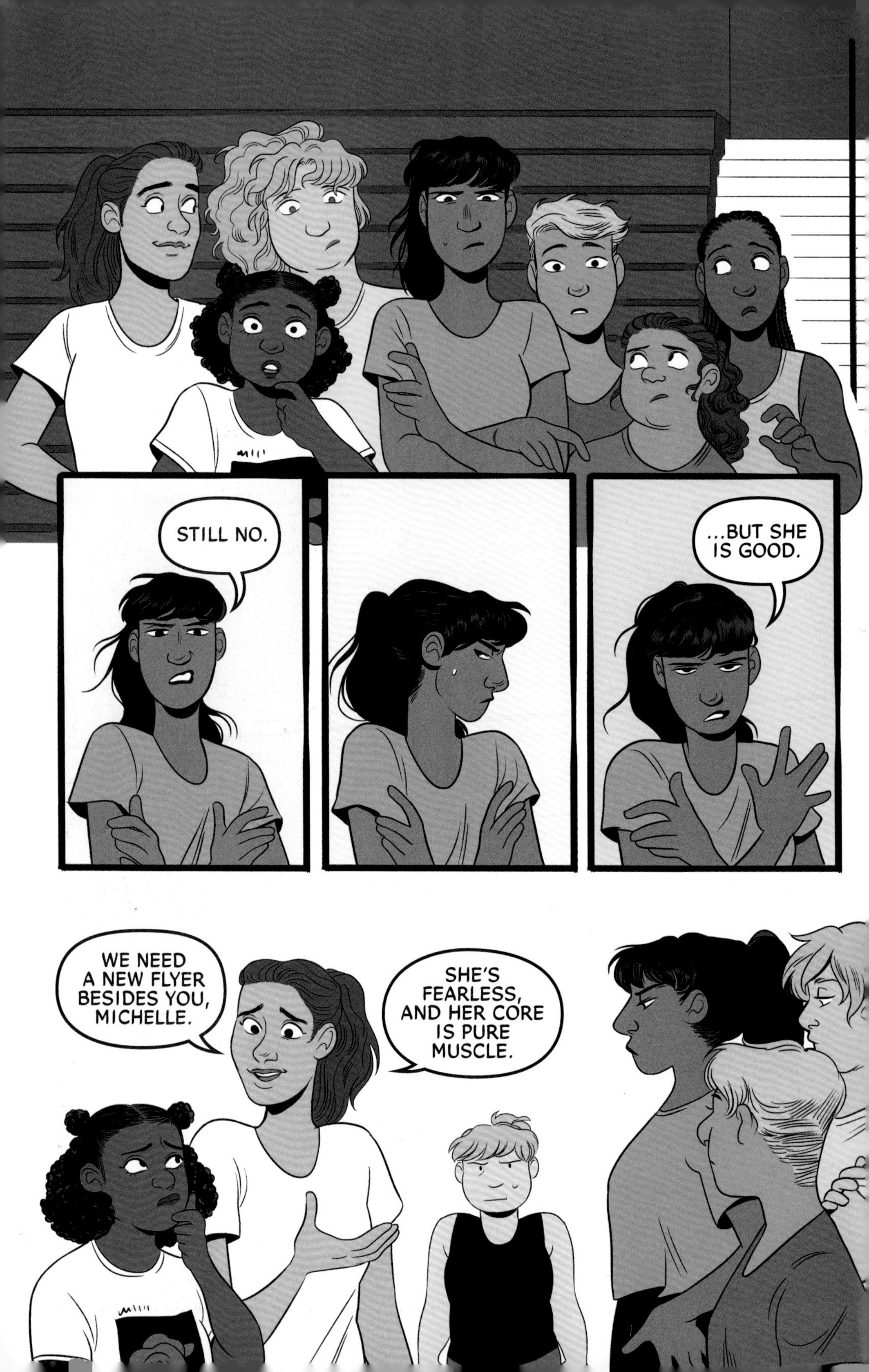
STILL NO.
...BUT SHE IS GOOD.
WE NEED A NEW FLYER BESIDES YOU, MICHELLE.
SHE'S FEARLESS, AND HER CORE IS PURE MUSCLE.

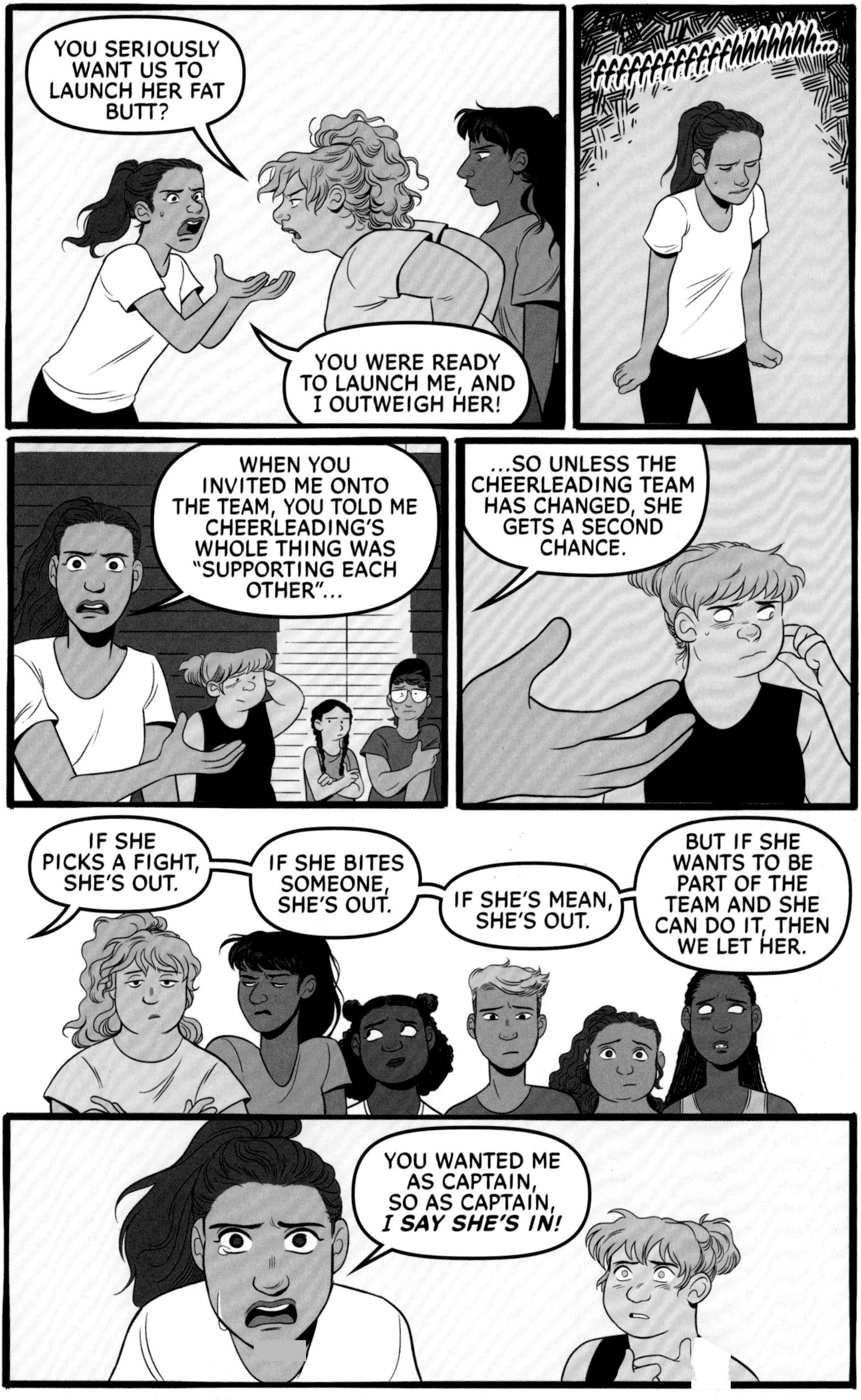
YOU SERIOUSLY WANT US TO LAUNCH HER FAT BUTT?
YOU WERE READY TO LAUNCH ME, AND I OUTWEIGH HER!
ffffffffffffhhhhhhh...
WHEN YOU INVITED ME ONTO THE TEAM, YOU TOLD ME CHEERLEADING'S WHOLE THING WAS "SUPPORTING EACH OTHER"...
...SO UNLESS THE CHEERLEADING TEAM HAS CHANGED, SHE GETS A SECOND CHANCE.
IF SHE PICKS A FIGHT, SHE'S OUT.
IF SHE BITES SOMEONE, SHE'S OUT.
IF SHE'S MEAN, SHE'S OUT.
BUT IF SHE WANTS TO BE PART OF THE TEAM AND SHE CAN DO IT, THEN WE LET HER.
YOU WANTED ME AS CAPTAIN, SO AS CAPTAIN, *I SAY SHE'S IN!*

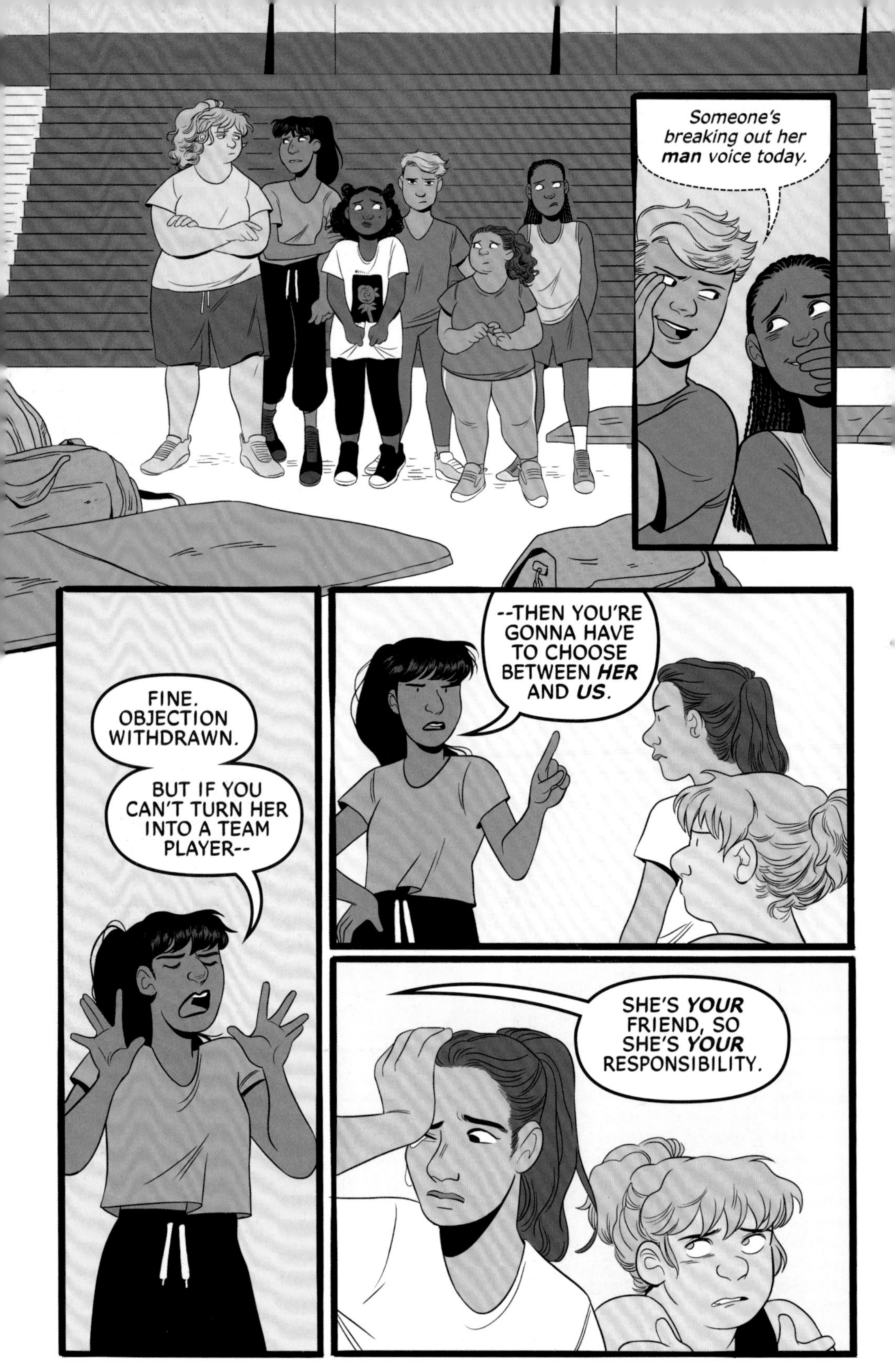
Someone's breaking out her *man* voice today.
FINE. OBJECTION WITHDRAWN.
BUT IF YOU CAN'T TURN HER INTO A TEAM PLAYER--
--THEN YOU'RE GONNA HAVE TO CHOOSE BETWEEN ***HER*** AND ***US***.
SHE'S ***YOUR*** FRIEND, SO SHE'S ***YOUR*** RESPONSIBILITY.

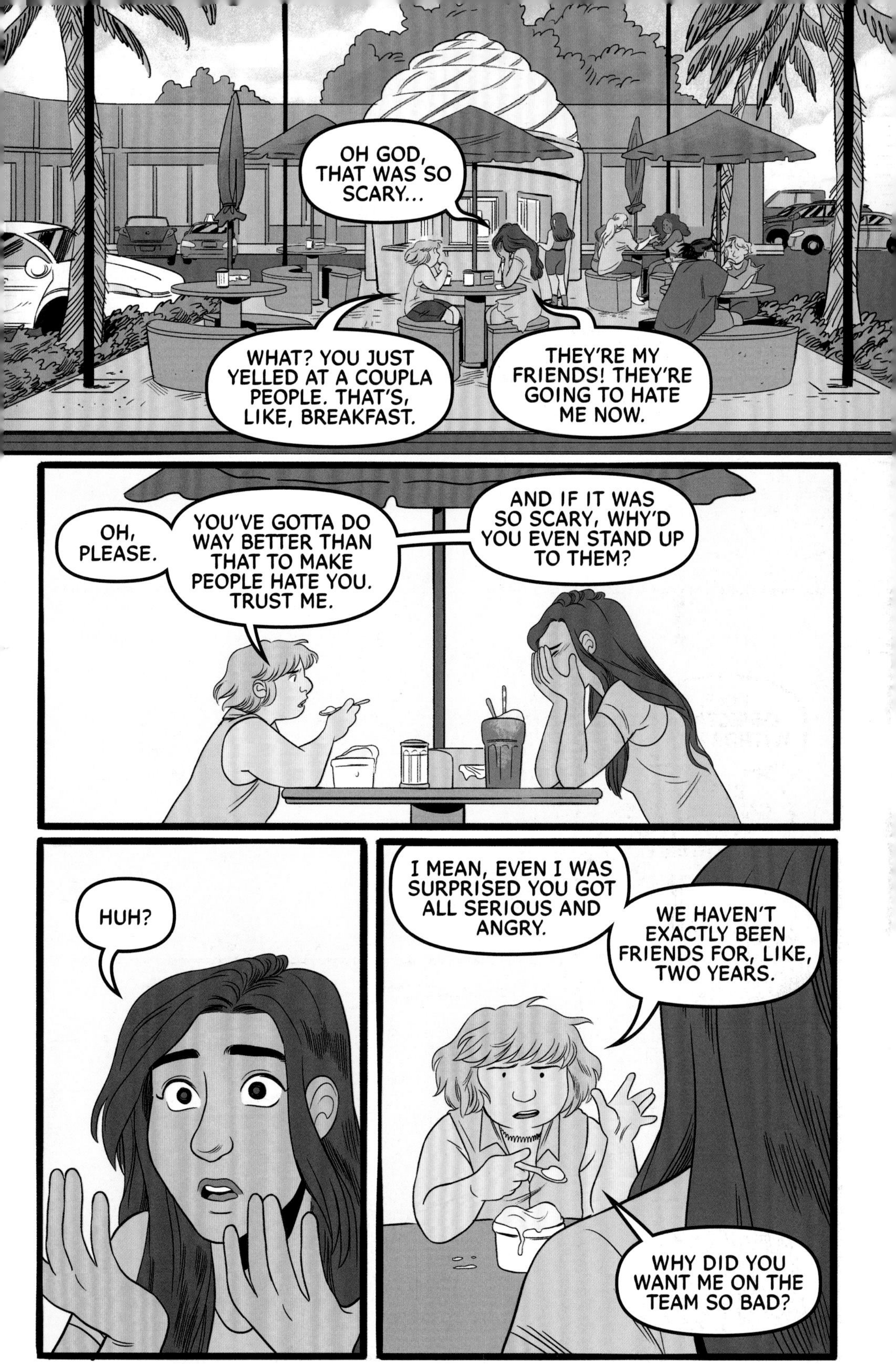
OH GOD, THAT WAS SO SCARY...
WHAT? YOU JUST YELLED AT A COUPLA PEOPLE. THAT'S, LIKE, BREAKFAST.
THEY'RE MY FRIENDS! THEY'RE GOING TO HATE ME NOW.
OH, PLEASE.
YOU'VE GOTTA DO WAY BETTER THAN THAT TO MAKE PEOPLE HATE YOU. TRUST ME.
AND IF IT WAS SO SCARY, WHY'D YOU EVEN STAND UP TO THEM?
HUH?
I MEAN, EVEN I WAS SURPRISED YOU GOT ALL SERIOUS AND ANGRY.
WE HAVEN'T EXACTLY BEEN FRIENDS FOR, LIKE, TWO YEARS.
WHY DID YOU WANT ME ON THE TEAM SO BAD?

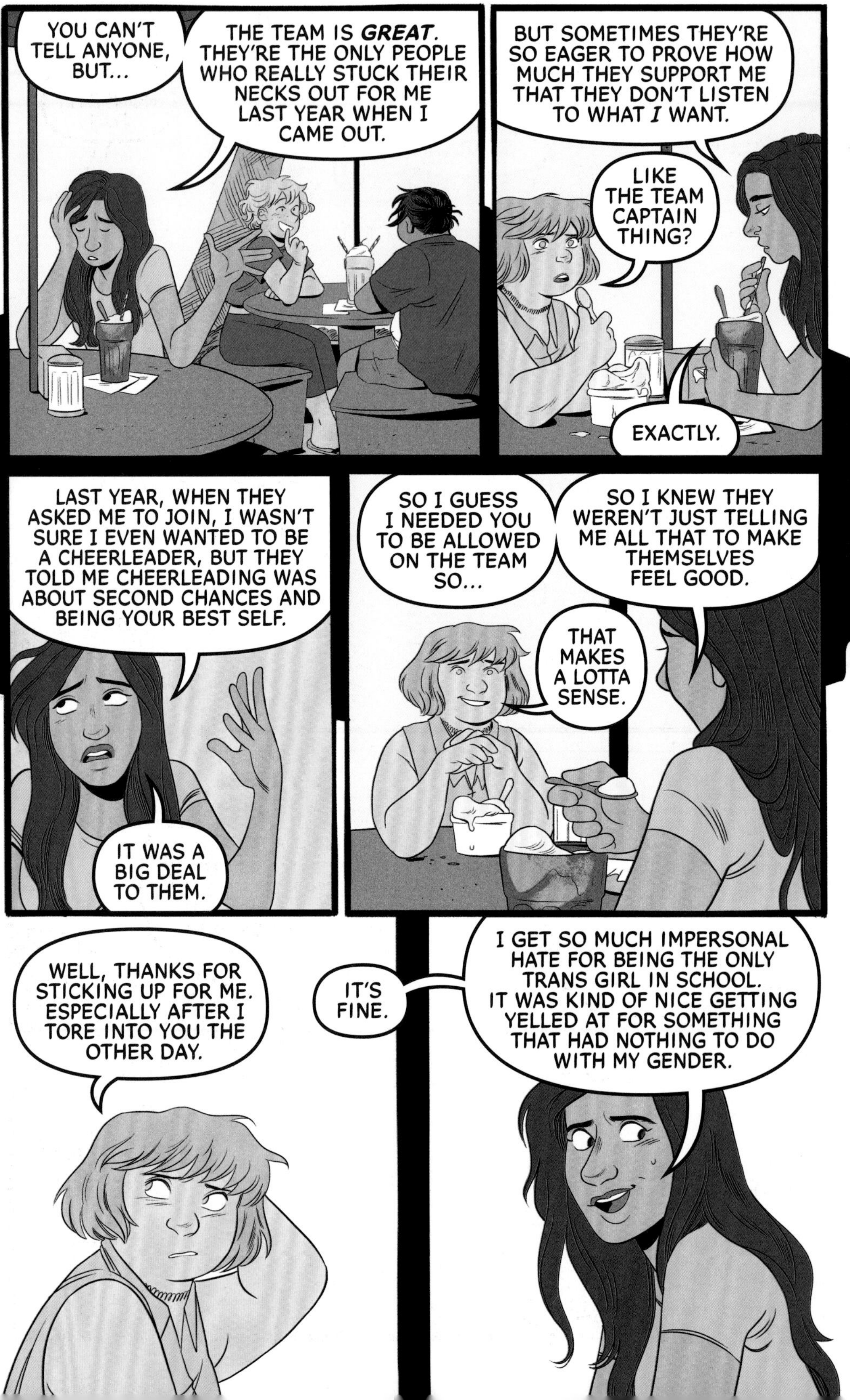
YOU CAN'T TELL ANYONE, BUT...
THE TEAM IS ***GREAT***. THEY'RE THE ONLY PEOPLE WHO REALLY STUCK THEIR NECKS OUT FOR ME LAST YEAR WHEN I CAME OUT.
BUT SOMETIMES THEY'RE SO EAGER TO PROVE HOW MUCH THEY SUPPORT ME THAT THEY DON'T LISTEN TO WHAT *I* WANT.
LIKE THE TEAM CAPTAIN THING?
EXACTLY.
LAST YEAR, WHEN THEY ASKED ME TO JOIN, I WASN'T SURE I EVEN WANTED TO BE A CHEERLEADER, BUT THEY TOLD ME CHEERLEADING WAS ABOUT SECOND CHANCES AND BEING YOUR BEST SELF.
IT WAS A BIG DEAL TO THEM.
SO I KNEW THEY WEREN'T JUST TELLING ME ALL THAT TO MAKE THEMSELVES FEEL GOOD.
SO I GUESS I NEEDED YOU TO BE ALLOWED ON THE TEAM SO...
THAT MAKES A LOTTA SENSE.
WELL, THANKS FOR STICKING UP FOR ME. ESPECIALLY AFTER I TORE INTO YOU THE OTHER DAY.
IT'S FINE.
I GET SO MUCH IMPERSONAL HATE FOR BEING THE ONLY TRANS GIRL IN SCHOOL. IT WAS KIND OF NICE GETTING YELLED AT FOR SOMETHING THAT HAD NOTHING TO DO WITH MY GENDER.

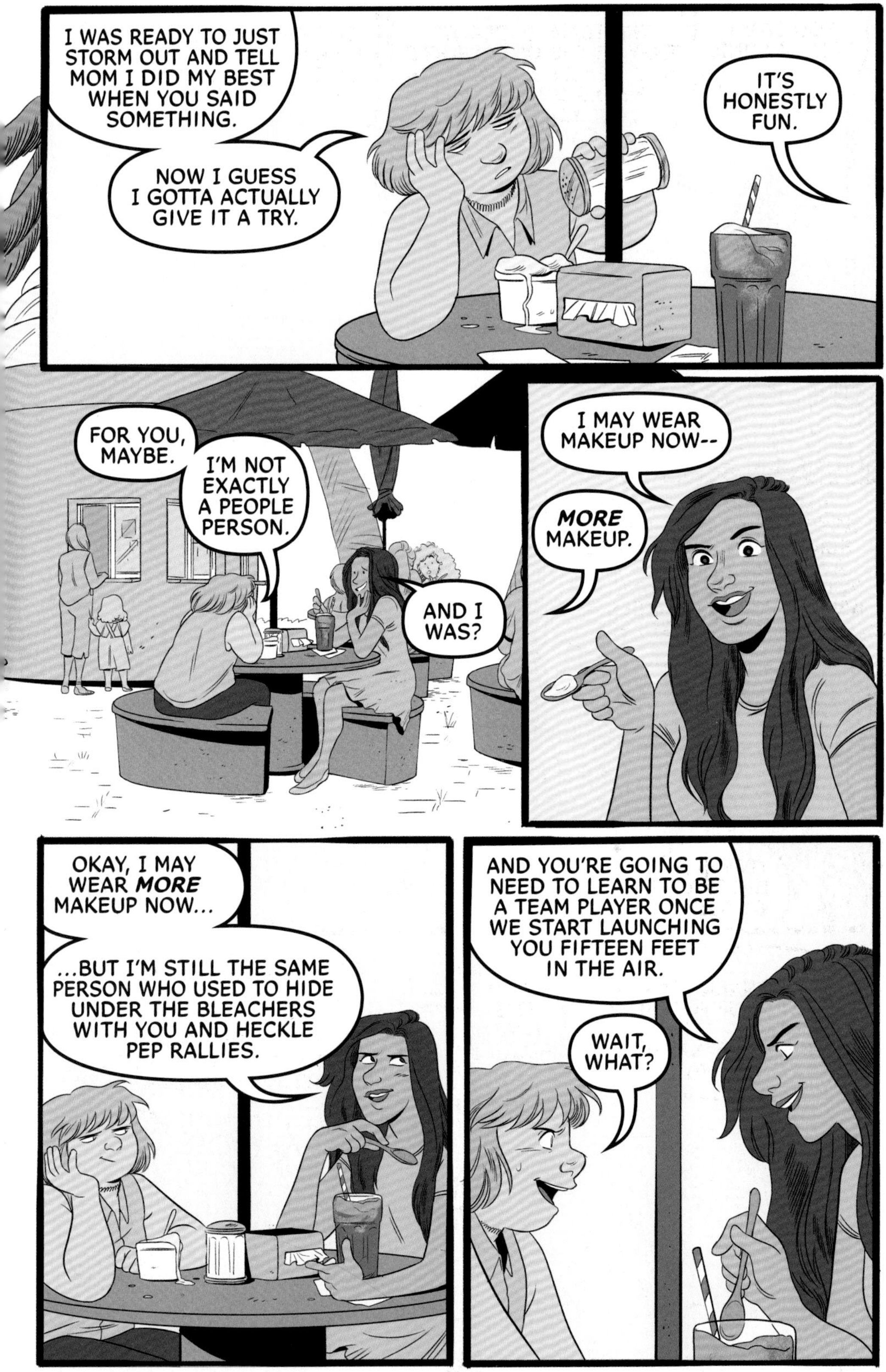
I WAS READY TO JUST STORM OUT AND TELL MOM I DID MY BEST WHEN YOU SAID SOMETHING.
NOW I GUESS I GOTTA ACTUALLY GIVE IT A TRY.
IT'S HONESTLY FUN.
FOR YOU, MAYBE.
I'M NOT EXACTLY A PEOPLE PERSON.
AND I WAS?
I MAY WEAR MAKEUP NOW--
MORE MAKEUP.
OKAY, I MAY WEAR *MORE* MAKEUP NOW...
...BUT I'M STILL THE SAME PERSON WHO USED TO HIDE UNDER THE BLEACHERS WITH YOU AND HECKLE PEP RALLIES.
AND YOU'RE GOING TO NEED TO LEARN TO BE A TEAM PLAYER ONCE WE START LAUNCHING YOU FIFTEEN FEET IN THE AIR.
WAIT, WHAT?

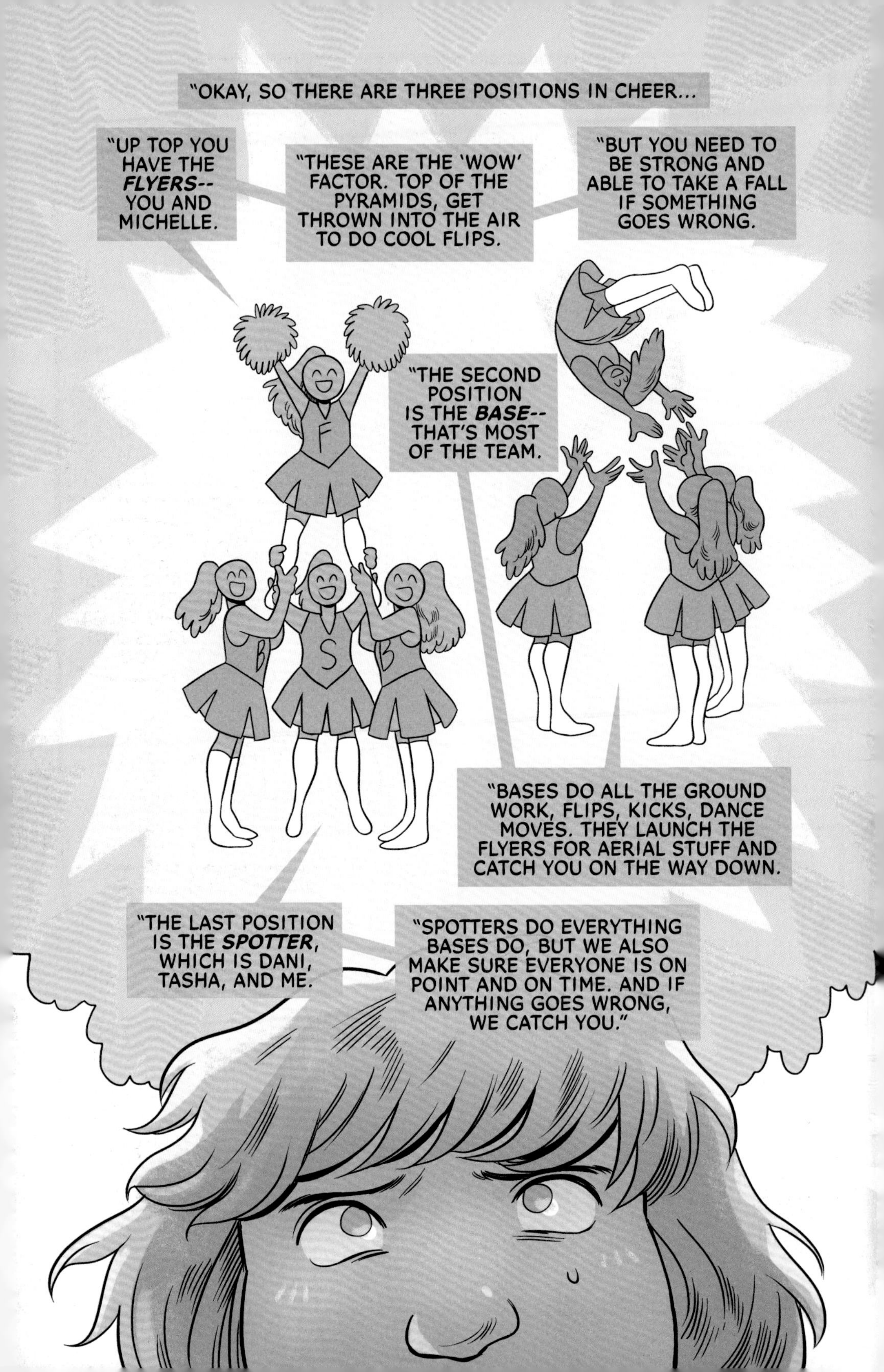
"OKAY, SO THERE ARE THREE POSITIONS IN CHEER...
"UP TOP YOU HAVE THE FLYERS-- YOU AND MICHELLE.
"THESE ARE THE 'WOW' FACTOR. TOP OF THE PYRAMIDS, GET THROWN INTO THE AIR TO DO COOL FLIPS.
"BUT YOU NEED TO BE STRONG AND ABLE TO TAKE A FALL IF SOMETHING GOES WRONG.
F
"THE SECOND POSITION IS THE BASE-- THAT'S MOST OF THE TEAM.
B
S
B
"BASES DO ALL THE GROUND WORK, FLIPS, KICKS, DANCE MOVES. THEY LAUNCH THE FLYERS FOR AERIAL STUFF AND CATCH YOU ON THE WAY DOWN.
"THE LAST POSITION IS THE SPOTTER, WHICH IS DANI, TASHA, AND ME.
"SPOTTERS DO EVERYTHING BASES DO, BUT WE ALSO MAKE SURE EVERYONE IS ON POINT AND ON TIME. AND IF ANYTHING GOES WRONG, WE CATCH YOU."

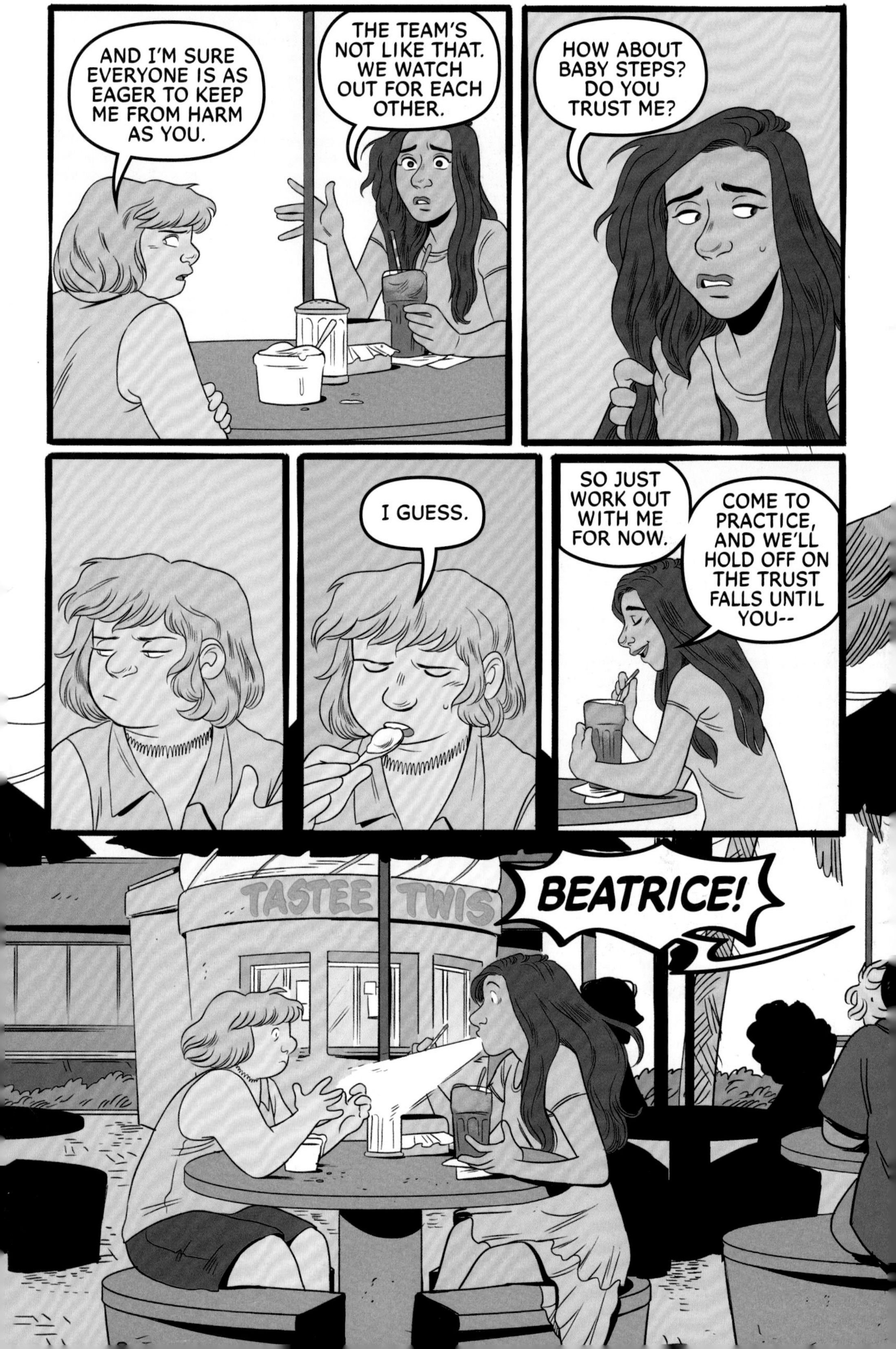
AND I'M SURE EVERYONE IS AS EAGER TO KEEP ME FROM HARM AS YOU.
THE TEAM'S NOT LIKE THAT. WE WATCH OUT FOR EACH OTHER.
HOW ABOUT BABY STEPS? DO YOU TRUST ME?
I GUESS.
SO JUST WORK OUT WITH ME FOR NOW.
COME TO PRACTICE, AND WE'LL HOLD OFF ON THE TRUST FALLS UNTIL YOU--
TASTEE TWIS
BEATRICE!

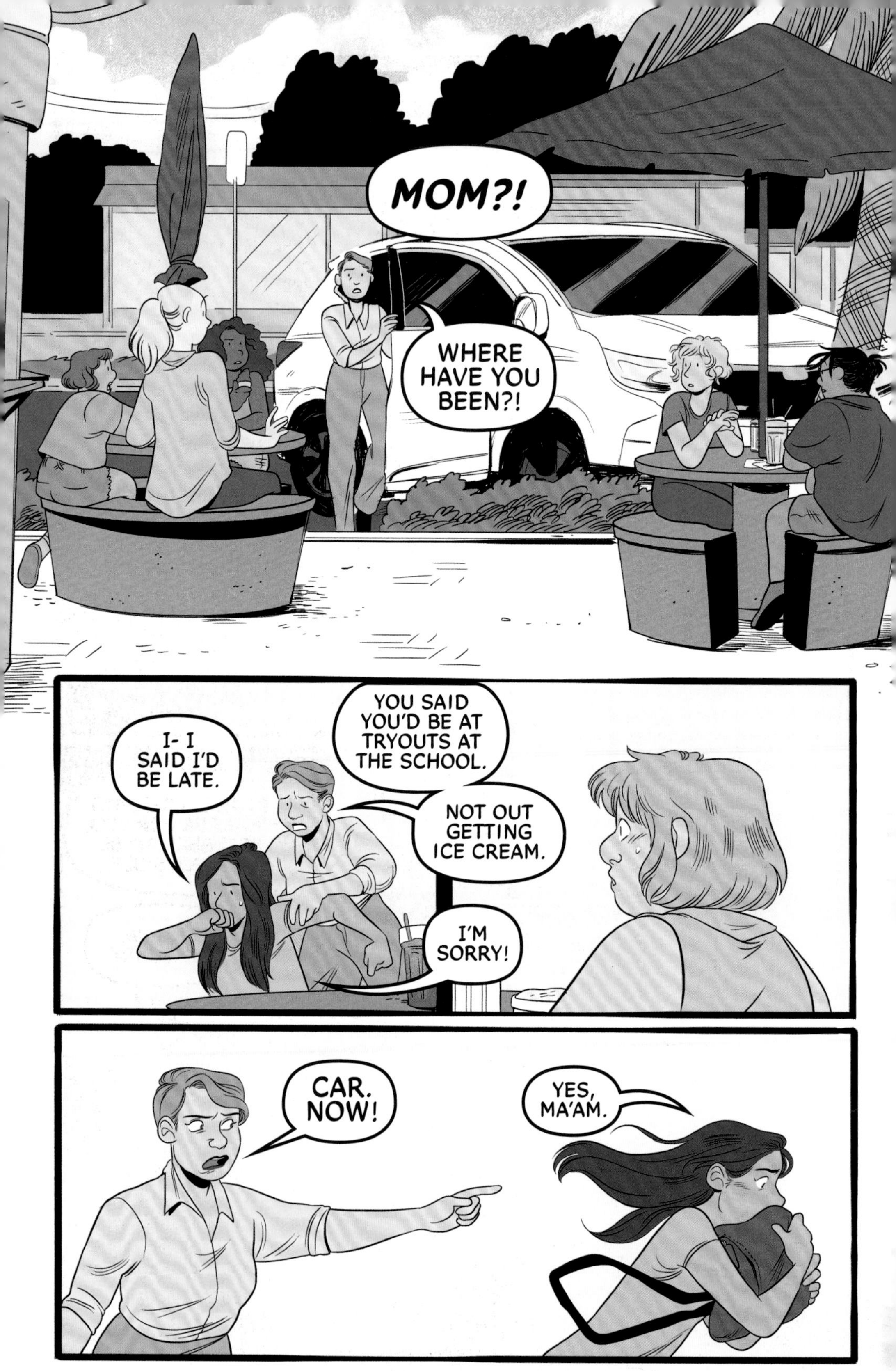
MOM?!
WHERE HAVE YOU BEEN?!
YOU SAID YOU'D BE AT TRYOUTS AT THE SCHOOL.
I- I SAID I'D BE LATE.
NOT OUT GETTING ICE CREAM.
I'M SORRY!
CAR. NOW!
YES, MA'AM.

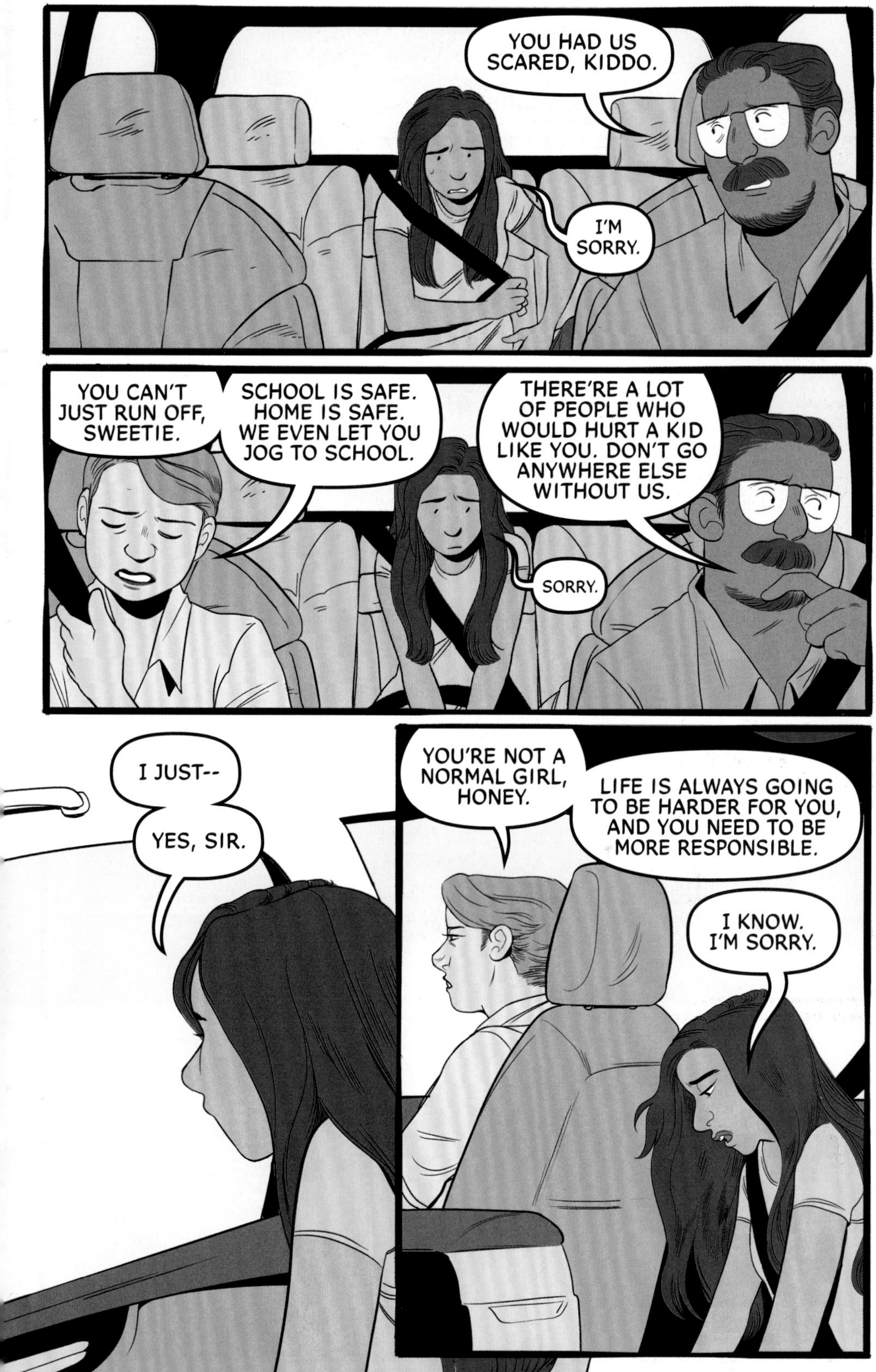
YOU HAD US SCARED, KIDDO.
I'M SORRY.
YOU CAN'T JUST RUN OFF, SWEETIE.
SCHOOL IS SAFE. HOME IS SAFE. WE EVEN LET YOU JOG TO SCHOOL.
THERE'RE A LOT OF PEOPLE WHO WOULD HURT A KID LIKE YOU. DON'T GO ANYWHERE ELSE WITHOUT US.
SORRY.
I JUST--
YES, SIR.
YOU'RE NOT A NORMAL GIRL, HONEY.
LIFE IS ALWAYS GOING TO BE HARDER FOR YOU, AND YOU NEED TO BE MORE RESPONSIBLE.
I KNOW. I'M SORRY.

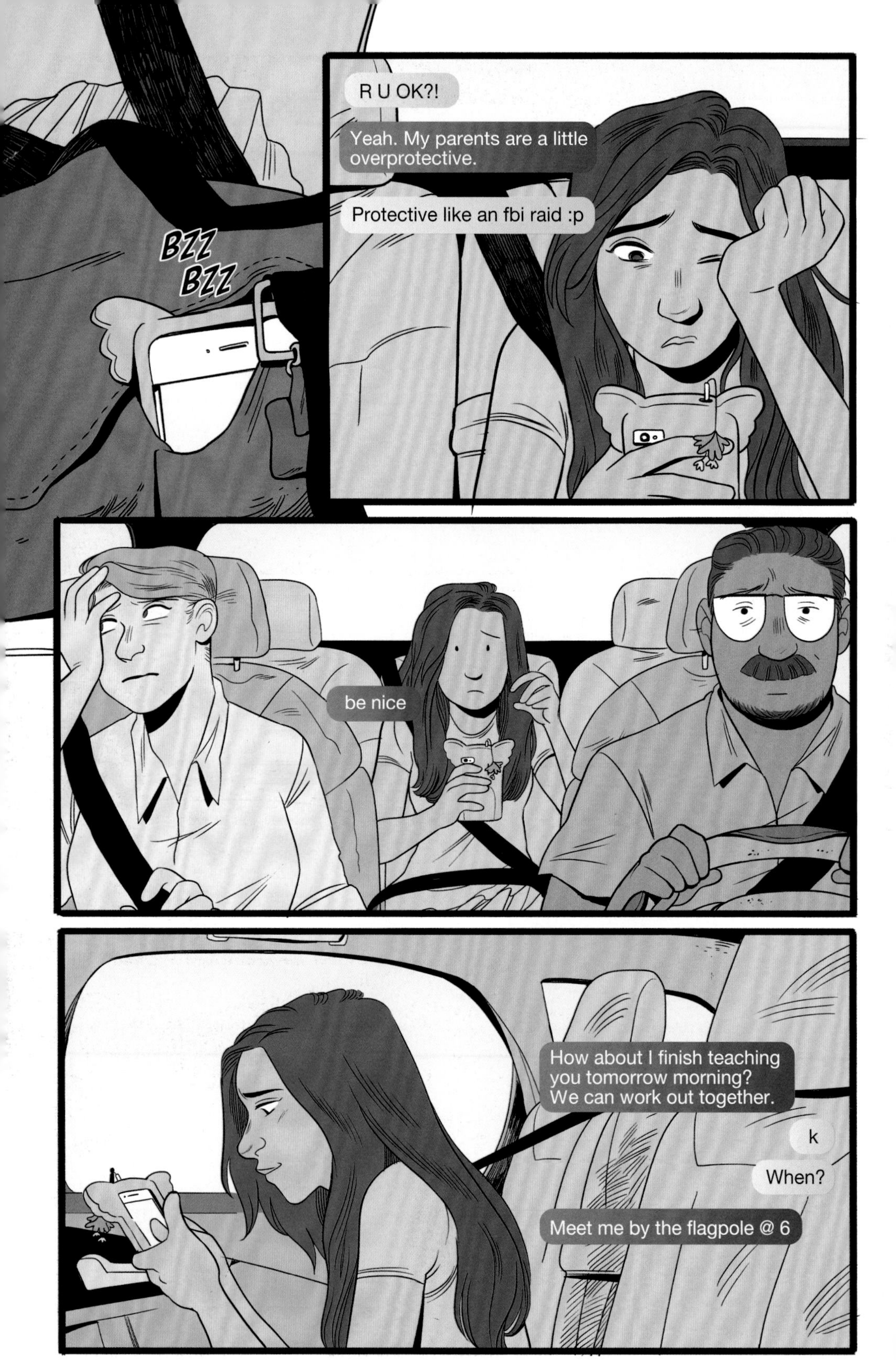
BZZ
BZZ
R U OK?!
Yeah. My parents are a little overprotective.
Protective like an fbi raid :p
be nice
How about I finish teaching you tomorrow morning? We can work out together.
k
When?
Meet me by the flagpole @ 6

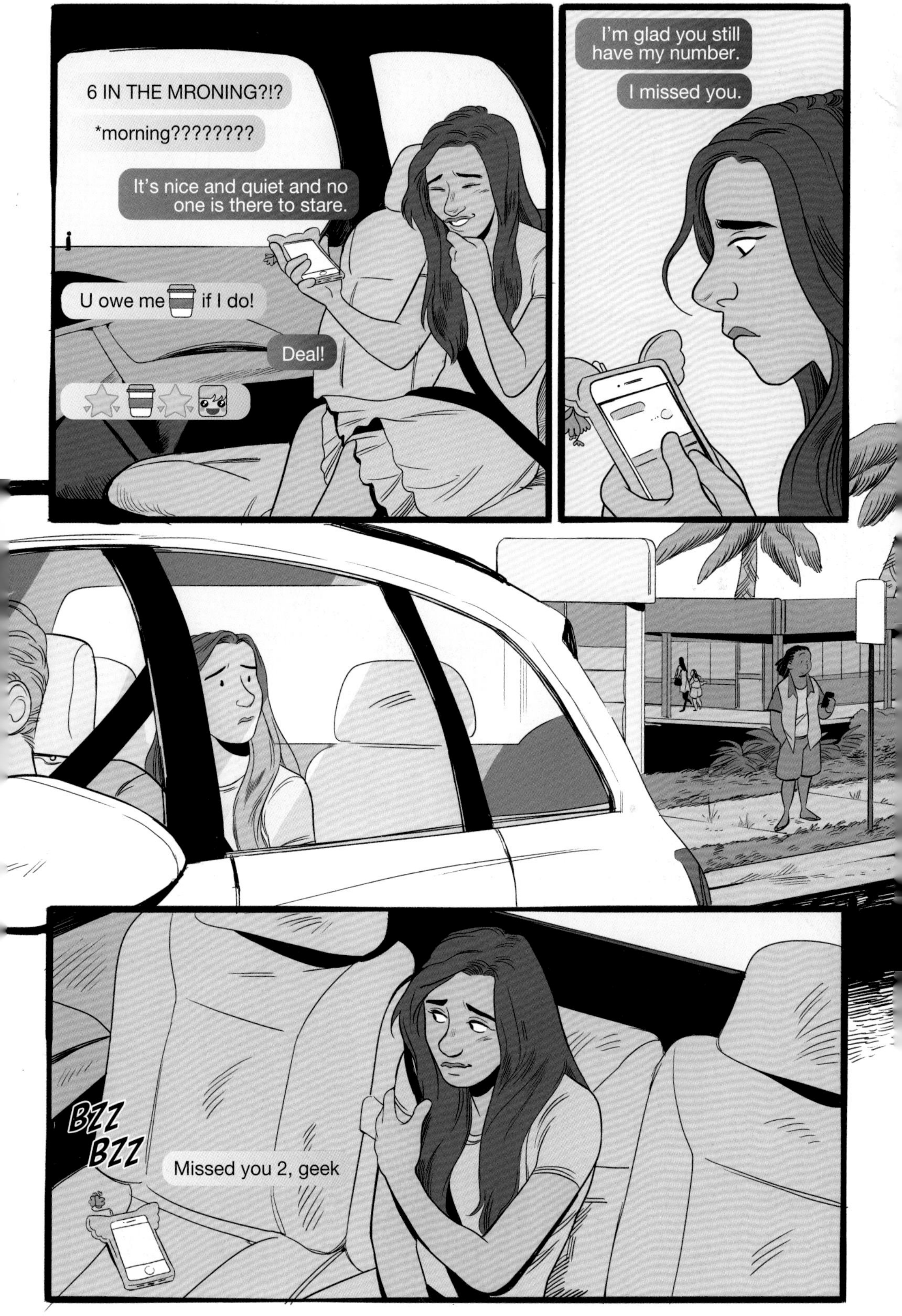
6 IN THE MRONING?!?
*morning????????
It's nice and quiet and no one is there to stare.
U owe me if I do!
Deal!
I'm glad you still have my number.
I missed you.
BZZ BZZ
Missed you 2, geek

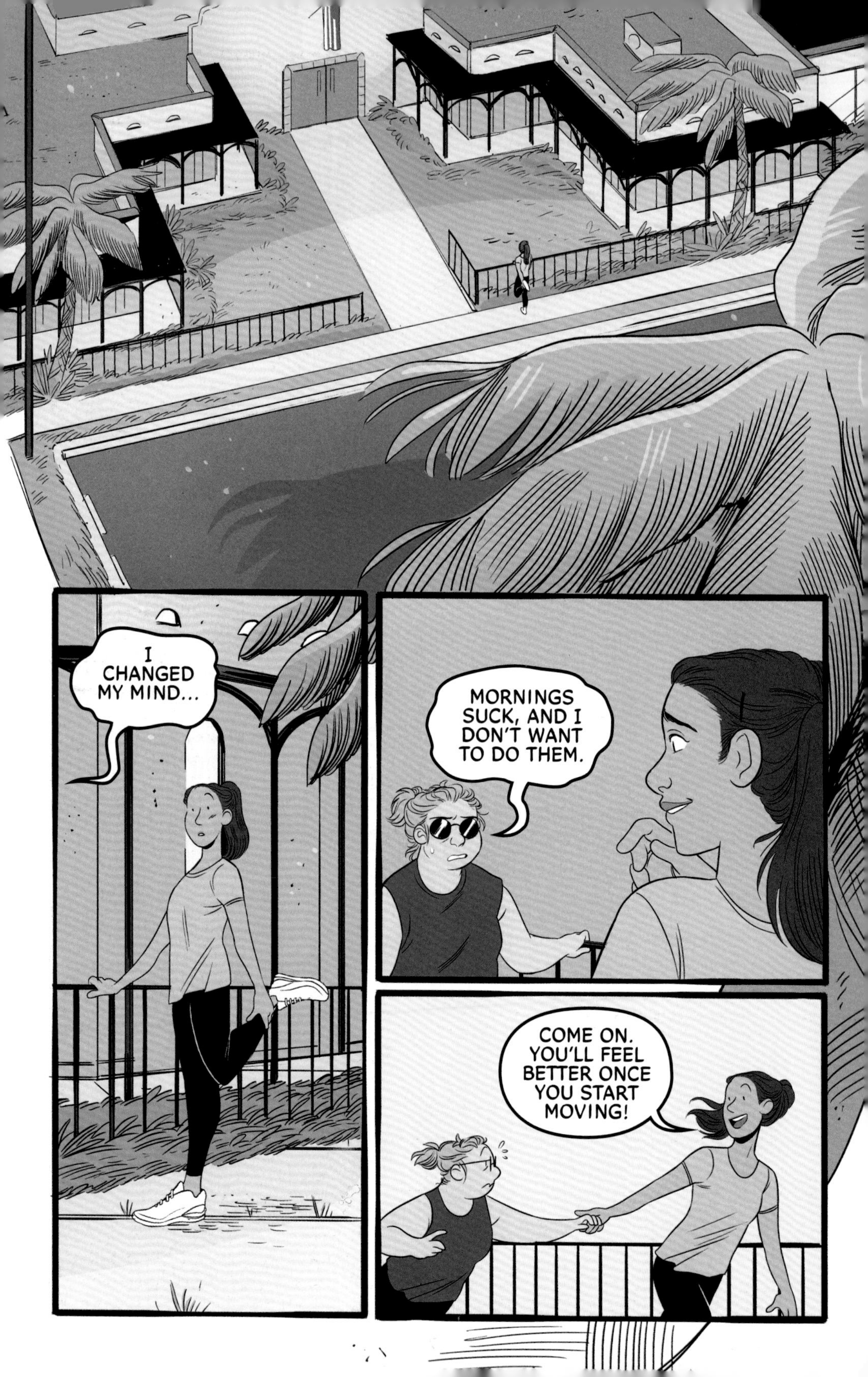
I CHANGED MY MIND...
MORNINGS SUCK, AND I DON'T WANT TO DO THEM.
COME ON. YOU'LL FEEL BETTER ONCE YOU START MOVING!

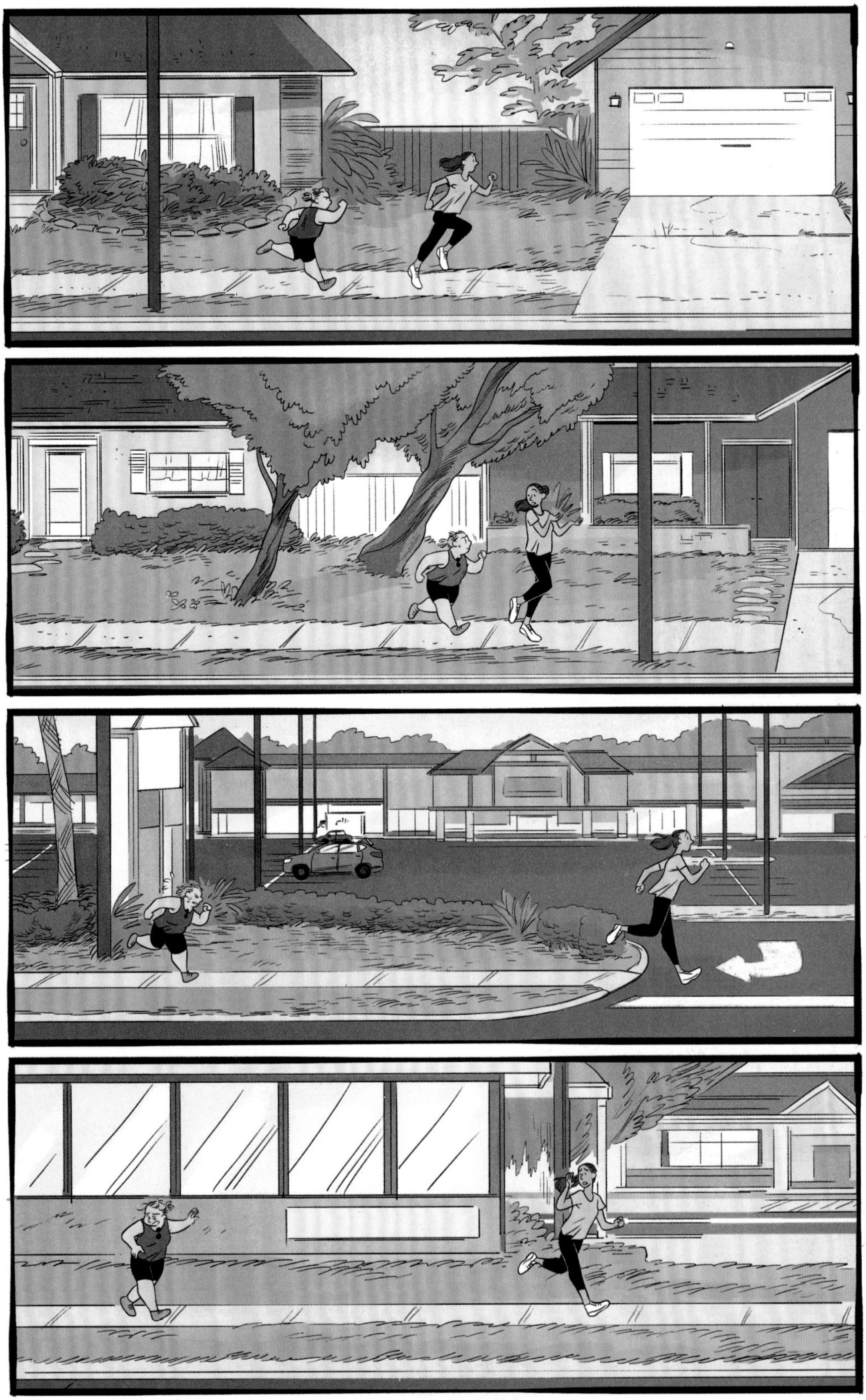

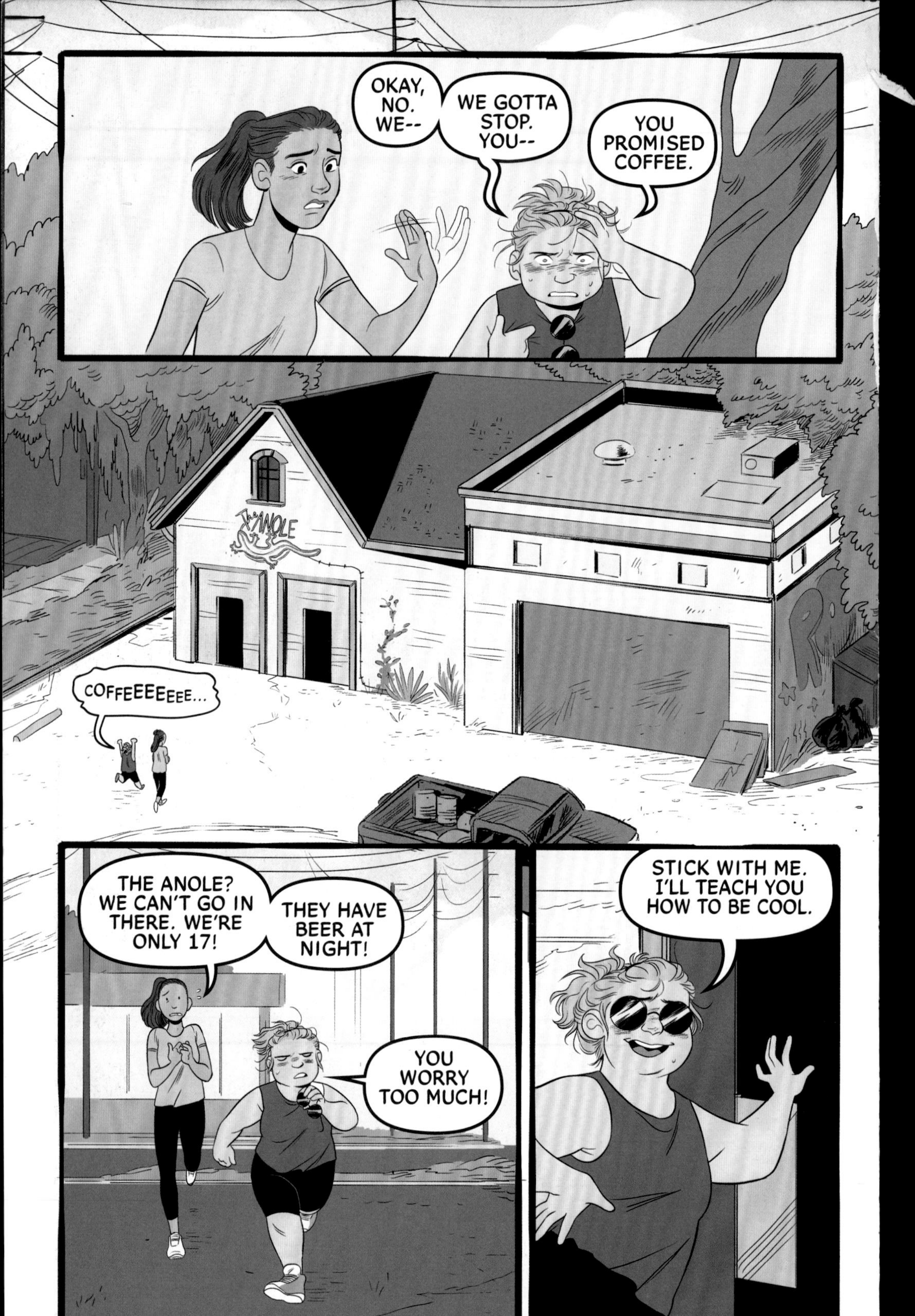
OKAY, NO. WE--
WE GOTTA STOP. YOU--
YOU PROMISED COFFEE.
The ANOLE
COFFEEEEEEEE...
THE ANOLE? WE CAN'T GO IN THERE. WE'RE ONLY 17!
THEY HAVE BEER AT NIGHT!
YOU WORRY TOO MUCH!
STICK WITH ME. I'LL TEACH YOU HOW TO BE COOL.

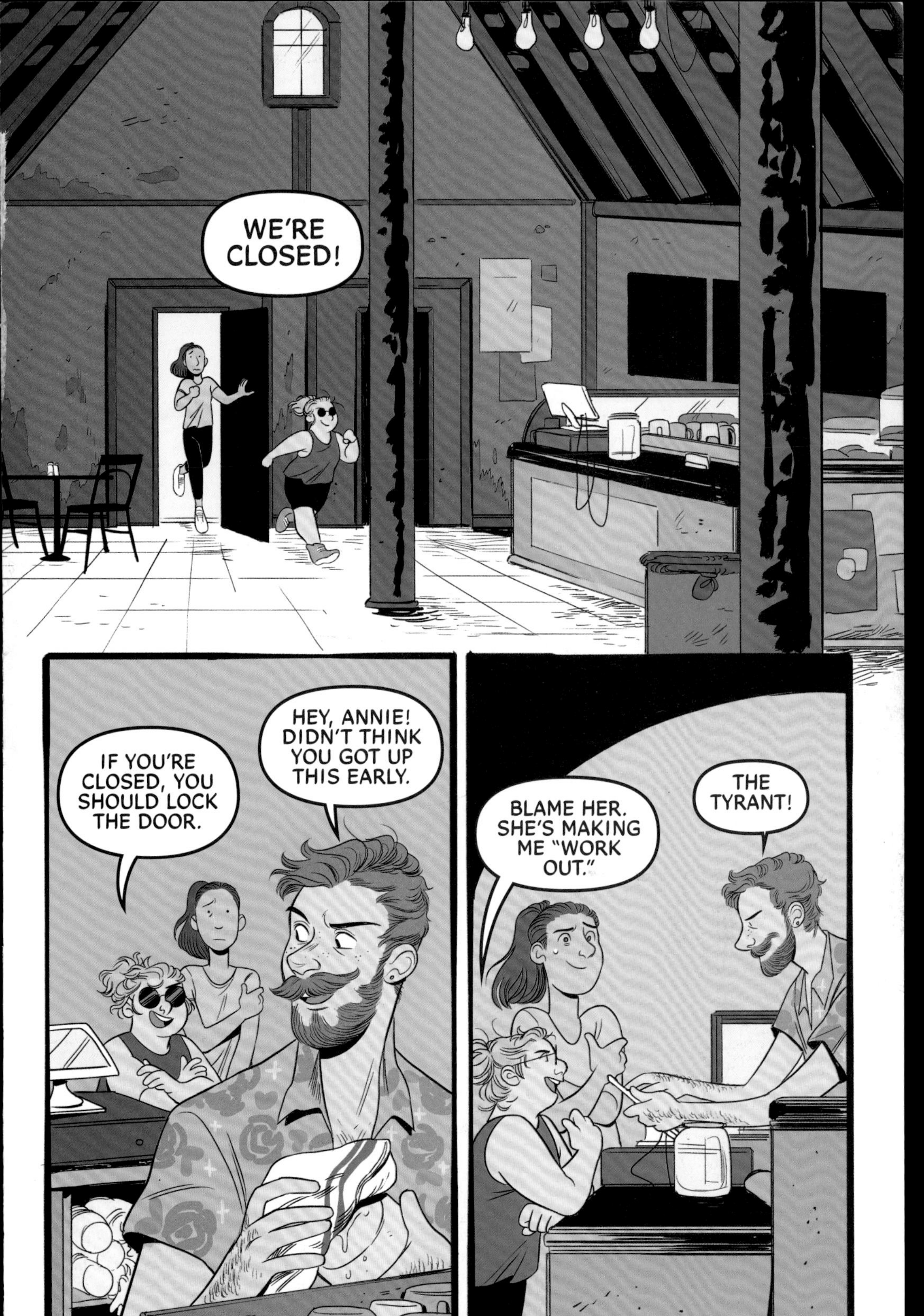
WE'RE CLOSED!
IF YOU'RE CLOSED, YOU SHOULD LOCK THE DOOR.
HEY, ANNIE! DIDN'T THINK YOU GOT UP THIS EARLY.
BLAME HER. SHE'S MAKING ME "WORK OUT."
THE TYRANT!

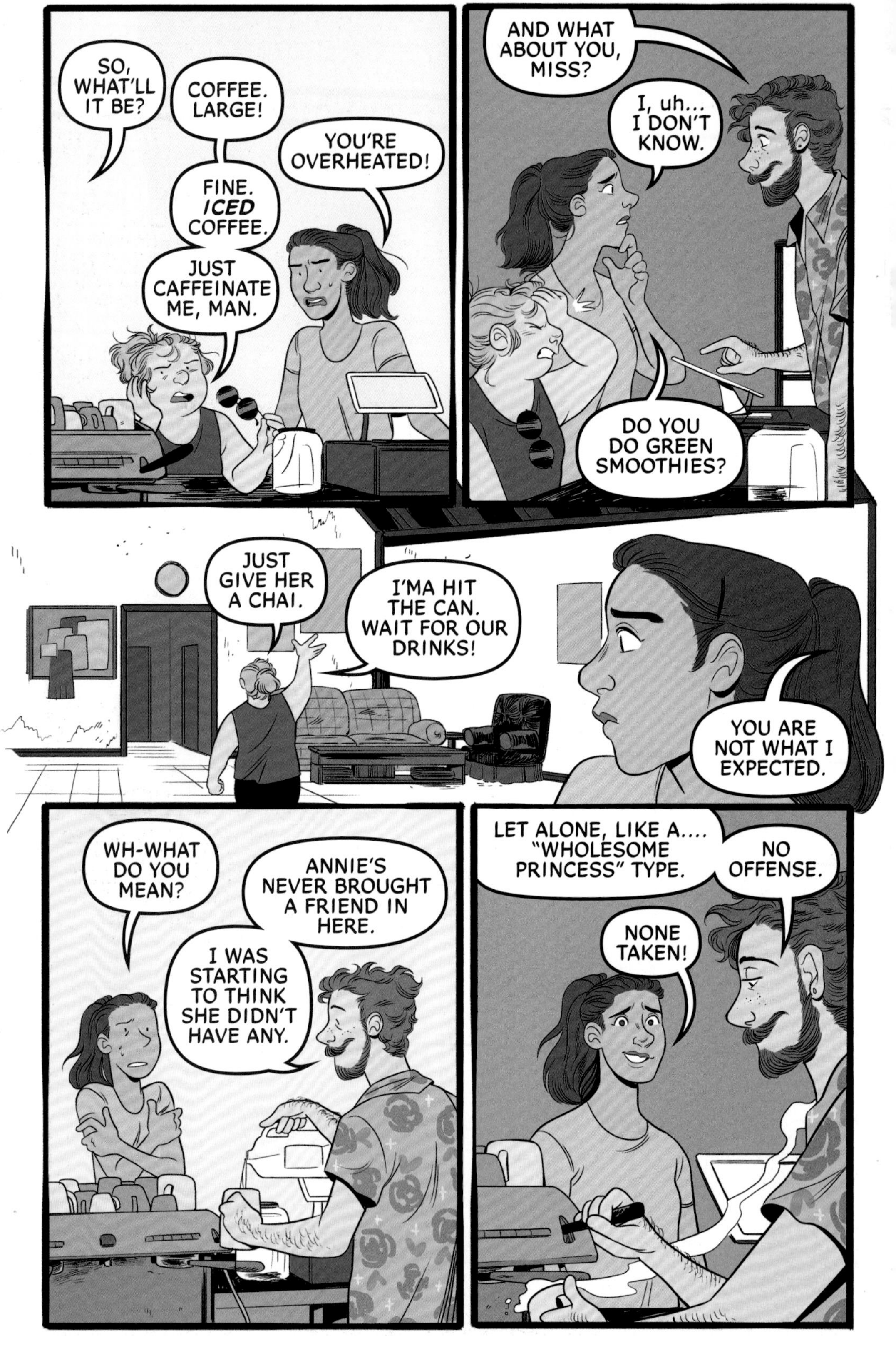
SO, WHAT'LL IT BE?
COFFEE. LARGE!
YOU'RE OVERHEATED!
FINE. *ICED* COFFEE.
JUST CAFFEINATE ME, MAN.
AND WHAT ABOUT YOU, MISS?
I, uh... I DON'T KNOW.
DO YOU DO GREEN SMOOTHIES?
JUST GIVE HER A CHAI.
I'MA HIT THE CAN. WAIT FOR OUR DRINKS!
YOU ARE NOT WHAT I EXPECTED.
WH-WHAT DO YOU MEAN?
ANNIE'S NEVER BROUGHT A FRIEND IN HERE.
I WAS STARTING TO THINK SHE DIDN'T HAVE ANY.
LET ALONE, LIKE A.... "WHOLESOME PRINCESS" TYPE.
NO OFFENSE.
NONE TAKEN!

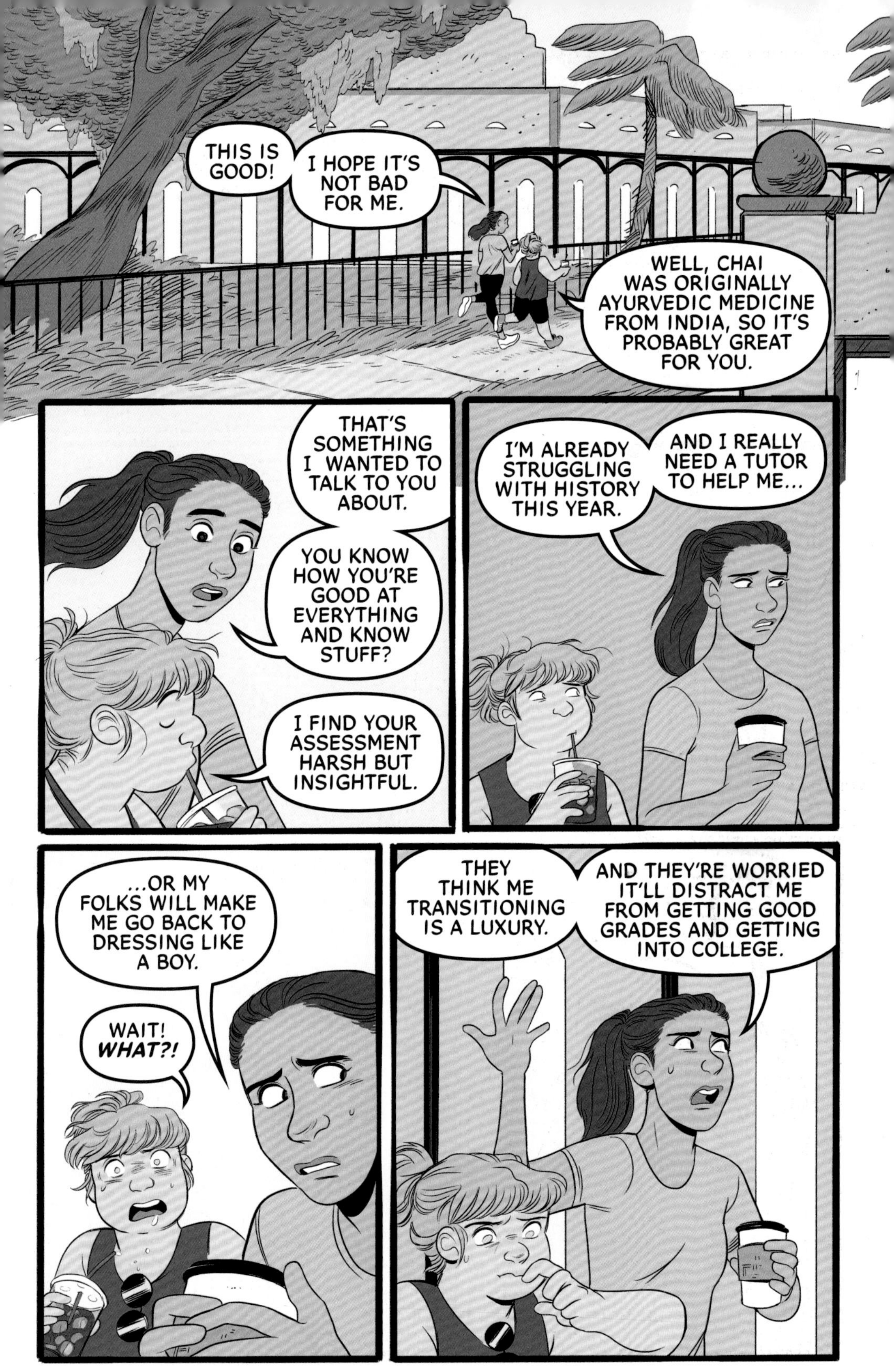
THIS IS GOOD!
I HOPE IT'S NOT BAD FOR ME.
WELL, CHAI WAS ORIGINALLY AYURVEDIC MEDICINE FROM INDIA, SO IT'S PROBABLY GREAT FOR YOU.
THAT'S SOMETHING I WANTED TO TALK TO YOU ABOUT.
YOU KNOW HOW YOU'RE GOOD AT EVERYTHING AND KNOW STUFF?
I FIND YOUR ASSESSMENT HARSH BUT INSIGHTFUL.
I'M ALREADY STRUGGLING WITH HISTORY THIS YEAR.
AND I REALLY NEED A TUTOR TO HELP ME...
...OR MY FOLKS WILL MAKE ME GO BACK TO DRESSING LIKE A BOY.
WAIT! ***WHAT?!***
THEY THINK ME TRANSITIONING IS A LUXURY.
AND THEY'RE WORRIED IT'LL DISTRACT ME FROM GETTING GOOD GRADES AND GETTING INTO COLLEGE.

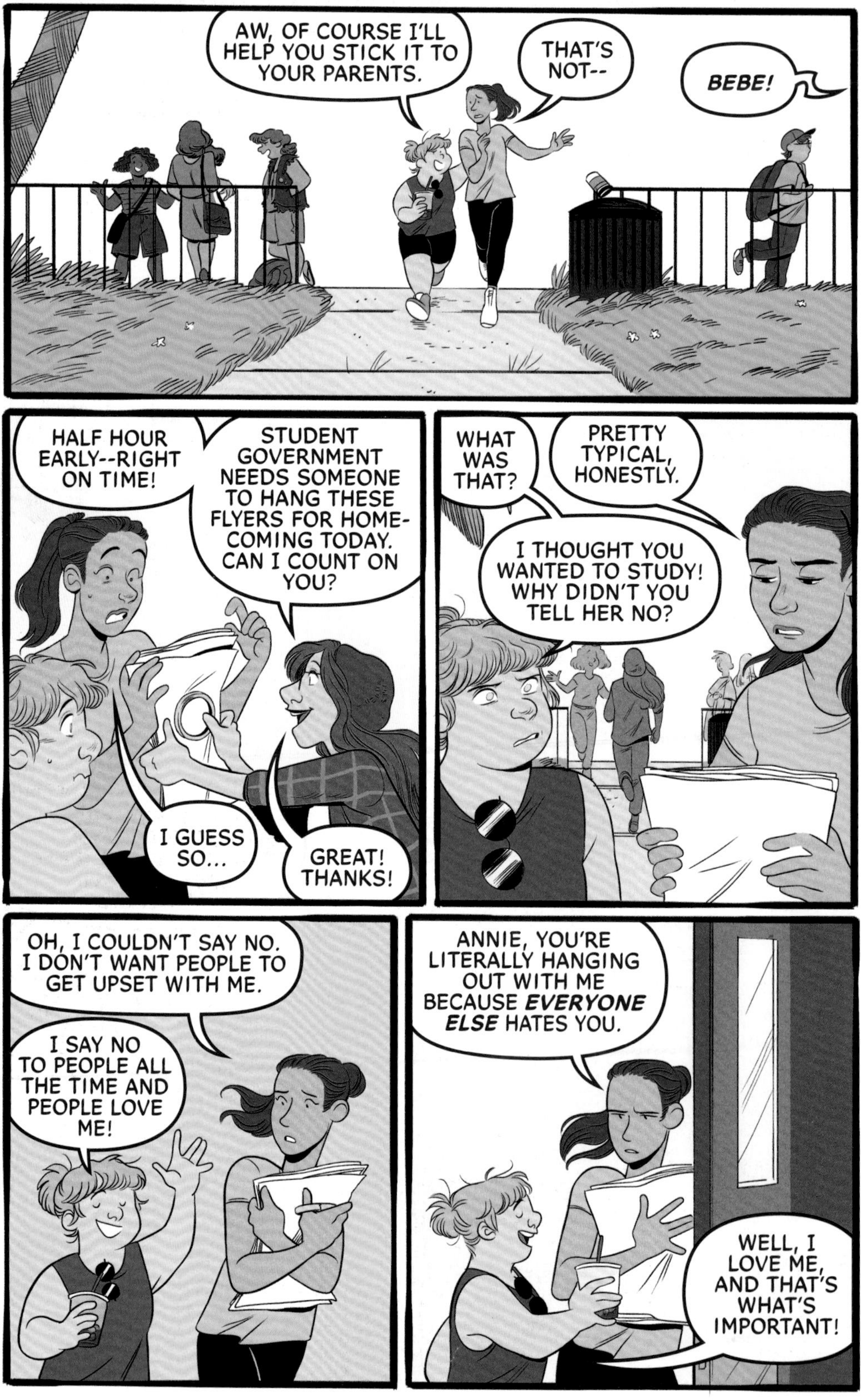
AW, OF COURSE I'LL HELP YOU STICK IT TO YOUR PARENTS.
THAT'S NOT--
BEBE!
HALF HOUR EARLY--RIGHT ON TIME!
STUDENT GOVERNMENT NEEDS SOMEONE TO HANG THESE FLYERS FOR HOME-COMING TODAY. CAN I COUNT ON YOU?
I GUESS SO...
GREAT! THANKS!
WHAT WAS THAT?
PRETTY TYPICAL, HONESTLY.
I THOUGHT YOU WANTED TO STUDY! WHY DIDN'T YOU TELL HER NO?
OH, I COULDN'T SAY NO. I DON'T WANT PEOPLE TO GET UPSET WITH ME.
I SAY NO TO PEOPLE ALL THE TIME AND PEOPLE LOVE ME!
ANNIE, YOU'RE LITERALLY HANGING OUT WITH ME BECAUSE *EVERYONE ELSE* HATES YOU.
WELL, I LOVE ME, AND THAT'S WHAT'S IMPORTANT!

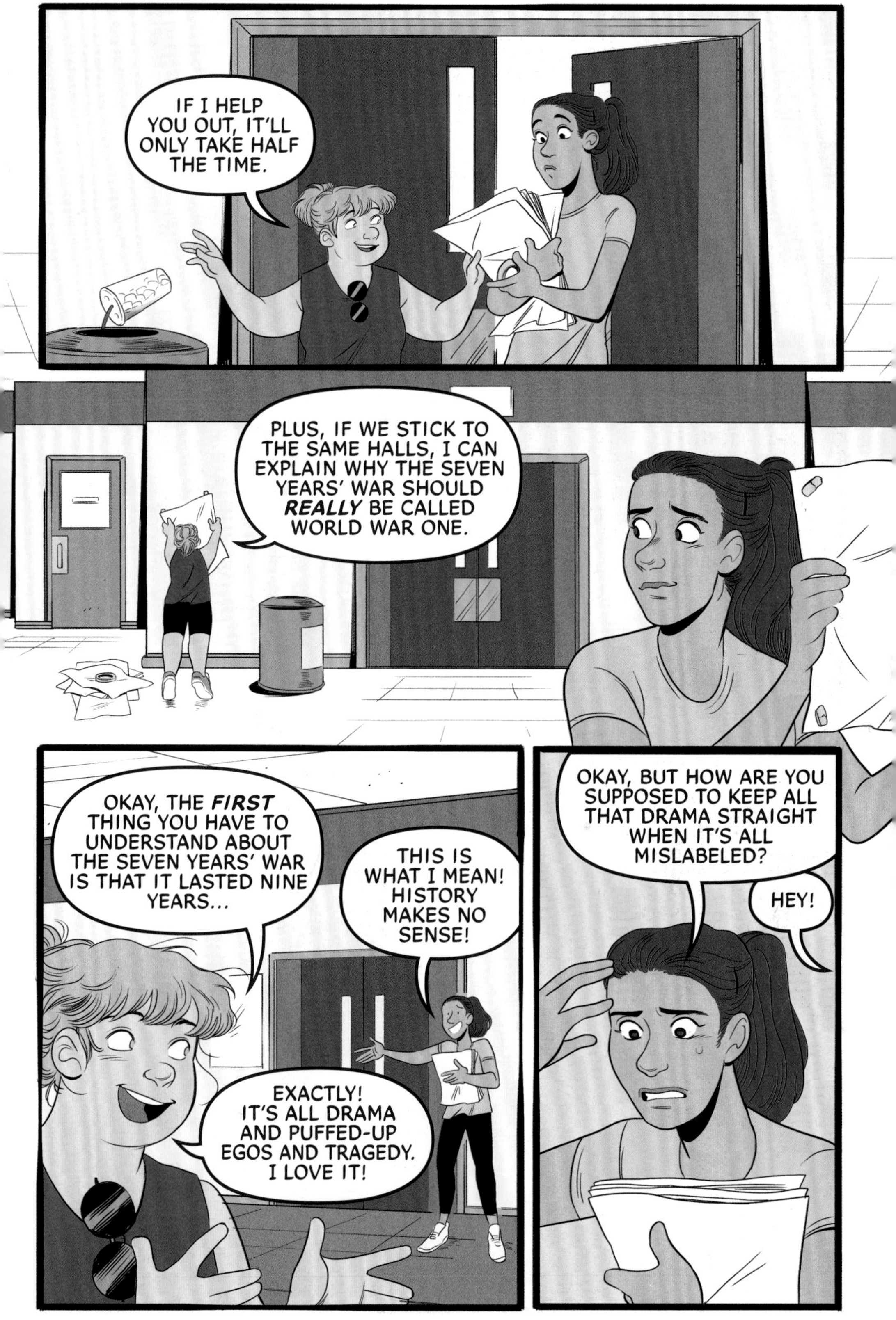
IF I HELP YOU OUT, IT'LL ONLY TAKE HALF THE TIME.
PLUS, IF WE STICK TO THE SAME HALLS, I CAN EXPLAIN WHY THE SEVEN YEARS' WAR SHOULD *REALLY* BE CALLED WORLD WAR ONE.
OKAY, THE *FIRST* THING YOU HAVE TO UNDERSTAND ABOUT THE SEVEN YEARS' WAR IS THAT IT LASTED NINE YEARS...
THIS IS WHAT I MEAN! HISTORY MAKES NO SENSE!
EXACTLY! IT'S ALL DRAMA AND PUFFED-UP EGOS AND TRAGEDY. I LOVE IT!
OKAY, BUT HOW ARE YOU SUPPOSED TO KEEP ALL THAT DRAMA STRAIGHT WHEN IT'S ALL MISLABELED?
HEY!

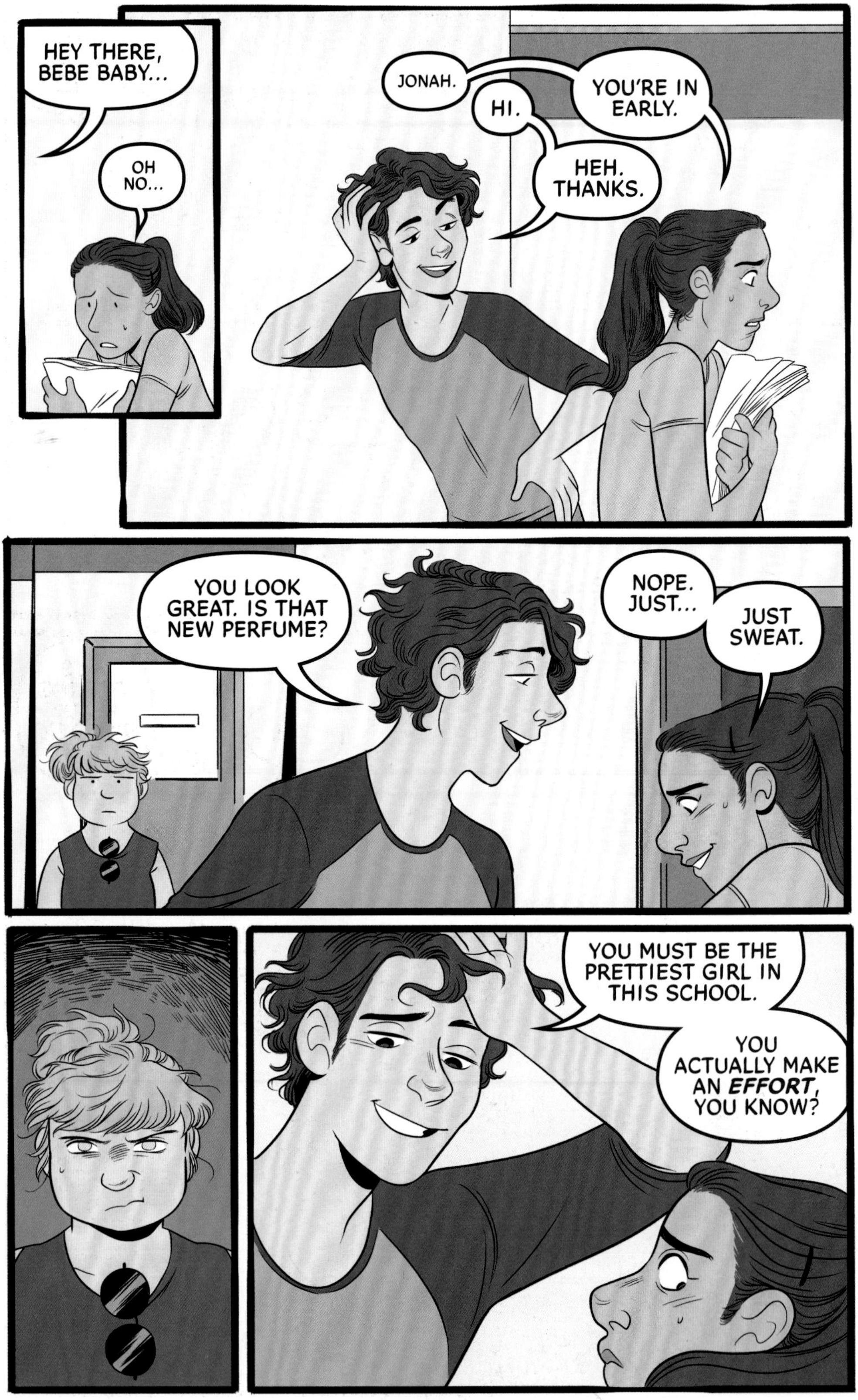
HEY THERE, BEBE BABY...
OH NO...
JONAH.
HI.
YOU'RE IN EARLY.
HEH. THANKS.
YOU LOOK GREAT. IS THAT NEW PERFUME?
NOPE. JUST...
JUST SWEAT.
YOU MUST BE THE PRETTIEST GIRL IN THIS SCHOOL.
YOU ACTUALLY MAKE AN *EFFORT*, YOU KNOW?

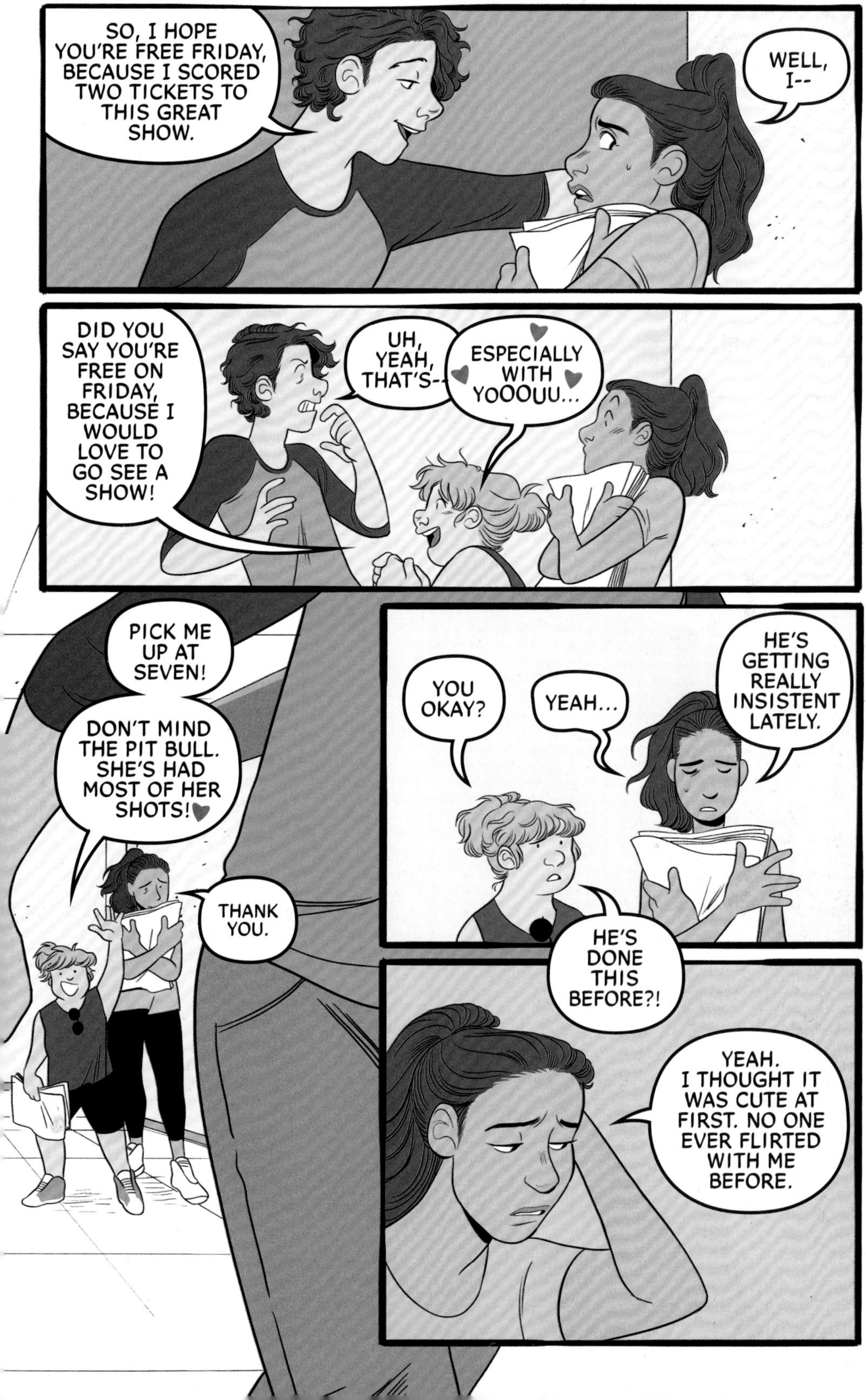
SO, I HOPE YOU'RE FREE FRIDAY, BECAUSE I SCORED TWO TICKETS TO THIS GREAT SHOW.
WELL, I--
DID YOU SAY YOU'RE FREE ON FRIDAY, BECAUSE I WOULD LOVE TO GO SEE A SHOW!
UH, YEAH, THAT'S--
ESPECIALLY WITH YOOOUU...
PICK ME UP AT SEVEN!
DON'T MIND THE PIT BULL. SHE'S HAD MOST OF HER SHOTS!
THANK YOU.
YOU OKAY?
YEAH...
HE'S GETTING REALLY INSISTENT LATELY.
HE'S DONE THIS BEFORE?!
YEAH. I THOUGHT IT WAS CUTE AT FIRST. NO ONE EVER FLIRTED WITH ME BEFORE.

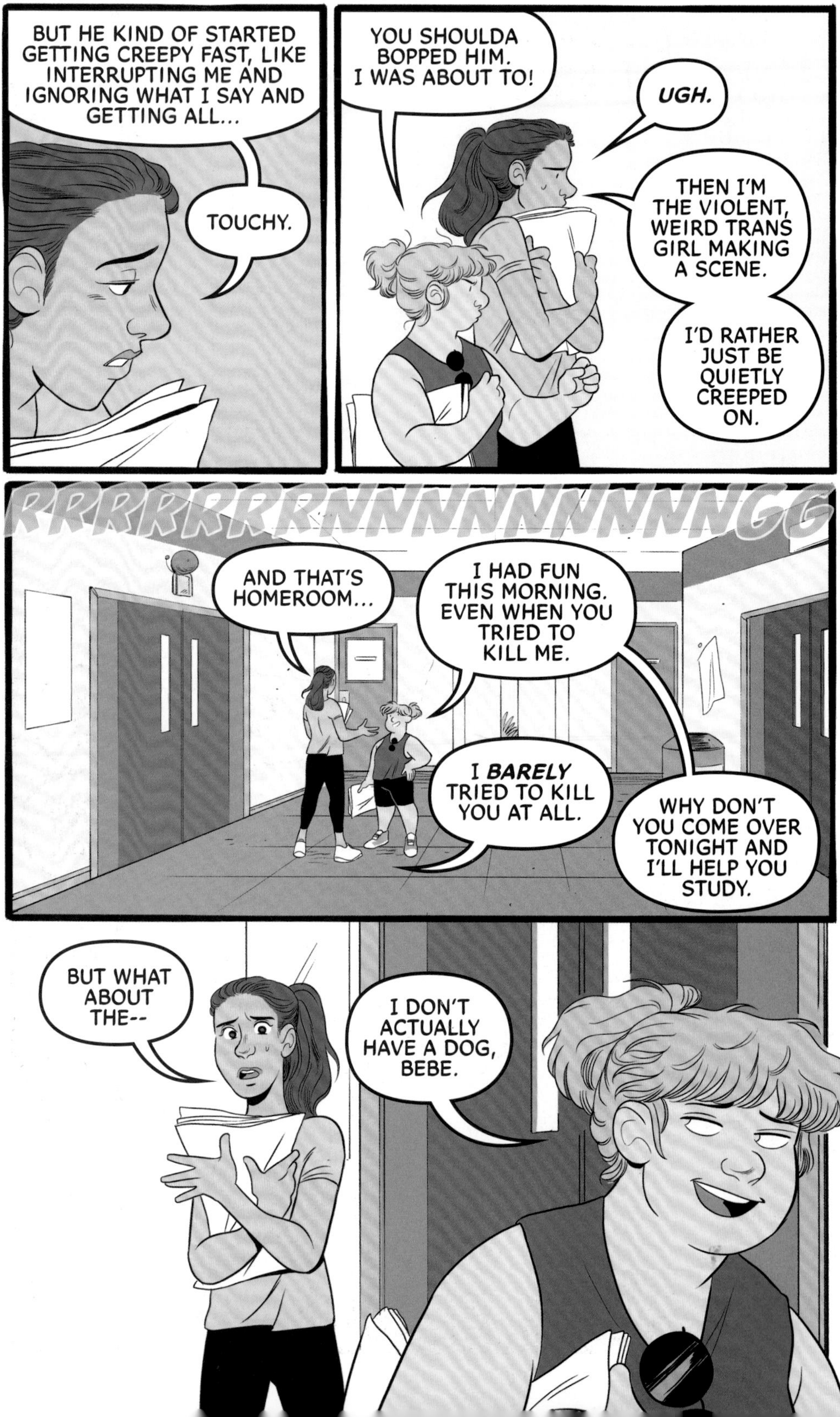
BUT HE KIND OF STARTED GETTING CREEPY FAST, LIKE INTERRUPTING ME AND IGNORING WHAT I SAY AND GETTING ALL...
TOUCHY.
YOU SHOULDA BOPPED HIM. I WAS ABOUT TO!
UGH.
THEN I'M THE VIOLENT, WEIRD TRANS GIRL MAKING A SCENE.
I'D RATHER JUST BE QUIETLY CREEPED ON.
RRRRRRRNNNNNNNNNNGG
AND THAT'S HOMEROOM...
I HAD FUN THIS MORNING. EVEN WHEN YOU TRIED TO KILL ME.
I BARELY TRIED TO KILL YOU AT ALL.
WHY DON'T YOU COME OVER TONIGHT AND I'LL HELP YOU STUDY.
BUT WHAT ABOUT THE--
I DON'T ACTUALLY HAVE A DOG, BEBE.

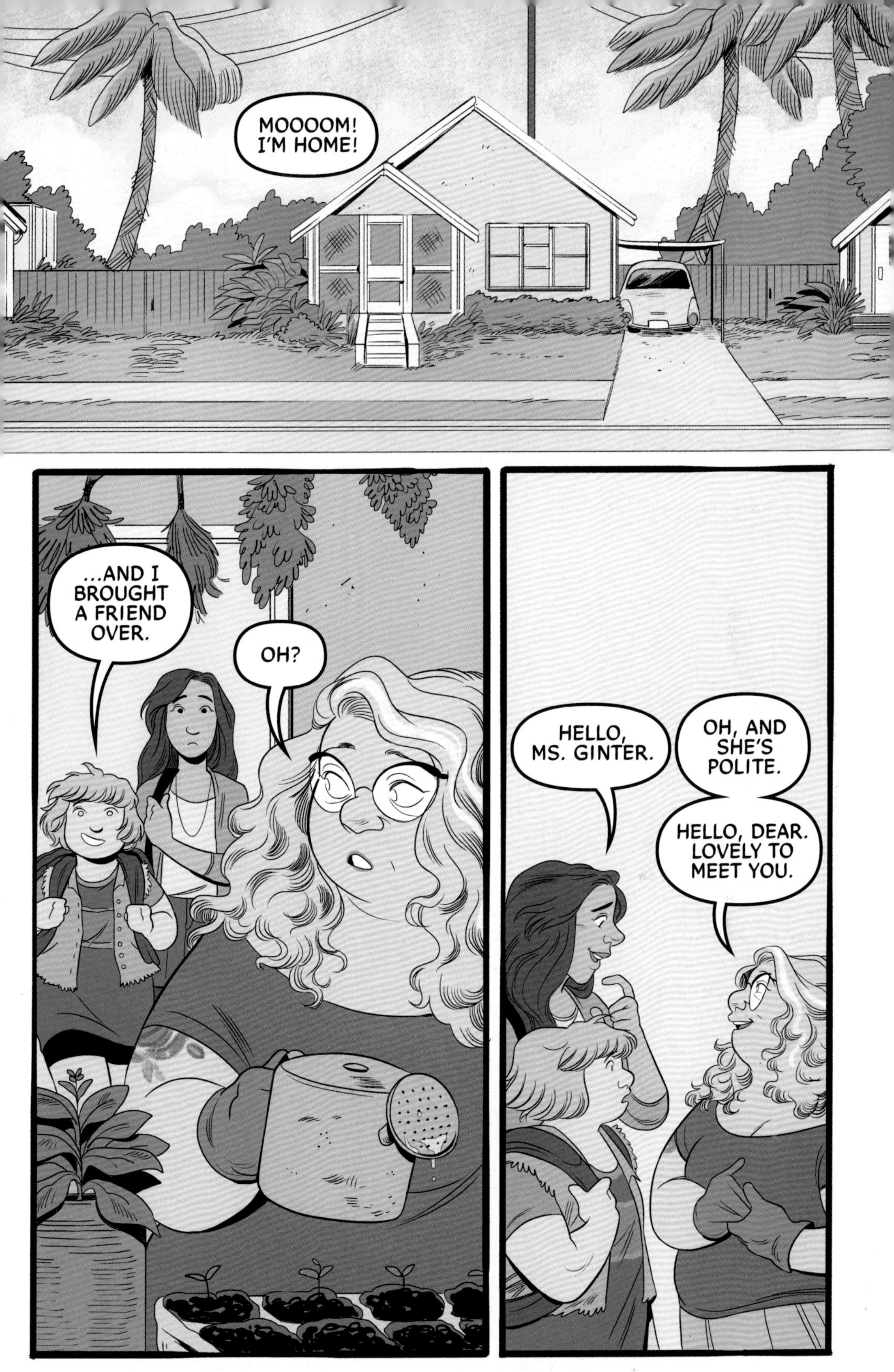
MOOOOM! I'M HOME!
...AND I BROUGHT A FRIEND OVER.
OH?
HELLO, MS. GINTER.
OH, AND SHE'S POLITE.
HELLO, DEAR. LOVELY TO MEET YOU.

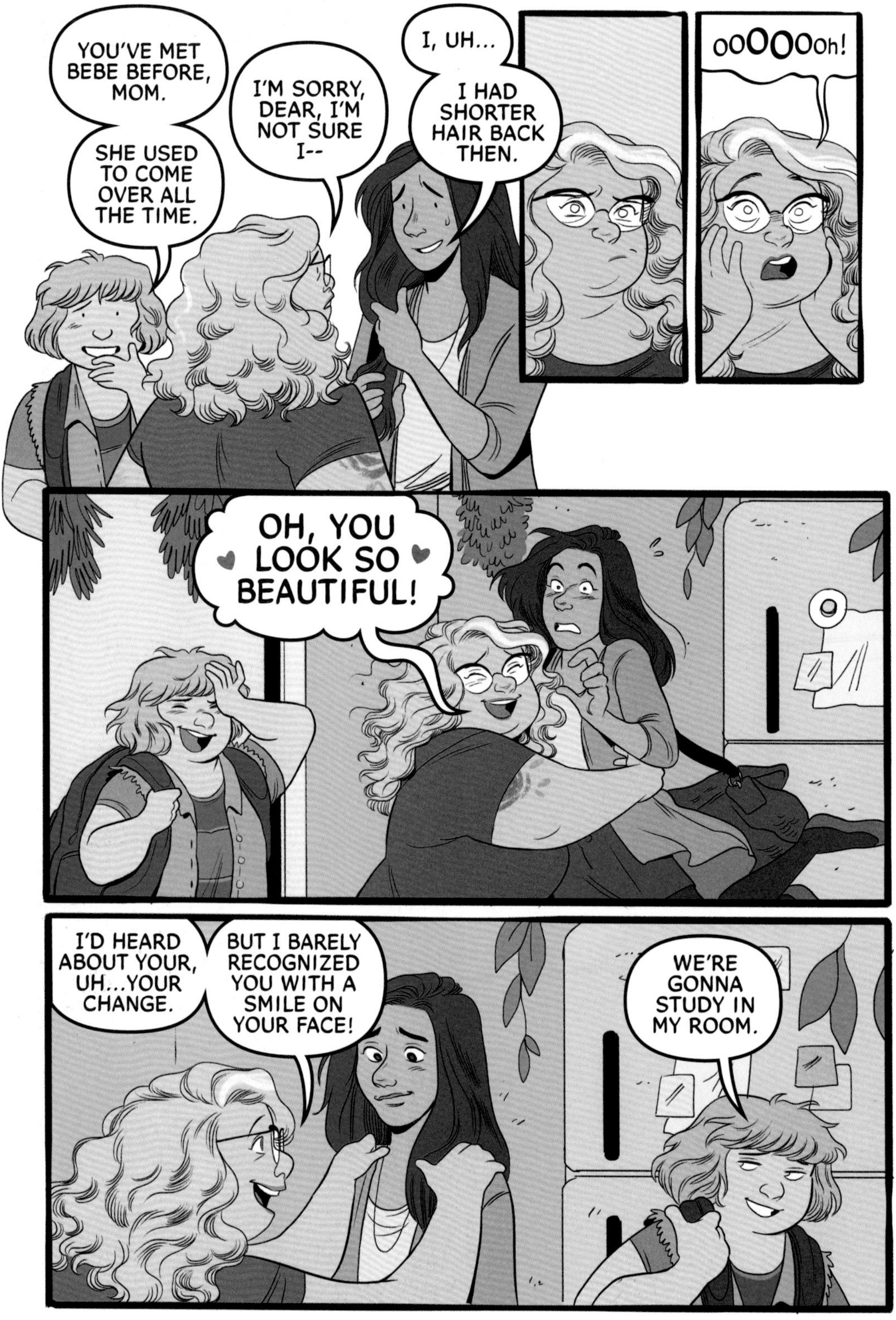
YOU'VE MET BEBE BEFORE, MOM.
SHE USED TO COME OVER ALL THE TIME.
I'M SORRY, DEAR, I'M NOT SURE I--
I, UH...
I HAD SHORTER HAIR BACK THEN.
ooOOOoh!
OH, YOU LOOK SO BEAUTIFUL!
I'D HEARD ABOUT YOUR, UH...YOUR CHANGE.
BUT I BARELY RECOGNIZED YOU WITH A SMILE ON YOUR FACE!
WE'RE GONNA STUDY IN MY ROOM.

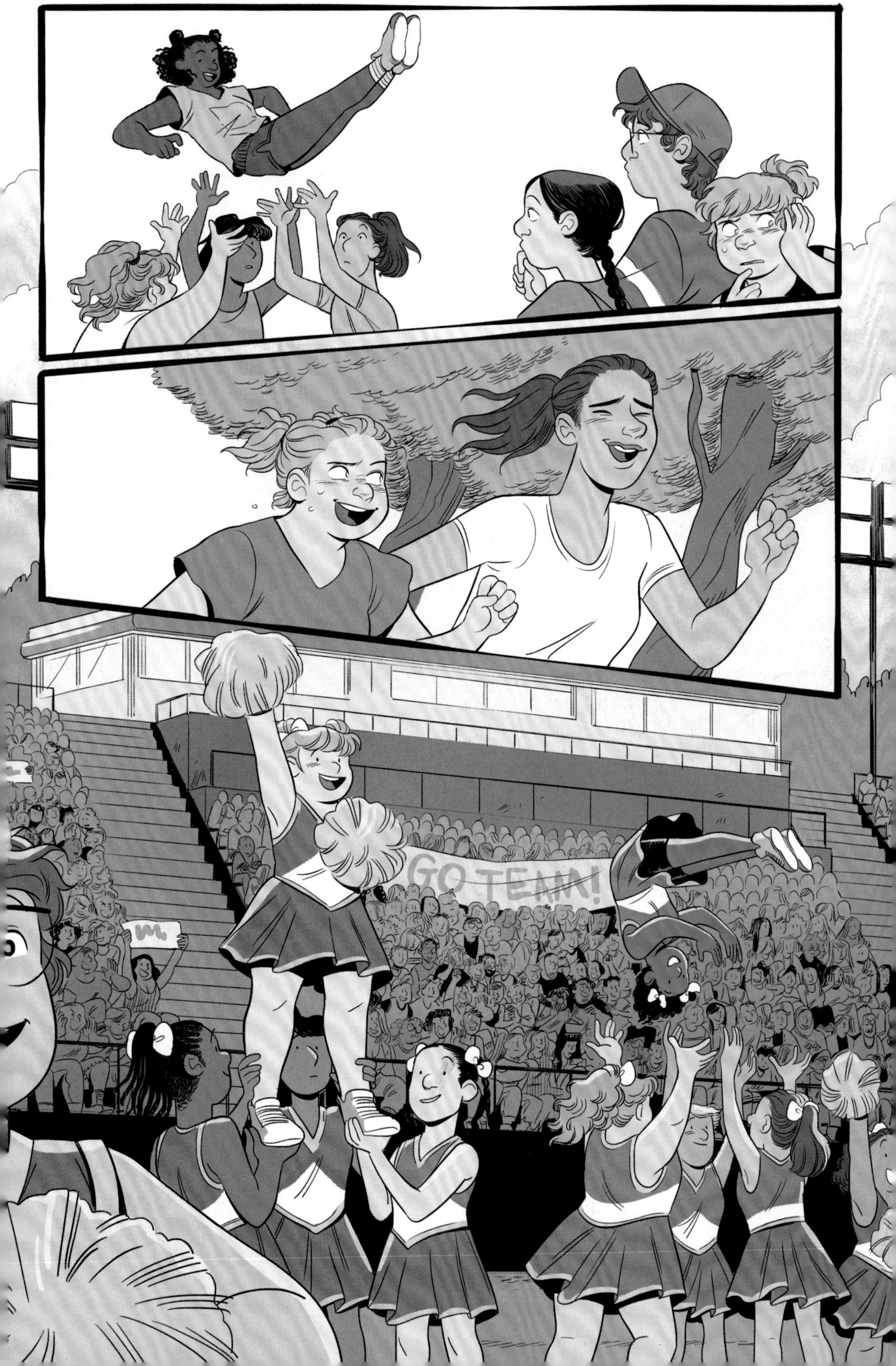
GO TEAM!

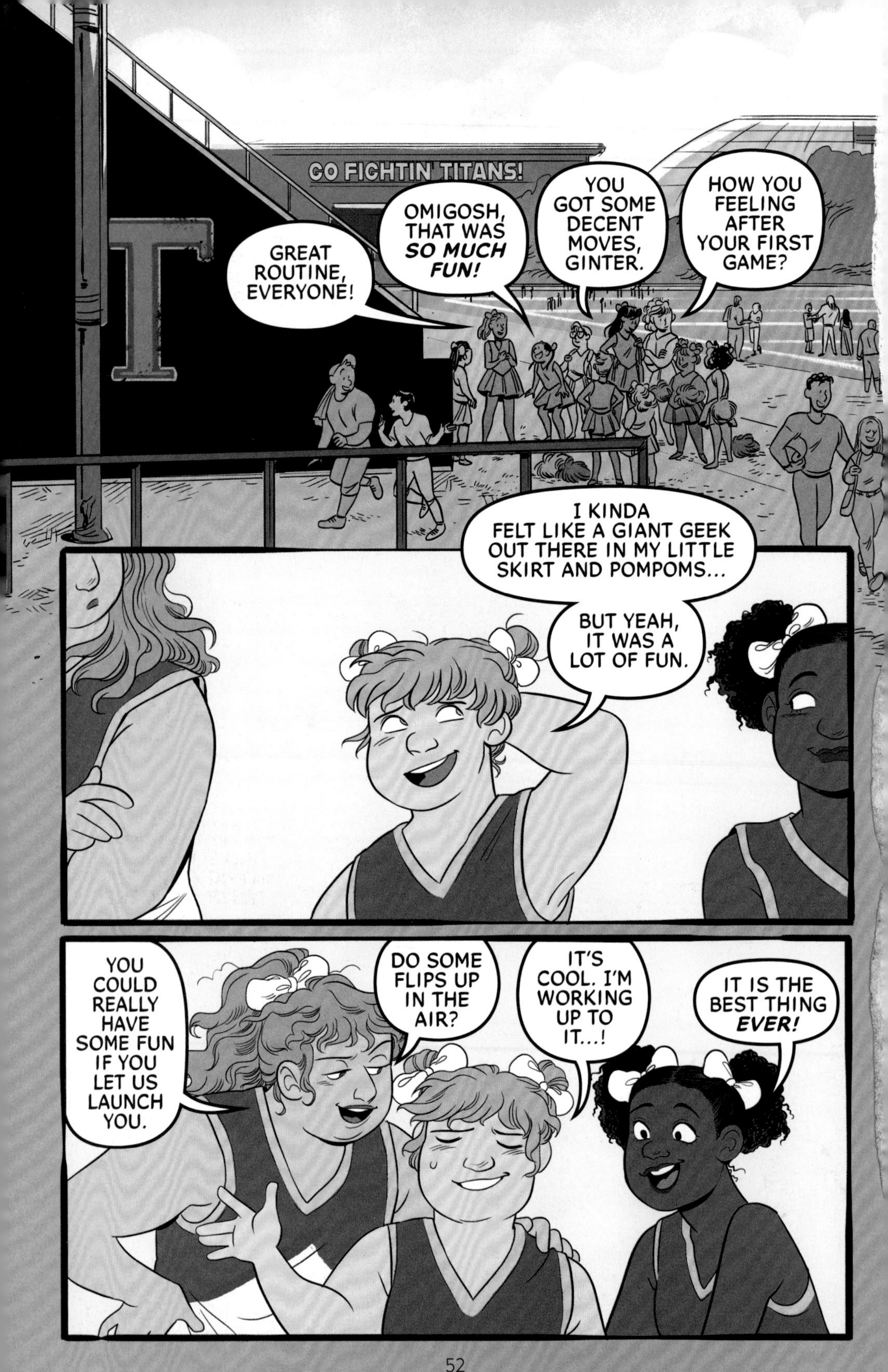
GO FIGHTIN' TITANS!
T
GREAT ROUTINE, EVERYONE!
OMIGOSH, THAT WAS *SO MUCH FUN!*
YOU GOT SOME DECENT MOVES, GINTER.
HOW YOU FEELING AFTER YOUR FIRST GAME?
I KINDA FELT LIKE A GIANT GEEK OUT THERE IN MY LITTLE SKIRT AND POMPOMS...
BUT YEAH, IT WAS A LOT OF FUN.
YOU COULD REALLY HAVE SOME FUN IF YOU LET US LAUNCH YOU.
DO SOME FLIPS UP IN THE AIR?
IT'S COOL. I'M WORKING UP TO IT...!
IT IS THE BEST THING *EVER!*

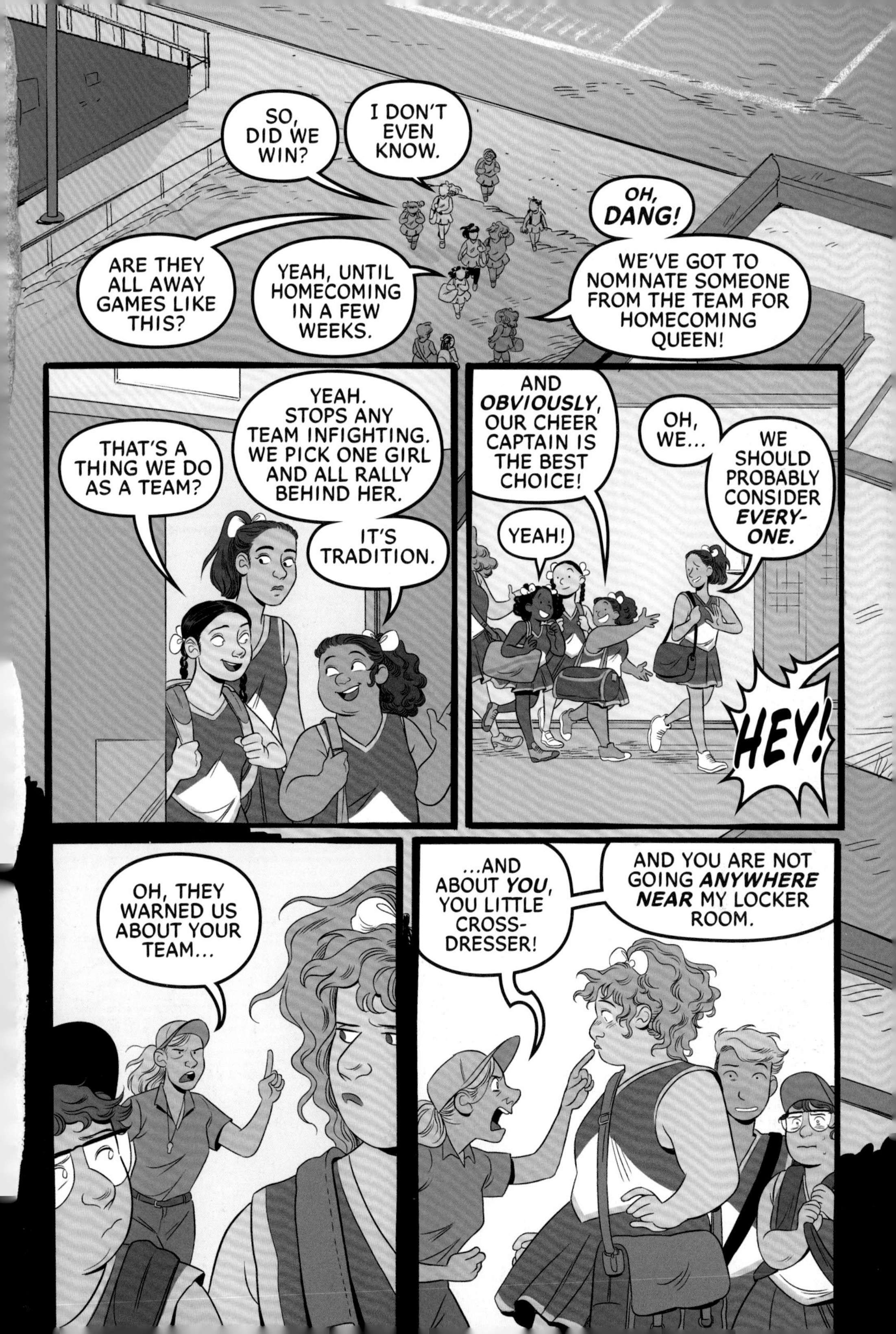
SO, DID WE WIN?
I DON'T EVEN KNOW.
ARE THEY ALL AWAY GAMES LIKE THIS?
YEAH, UNTIL HOMECOMING IN A FEW WEEKS.
OH, DANG!
WE'VE GOT TO NOMINATE SOMEONE FROM THE TEAM FOR HOMECOMING QUEEN!
THAT'S A THING WE DO AS A TEAM?
YEAH. STOPS ANY TEAM INFIGHTING. WE PICK ONE GIRL AND ALL RALLY BEHIND HER.
IT'S TRADITION.
AND OBVIOUSLY, OUR CHEER CAPTAIN IS THE BEST CHOICE!
YEAH!
OH, WE...
WE SHOULD PROBABLY CONSIDER EVERY-ONE.
HEY!
OH, THEY WARNED US ABOUT YOUR TEAM...
...AND ABOUT YOU, YOU LITTLE CROSS-DRESSER!
AND YOU ARE NOT GOING ANYWHERE NEAR MY LOCKER ROOM.

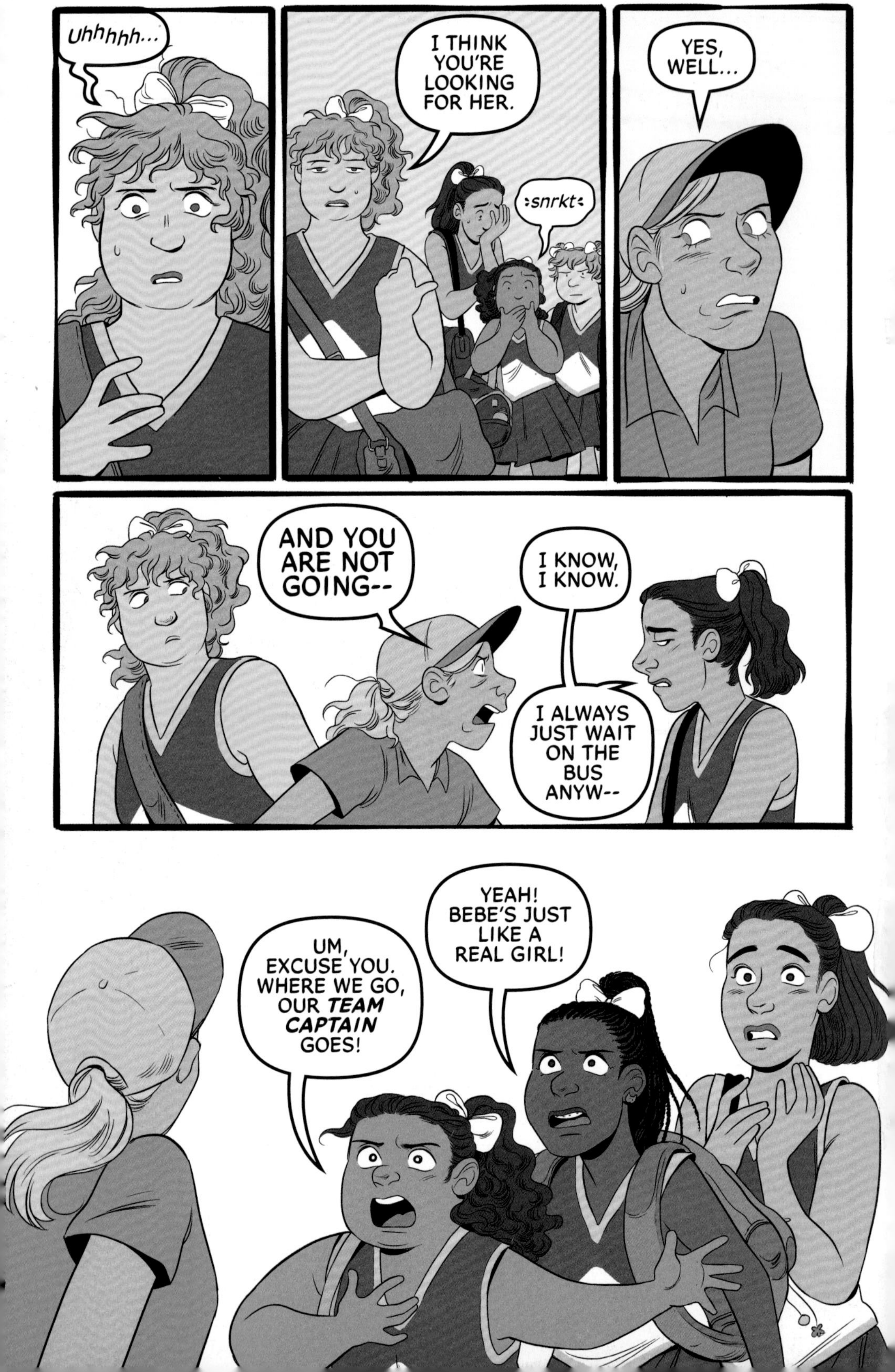
Uhhhhh...
I THINK YOU'RE LOOKING FOR HER.
:snrkt:
YES, WELL...
AND YOU ARE NOT GOING--
I KNOW, I KNOW.
I ALWAYS JUST WAIT ON THE BUS ANYW--
UM, EXCUSE YOU. WHERE WE GO, OUR *TEAM CAPTAIN* GOES!
YEAH! BEBE'S JUST LIKE A REAL GIRL!

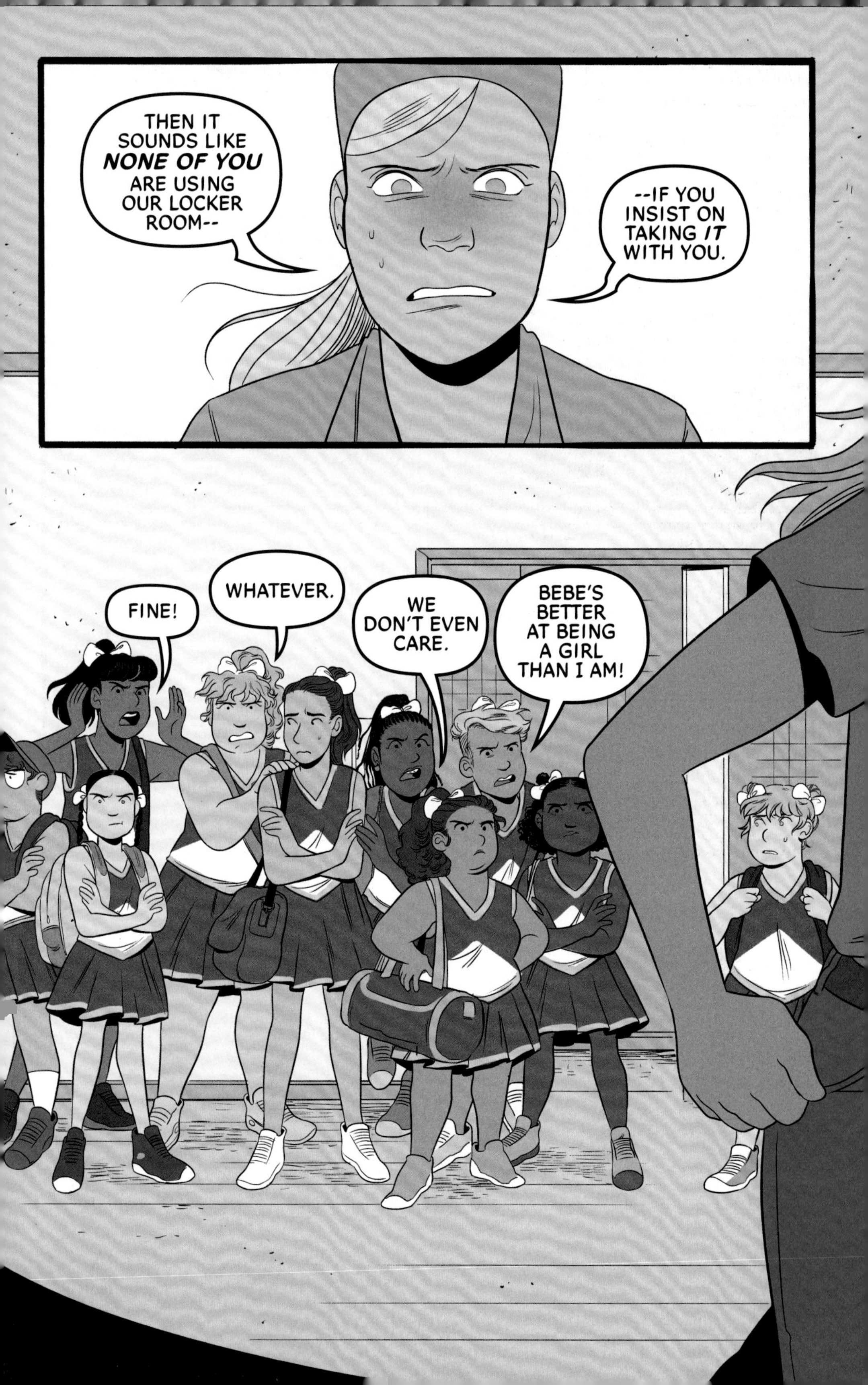
THEN IT SOUNDS LIKE NONE OF YOU ARE USING OUR LOCKER ROOM--
--IF YOU INSIST ON TAKING IT WITH YOU.
FINE!
WHATEVER.
WE DON'T EVEN CARE.
BEBE'S BETTER AT BEING A GIRL THAN I AM!

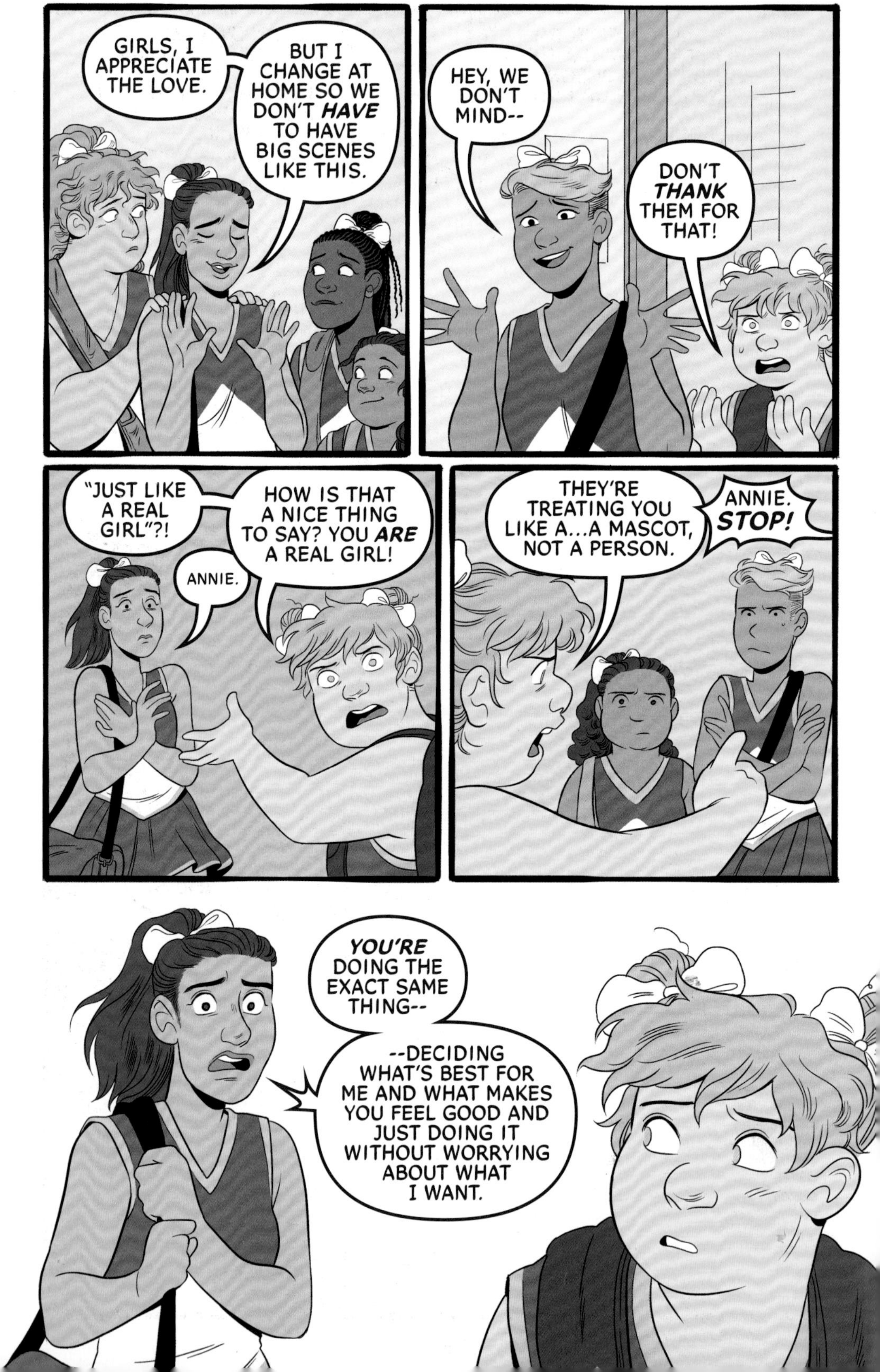
GIRLS, I APPRECIATE THE LOVE.
BUT I CHANGE AT HOME SO WE DON'T *HAVE* TO HAVE BIG SCENES LIKE THIS.
HEY, WE DON'T MIND--
DON'T *THANK* THEM FOR THAT!
"JUST LIKE A REAL GIRL"?!
HOW IS THAT A NICE THING TO SAY? YOU *ARE* A REAL GIRL!
ANNIE.
THEY'RE TREATING YOU LIKE A...A MASCOT, NOT A PERSON.
ANNIE. *STOP!*
YOU'RE DOING THE EXACT SAME THING--
--DECIDING WHAT'S BEST FOR ME AND WHAT MAKES YOU FEEL GOOD AND JUST DOING IT WITHOUT WORRYING ABOUT WHAT I WANT.

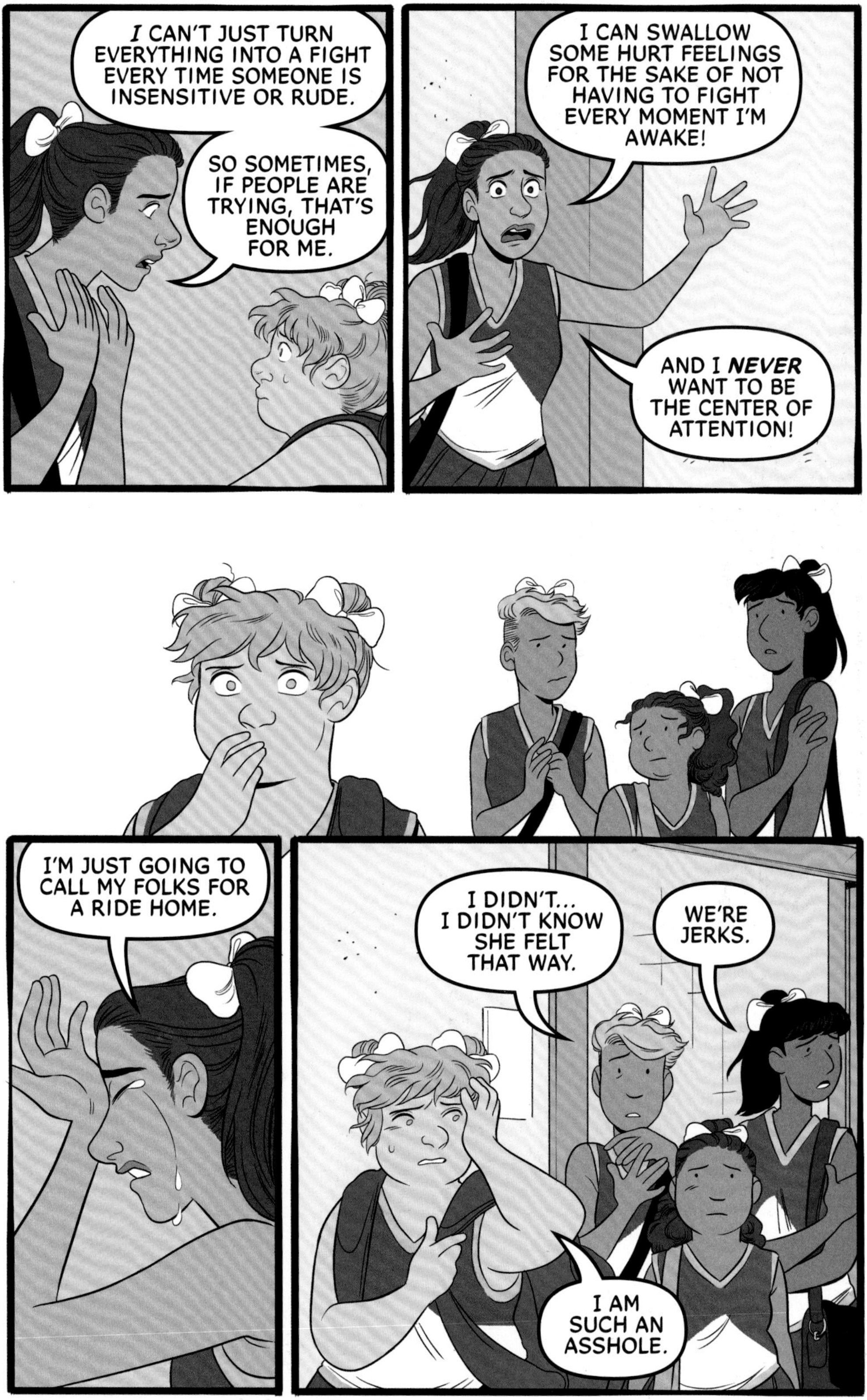
I CAN'T JUST TURN EVERYTHING INTO A FIGHT EVERY TIME SOMEONE IS INSENSITIVE OR RUDE.
SO SOMETIMES, IF PEOPLE ARE TRYING, THAT'S ENOUGH FOR ME.
I CAN SWALLOW SOME HURT FEELINGS FOR THE SAKE OF NOT HAVING TO FIGHT EVERY MOMENT I'M AWAKE!
AND I NEVER WANT TO BE THE CENTER OF ATTENTION!
I'M JUST GOING TO CALL MY FOLKS FOR A RIDE HOME.
I DIDN'T... I DIDN'T KNOW SHE FELT THAT WAY.
WE'RE JERKS.
I AM SUCH AN ASSHOLE.

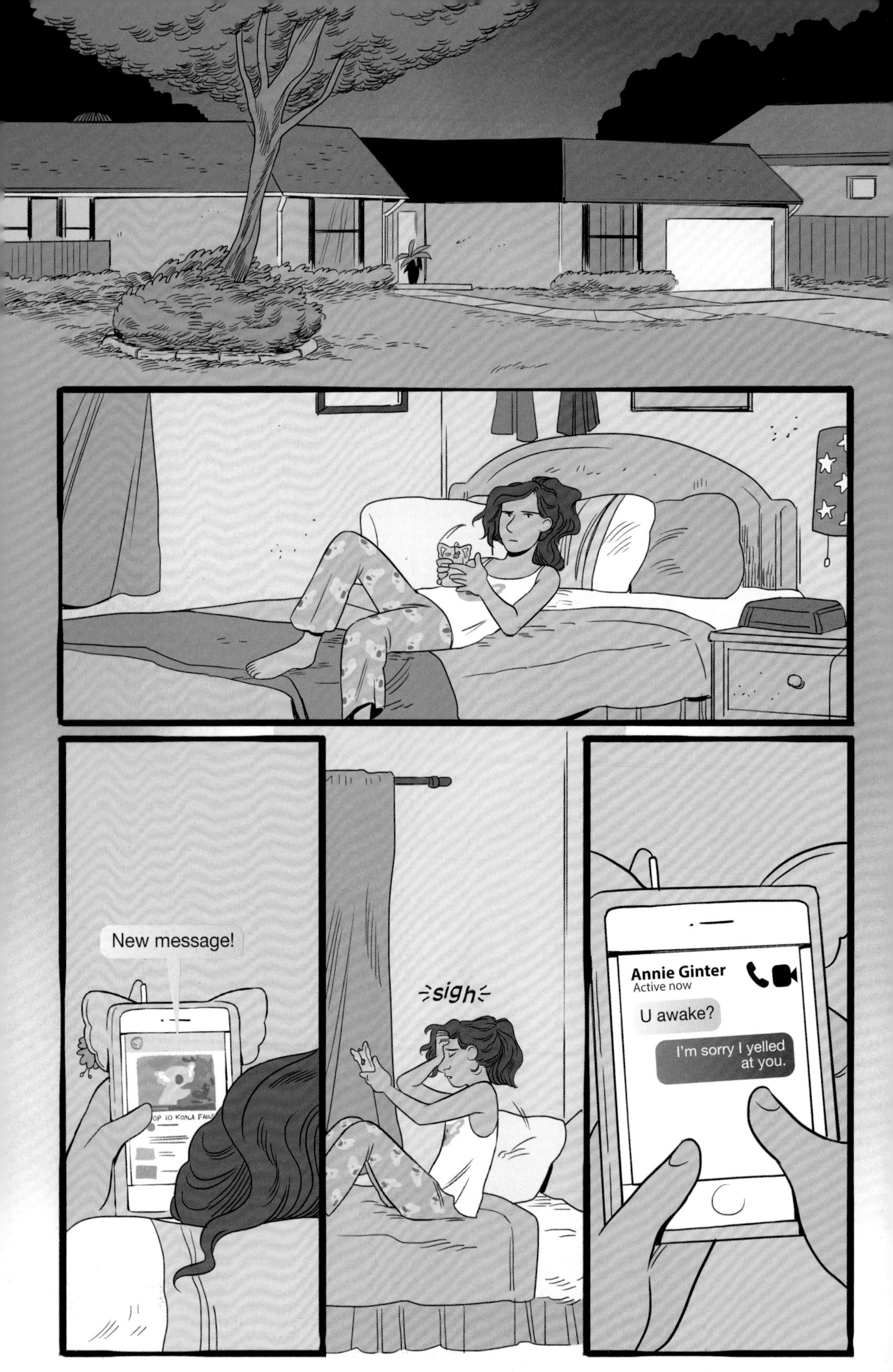
New message!
TOP 10 KOALA FAILS
sigh
Annie Ginter
Active now
U awake?
I'm sorry I yelled at you.

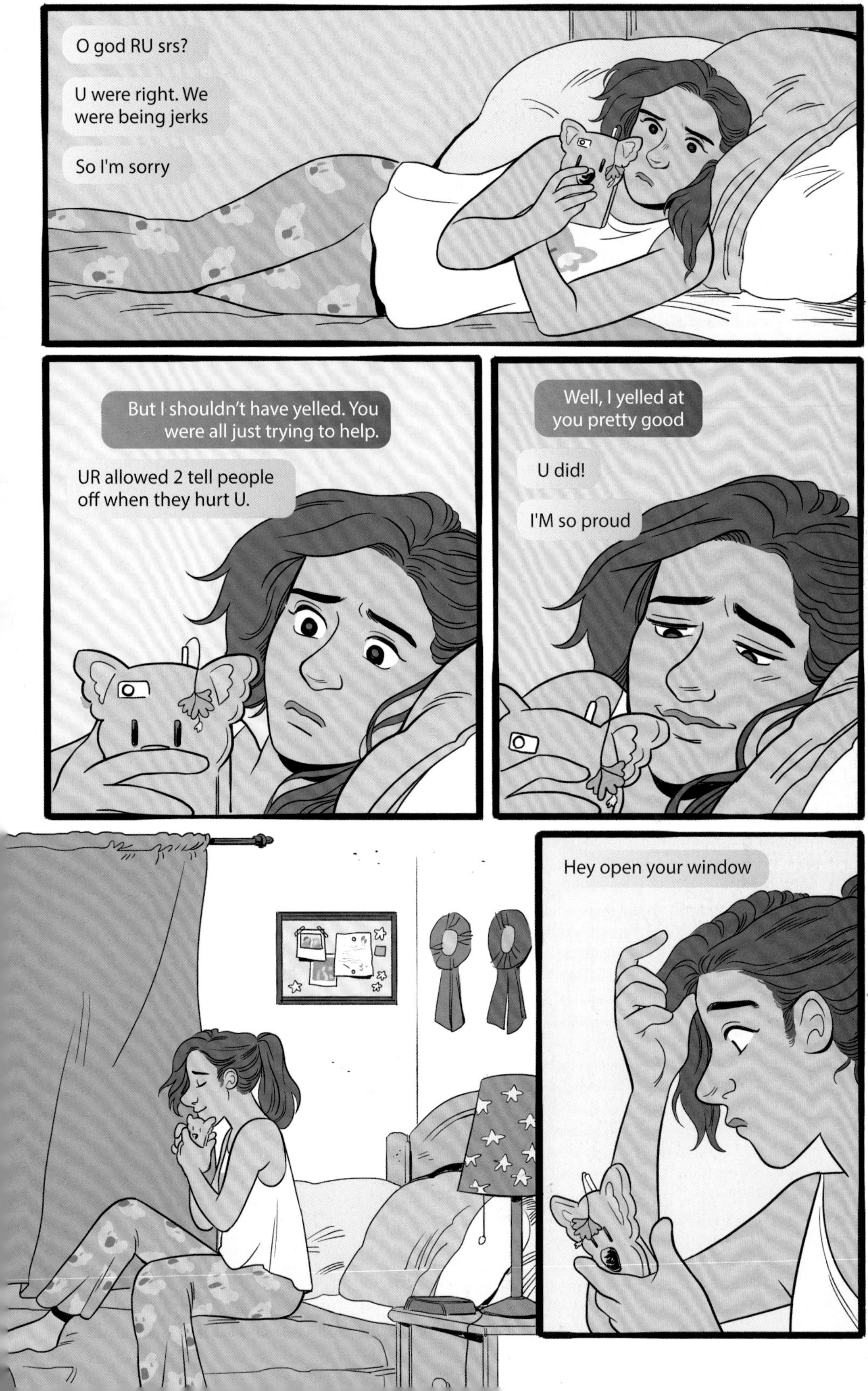

O god RU srs?
U were right. We were being jerks
So I'm sorry
But I shouldn't have yelled. You were all just trying to help.
UR allowed 2 tell people off when they hurt U.
Well, I yelled at you pretty good
U did!
I'M so proud
Hey open your window

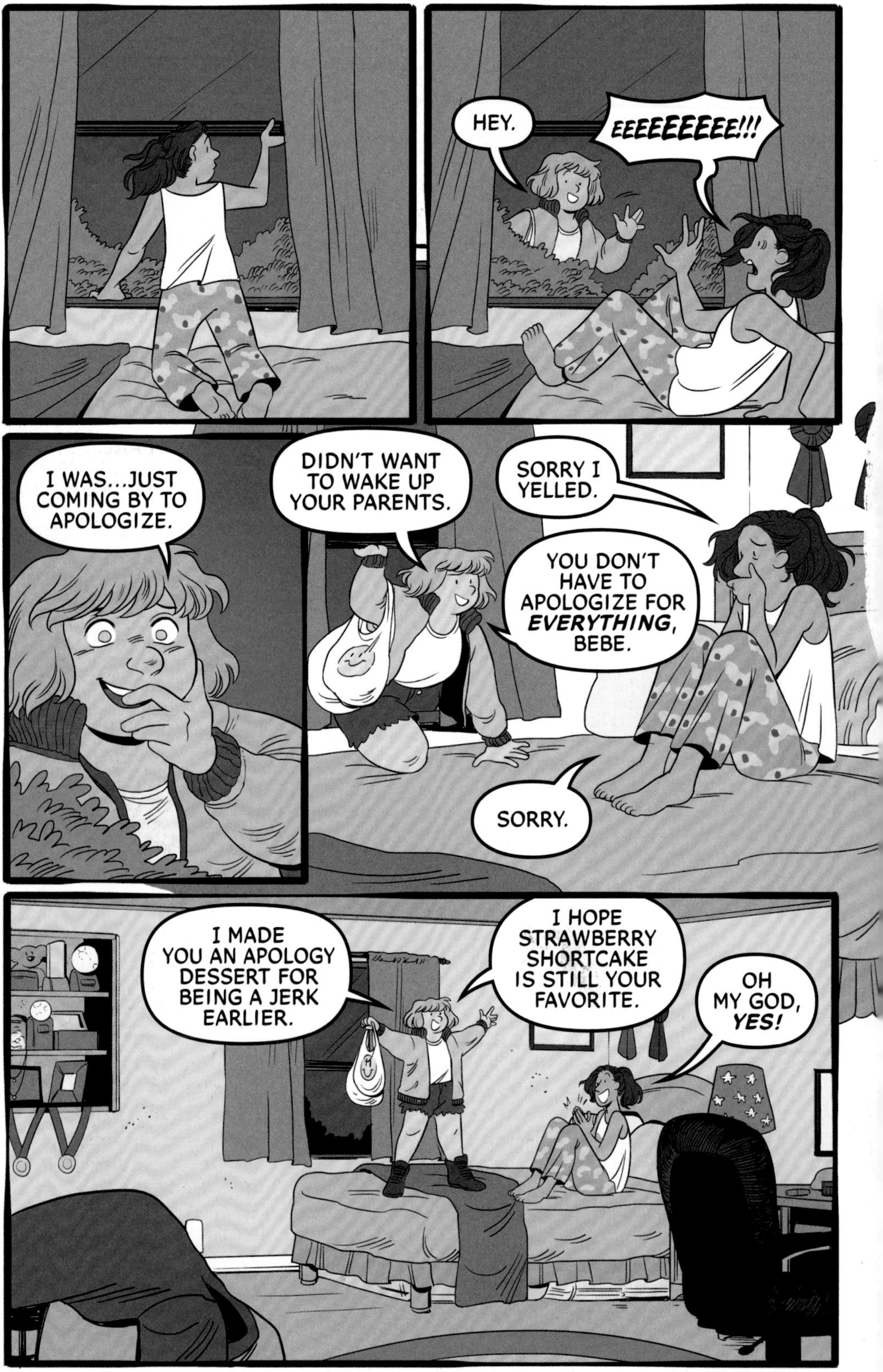
HEY.
EEEEEEEEE!!!
I WAS...JUST COMING BY TO APOLOGIZE.
DIDN'T WANT TO WAKE UP YOUR PARENTS.
SORRY I YELLED.
YOU DON'T HAVE TO APOLOGIZE FOR *EVERYTHING*, BEBE.
SORRY.
I MADE YOU AN APOLOGY DESSERT FOR BEING A JERK EARLIER.
I HOPE STRAWBERRY SHORTCAKE IS STILL YOUR FAVORITE.
OH MY GOD, *YES!*

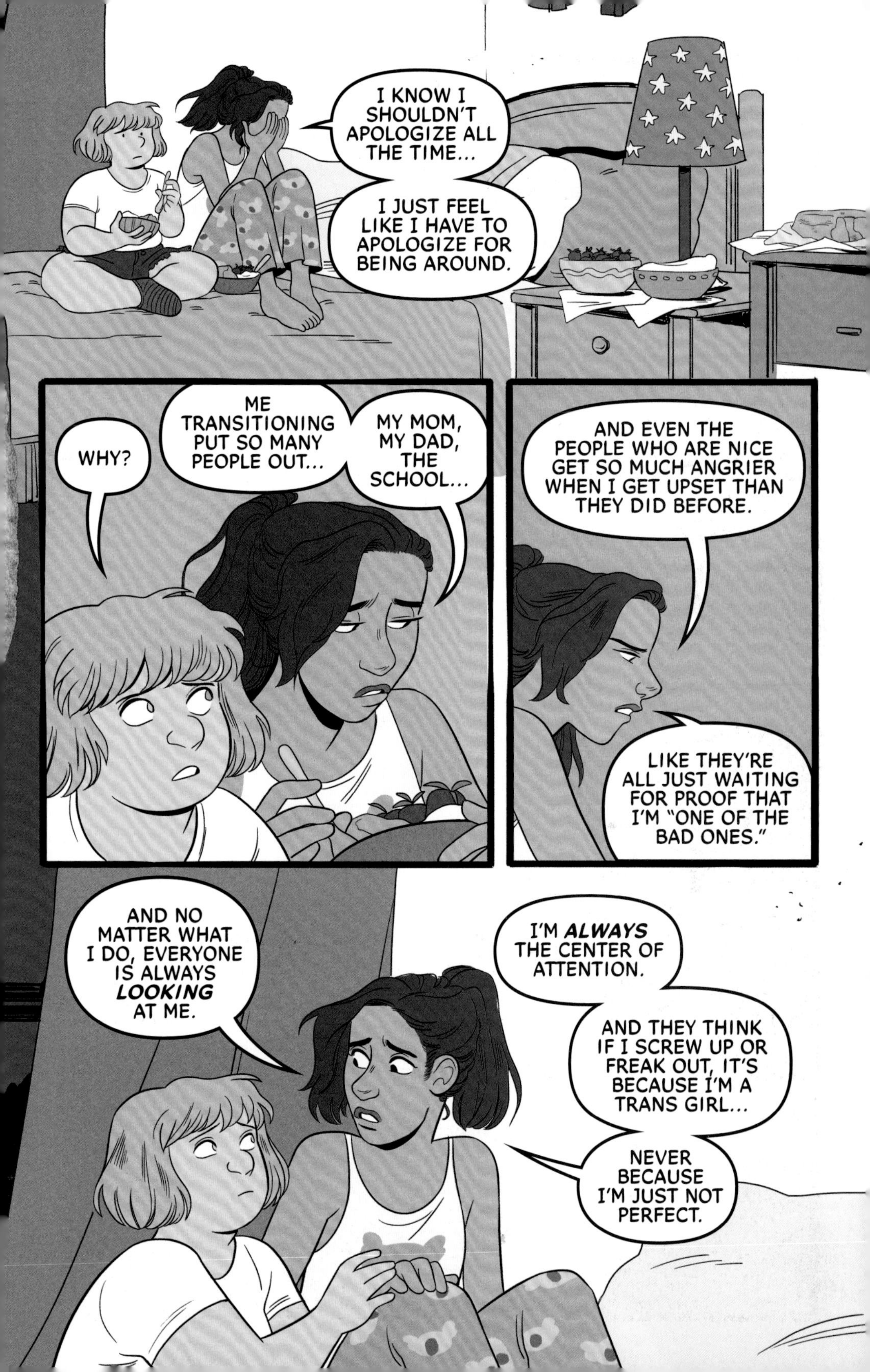
I KNOW I SHOULDN'T APOLOGIZE ALL THE TIME...
I JUST FEEL LIKE I HAVE TO APOLOGIZE FOR BEING AROUND.
WHY?
ME TRANSITIONING PUT SO MANY PEOPLE OUT...
MY MOM, MY DAD, THE SCHOOL...
AND EVEN THE PEOPLE WHO ARE NICE GET SO MUCH ANGRIER WHEN I GET UPSET THAN THEY DID BEFORE.
LIKE THEY'RE ALL JUST WAITING FOR PROOF THAT I'M "ONE OF THE BAD ONES."
AND NO MATTER WHAT I DO, EVERYONE IS ALWAYS ***LOOKING*** AT ME.
I'M ***ALWAYS*** THE CENTER OF ATTENTION.
AND THEY THINK IF I SCREW UP OR FREAK OUT, IT'S BECAUSE I'M A TRANS GIRL...
NEVER BECAUSE I'M JUST NOT PERFECT.

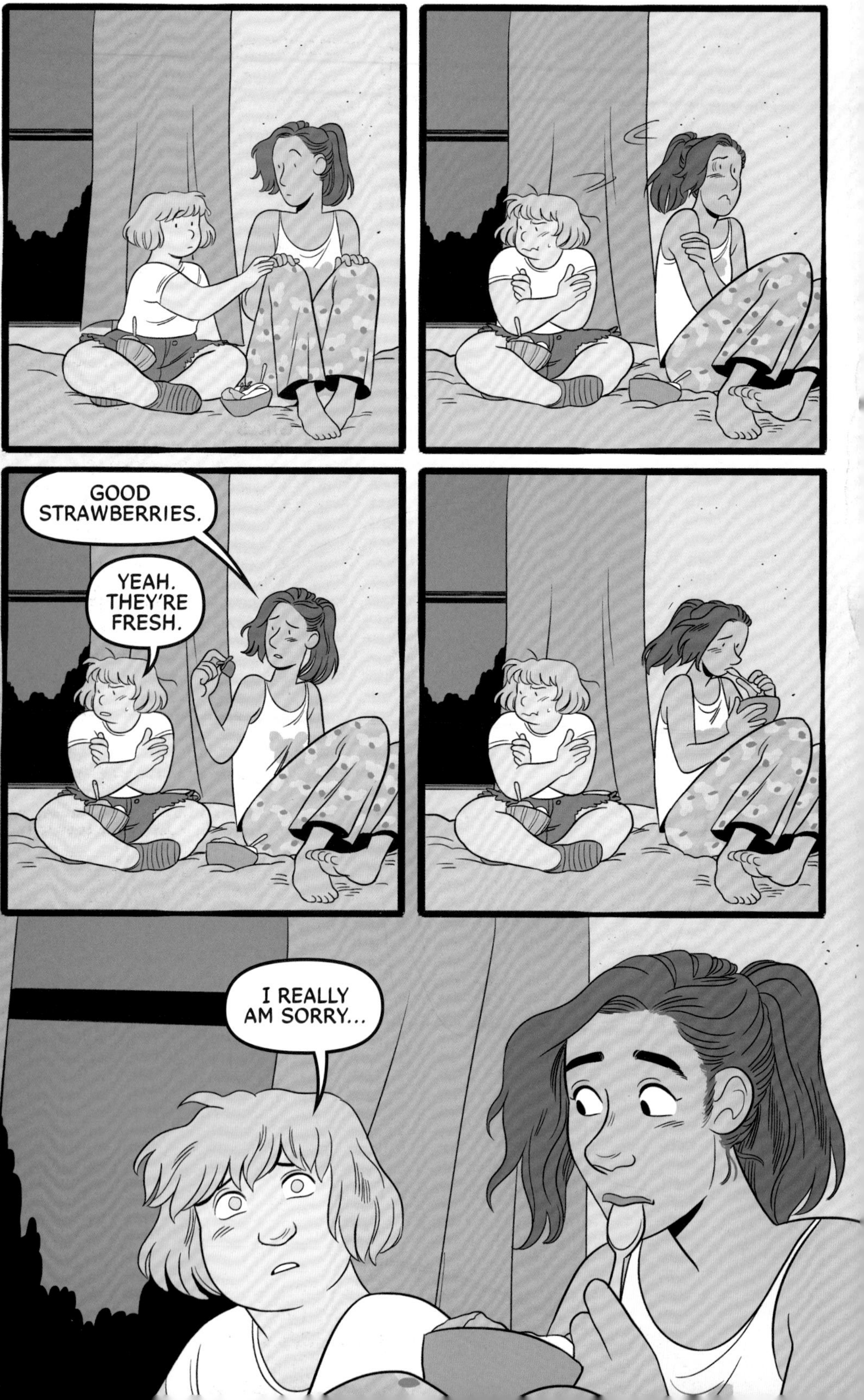
GOOD STRAWBERRIES.
YEAH. THEY'RE FRESH.
I REALLY AM SORRY...

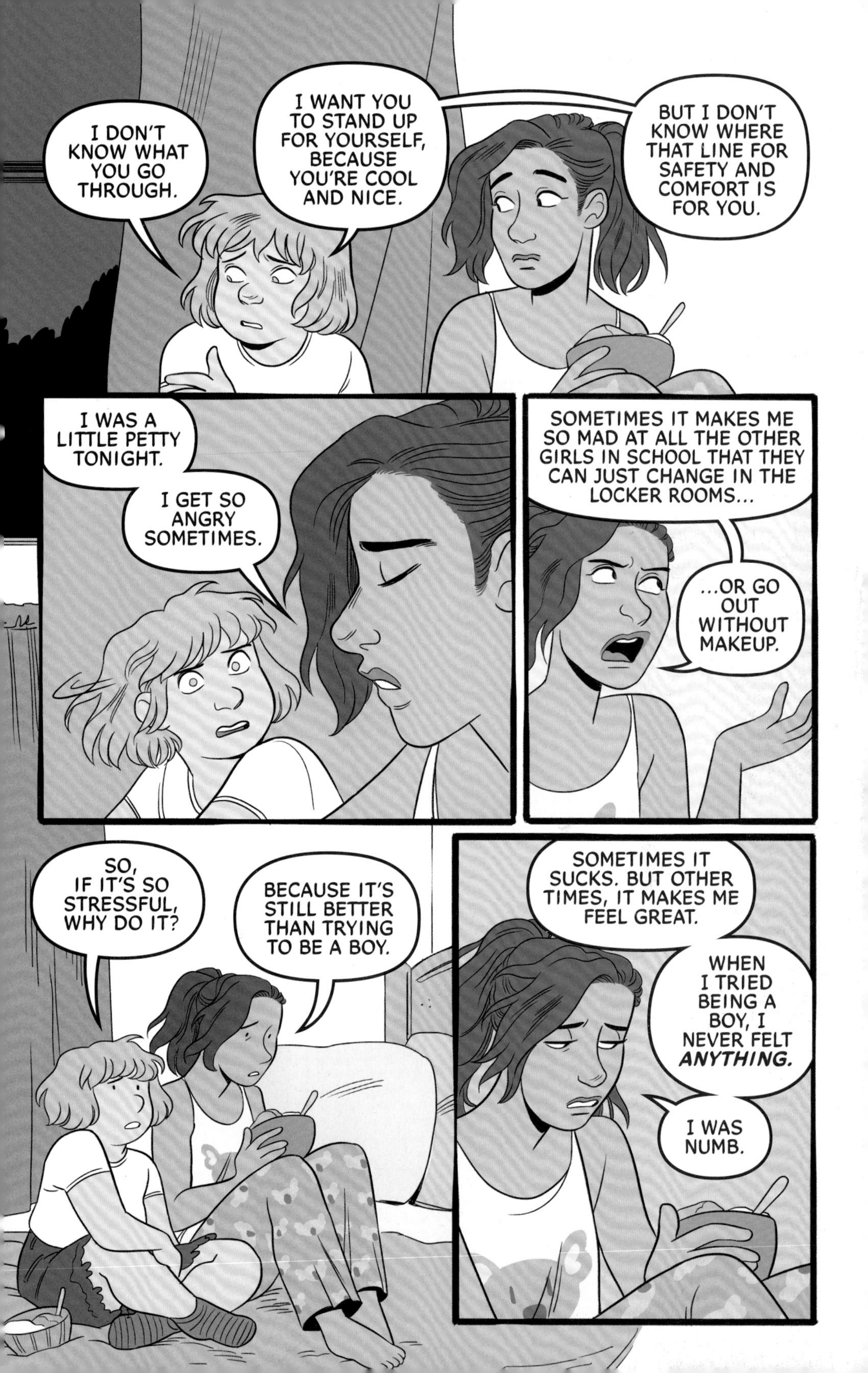
I DON'T KNOW WHAT YOU GO THROUGH.
I WANT YOU TO STAND UP FOR YOURSELF, BECAUSE YOU'RE COOL AND NICE.
BUT I DON'T KNOW WHERE THAT LINE FOR SAFETY AND COMFORT IS FOR YOU.
I WAS A LITTLE PETTY TONIGHT.
I GET SO ANGRY SOMETIMES.
SOMETIMES IT MAKES ME SO MAD AT ALL THE OTHER GIRLS IN SCHOOL THAT THEY CAN JUST CHANGE IN THE LOCKER ROOMS...
...OR GO OUT WITHOUT MAKEUP.
SO, IF IT'S SO STRESSFUL, WHY DO IT?
BECAUSE IT'S STILL BETTER THAN TRYING TO BE A BOY.
SOMETIMES IT SUCKS. BUT OTHER TIMES, IT MAKES ME FEEL GREAT.
WHEN I TRIED BEING A BOY, I NEVER FELT *ANYTHING.*
I WAS NUMB.

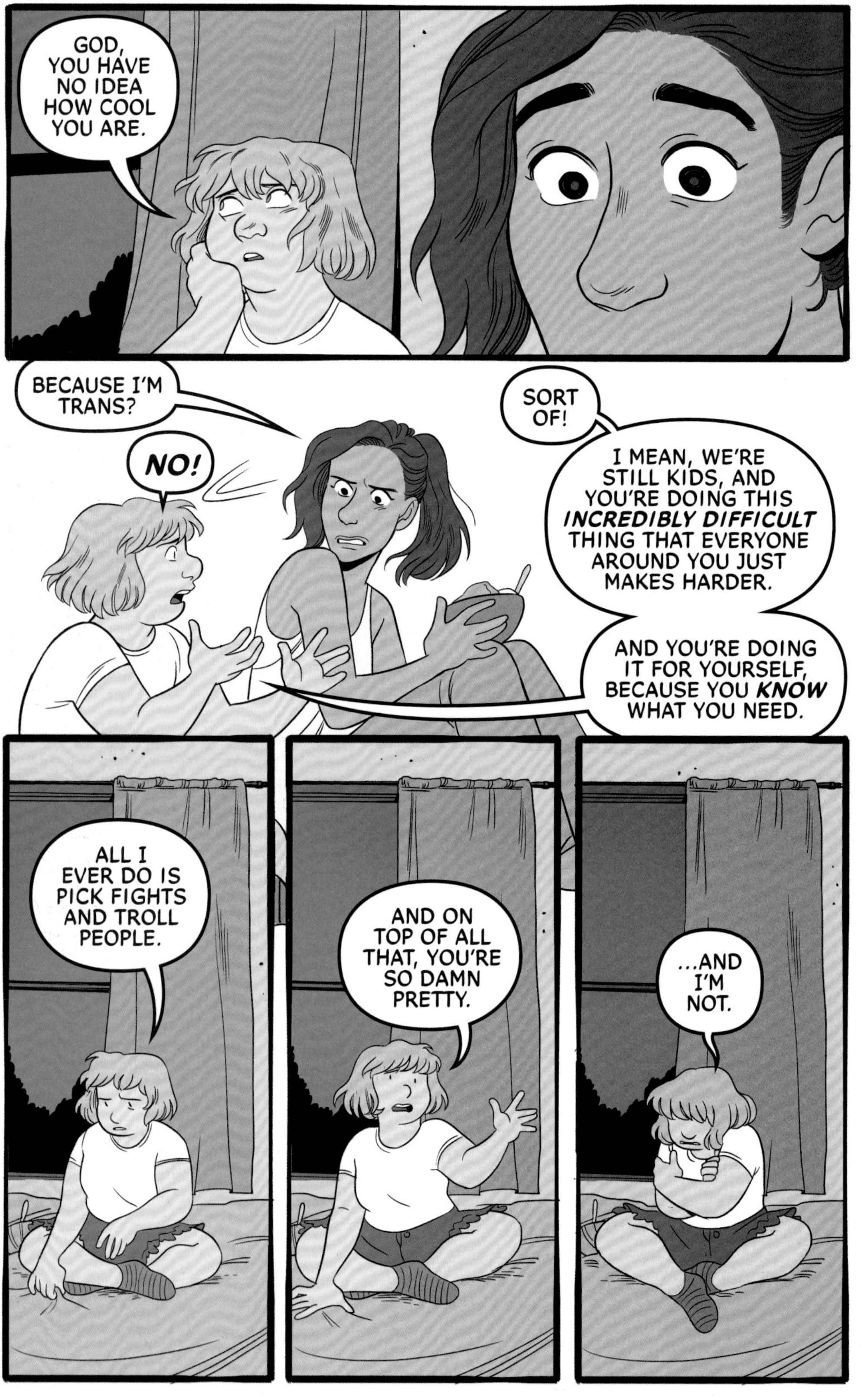
GOD, YOU HAVE NO IDEA HOW COOL YOU ARE.
BECAUSE I'M TRANS?
NO!
SORT OF!
I MEAN, WE'RE STILL KIDS, AND YOU'RE DOING THIS INCREDIBLY DIFFICULT THING THAT EVERYONE AROUND YOU JUST MAKES HARDER.
AND YOU'RE DOING IT FOR YOURSELF, BECAUSE YOU KNOW WHAT YOU NEED.
ALL I EVER DO IS PICK FIGHTS AND TROLL PEOPLE.
AND ON TOP OF ALL THAT, YOU'RE SO DAMN PRETTY.
...AND I'M NOT.

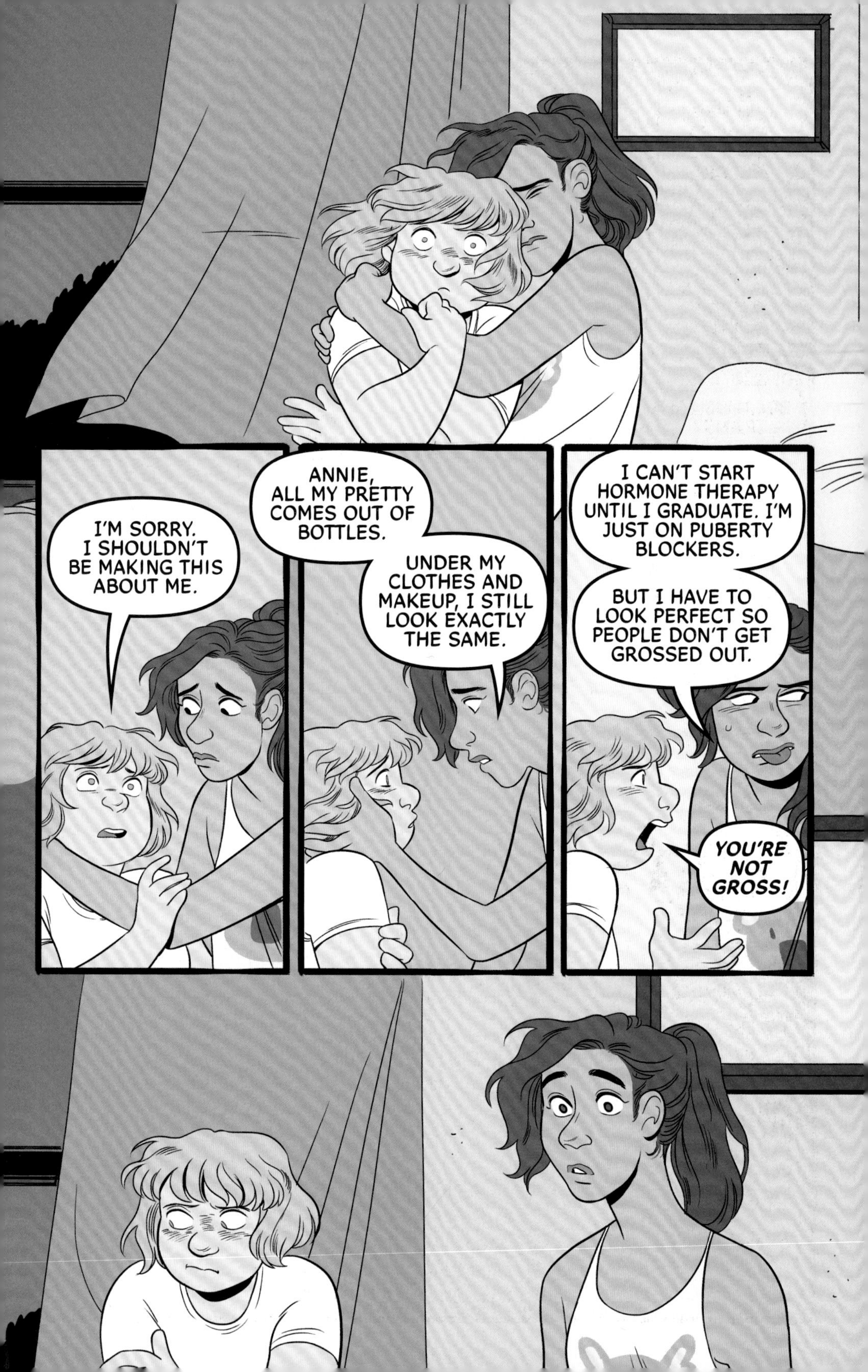
I'M SORRY. I SHOULDN'T BE MAKING THIS ABOUT ME.
ANNIE, ALL MY PRETTY COMES OUT OF BOTTLES.
UNDER MY CLOTHES AND MAKEUP, I STILL LOOK EXACTLY THE SAME.
I CAN'T START HORMONE THERAPY UNTIL I GRADUATE. I'M JUST ON PUBERTY BLOCKERS.
BUT I HAVE TO LOOK PERFECT SO PEOPLE DON'T GET GROSSED OUT.
YOU'RE NOT GROSS!

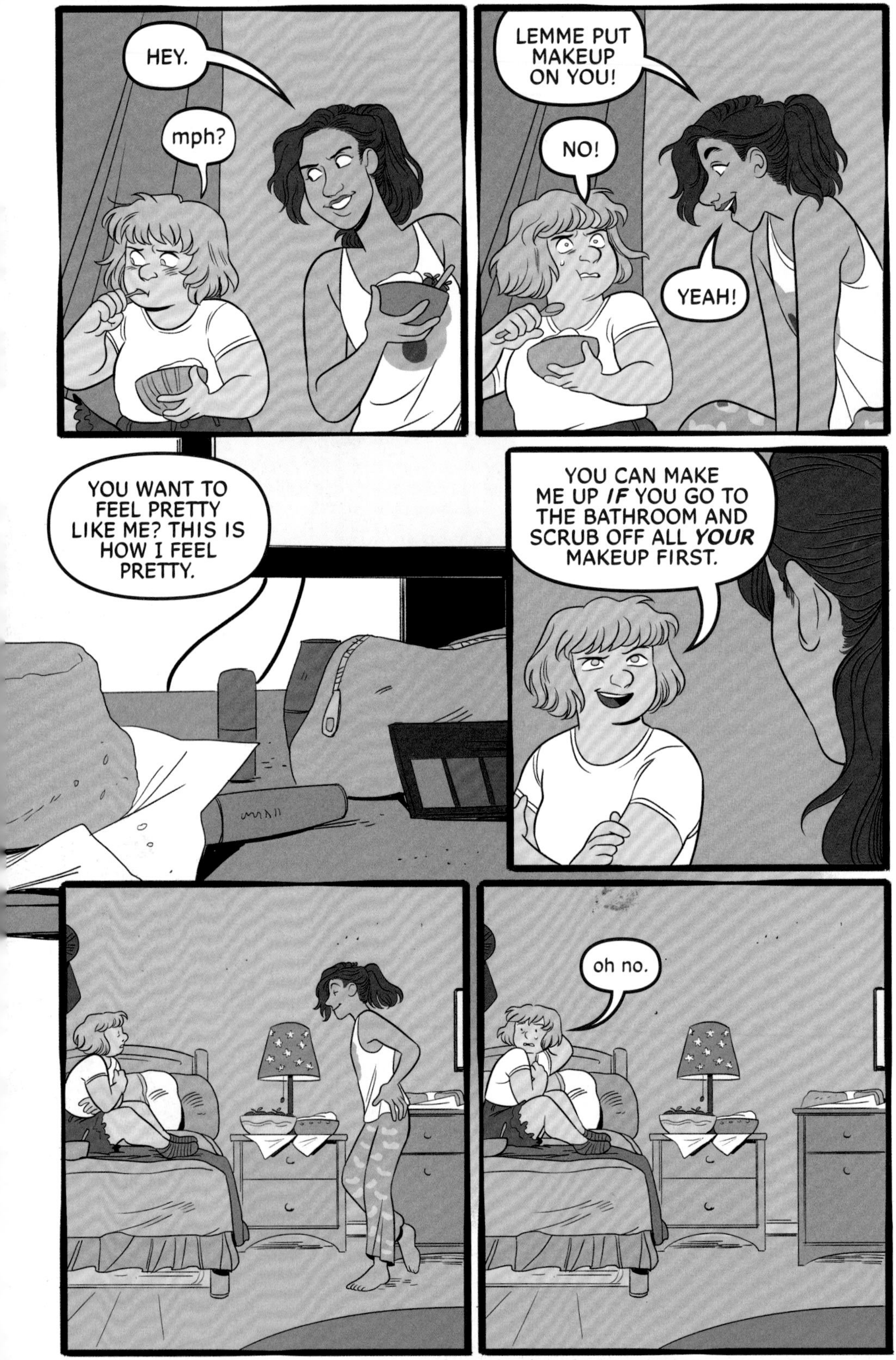
HEY.
mph?
LEMME PUT MAKEUP ON YOU!
NO!
YEAH!
YOU WANT TO FEEL PRETTY LIKE ME? THIS IS HOW I FEEL PRETTY.
YOU CAN MAKE ME UP *IF* YOU GO TO THE BATHROOM AND SCRUB OFF ALL *YOUR* MAKEUP FIRST.
oh no.

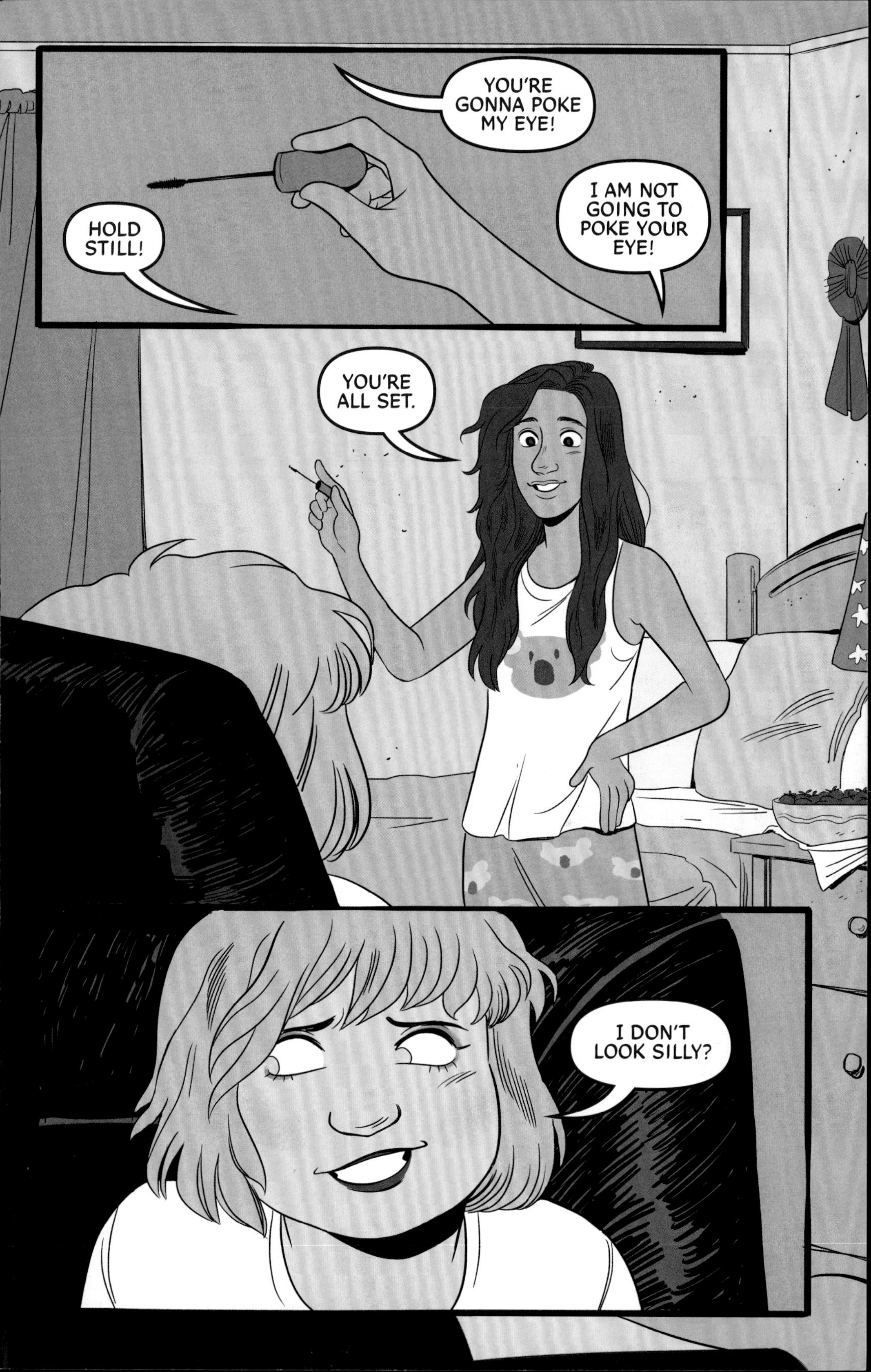
YOU'RE GONNA POKE MY EYE!
HOLD STILL!
I AM NOT GOING TO POKE YOUR EYE!
YOU'RE ALL SET.
I DON'T LOOK SILLY?

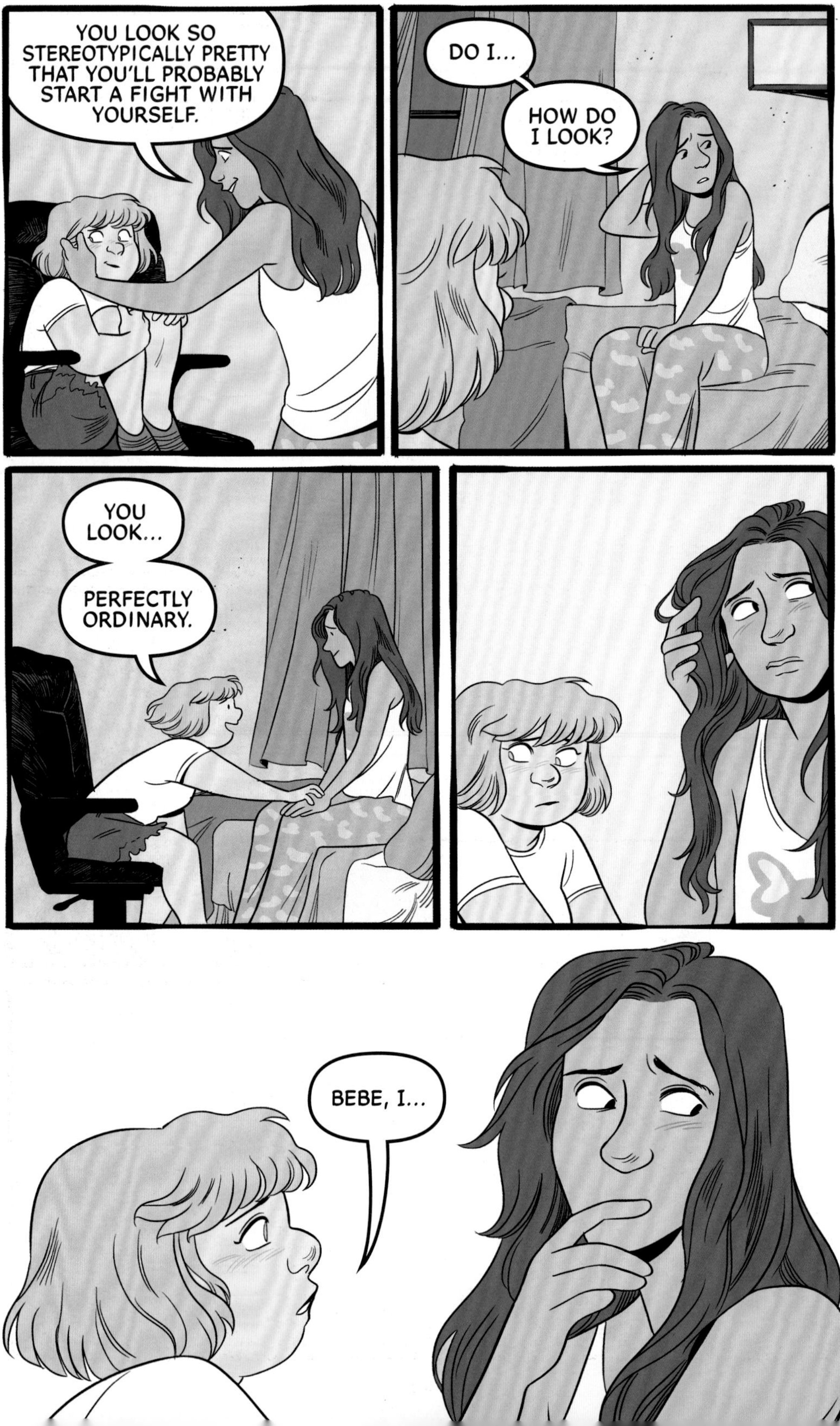
YOU LOOK SO STEREOTYPICALLY PRETTY THAT YOU'LL PROBABLY START A FIGHT WITH YOURSELF.
DO I...
HOW DO I LOOK?
YOU LOOK...
PERFECTLY ORDINARY.
BEBE, I...

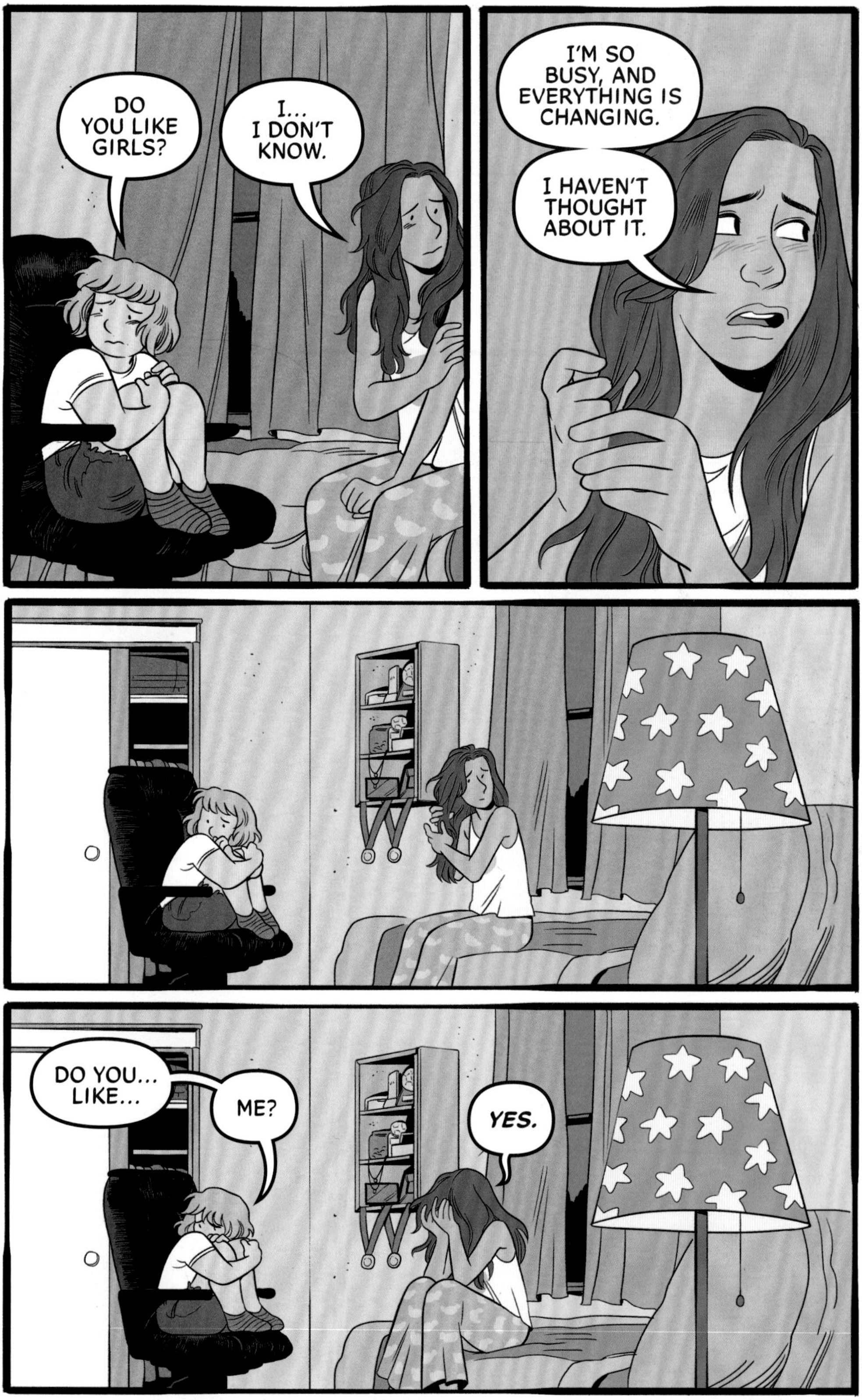
DO YOU LIKE GIRLS?
I... I DON'T KNOW.
I'M SO BUSY, AND EVERYTHING IS CHANGING.
I HAVEN'T THOUGHT ABOUT IT.
DO YOU... LIKE...
ME?
YES.

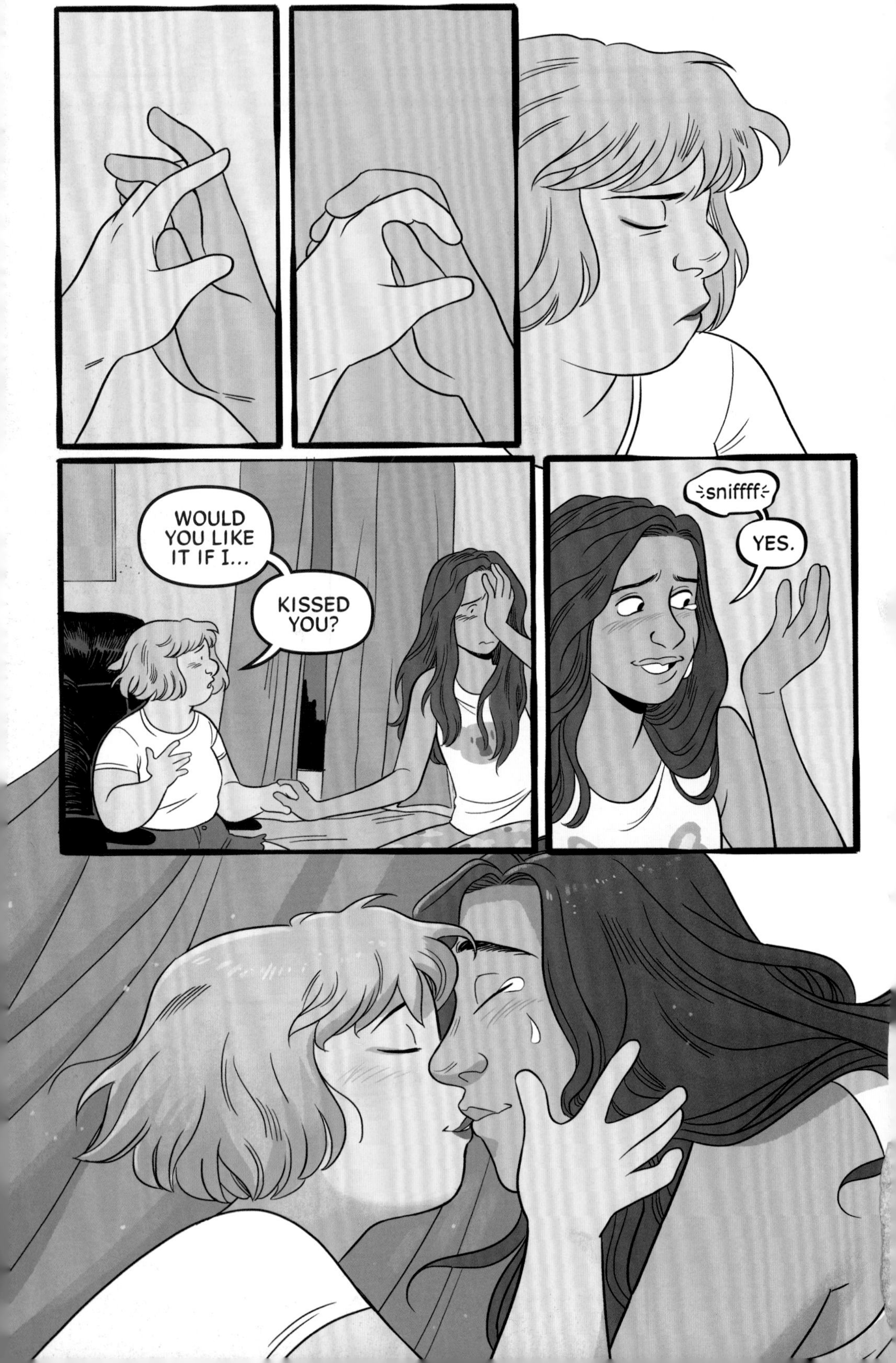
WOULD YOU LIKE IT IF I...
KISSED YOU?
sniffff
YES.

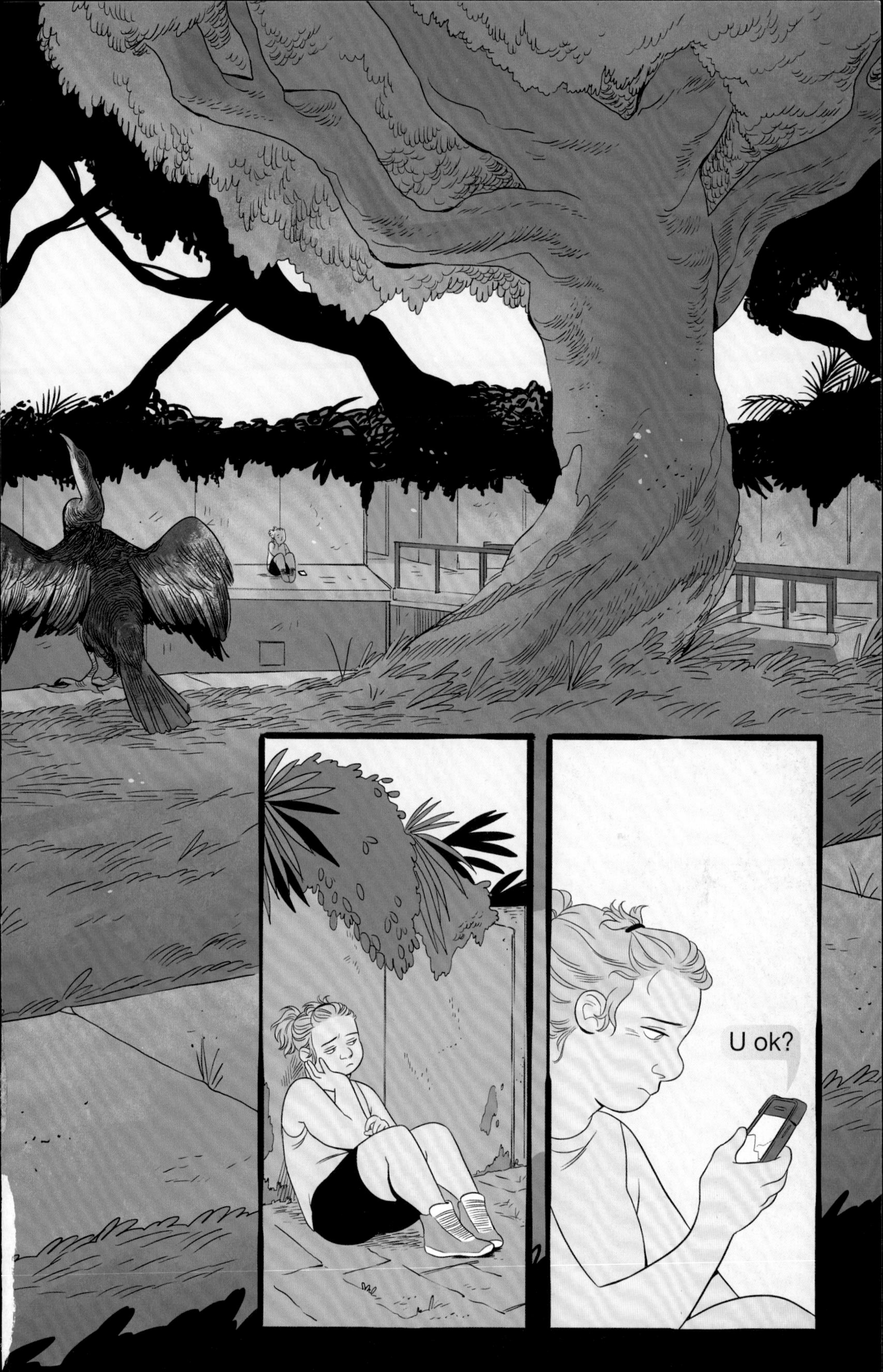
U ok?

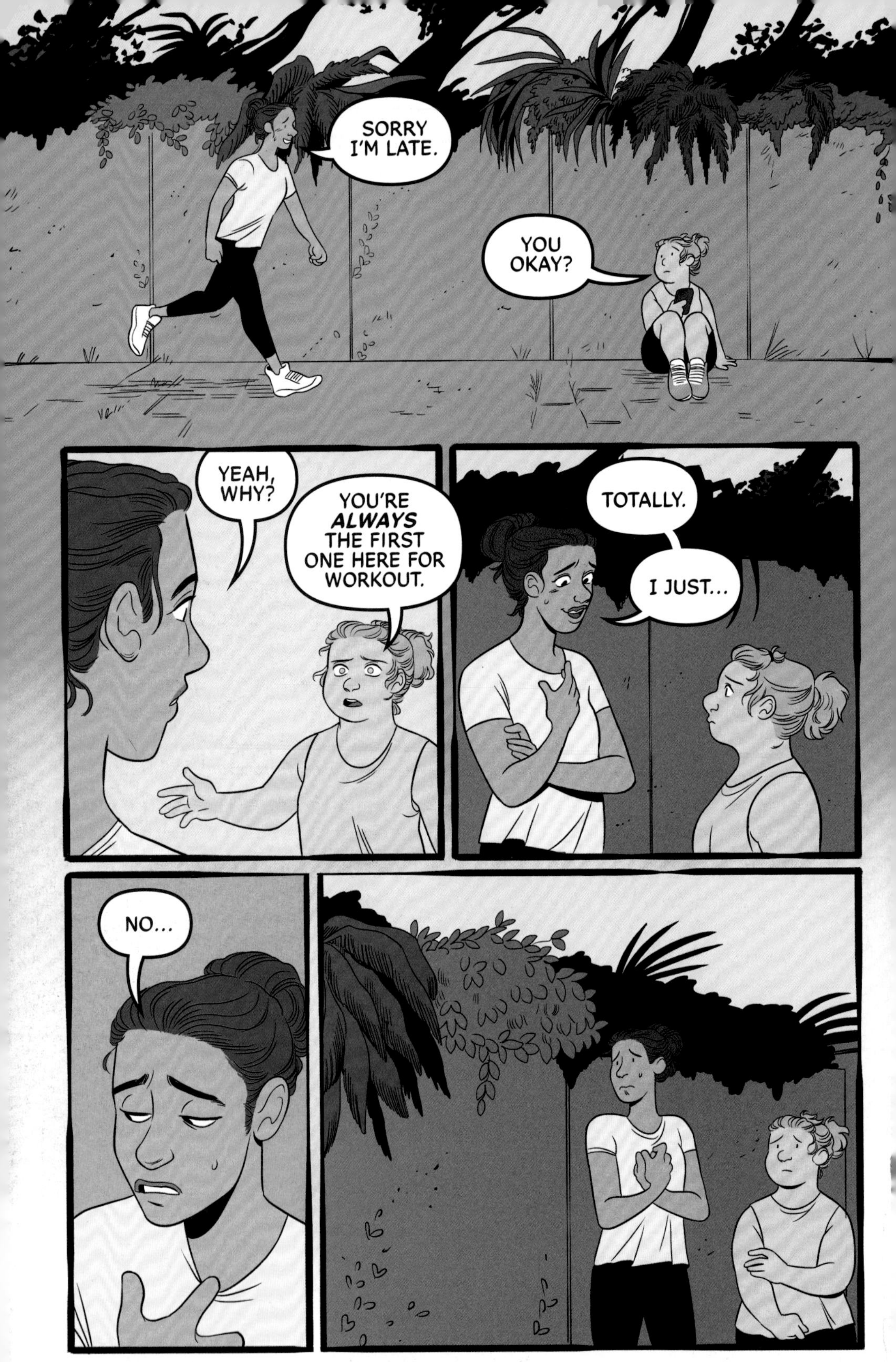
SORRY I'M LATE.
YOU OKAY?
YEAH, WHY?
YOU'RE *ALWAYS* THE FIRST ONE HERE FOR WORKOUT.
TOTALLY.
I JUST...
NO...

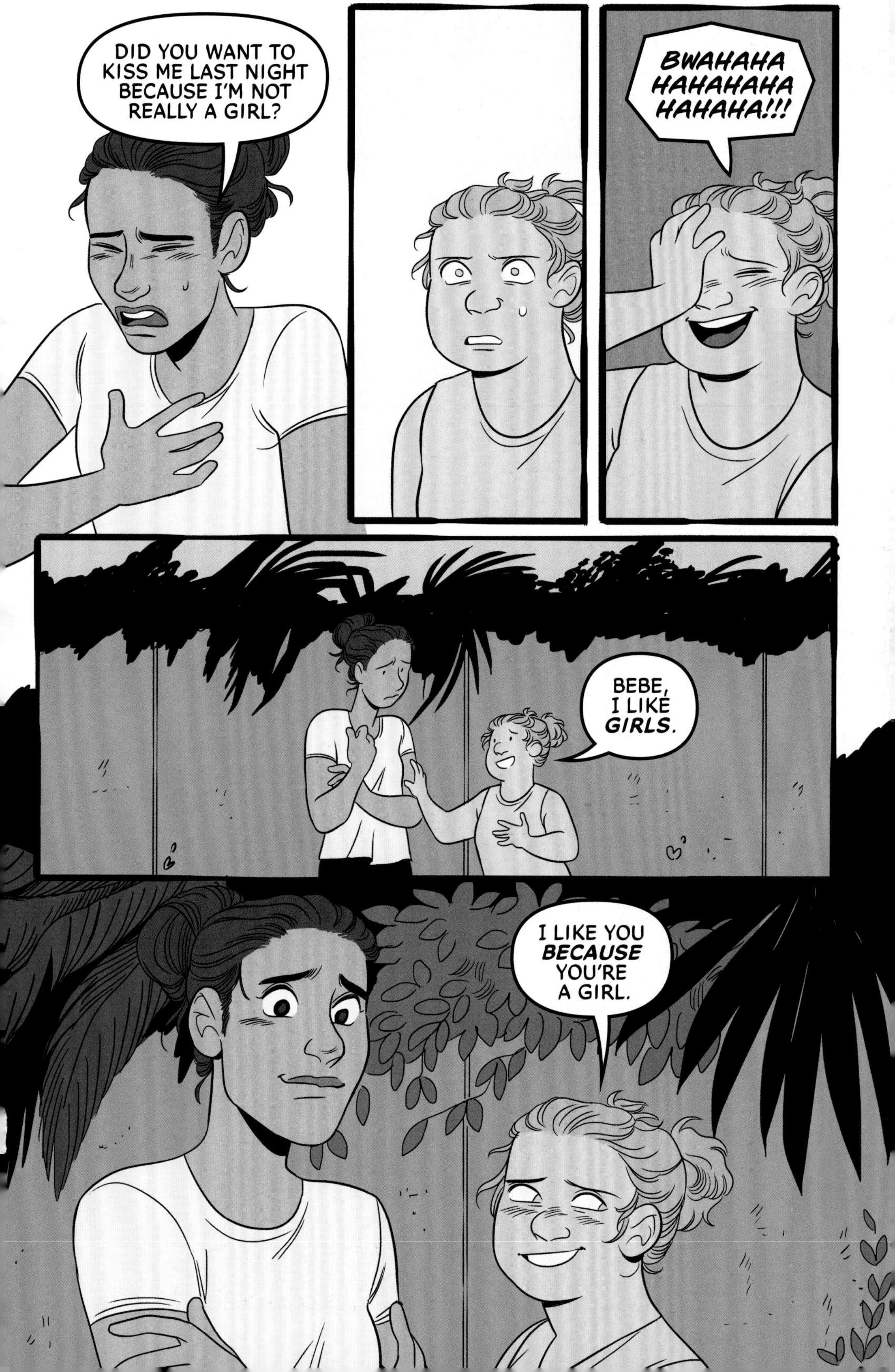
DID YOU WANT TO KISS ME LAST NIGHT BECAUSE I'M NOT REALLY A GIRL?
BWAHAHA HAHAHAHA HAHAHA!!!
BEBE, I LIKE *GIRLS*.
I LIKE YOU *BECAUSE* YOU'RE A GIRL.

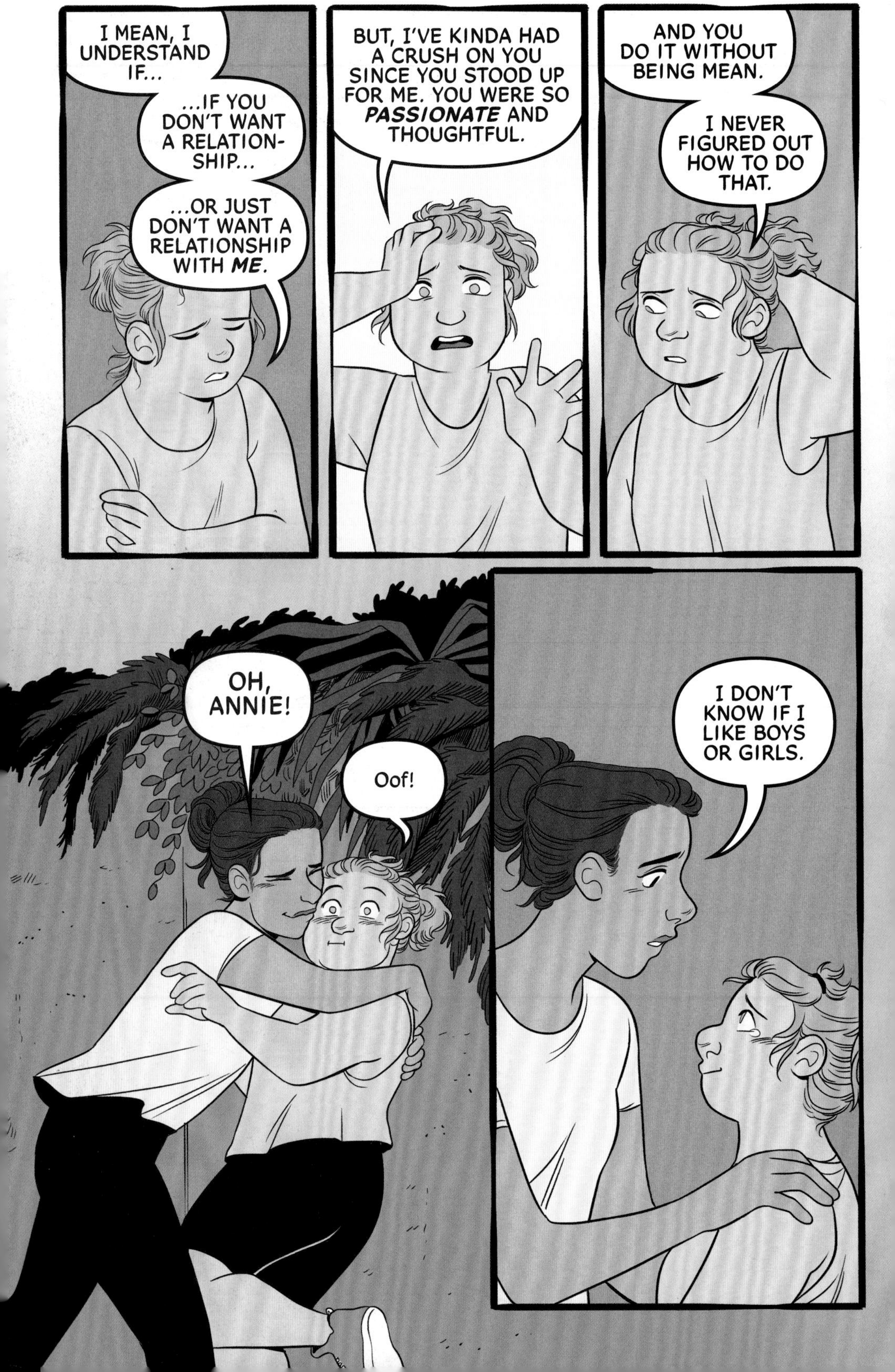
I MEAN, I UNDERSTAND IF...
...IF YOU DON'T WANT A RELATIONSHIP...
...OR JUST DON'T WANT A RELATIONSHIP WITH ME.
BUT, I'VE KINDA HAD A CRUSH ON YOU SINCE YOU STOOD UP FOR ME. YOU WERE SO PASSIONATE AND THOUGHTFUL.
AND YOU DO IT WITHOUT BEING MEAN.
I NEVER FIGURED OUT HOW TO DO THAT.
I DON'T KNOW IF I LIKE BOYS OR GIRLS.
OH, ANNIE!
Oof!

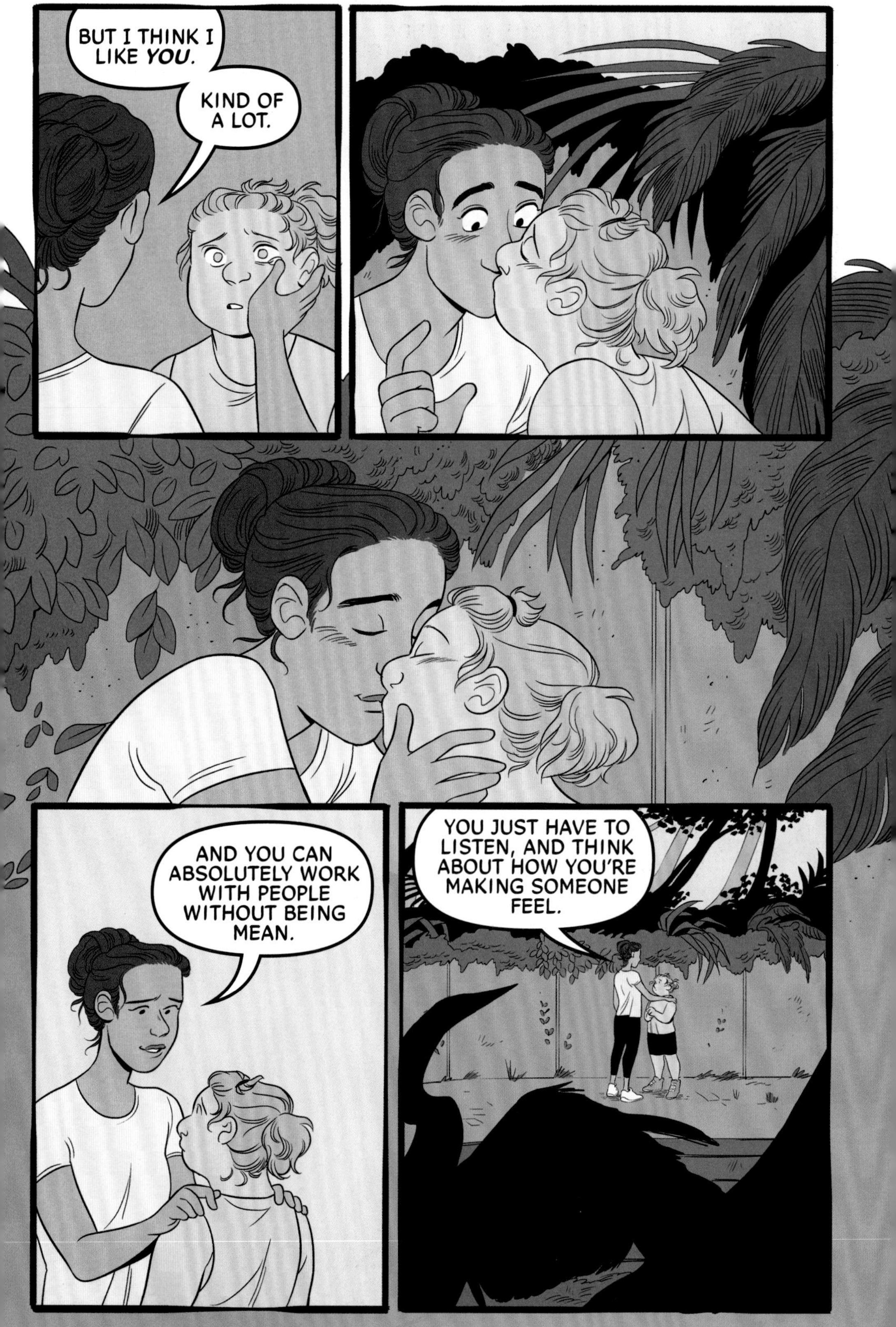
BUT I THINK I LIKE *YOU*.
KIND OF A LOT.
AND YOU CAN ABSOLUTELY WORK WITH PEOPLE WITHOUT BEING MEAN.
YOU JUST HAVE TO LISTEN, AND THINK ABOUT HOW YOU'RE MAKING SOMEONE FEEL.

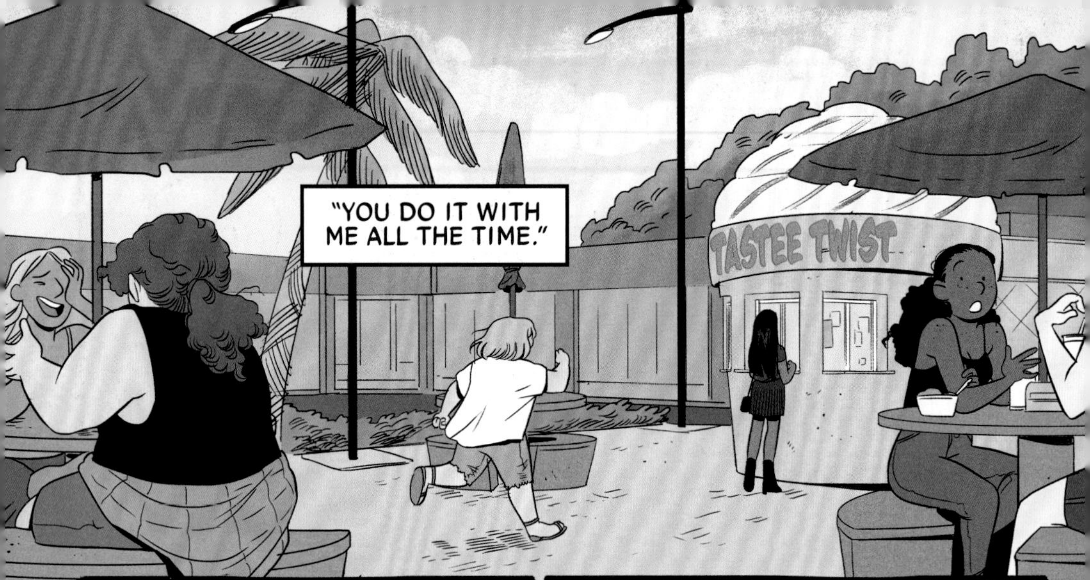
"YOU DO IT WITH ME ALL THE TIME."
TASTEE TWIST

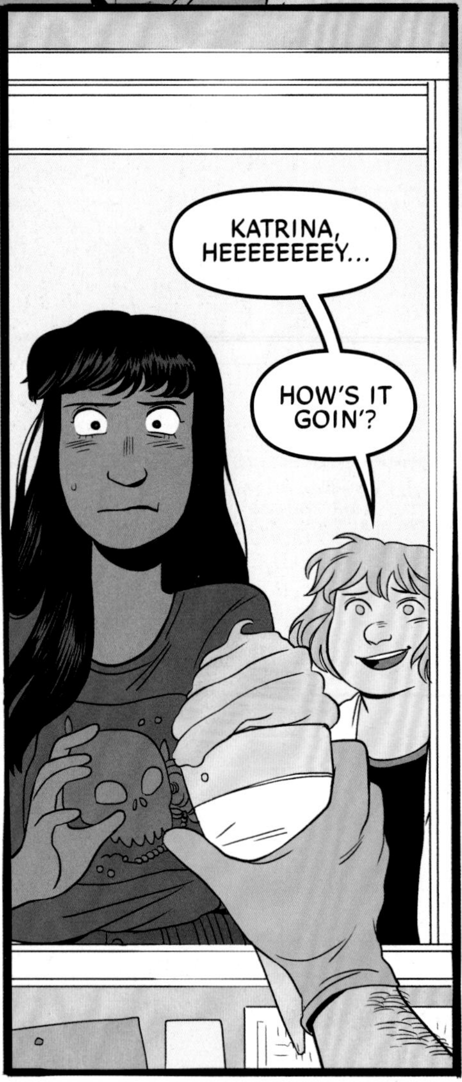
KATRINA, HEEEEEEEEY...
HOW'S IT GOIN'?

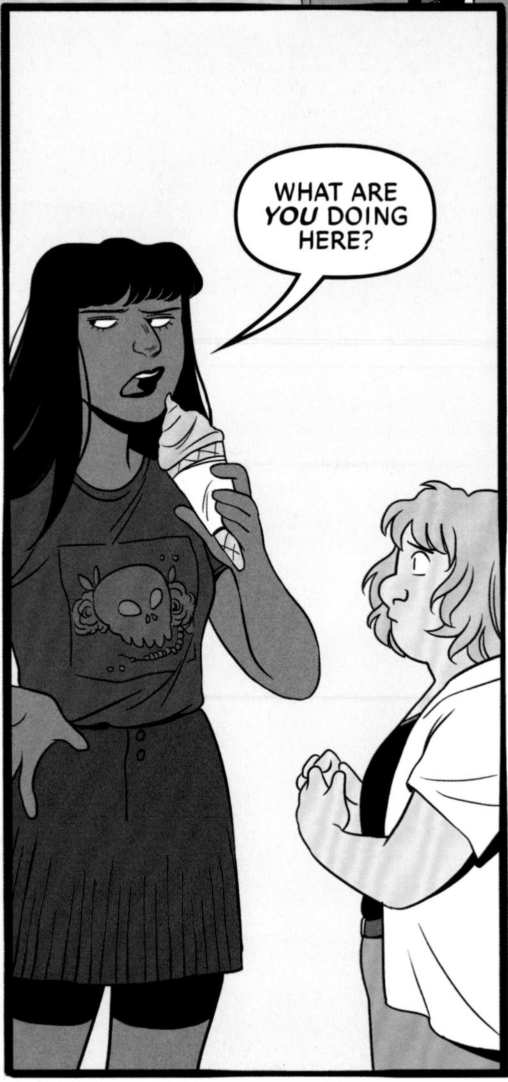
WHAT ARE *YOU* DOING HERE?

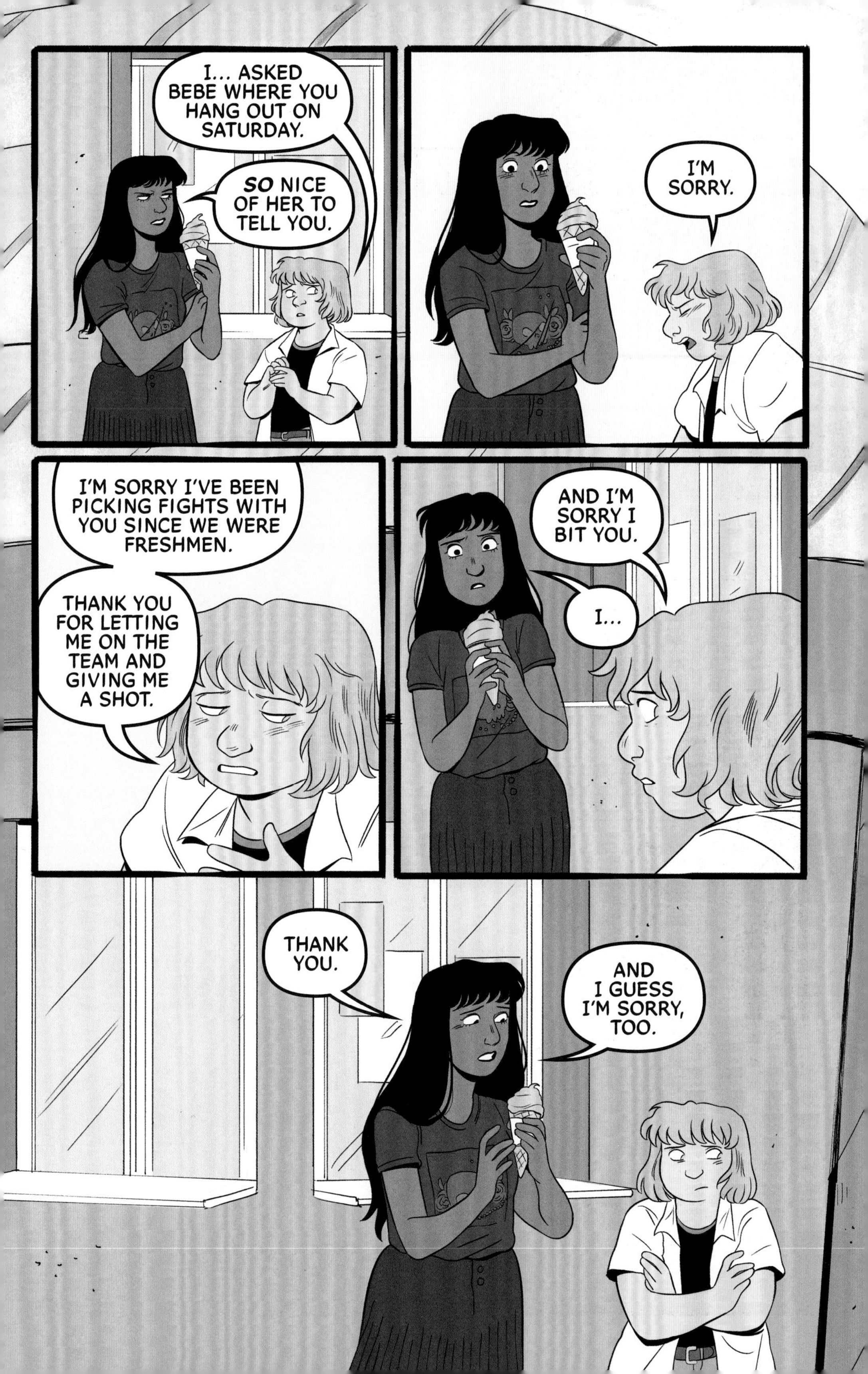
I... ASKED BEBE WHERE YOU HANG OUT ON SATURDAY.
SO NICE OF HER TO TELL YOU.
I'M SORRY.
I'M SORRY I'VE BEEN PICKING FIGHTS WITH YOU SINCE WE WERE FRESHMEN.
THANK YOU FOR LETTING ME ON THE TEAM AND GIVING ME A SHOT.
AND I'M SORRY I BIT YOU.
I...
THANK YOU.
AND I GUESS I'M SORRY, TOO.

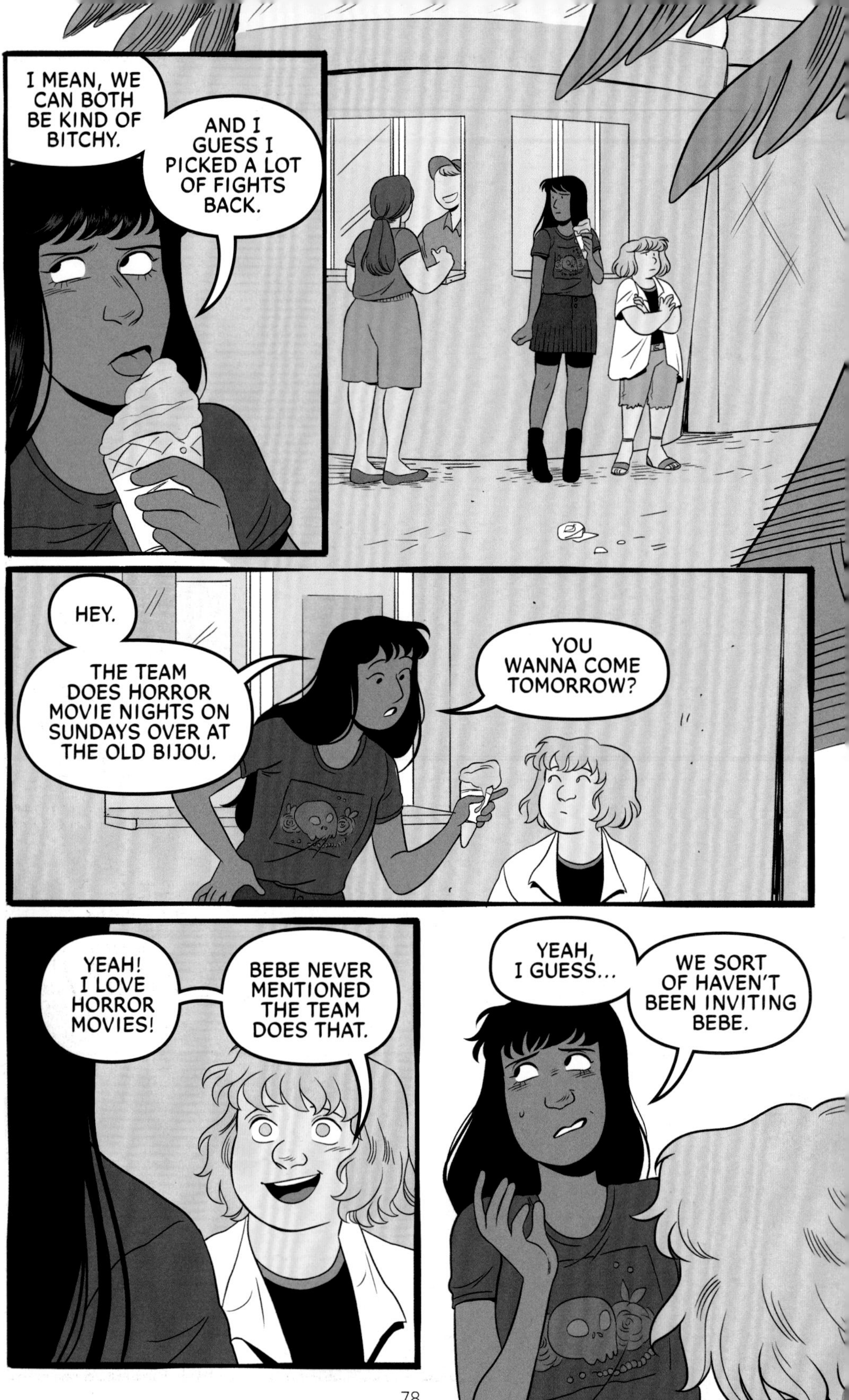

I MEAN, WE CAN BOTH BE KIND OF BITCHY.
AND I GUESS I PICKED A LOT OF FIGHTS BACK.
HEY.
THE TEAM DOES HORROR MOVIE NIGHTS ON SUNDAYS OVER AT THE OLD BIJOU.
YOU WANNA COME TOMORROW?
YEAH! I LOVE HORROR MOVIES!
BEBE NEVER MENTIONED THE TEAM DOES THAT.
YEAH, I GUESS...
WE SORT OF HAVEN'T BEEN INVITING BEBE.

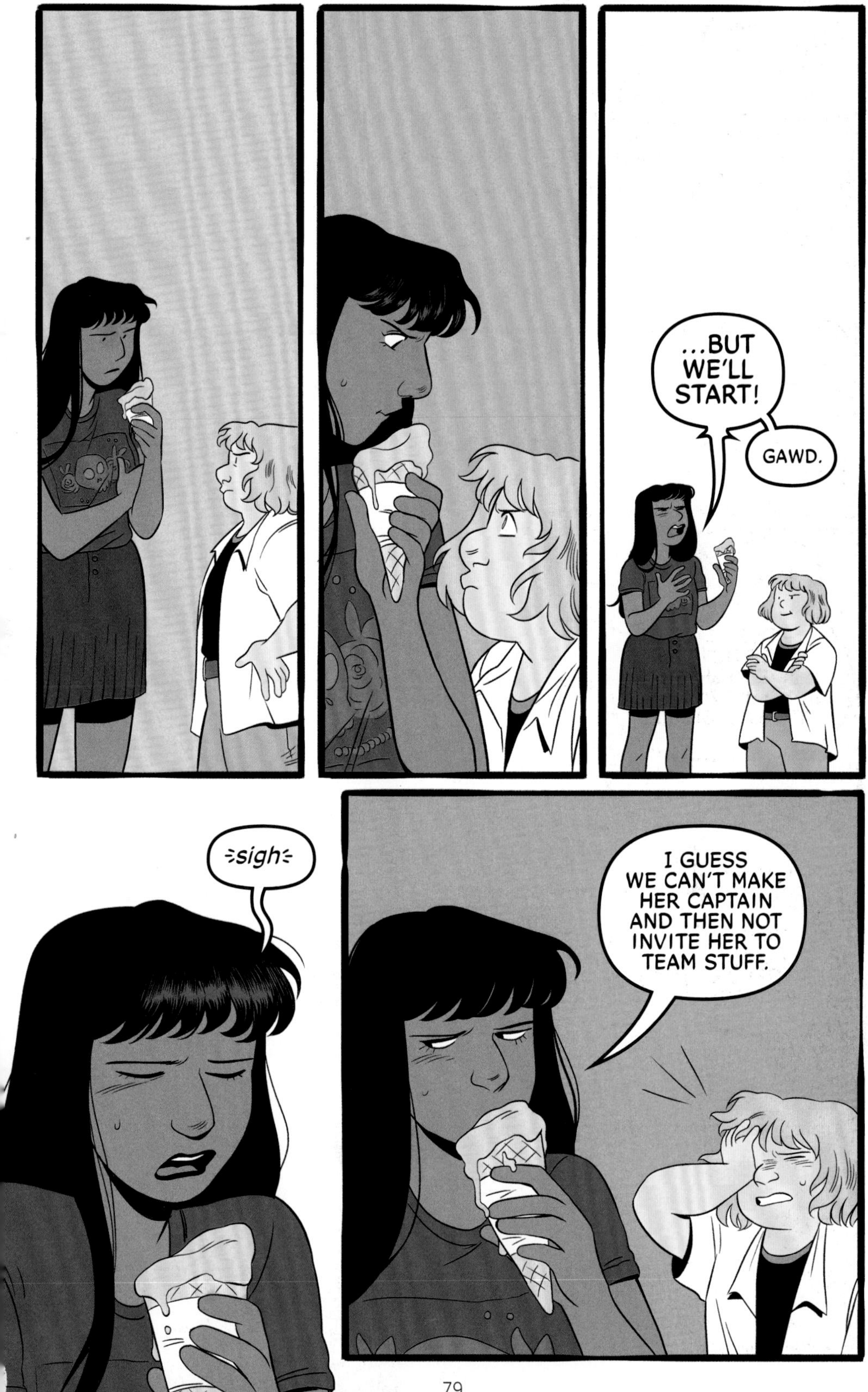
...BUT WE'LL START!
GAWD.
sigh
I GUESS WE CAN'T MAKE HER CAPTAIN AND THEN NOT INVITE HER TO TEAM STUFF.

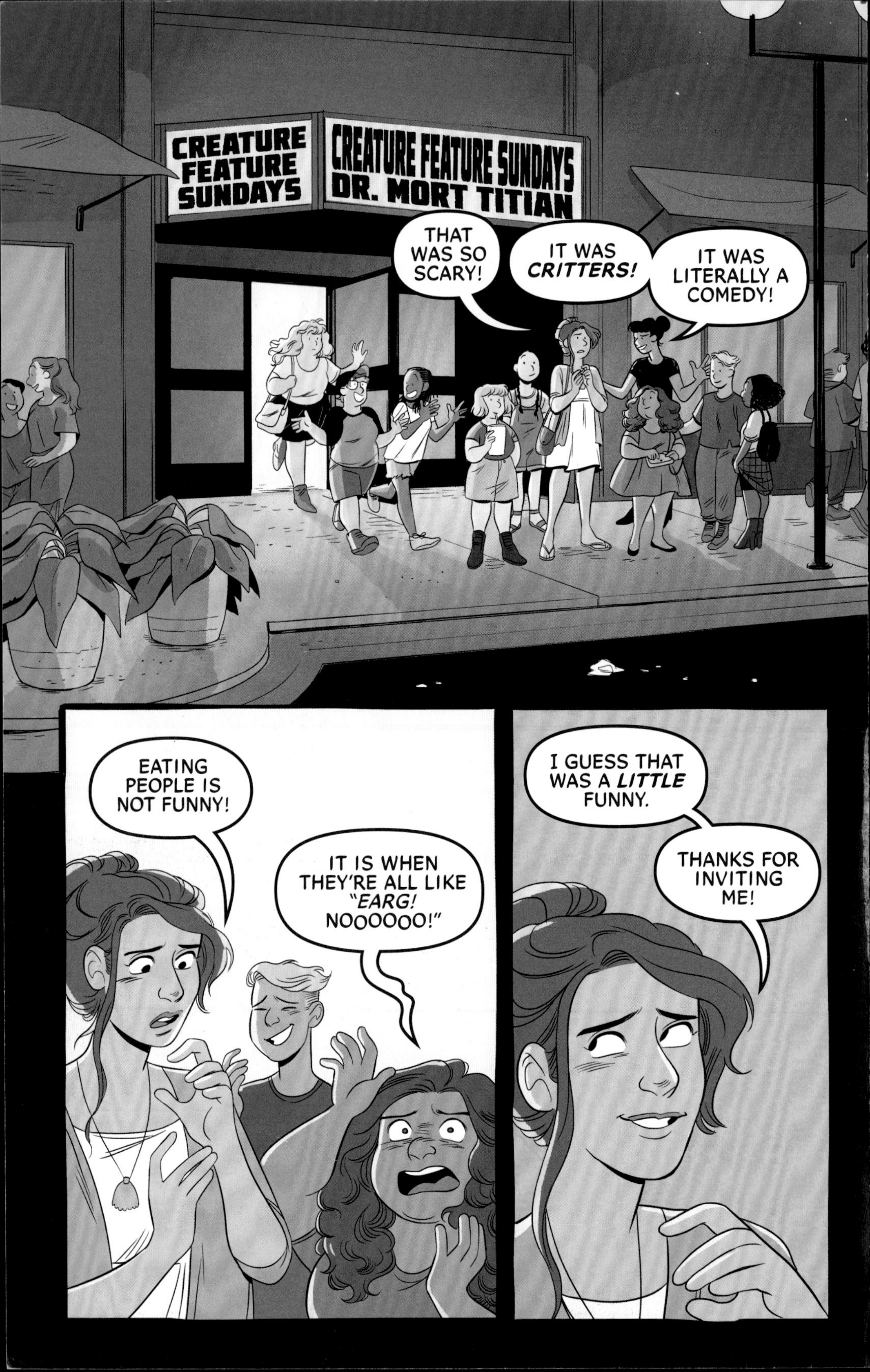
CREATURE FEATURE SUNDAYS
CREATURE FEATURE SUNDAYS DR. MORT TITIAN
THAT WAS SO SCARY!
IT WAS *CRITTERS!*
IT WAS LITERALLY A COMEDY!
EATING PEOPLE IS NOT FUNNY!
IT IS WHEN THEY'RE ALL LIKE "*EARG!* NOOOOOO!"
I GUESS THAT WAS A *LITTLE* FUNNY.
THANKS FOR INVITING ME!

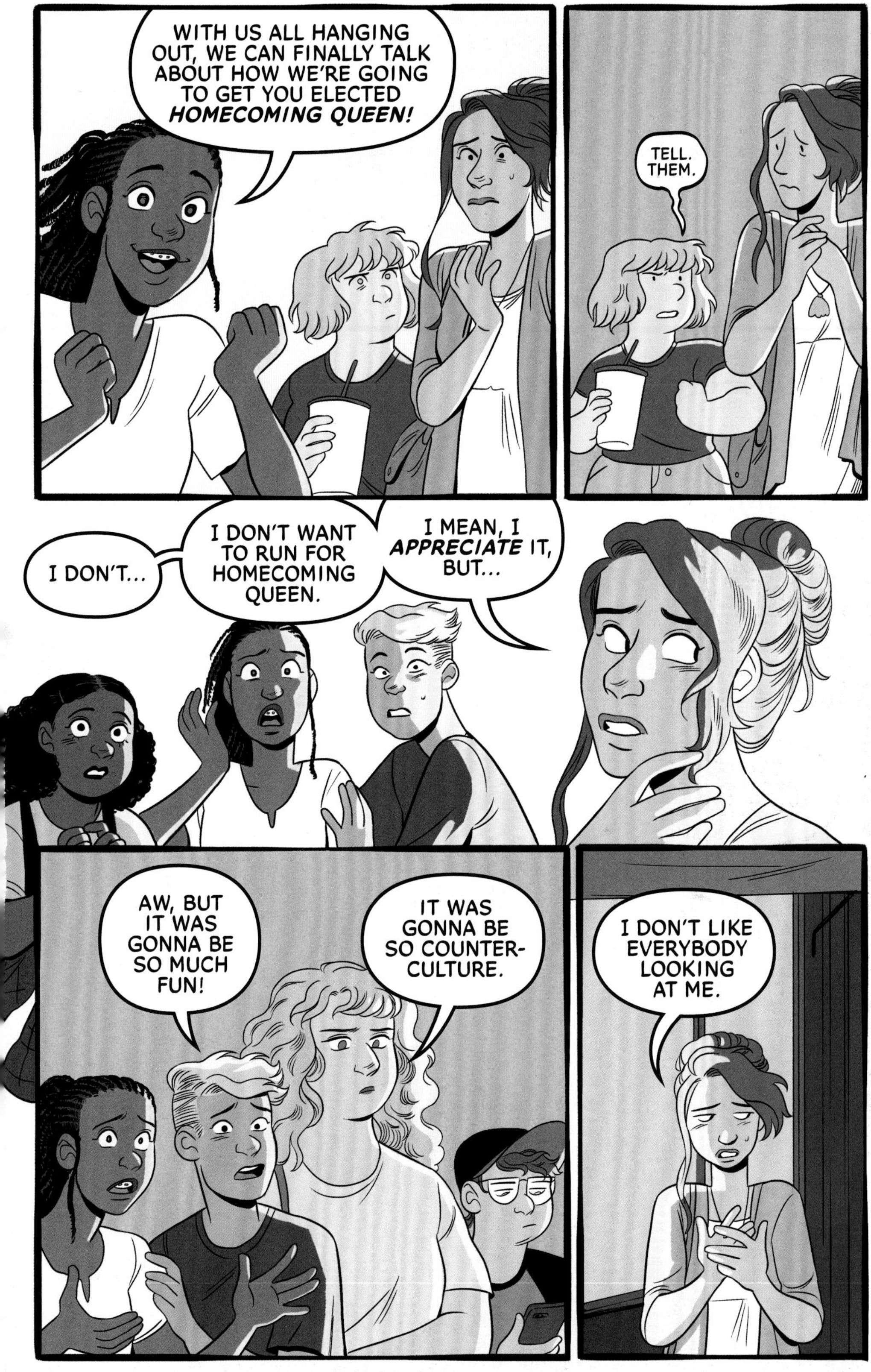
WITH US ALL HANGING OUT, WE CAN FINALLY TALK ABOUT HOW WE'RE GOING TO GET YOU ELECTED *HOMECOMING QUEEN!*
TELL. THEM.
I DON'T...
I DON'T WANT TO RUN FOR HOMECOMING QUEEN.
I MEAN, I *APPRECIATE* IT, BUT...
AW, BUT IT WAS GONNA BE SO MUCH FUN!
IT WAS GONNA BE SO COUNTER-CULTURE.
I DON'T LIKE EVERYBODY LOOKING AT ME.

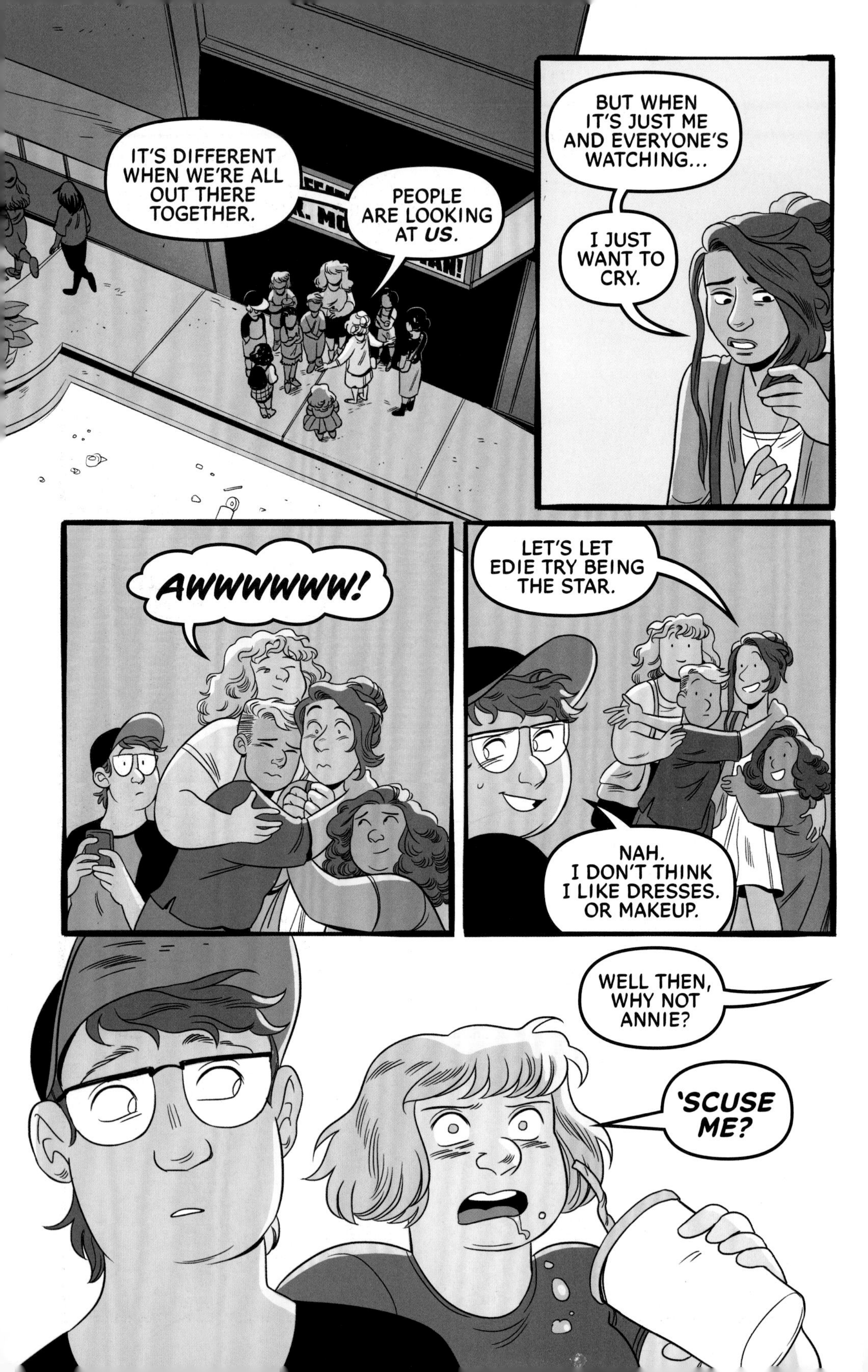
IT'S DIFFERENT WHEN WE'RE ALL OUT THERE TOGETHER.
PEOPLE ARE LOOKING AT *US*.
BUT WHEN IT'S JUST ME AND EVERYONE'S WATCHING...
I JUST WANT TO CRY.
AWWWWWW!
LET'S LET EDIE TRY BEING THE STAR.
NAH. I DON'T THINK I LIKE DRESSES. OR MAKEUP.
WELL THEN, WHY NOT ANNIE?
'SCUSE ME?

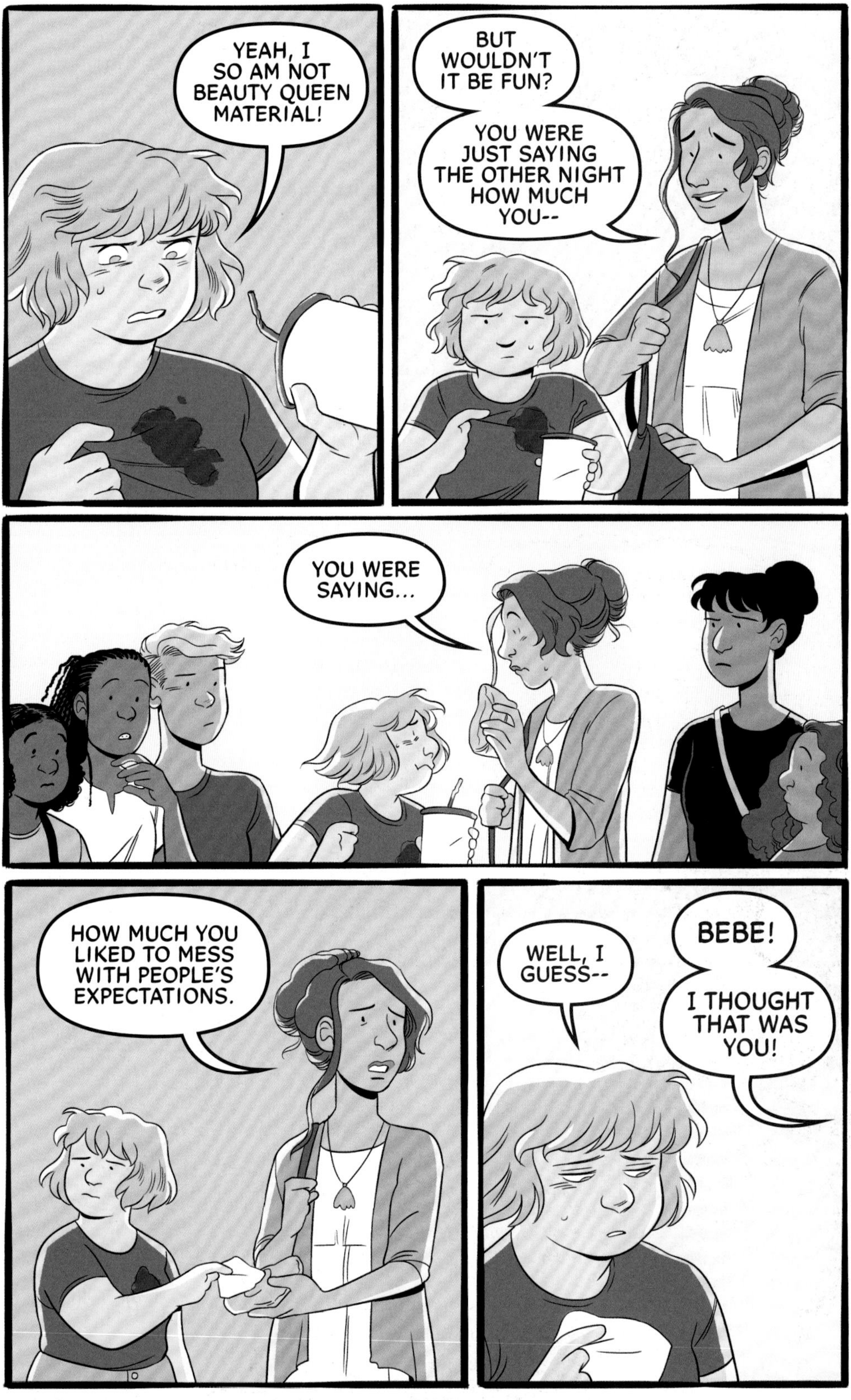
YEAH, I SO AM NOT BEAUTY QUEEN MATERIAL!
BUT WOULDN'T IT BE FUN?
YOU WERE JUST SAYING THE OTHER NIGHT HOW MUCH YOU--
YOU WERE SAYING...
HOW MUCH YOU LIKED TO MESS WITH PEOPLE'S EXPECTATIONS.
WELL, I GUESS--
BEBE!
I THOUGHT THAT WAS YOU!

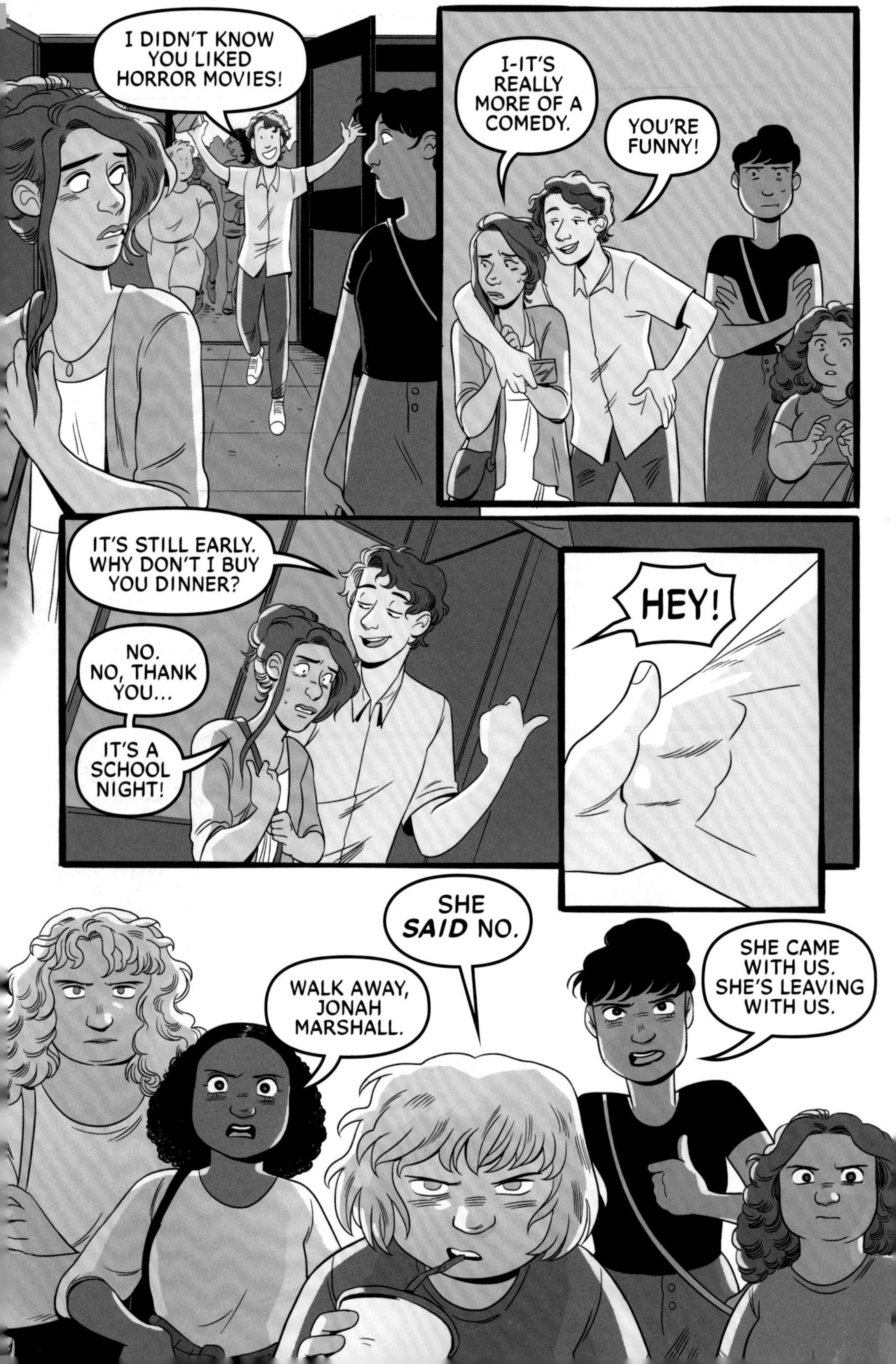
I DIDN'T KNOW YOU LIKED HORROR MOVIES!
I-IT'S REALLY MORE OF A COMEDY.
YOU'RE FUNNY!
IT'S STILL EARLY. WHY DON'T I BUY YOU DINNER?
NO. NO, THANK YOU...
IT'S A SCHOOL NIGHT!
HEY!
WALK AWAY, JONAH MARSHALL.
SHE *SAID* NO.
SHE CAME WITH US. SHE'S LEAVING WITH US.

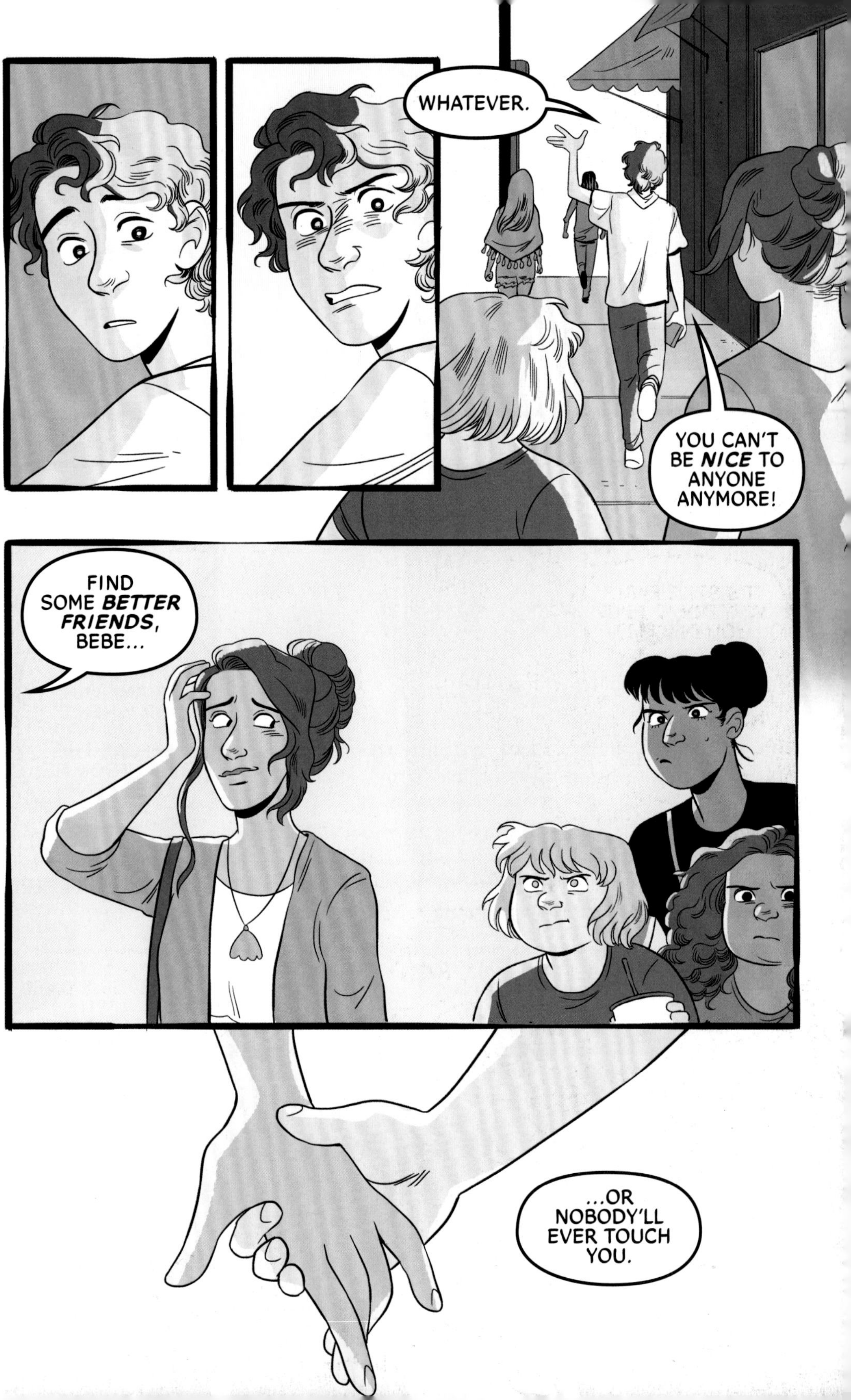
WHATEVER.
YOU CAN'T BE *NICE* TO ANYONE ANYMORE!
FIND SOME ***BETTER FRIENDS***, BEBE...
...OR NOBODY'LL EVER TOUCH YOU.

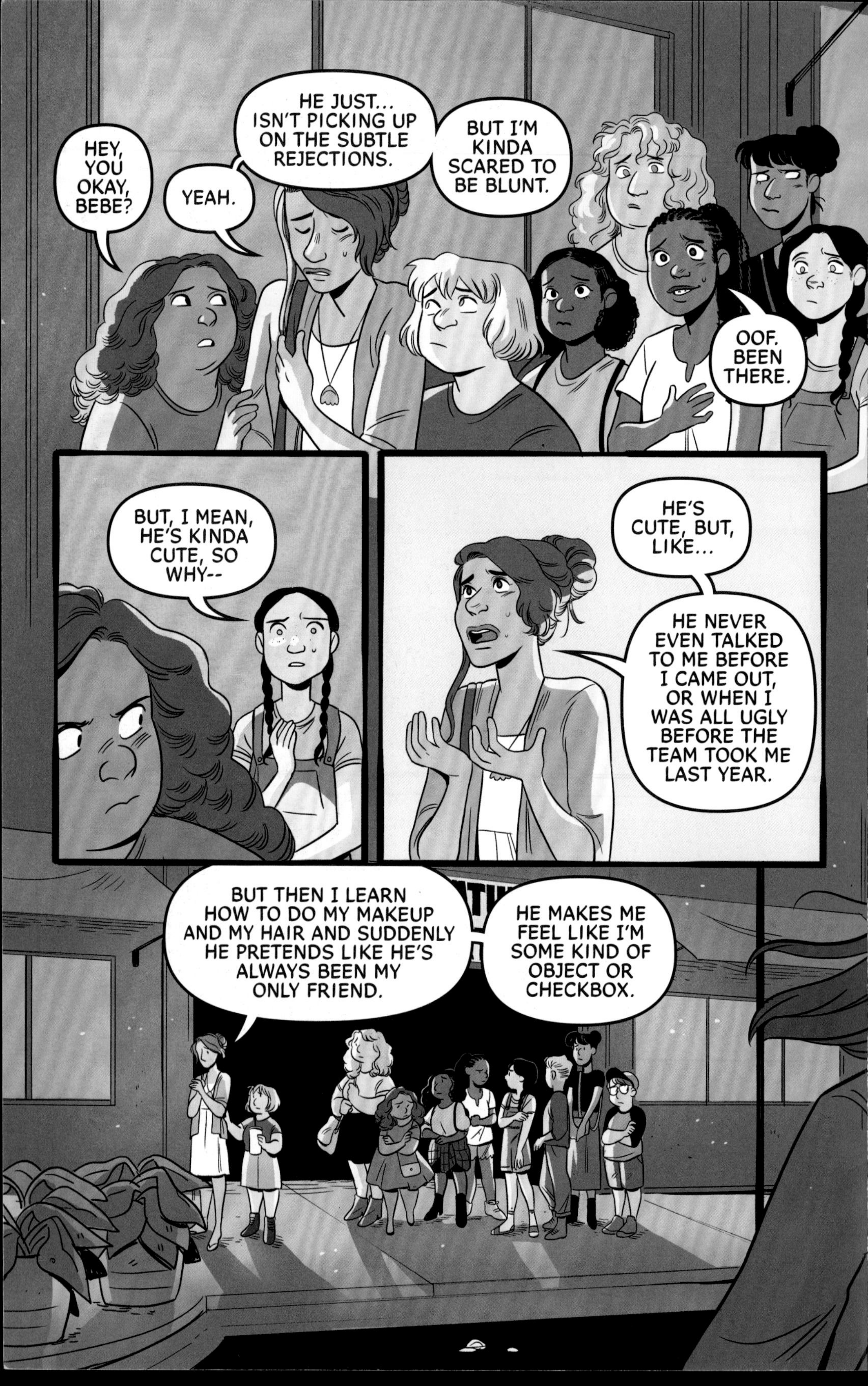
HEY, YOU OKAY, BEBE?
YEAH.
HE JUST... ISN'T PICKING UP ON THE SUBTLE REJECTIONS.
BUT I'M KINDA SCARED TO BE BLUNT.
OOF. BEEN THERE.
BUT, I MEAN, HE'S KINDA CUTE, SO WHY--
HE'S CUTE, BUT, LIKE...
HE NEVER EVEN TALKED TO ME BEFORE I CAME OUT, OR WHEN I WAS ALL UGLY BEFORE THE TEAM TOOK ME LAST YEAR.
BUT THEN I LEARN HOW TO DO MY MAKEUP AND MY HAIR AND SUDDENLY HE PRETENDS LIKE HE'S ALWAYS BEEN MY ONLY FRIEND.
HE MAKES ME FEEL LIKE I'M SOME KIND OF OBJECT OR CHECKBOX.

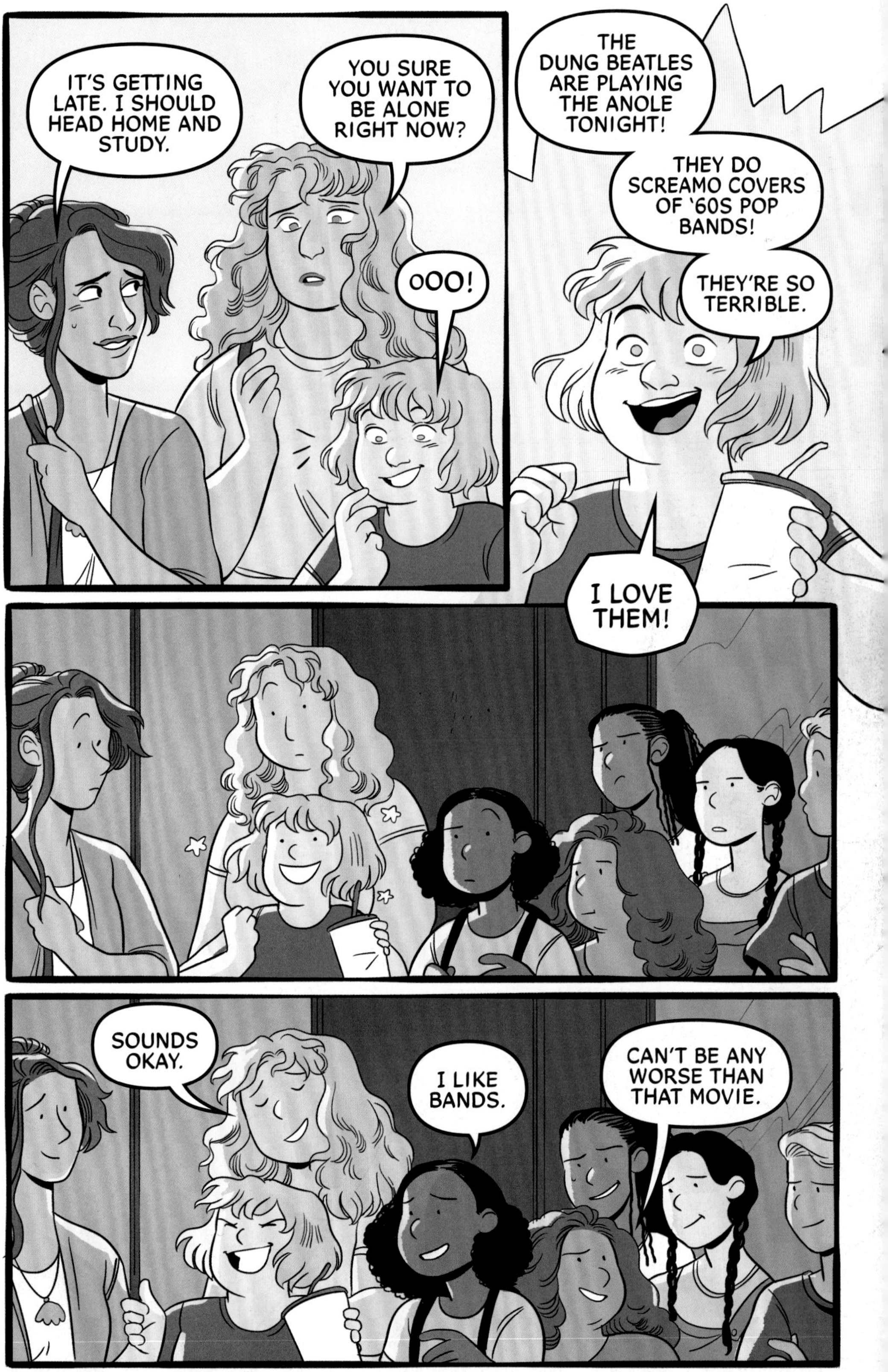
IT'S GETTING LATE. I SHOULD HEAD HOME AND STUDY.
YOU SURE YOU WANT TO BE ALONE RIGHT NOW?
OOO!
THE DUNG BEATLES ARE PLAYING THE ANOLE TONIGHT!
THEY DO SCREAMO COVERS OF '60S POP BANDS!
THEY'RE SO TERRIBLE.
I LOVE THEM!
SOUNDS OKAY.
I LIKE BANDS.
CAN'T BE ANY WORSE THAN THAT MOVIE.

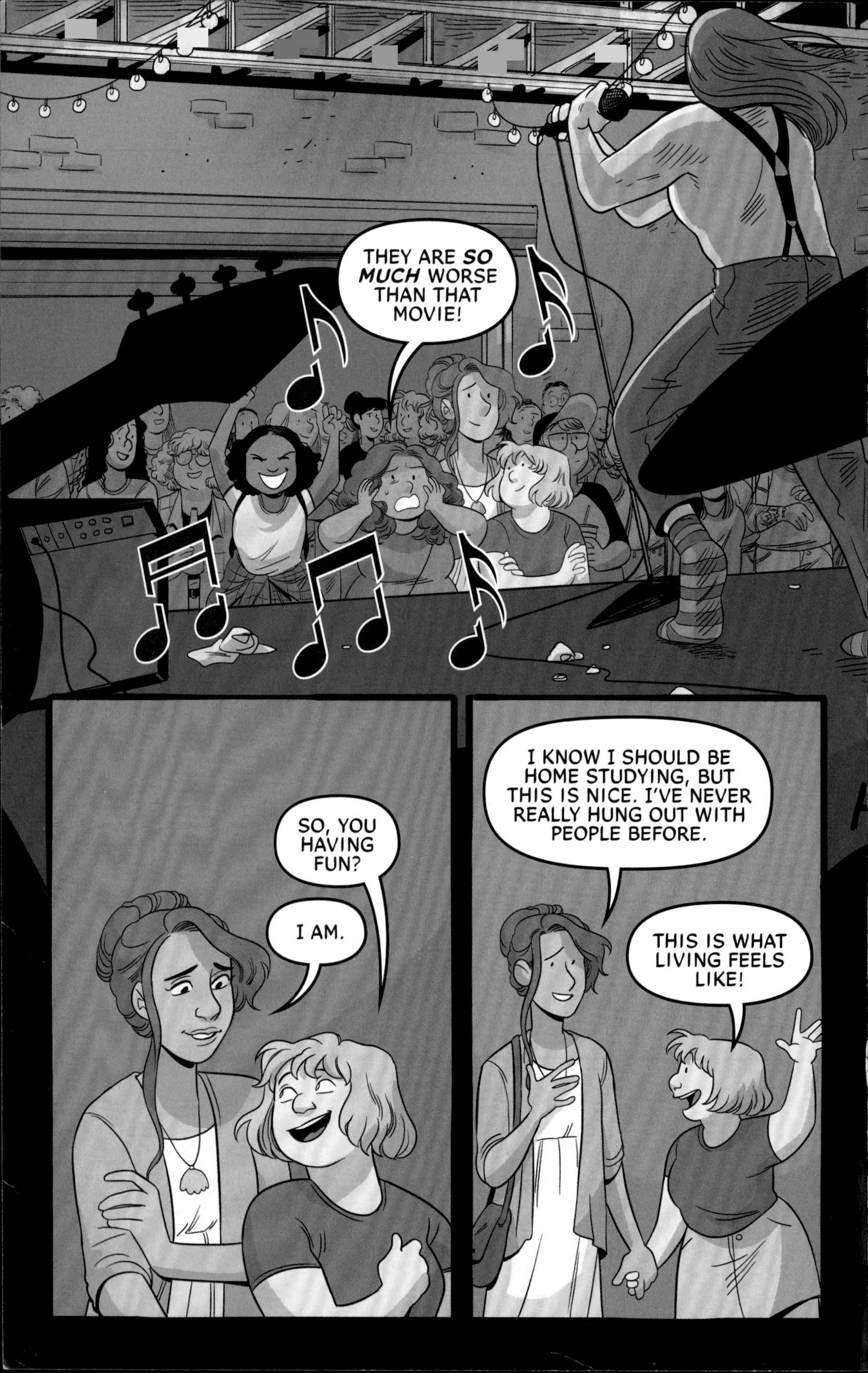
THEY ARE *SO MUCH* WORSE THAN THAT MOVIE!
SO, YOU HAVING FUN?
I AM.
I KNOW I SHOULD BE HOME STUDYING, BUT THIS IS NICE. I'VE NEVER REALLY HUNG OUT WITH PEOPLE BEFORE.
THIS IS WHAT LIVING FEELS LIKE!

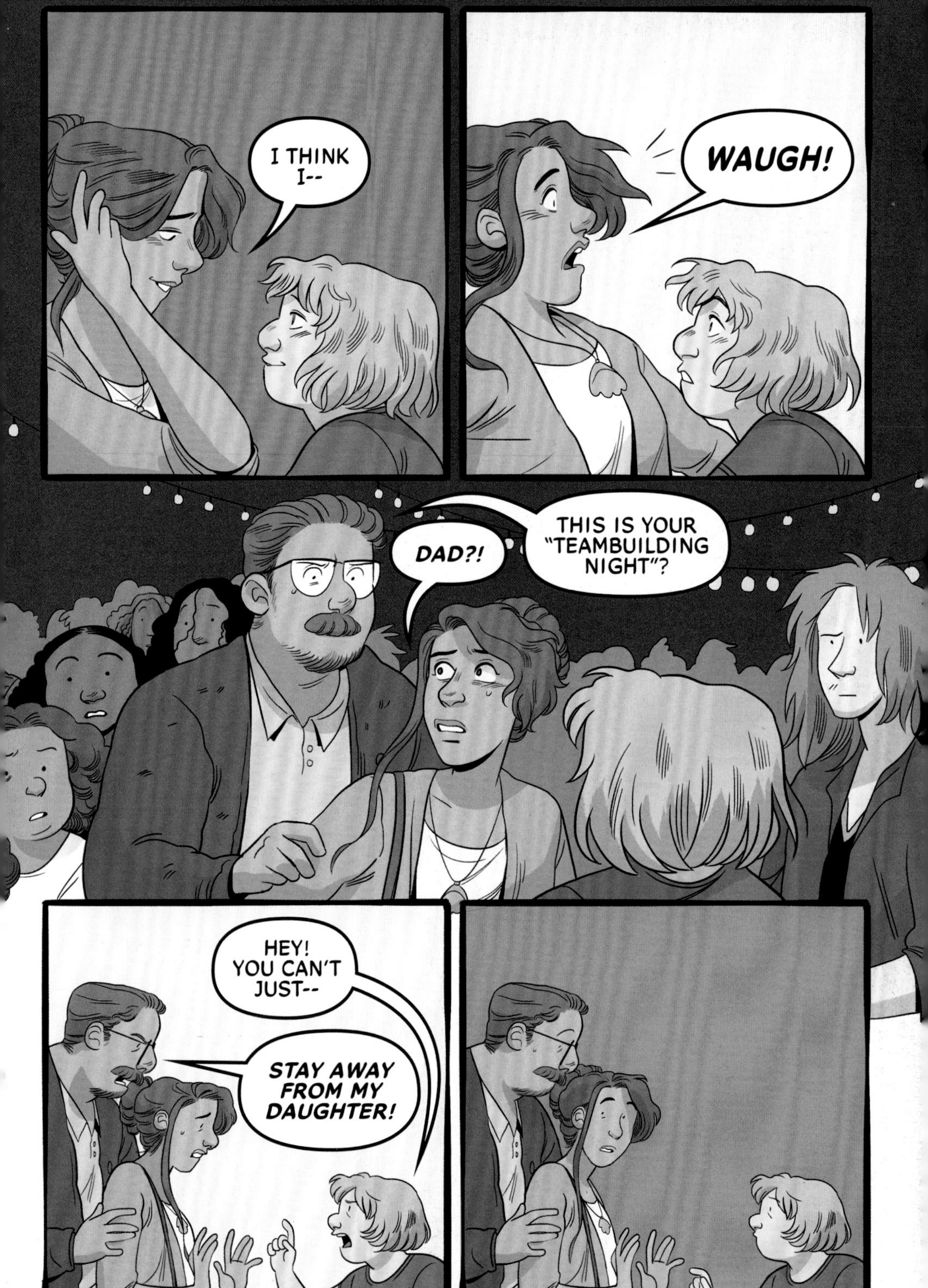
I THINK I--
WAUGH!
DAD?!
THIS IS YOUR "TEAMBUILDING NIGHT"?
HEY! YOU CAN'T JUST--
STAY AWAY FROM MY DAUGHTER!

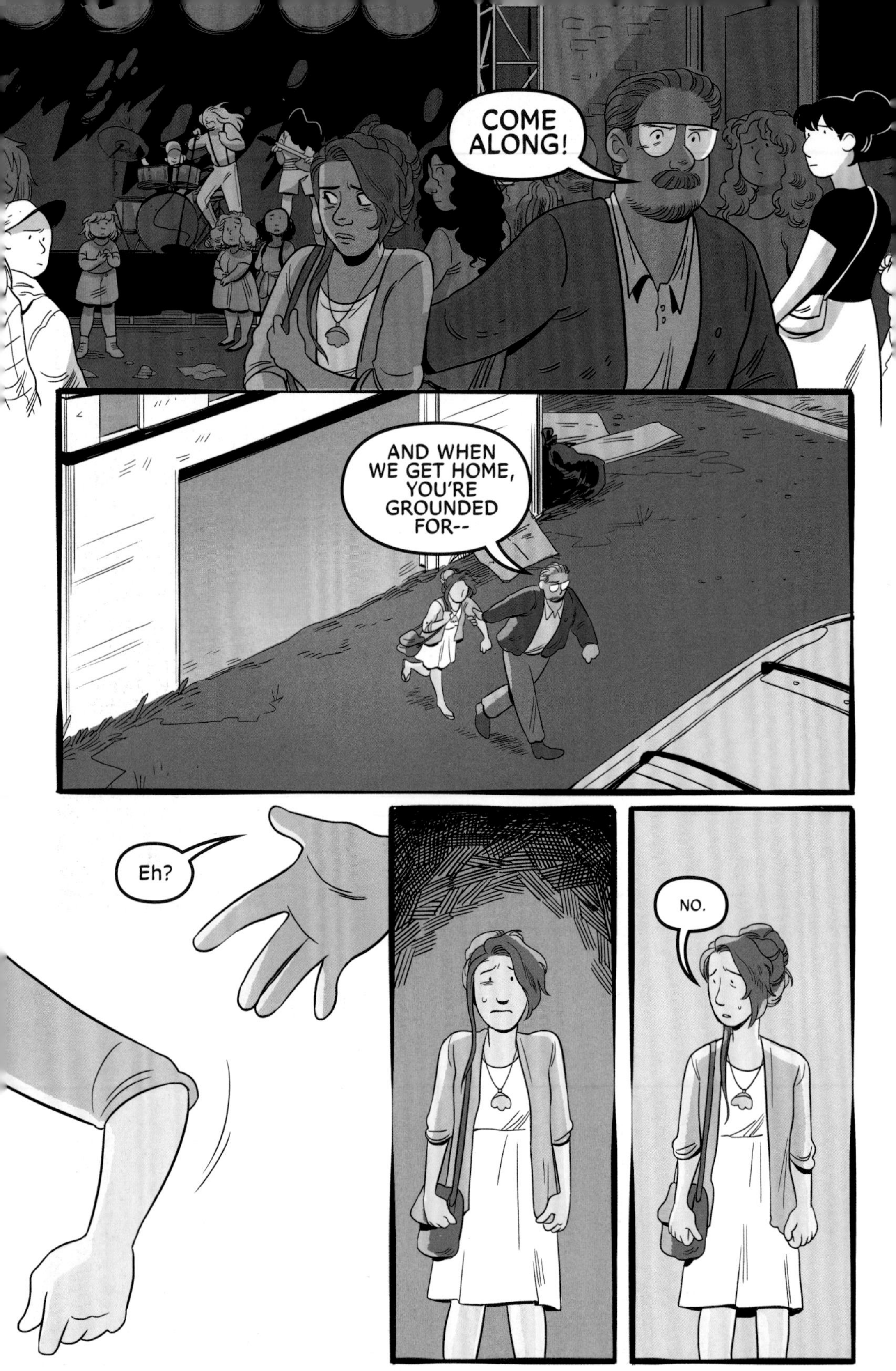
COME ALONG!
AND WHEN WE GET HOME, YOU'RE GROUNDED FOR--
Eh?
NO.

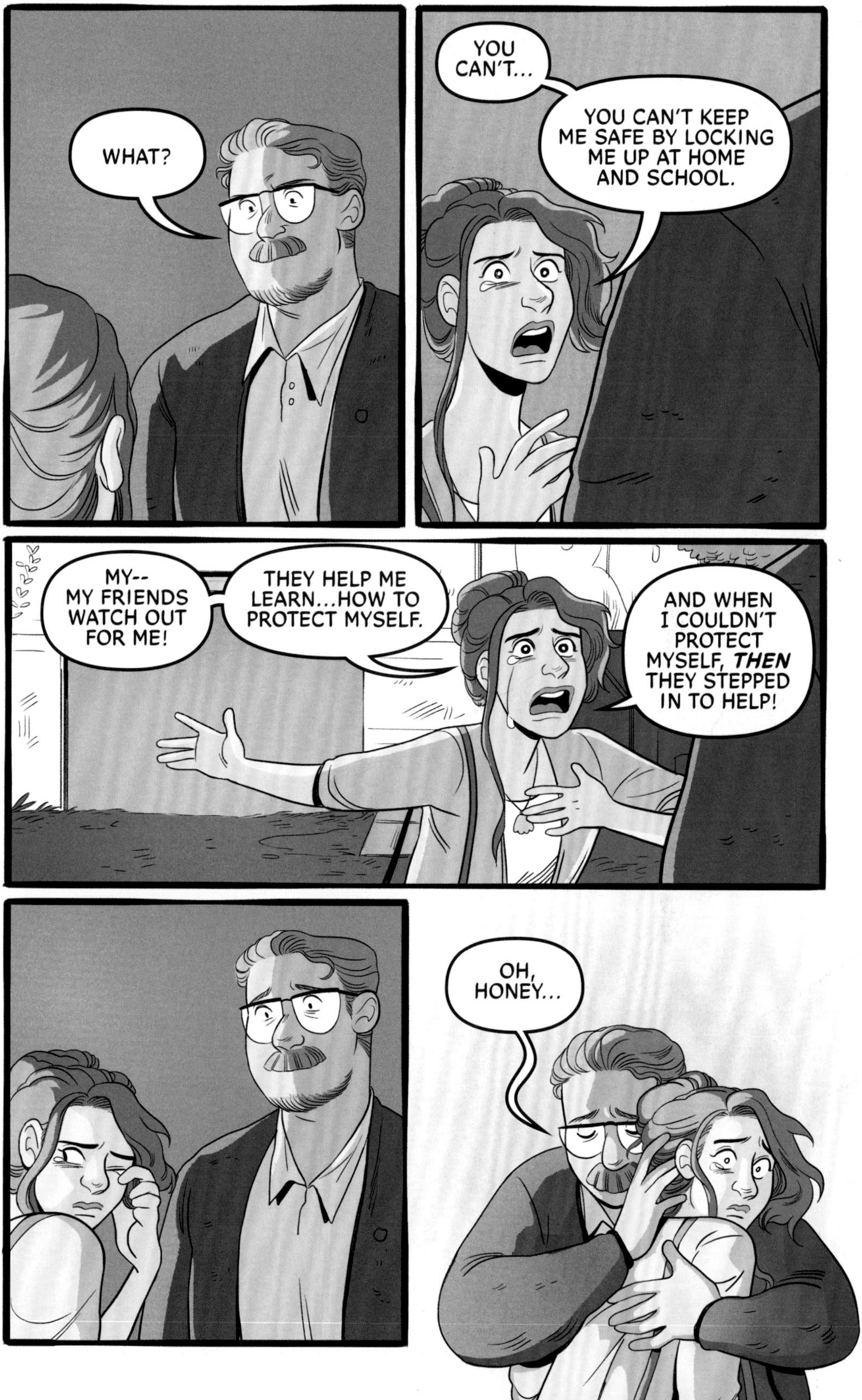
WHAT?
YOU CAN'T...
YOU CAN'T KEEP ME SAFE BY LOCKING ME UP AT HOME AND SCHOOL.
MY-- MY FRIENDS WATCH OUT FOR ME!
THEY HELP ME LEARN...HOW TO PROTECT MYSELF.
AND WHEN I COULDN'T PROTECT MYSELF, *THEN* THEY STEPPED IN TO HELP!
OH, HONEY...

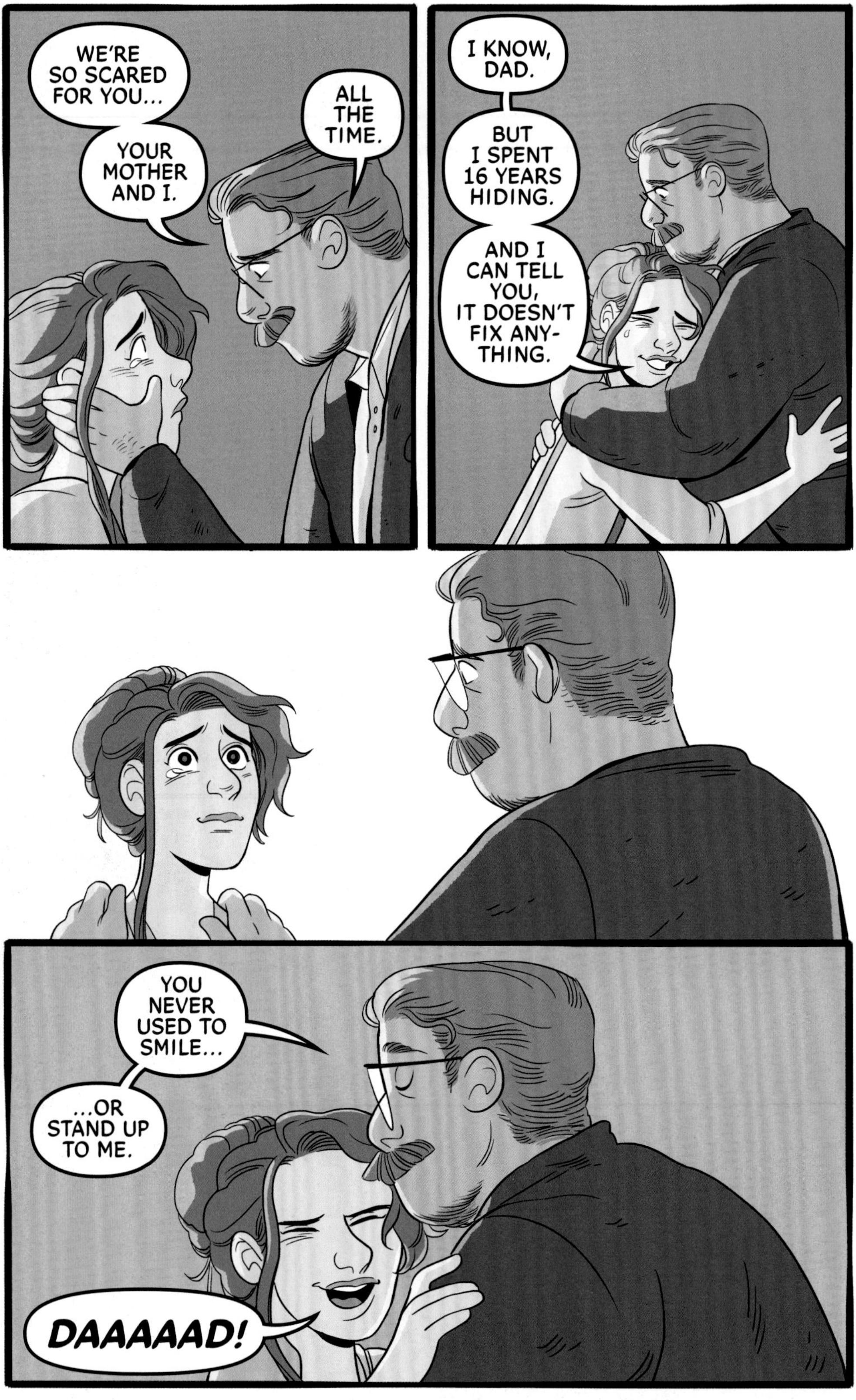
WE'RE SO SCARED FOR YOU...
YOUR MOTHER AND I.
ALL THE TIME.
I KNOW, DAD.
BUT I SPENT 16 YEARS HIDING.
AND I CAN TELL YOU, IT DOESN'T FIX ANY-THING.
YOU NEVER USED TO SMILE...
...OR STAND UP TO ME.
DAAAAAD!

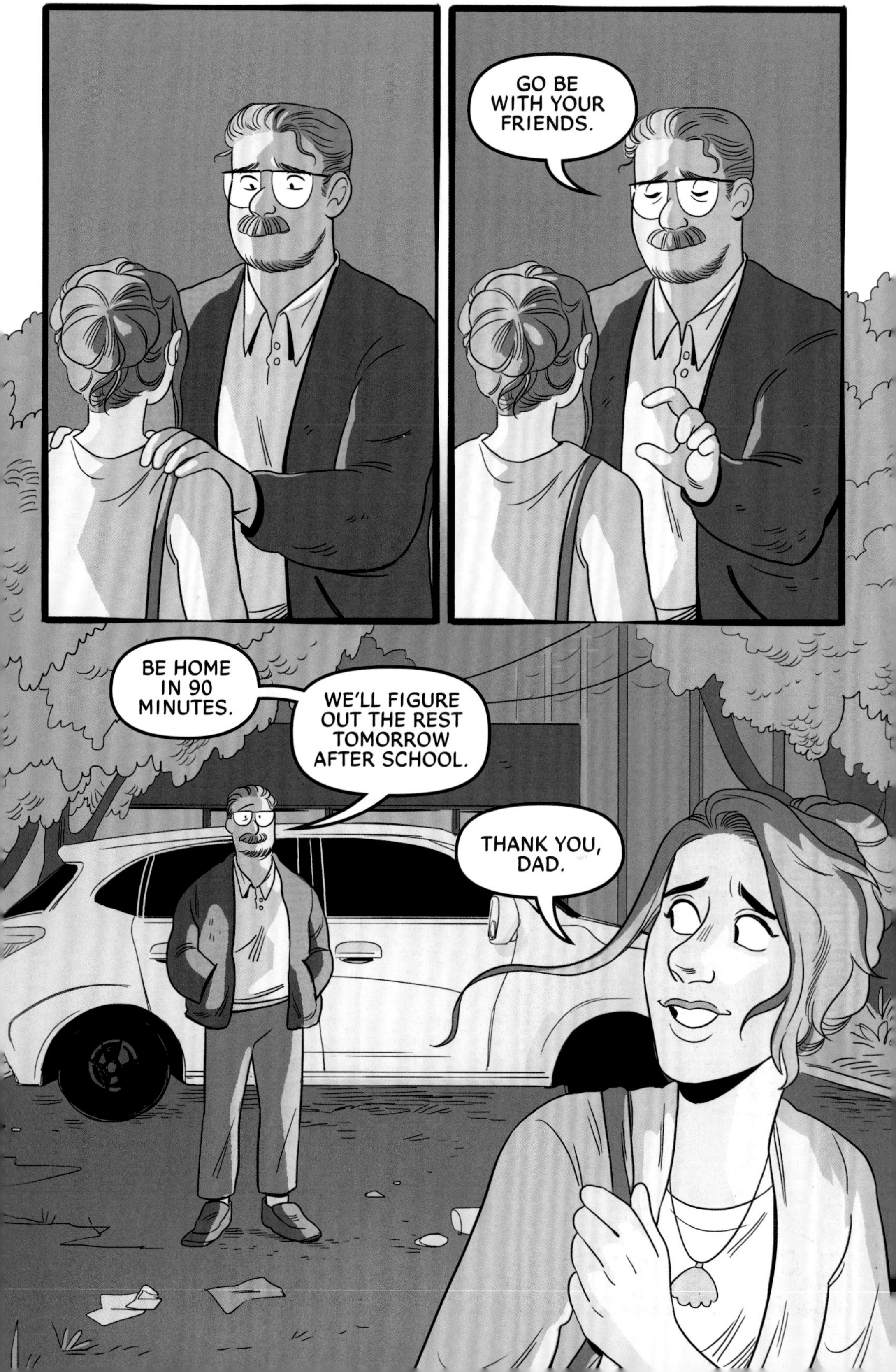
GO BE WITH YOUR FRIENDS.
BE HOME IN 90 MINUTES.
WE'LL FIGURE OUT THE REST TOMORROW AFTER SCHOOL.
THANK YOU, DAD.

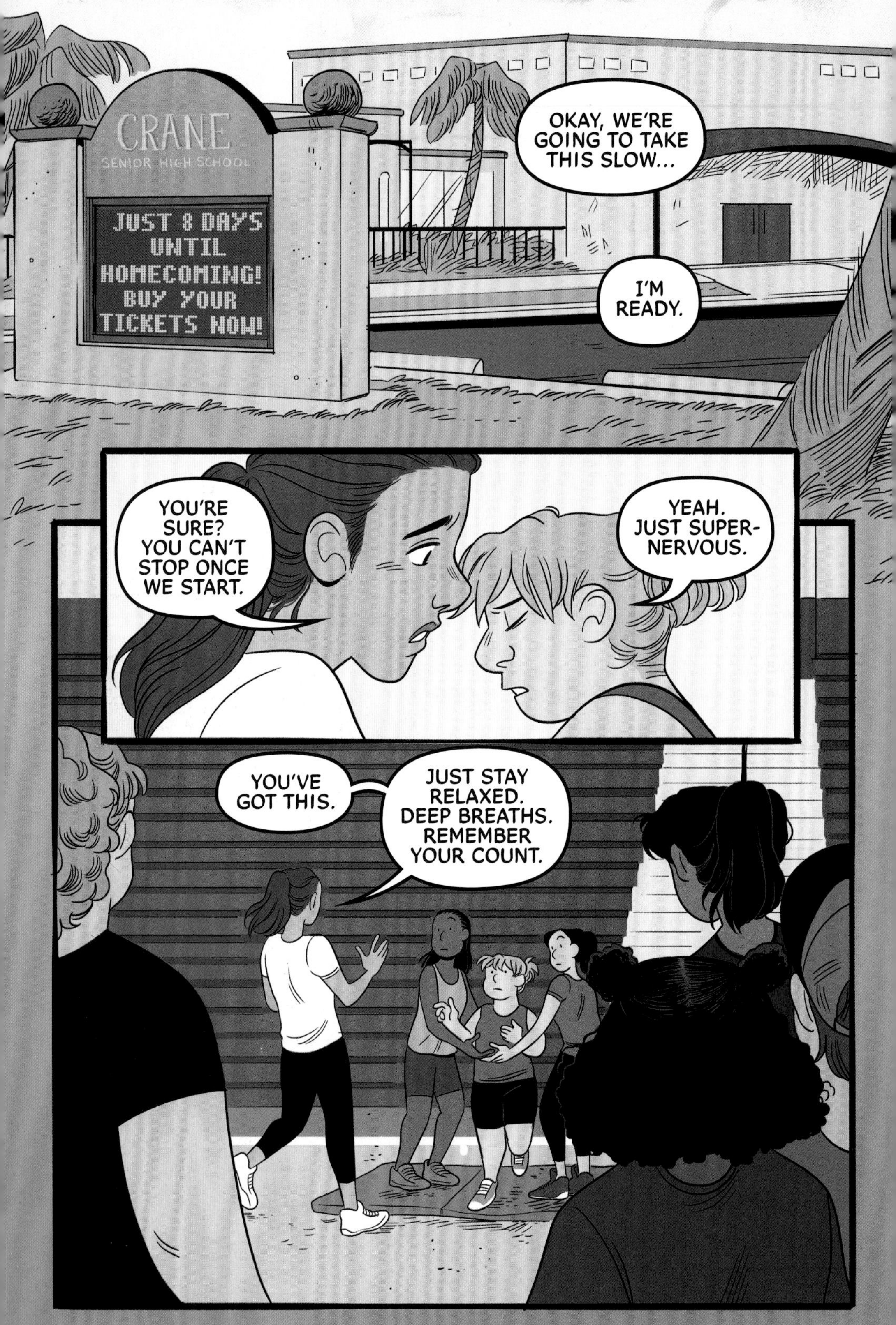
CRANE
SENIOR HIGH SCHOOL
JUST 8 DAYS UNTIL HOMECOMING! BUY YOUR TICKETS NOW!
OKAY, WE'RE GOING TO TAKE THIS SLOW...
I'M READY.
YOU'RE SURE? YOU CAN'T STOP ONCE WE START.
YEAH. JUST SUPER-NERVOUS.
YOU'VE GOT THIS.
JUST STAY RELAXED. DEEP BREATHS. REMEMBER YOUR COUNT.

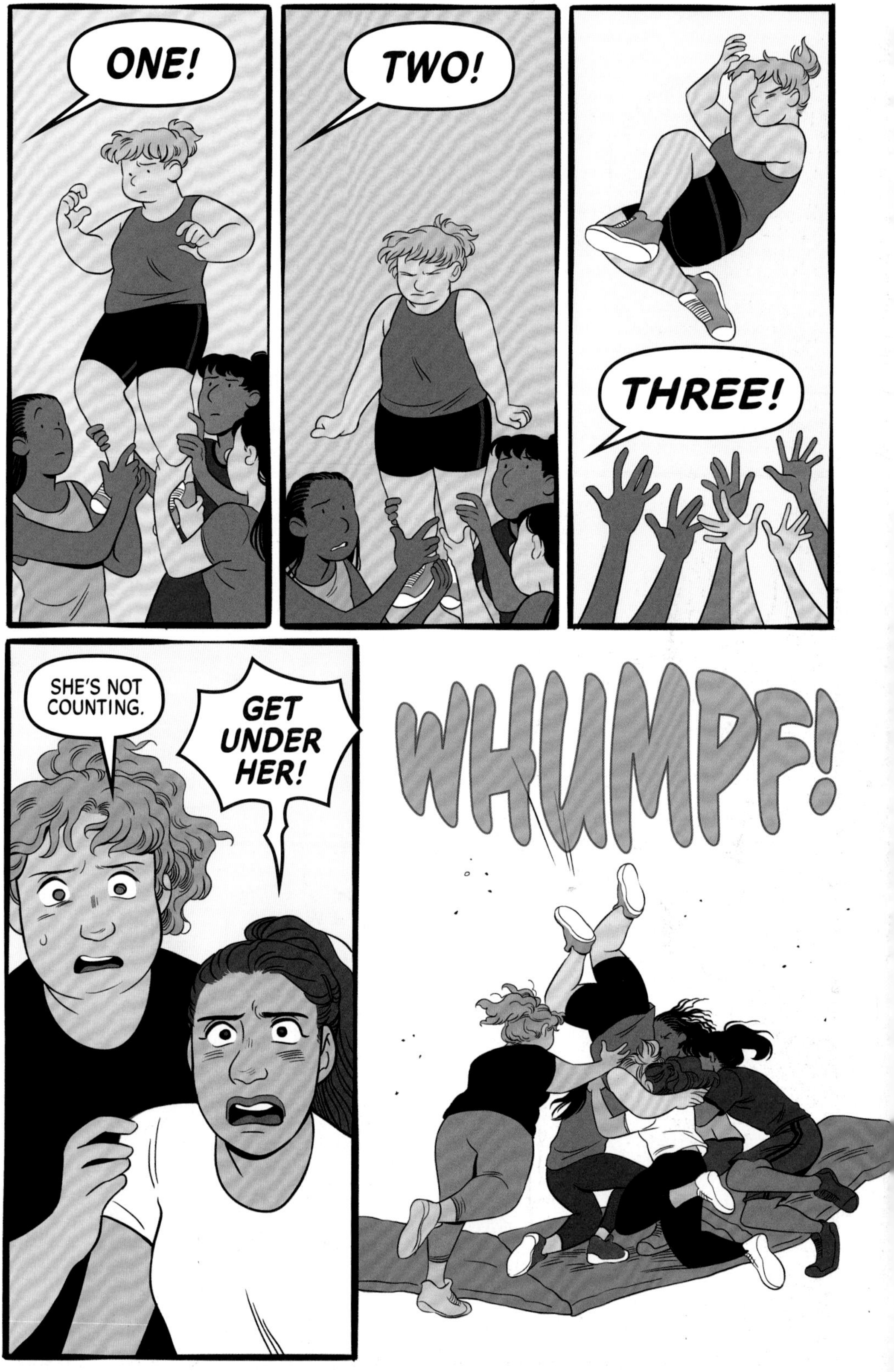
ONE!
TWO!
THREE!
SHE'S NOT COUNTING.
GET UNDER HER!
WHUMPF!

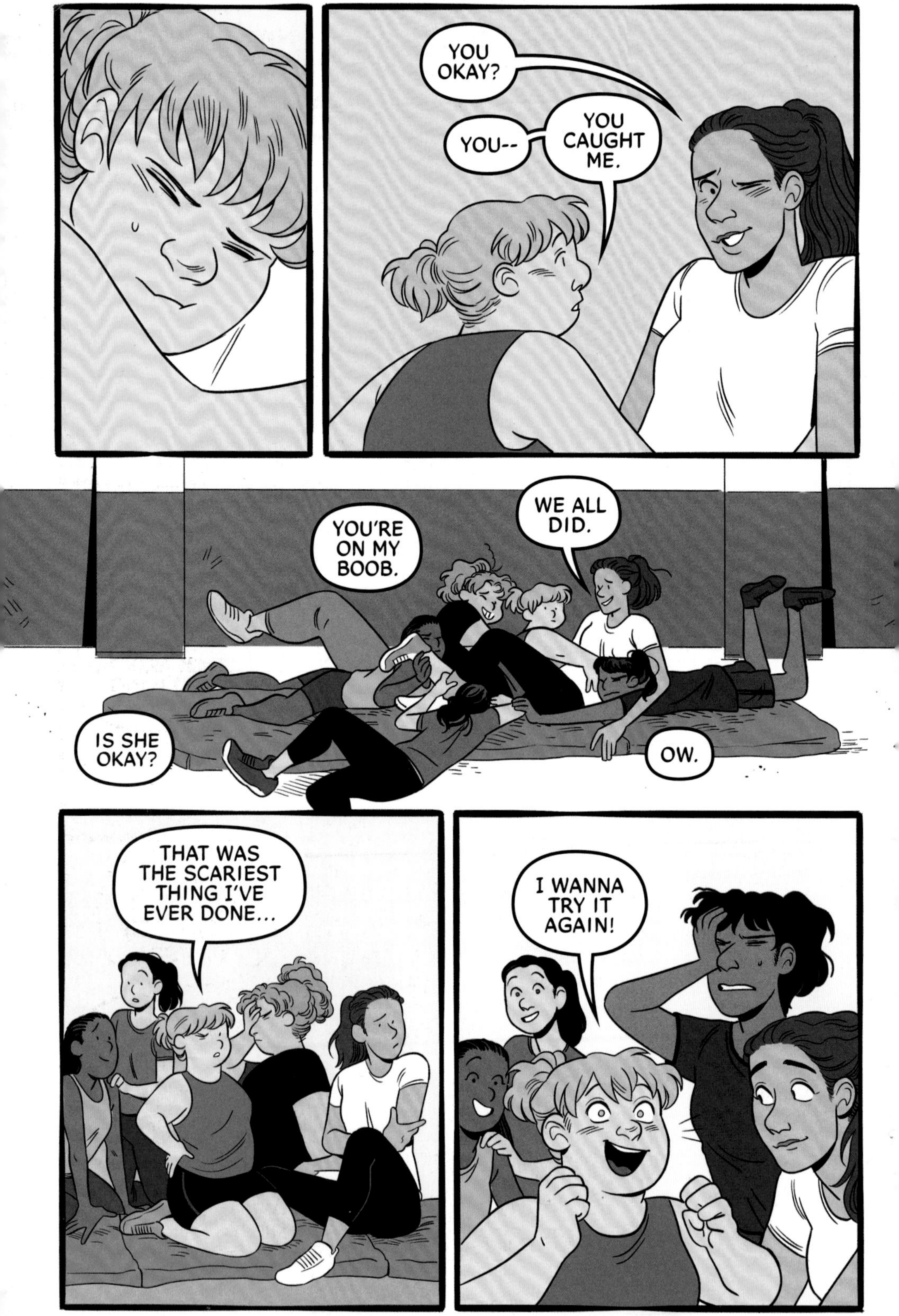
YOU OKAY?
YOU--
YOU CAUGHT ME.
YOU'RE ON MY BOOB.
WE ALL DID.
IS SHE OKAY?
OW.
THAT WAS THE SCARIEST THING I'VE EVER DONE...
I WANNA TRY IT AGAIN!

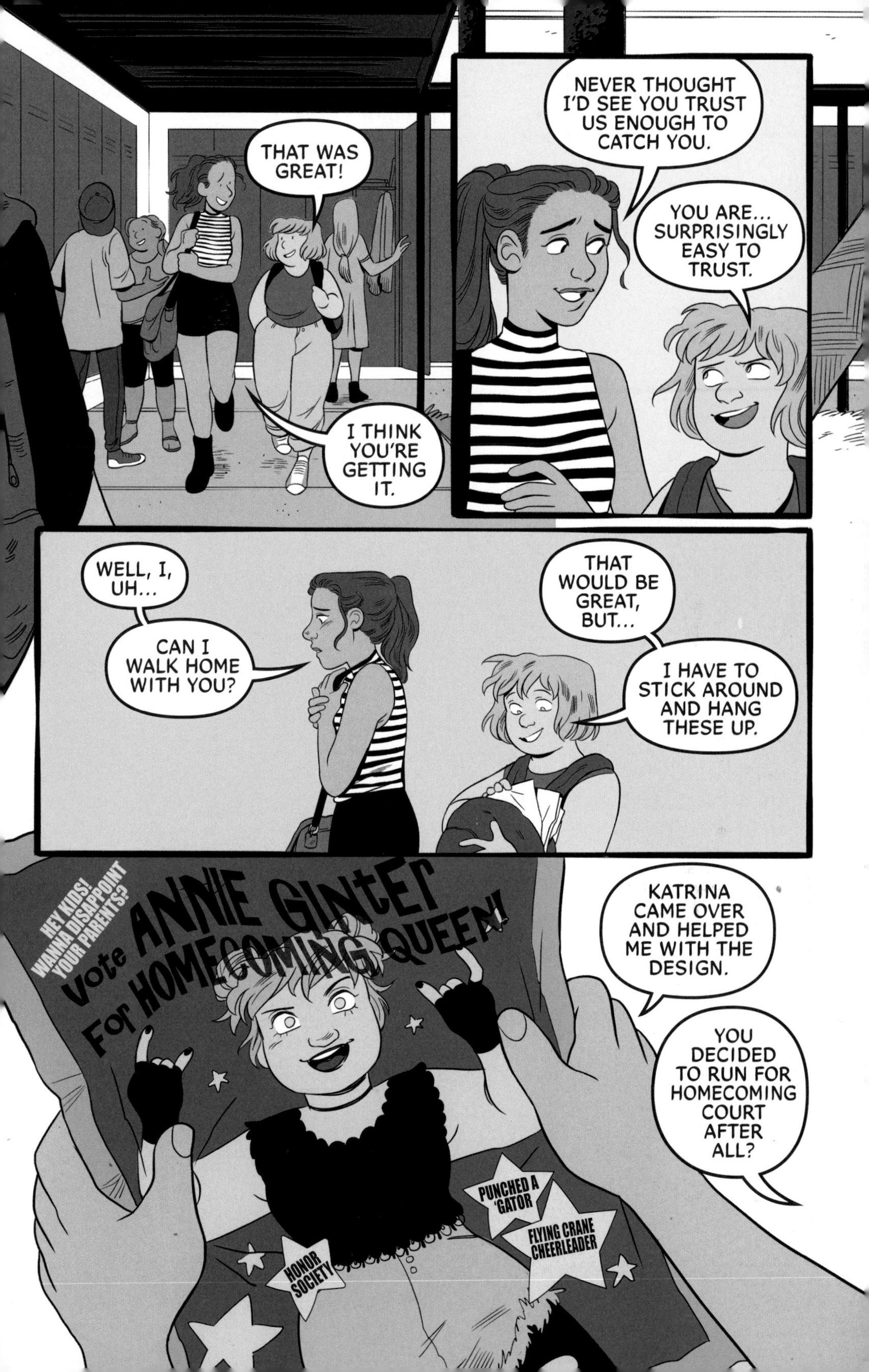
THAT WAS GREAT!
I THINK YOU'RE GETTING IT.
NEVER THOUGHT I'D SEE YOU TRUST US ENOUGH TO CATCH YOU.
YOU ARE... SURPRISINGLY EASY TO TRUST.
WELL, I, UH...
CAN I WALK HOME WITH YOU?
THAT WOULD BE GREAT, BUT...
I HAVE TO STICK AROUND AND HANG THESE UP.
HEY KIDS! WANNA DISAPPOINT YOUR PARENTS?
Vote ANNIE GINTER For HOMECOMING QUEEN!
PUNCHED A 'GATOR
FLYING CRANE CHEERLEADER
HONOR SOCIETY
KATRINA CAME OVER AND HELPED ME WITH THE DESIGN.
YOU DECIDED TO RUN FOR HOMECOMING COURT AFTER ALL?

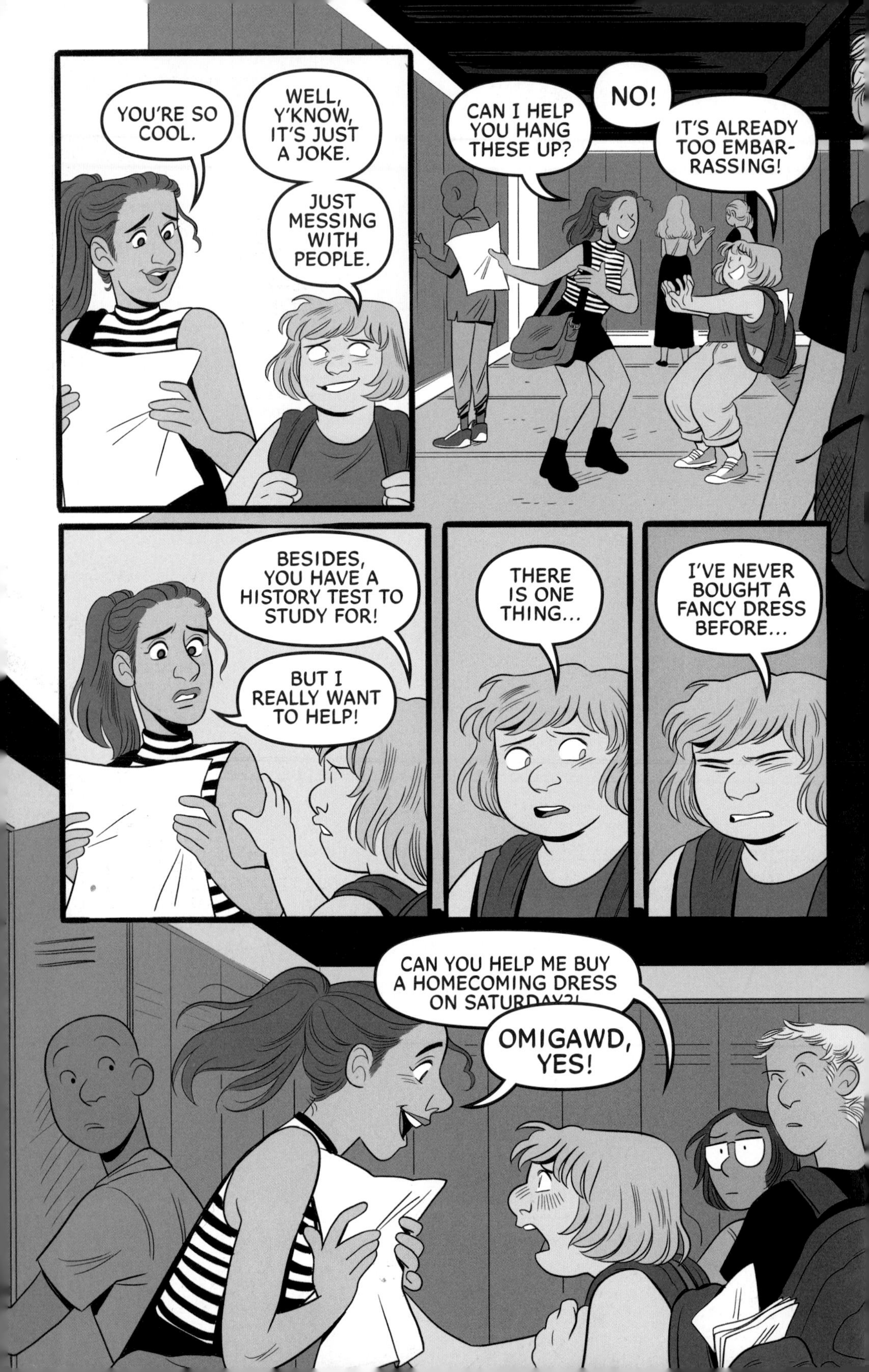
YOU'RE SO COOL.
WELL, Y'KNOW, IT'S JUST A JOKE.
JUST MESSING WITH PEOPLE.
CAN I HELP YOU HANG THESE UP?
NO!
IT'S ALREADY TOO EMBAR-RASSING!
BESIDES, YOU HAVE A HISTORY TEST TO STUDY FOR!
BUT I REALLY WANT TO HELP!
THERE IS ONE THING...
I'VE NEVER BOUGHT A FANCY DRESS BEFORE...
CAN YOU HELP ME BUY A HOMECOMING DRESS
OMIGAWD, YES!

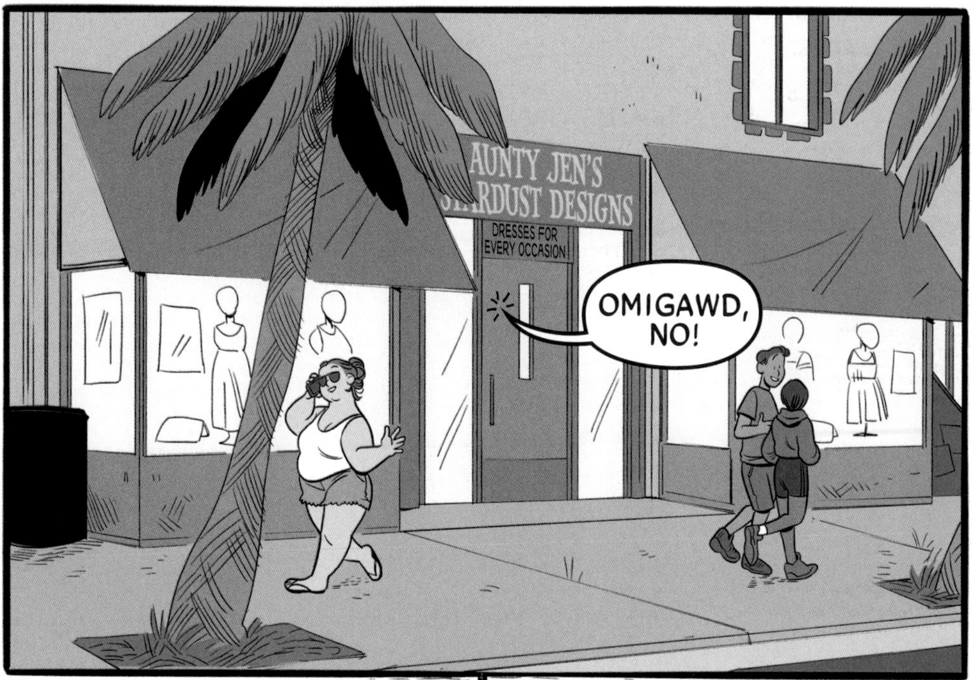
AUNTY JEN'S
STARDUST DESIGNS
DRESSES FOR EVERY OCCASION
OMIGAWD, NO!

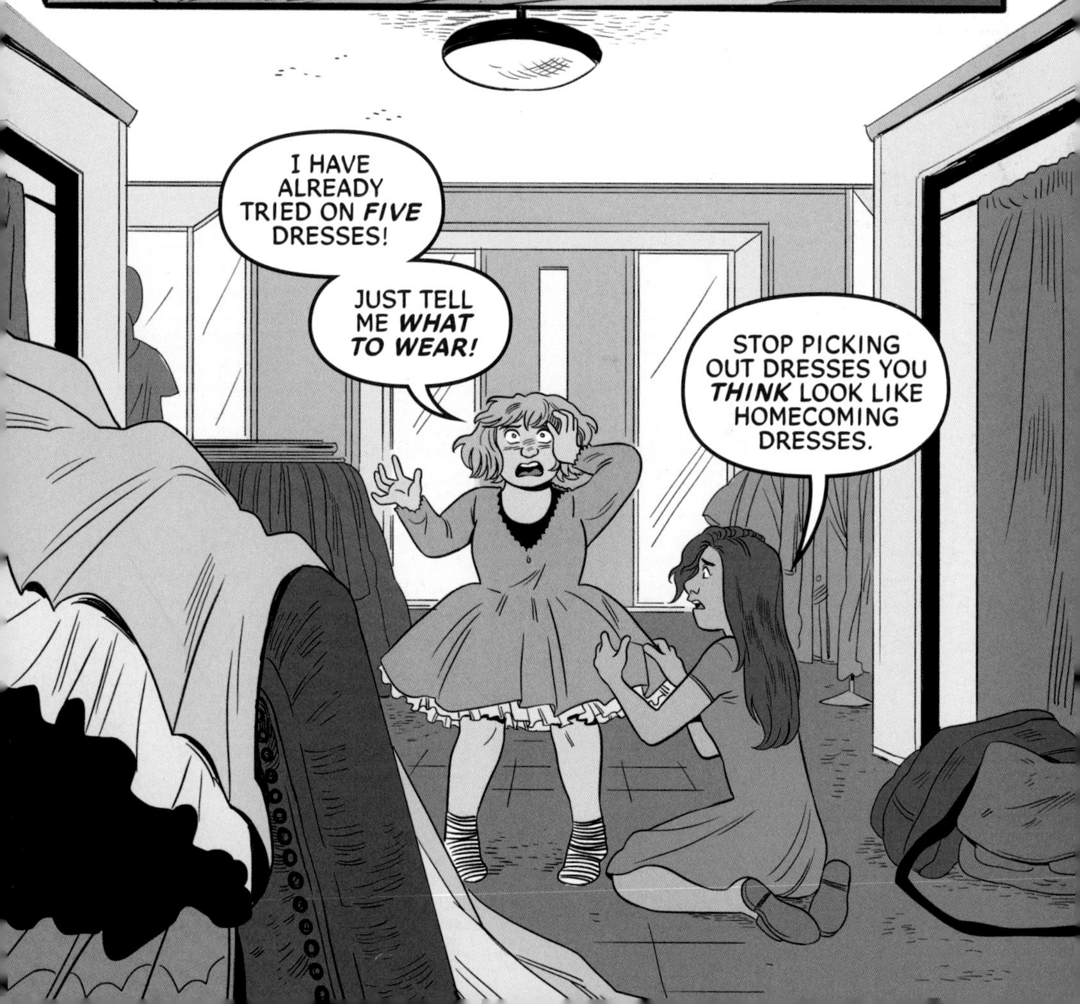
I HAVE ALREADY TRIED ON *FIVE* DRESSES!
JUST TELL ME ***WHAT TO WEAR!***
STOP PICKING OUT DRESSES YOU ***THINK*** LOOK LIKE HOMECOMING DRESSES.

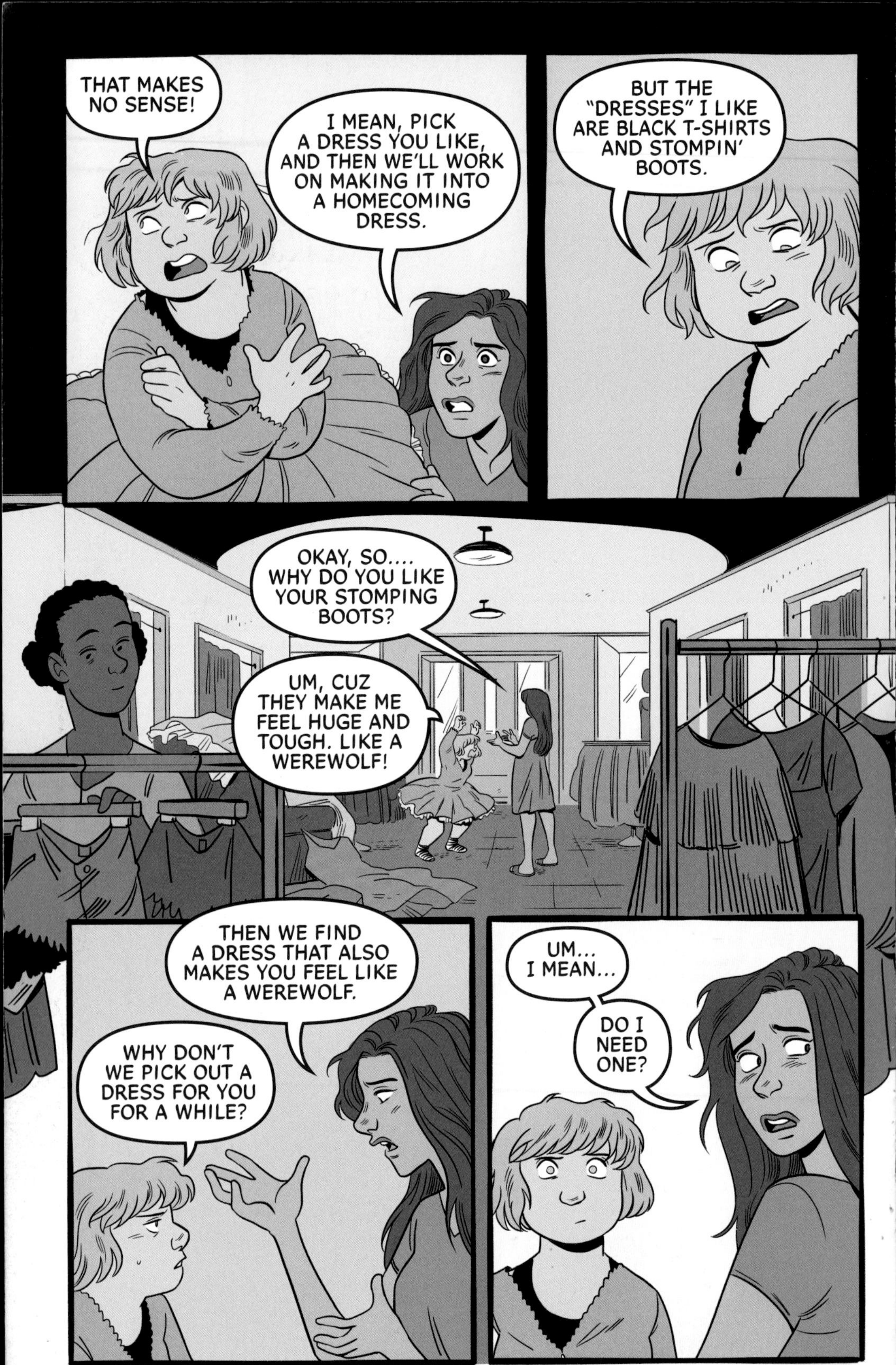

THAT MAKES NO SENSE!
I MEAN, PICK A DRESS YOU LIKE, AND THEN WE'LL WORK ON MAKING IT INTO A HOMECOMING DRESS.
BUT THE "DRESSES" I LIKE ARE BLACK T-SHIRTS AND STOMPIN' BOOTS.
OKAY, SO.... WHY DO YOU LIKE YOUR STOMPING BOOTS?
UM, CUZ THEY MAKE ME FEEL HUGE AND TOUGH. LIKE A WEREWOLF!
THEN WE FIND A DRESS THAT ALSO MAKES YOU FEEL LIKE A WEREWOLF.
WHY DON'T WE PICK OUT A DRESS FOR YOU FOR A WHILE?
UM... I MEAN...
DO I NEED ONE?

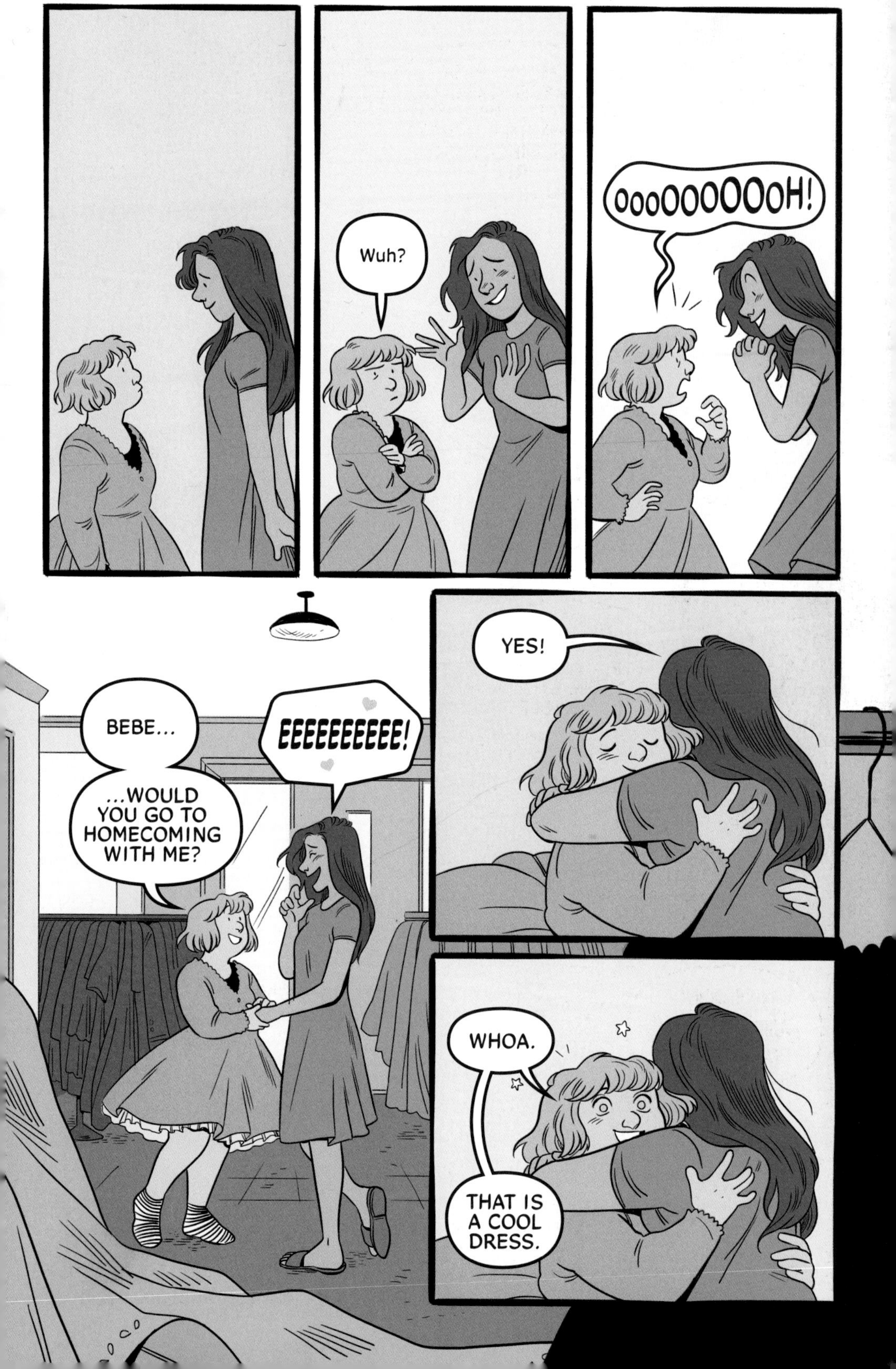
Wuh?
OOOOOOOOOOH!
BEBE...
...WOULD YOU GO TO HOMECOMING WITH ME?
EEEEEEEEEE!
YES!
WHOA.
THAT IS A COOL DRESS.

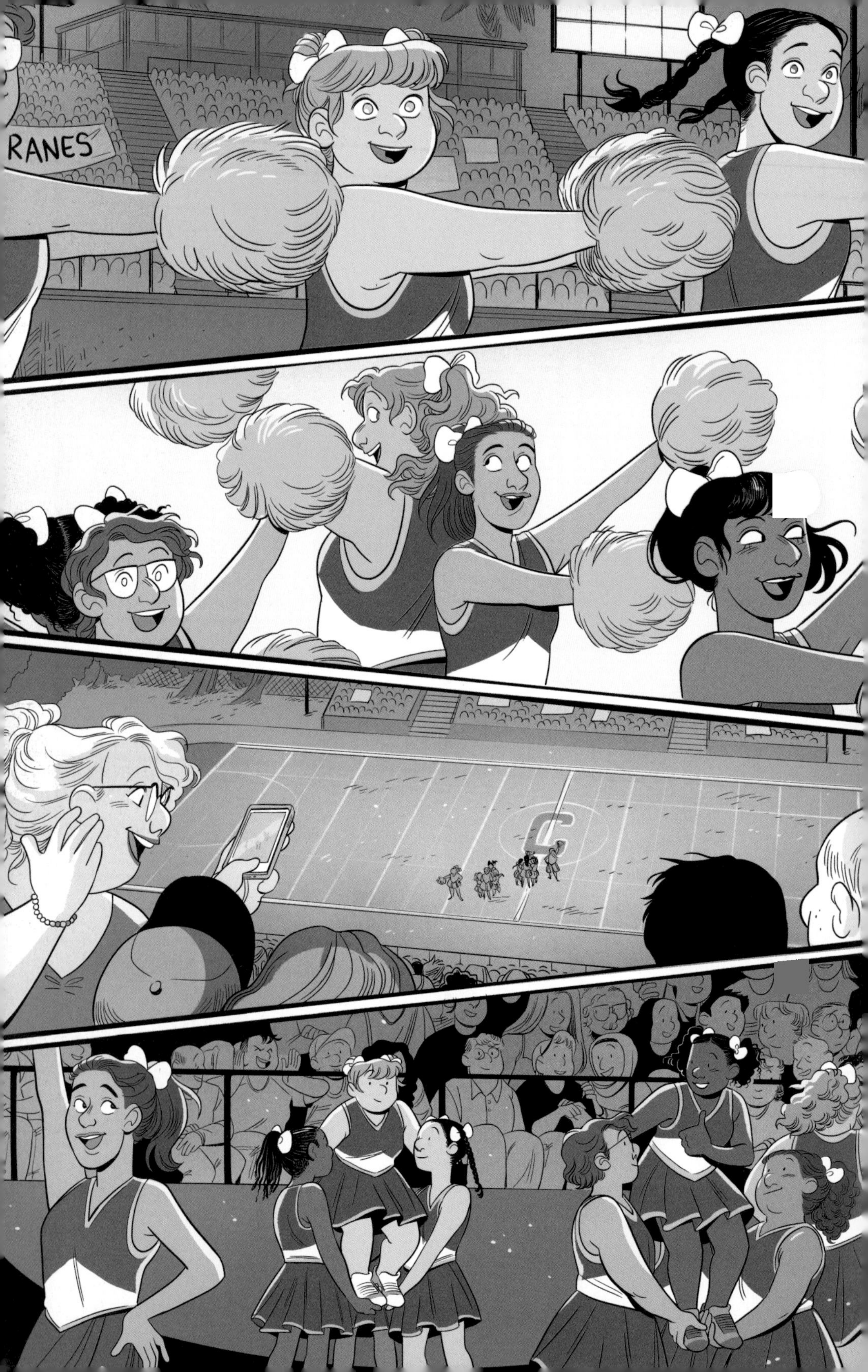
RANES

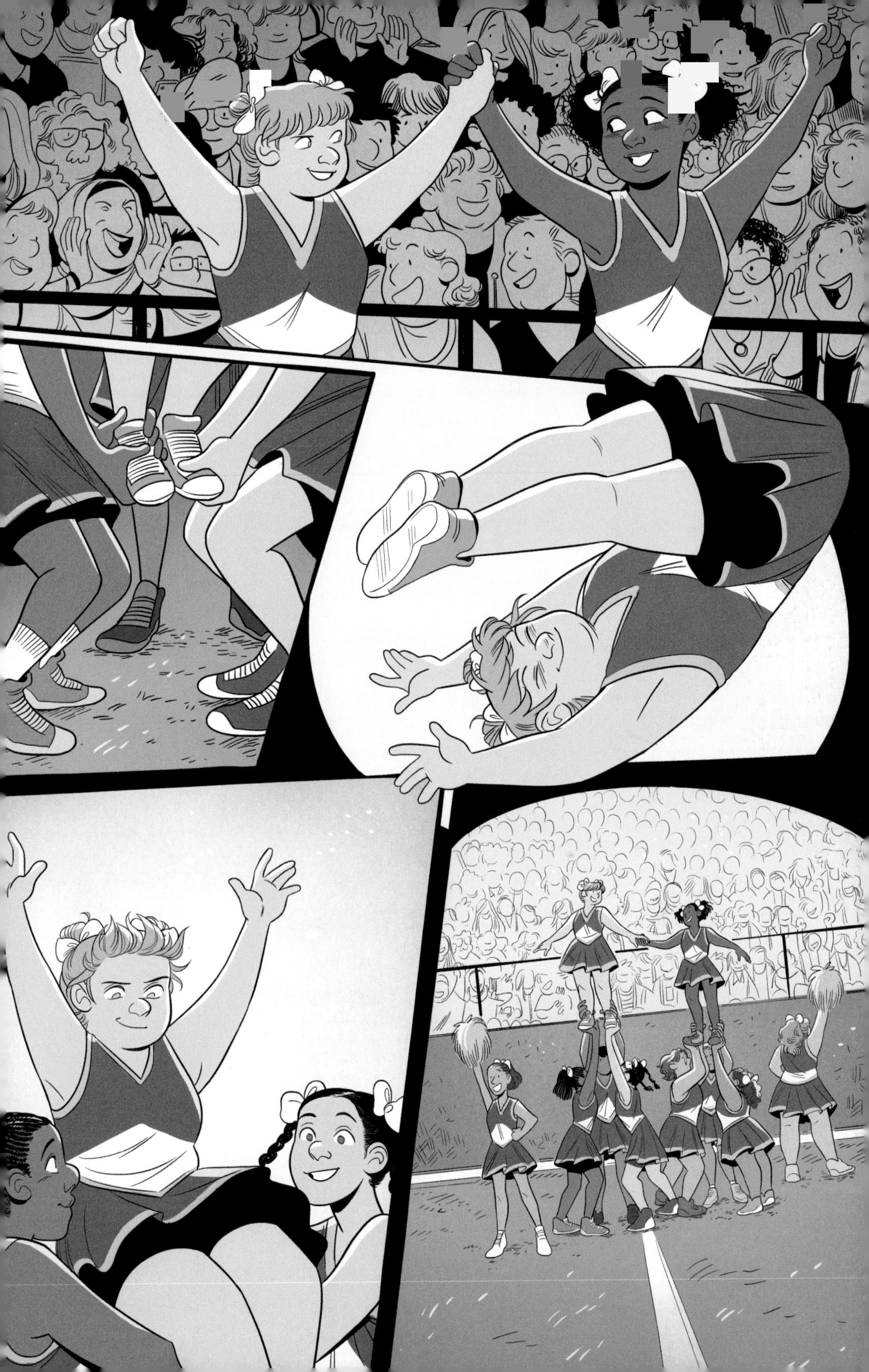

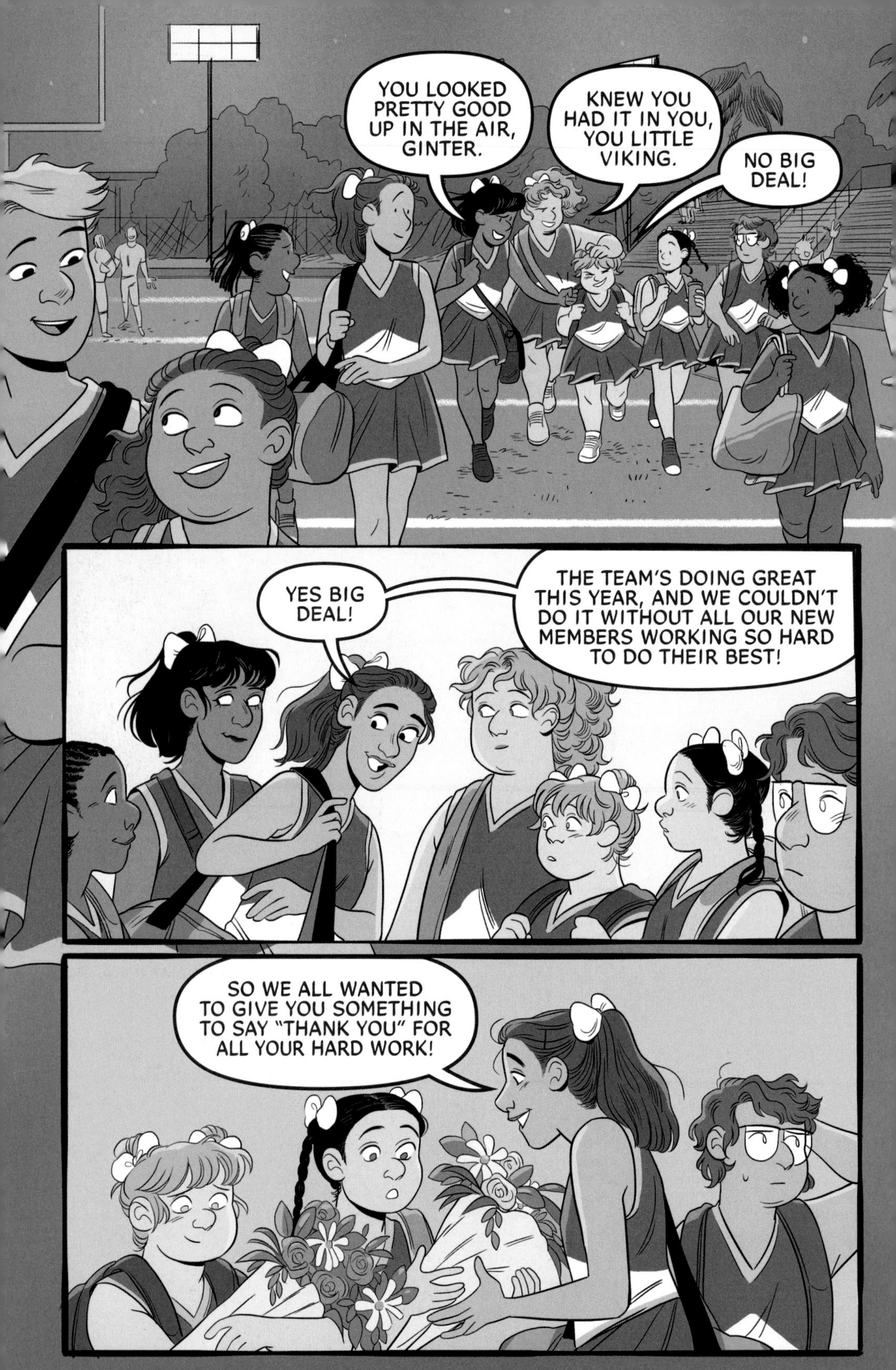
YOU LOOKED PRETTY GOOD UP IN THE AIR, GINTER.
KNEW YOU HAD IT IN YOU, YOU LITTLE VIKING.
NO BIG DEAL!
YES BIG DEAL!
THE TEAM'S DOING GREAT THIS YEAR, AND WE COULDN'T DO IT WITHOUT ALL OUR NEW MEMBERS WORKING SO HARD TO DO THEIR BEST!
SO WE ALL WANTED TO GIVE YOU SOMETHING TO SAY "THANK YOU" FOR ALL YOUR HARD WORK!

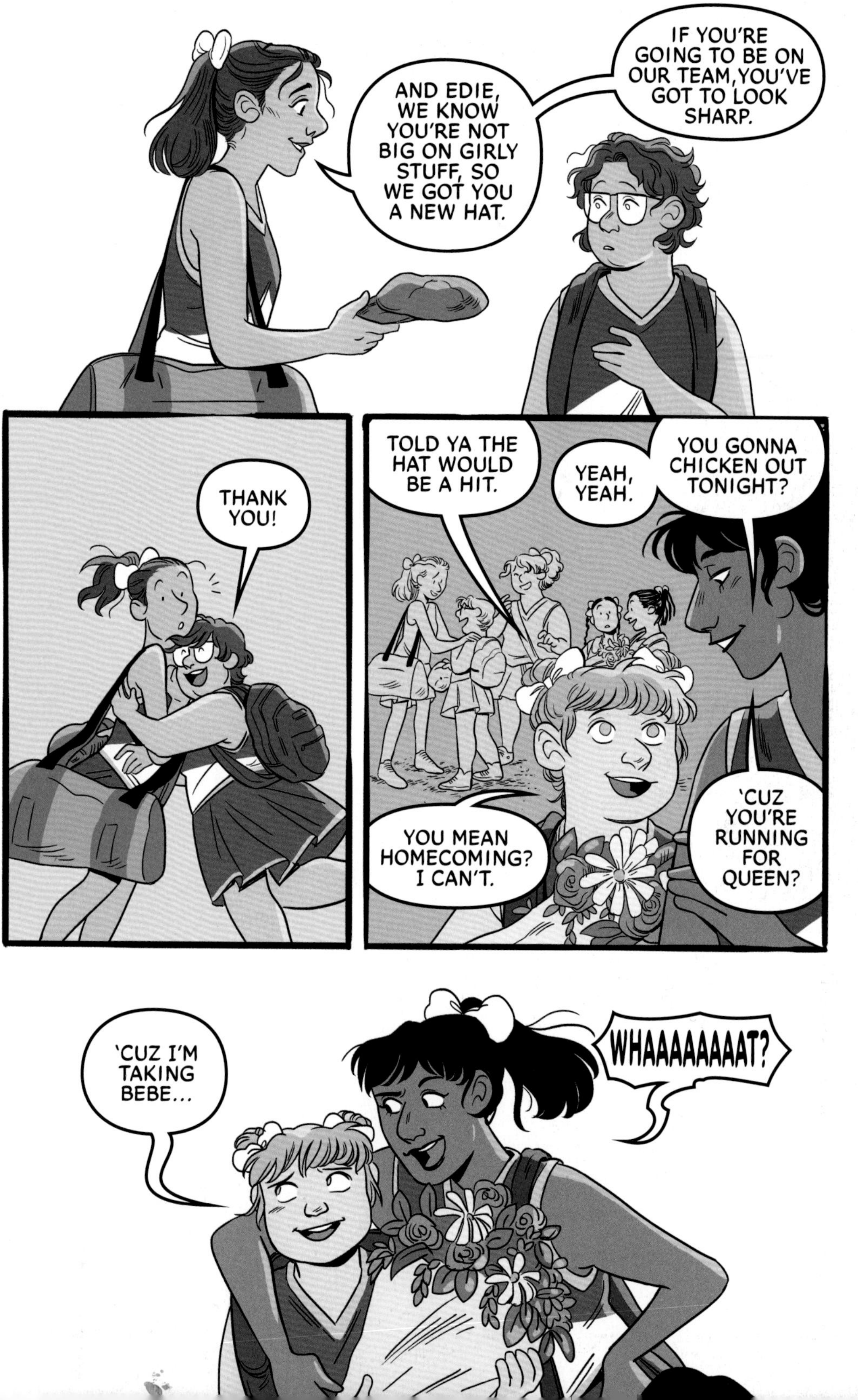
AND EDIE, WE KNOW YOU'RE NOT BIG ON GIRLY STUFF, SO WE GOT YOU A NEW HAT.
IF YOU'RE GOING TO BE ON OUR TEAM, YOU'VE GOT TO LOOK SHARP.
THANK YOU!
TOLD YA THE HAT WOULD BE A HIT.
YEAH, YEAH.
YOU GONNA CHICKEN OUT TONIGHT?
'CUZ YOU'RE RUNNING FOR QUEEN?
YOU MEAN HOMECOMING? I CAN'T.
'CUZ I'M TAKING BEBE...
WHAAAAAAAAT?

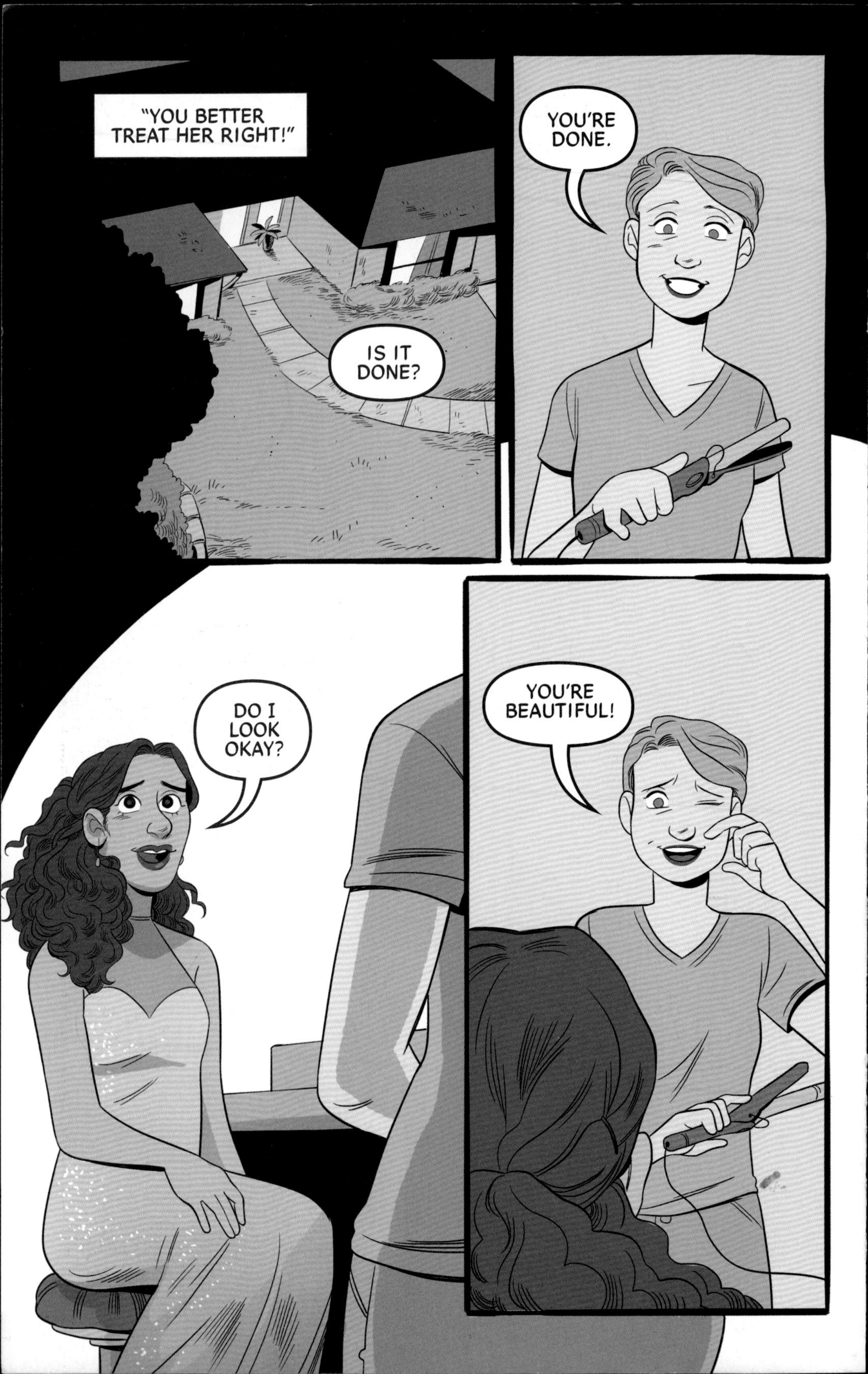
"YOU BETTER TREAT HER RIGHT!"
IS IT DONE?
YOU'RE DONE.
DO I LOOK OKAY?
YOU'RE BEAUTIFUL!

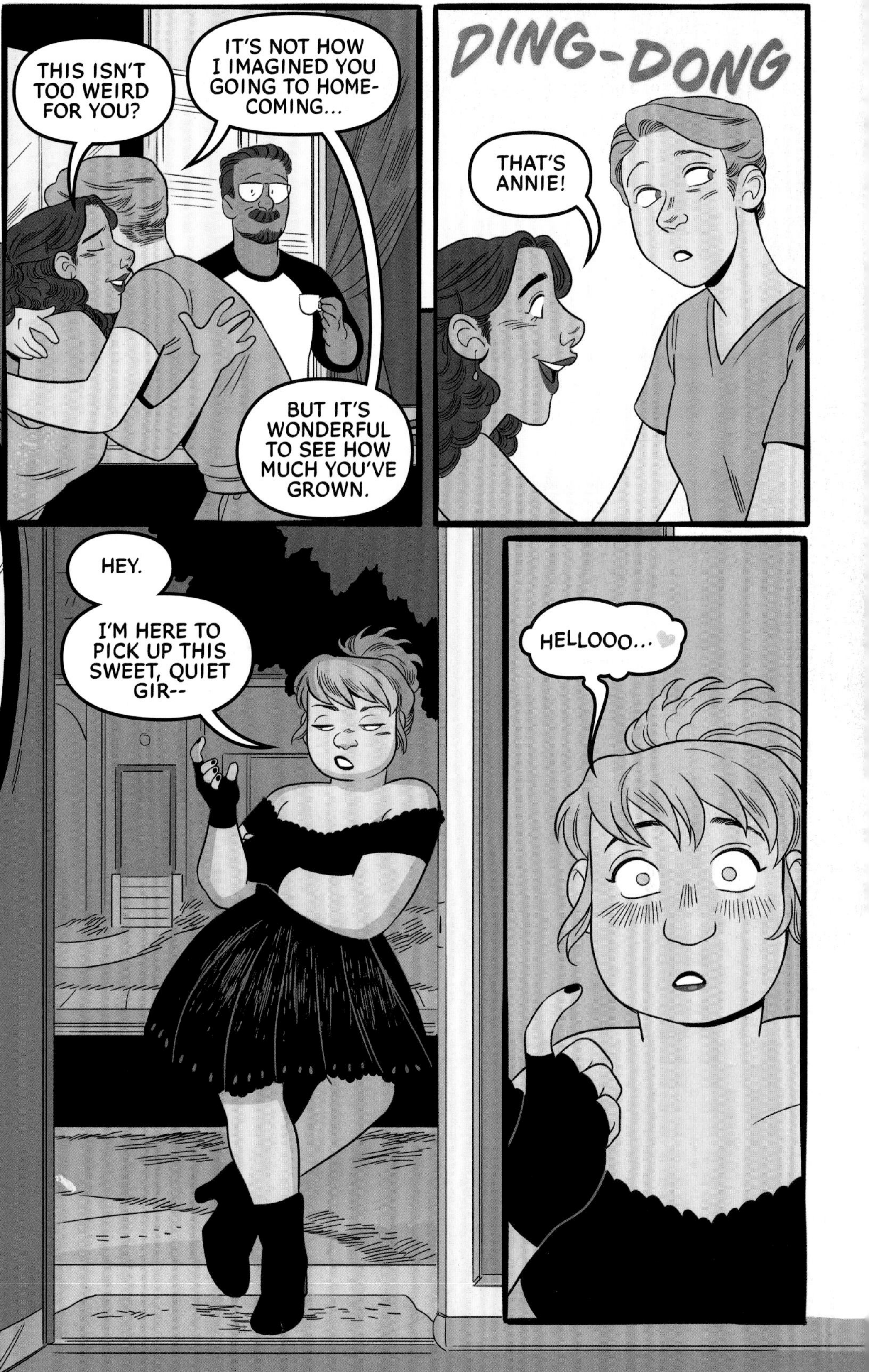
THIS ISN'T TOO WEIRD FOR YOU?
IT'S NOT HOW I IMAGINED YOU GOING TO HOME-COMING...
BUT IT'S WONDERFUL TO SEE HOW MUCH YOU'VE GROWN.
DING-DONG
THAT'S ANNIE!
HEY.
I'M HERE TO PICK UP THIS SWEET, QUIET GIR--
HELLOOO...

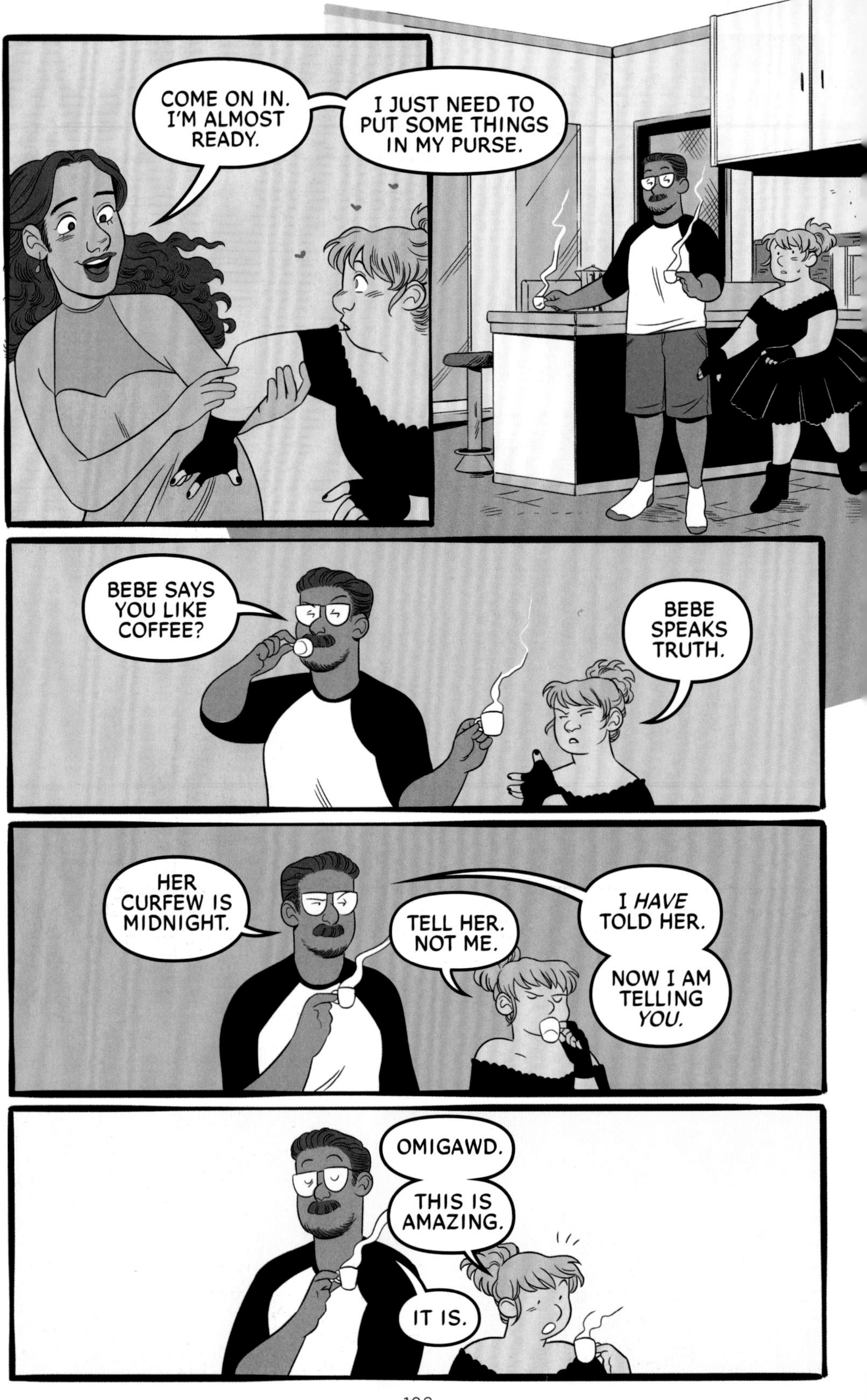
COME ON IN. I'M ALMOST READY.
I JUST NEED TO PUT SOME THINGS IN MY PURSE.
BEBE SAYS YOU LIKE COFFEE?
BEBE SPEAKS TRUTH.
HER CURFEW IS MIDNIGHT.
TELL HER. NOT ME.
I *HAVE* TOLD HER.
NOW I AM TELLING *YOU.*
OMIGAWD.
THIS IS AMAZING.
IT IS.

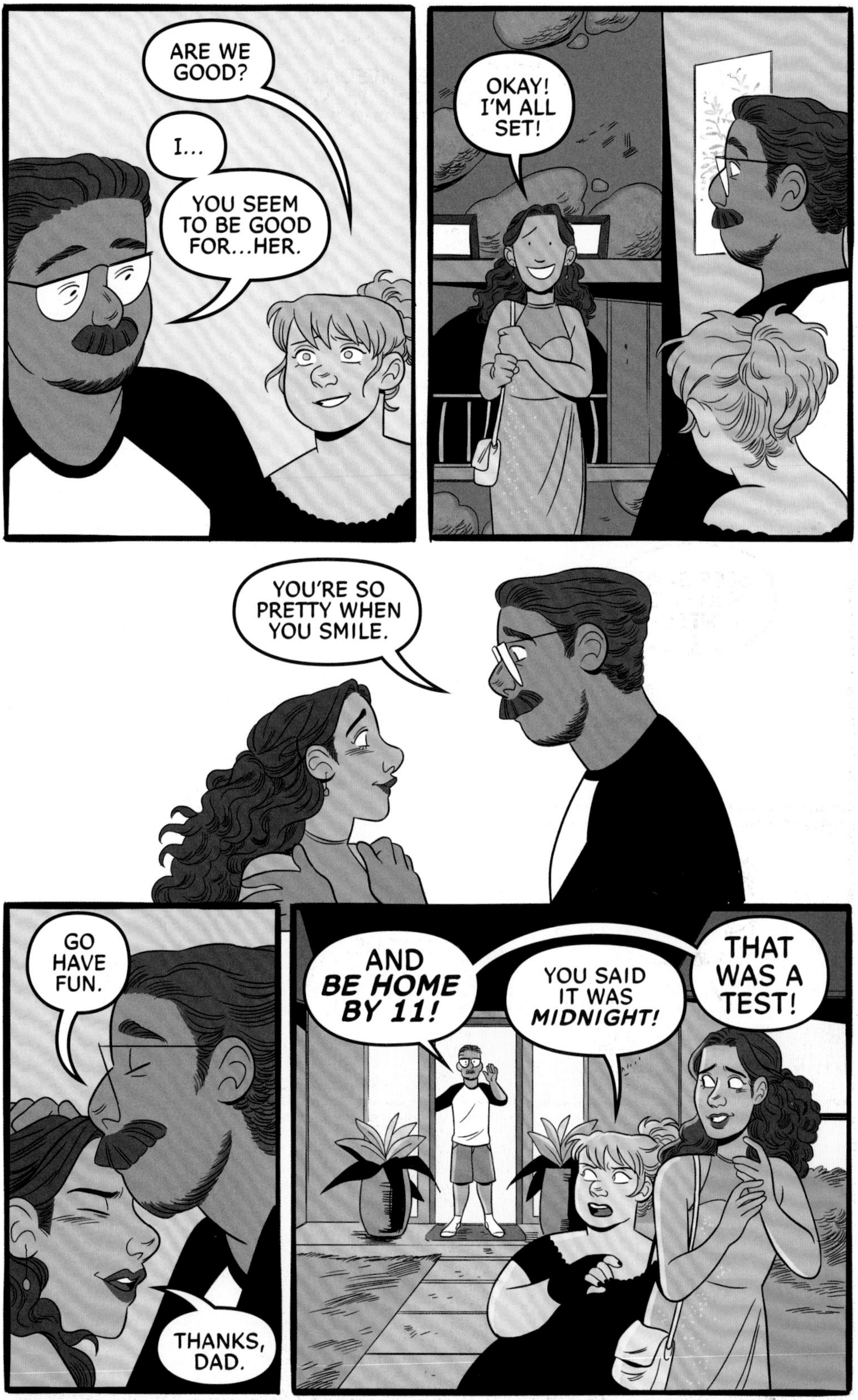
ARE WE GOOD?
I...
YOU SEEM TO BE GOOD FOR...HER.
OKAY! I'M ALL SET!
YOU'RE SO PRETTY WHEN YOU SMILE.
GO HAVE FUN.
THANKS, DAD.
AND *BE HOME BY 11!*
YOU SAID IT WAS *MIDNIGHT!*
THAT WAS A TEST!

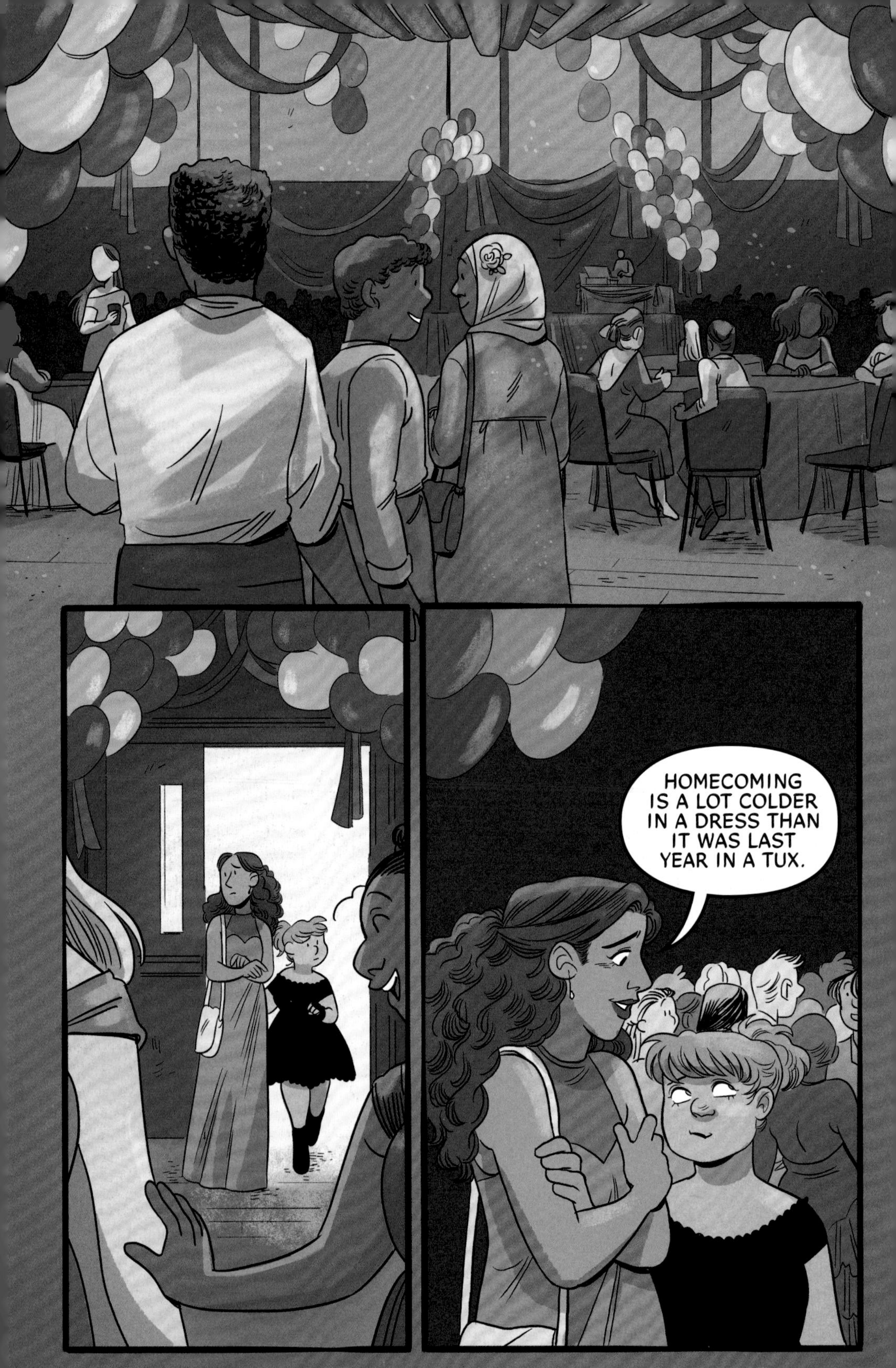
HOMECOMING IS A LOT COLDER IN A DRESS THAN IT WAS LAST YEAR IN A TUX.

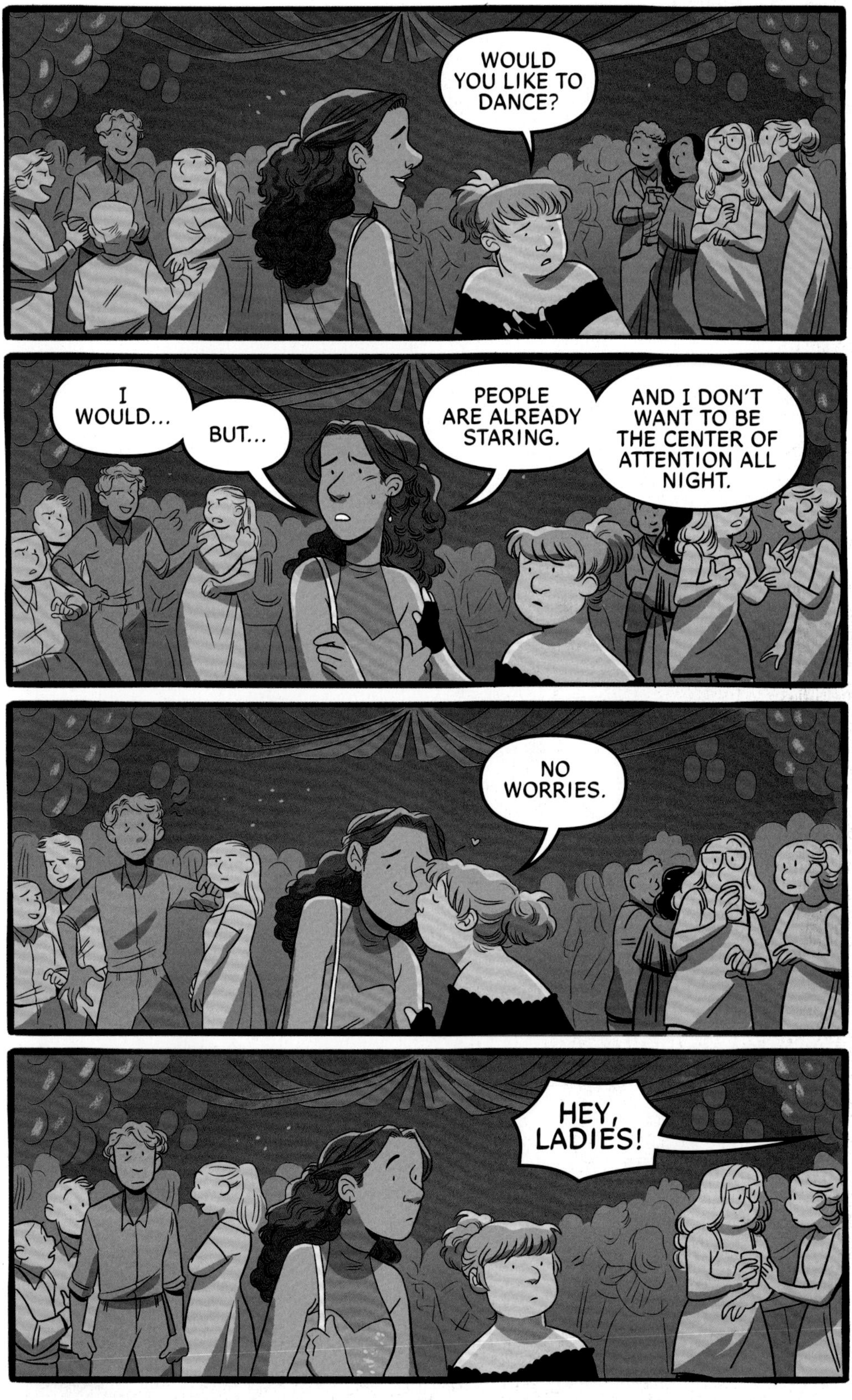
WOULD YOU LIKE TO DANCE?
I WOULD...
BUT...
PEOPLE ARE ALREADY STARING.
AND I DON'T WANT TO BE THE CENTER OF ATTENTION ALL NIGHT.
NO WORRIES.
HEY, LADIES!

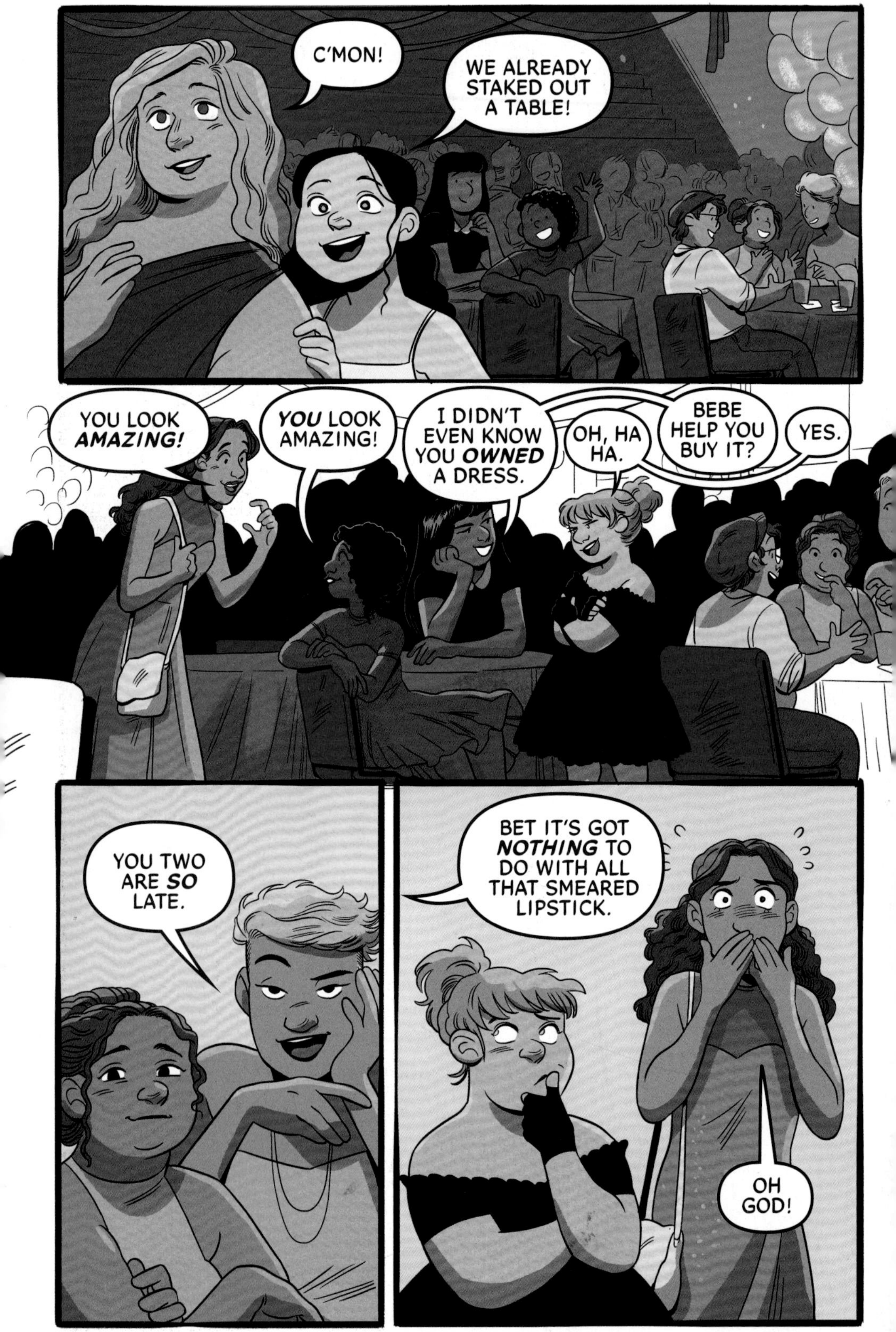
C'MON!
WE ALREADY STAKED OUT A TABLE!
YOU LOOK **AMAZING!**
YOU LOOK AMAZING!
I DIDN'T EVEN KNOW YOU ***OWNED*** A DRESS.
OH, HA HA.
BEBE HELP YOU BUY IT?
YES.
YOU TWO ARE ***SO*** LATE.
BET IT'S GOT ***NOTHING*** TO DO WITH ALL THAT SMEARED LIPSTICK.
OH GOD!

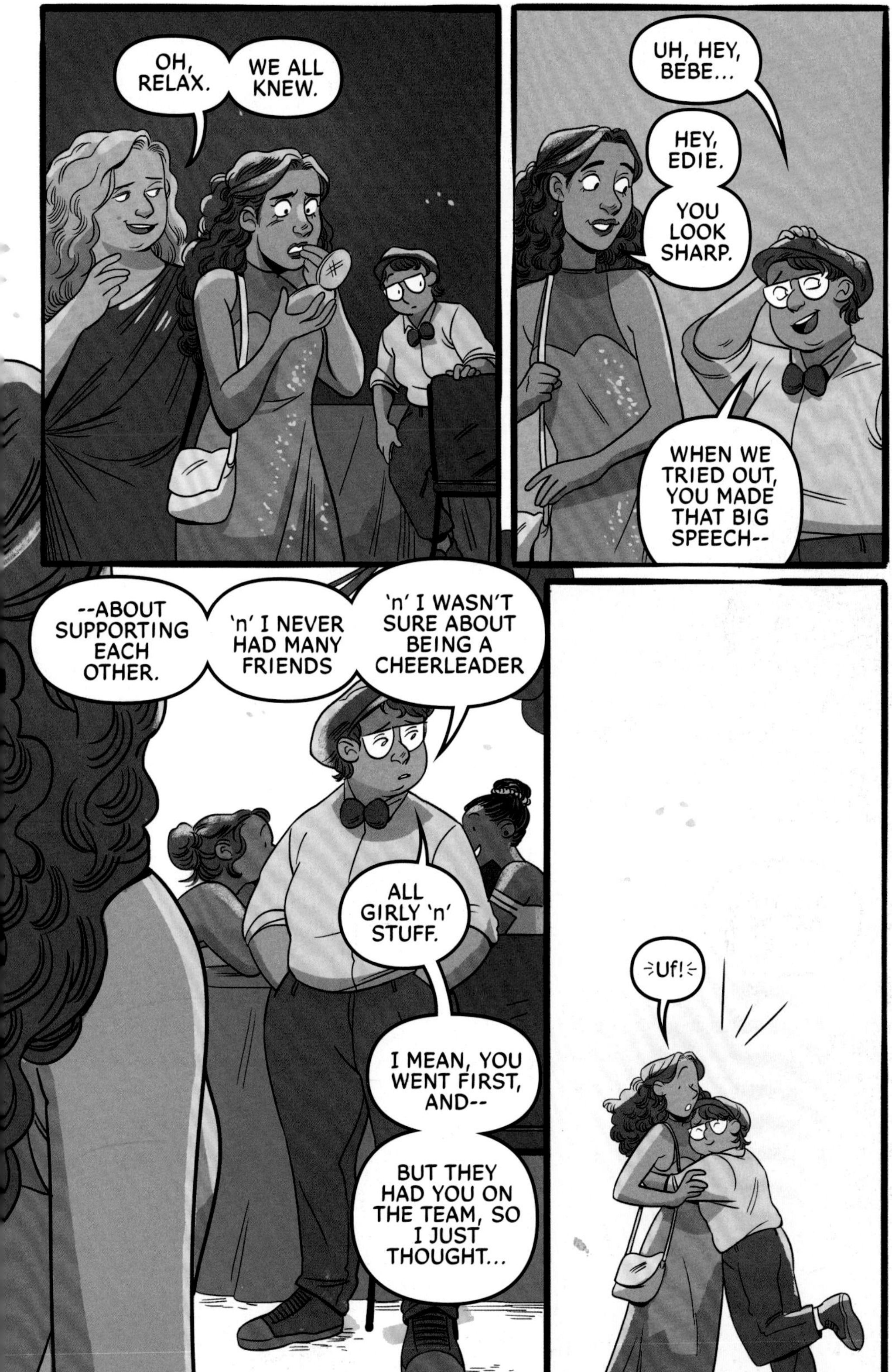
OH, RELAX.
WE ALL KNEW.
UH, HEY, BEBE...
HEY, EDIE.
YOU LOOK SHARP.
WHEN WE TRIED OUT, YOU MADE THAT BIG SPEECH--
--ABOUT SUPPORTING EACH OTHER.
'n' I NEVER HAD MANY FRIENDS
'n' I WASN'T SURE ABOUT BEING A CHEERLEADER
ALL GIRLY 'n' STUFF.
I MEAN, YOU WENT FIRST, AND--
BUT THEY HAD YOU ON THE TEAM, SO I JUST THOUGHT...
Uf!

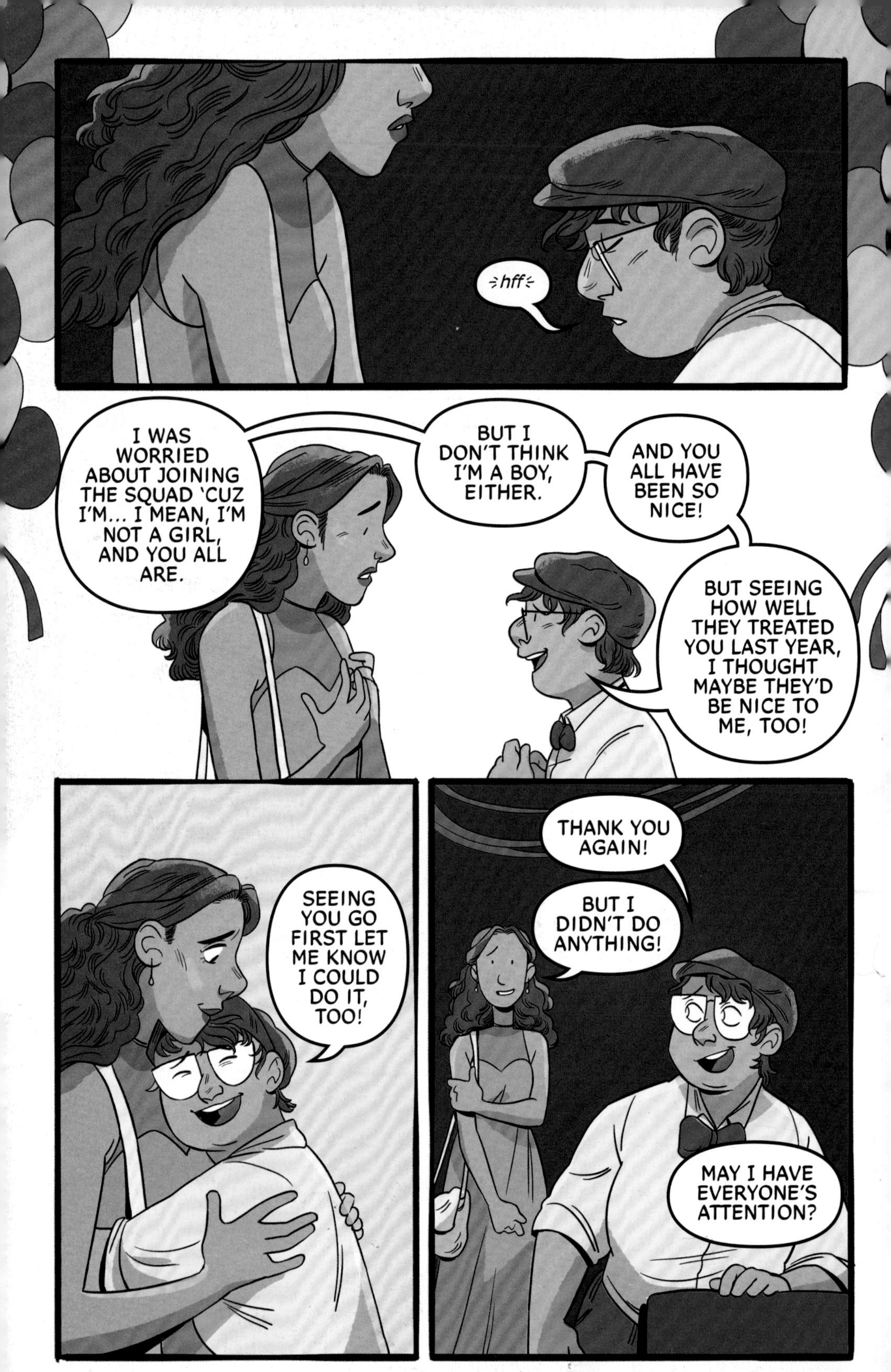
hff
I WAS WORRIED ABOUT JOINING THE SQUAD 'CUZ I'M... I MEAN, I'M NOT A GIRL, AND YOU ALL ARE.
BUT I DON'T THINK I'M A BOY, EITHER.
AND YOU ALL HAVE BEEN SO NICE!
BUT SEEING HOW WELL THEY TREATED YOU LAST YEAR, I THOUGHT MAYBE THEY'D BE NICE TO ME, TOO!
SEEING YOU GO FIRST LET ME KNOW I COULD DO IT, TOO!
THANK YOU AGAIN!
BUT I DIDN'T DO ANYTHING!
MAY I HAVE EVERYONE'S ATTENTION?

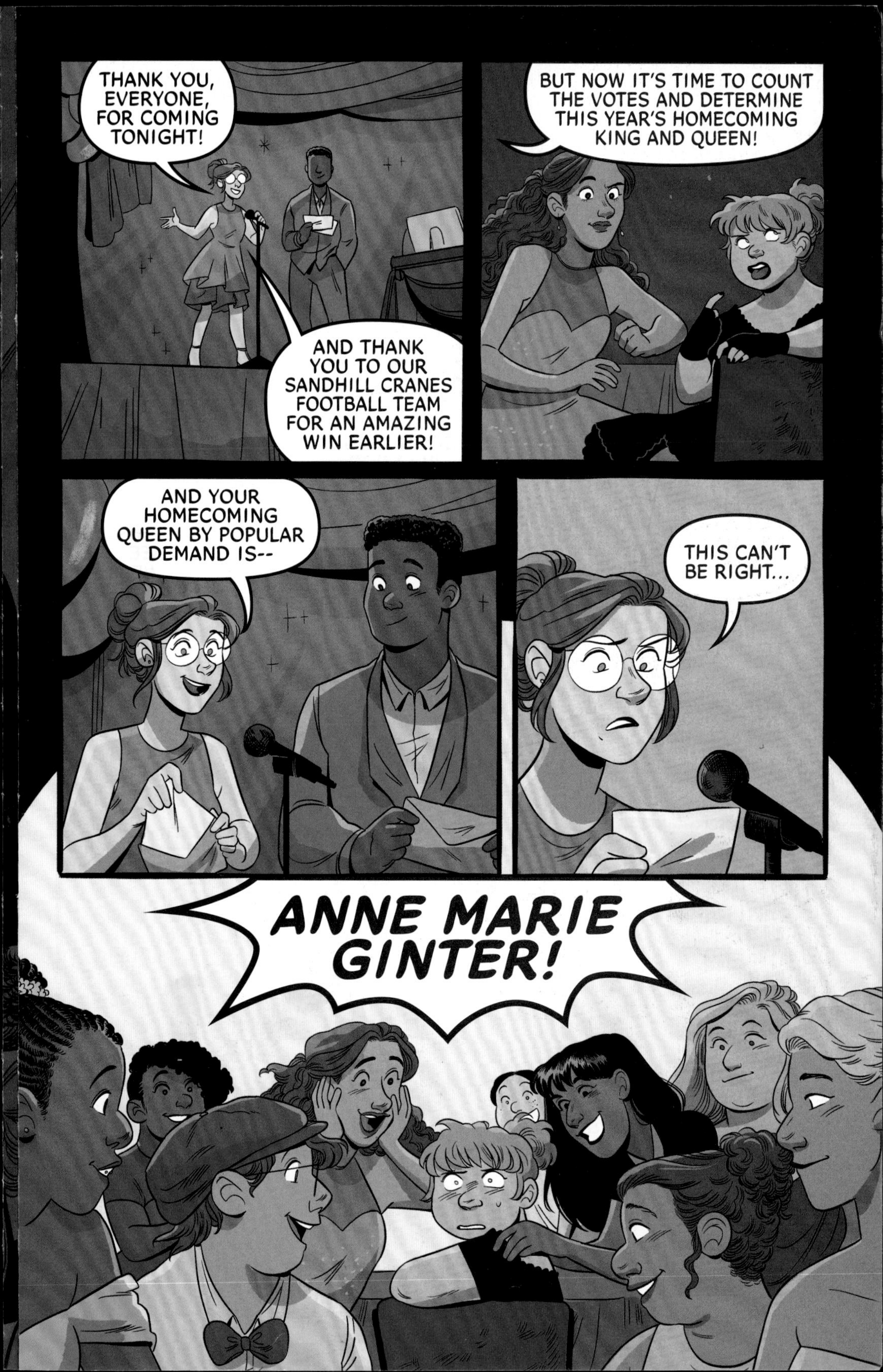
THANK YOU, EVERYONE, FOR COMING TONIGHT!
AND THANK YOU TO OUR SANDHILL CRANES FOOTBALL TEAM FOR AN AMAZING WIN EARLIER!
BUT NOW IT'S TIME TO COUNT THE VOTES AND DETERMINE THIS YEAR'S HOMECOMING KING AND QUEEN!
AND YOUR HOMECOMING QUEEN BY POPULAR DEMAND IS--
THIS CAN'T BE RIGHT...
ANNE MARIE GINTER!

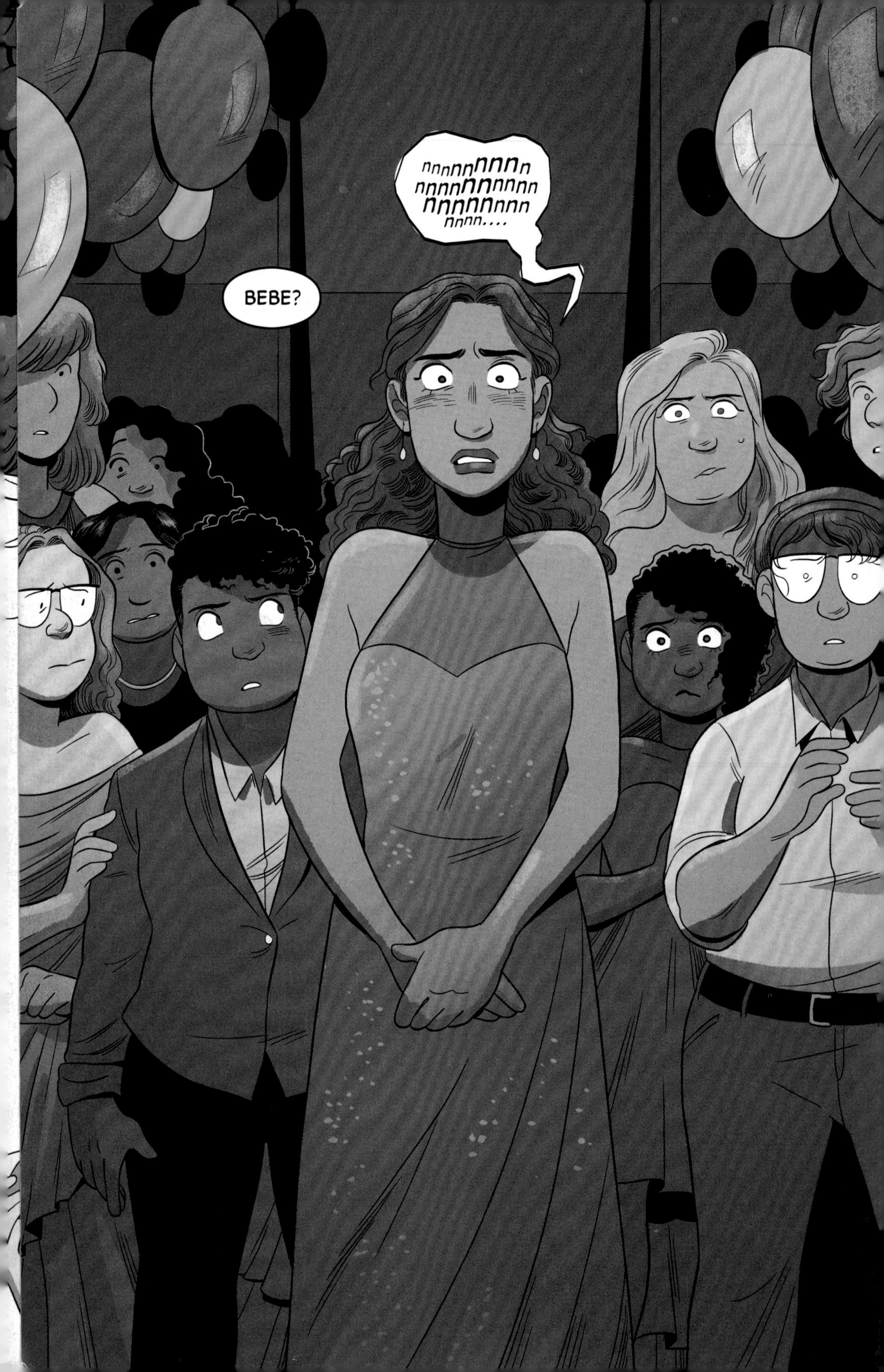

nnnnnnnnn nnnnnnnnnnn nnnnnnnnnn nnnn....
BEBE?

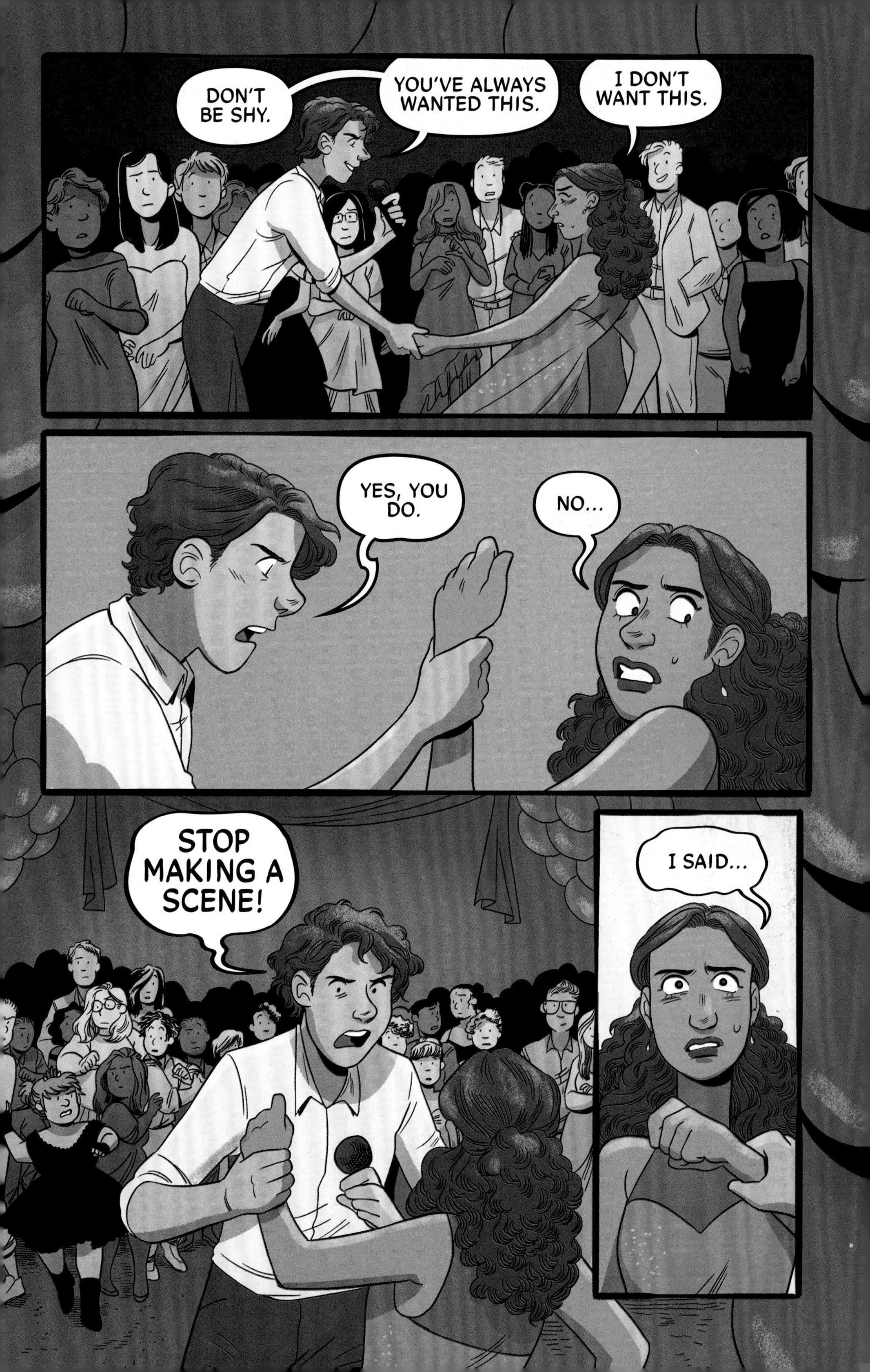
DON'T BE SHY.
YOU'VE ALWAYS WANTED THIS.
I DON'T WANT THIS.
YES, YOU DO.
NO...
STOP MAKING A SCENE!
I SAID...

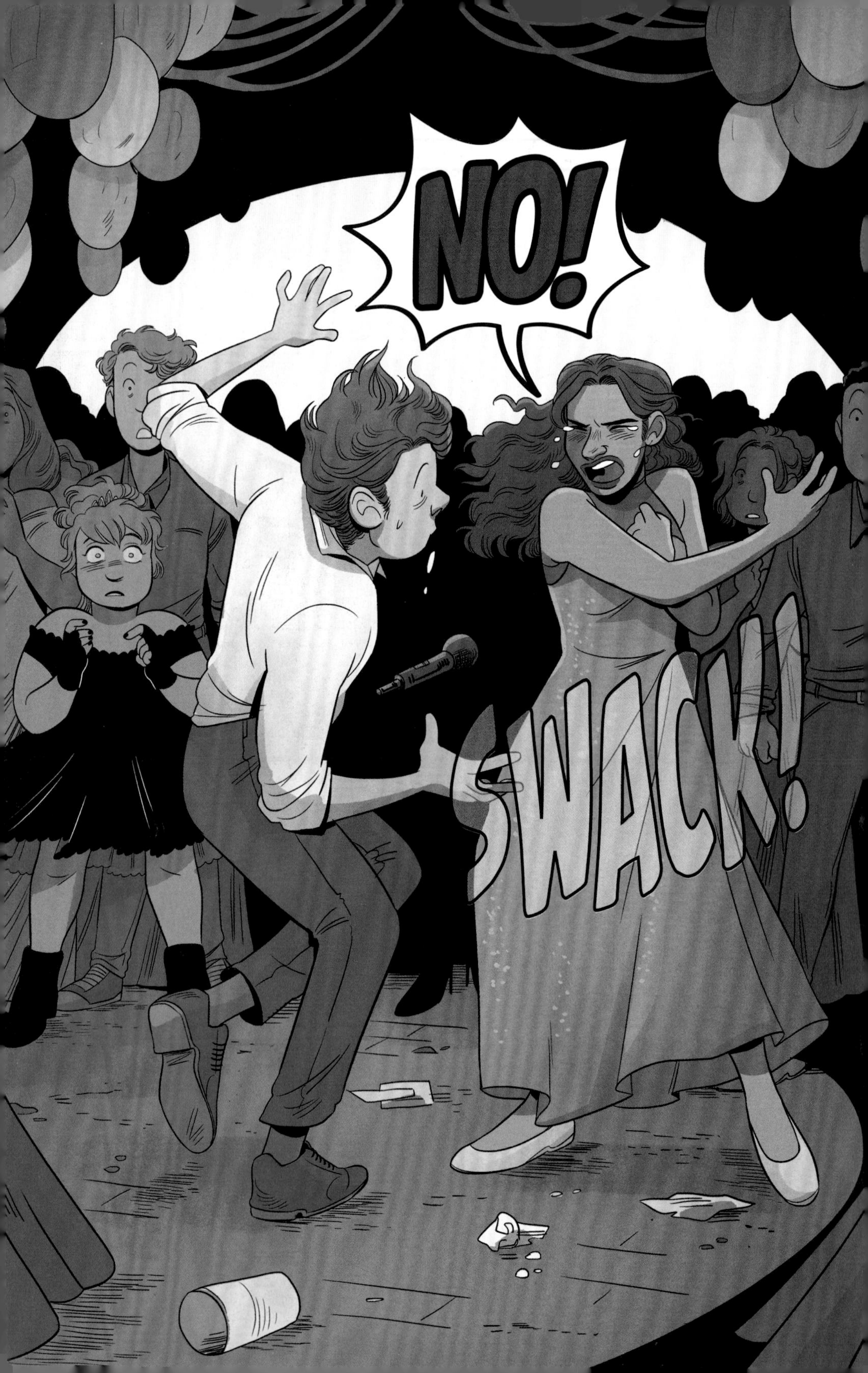
NO!
SWACK!

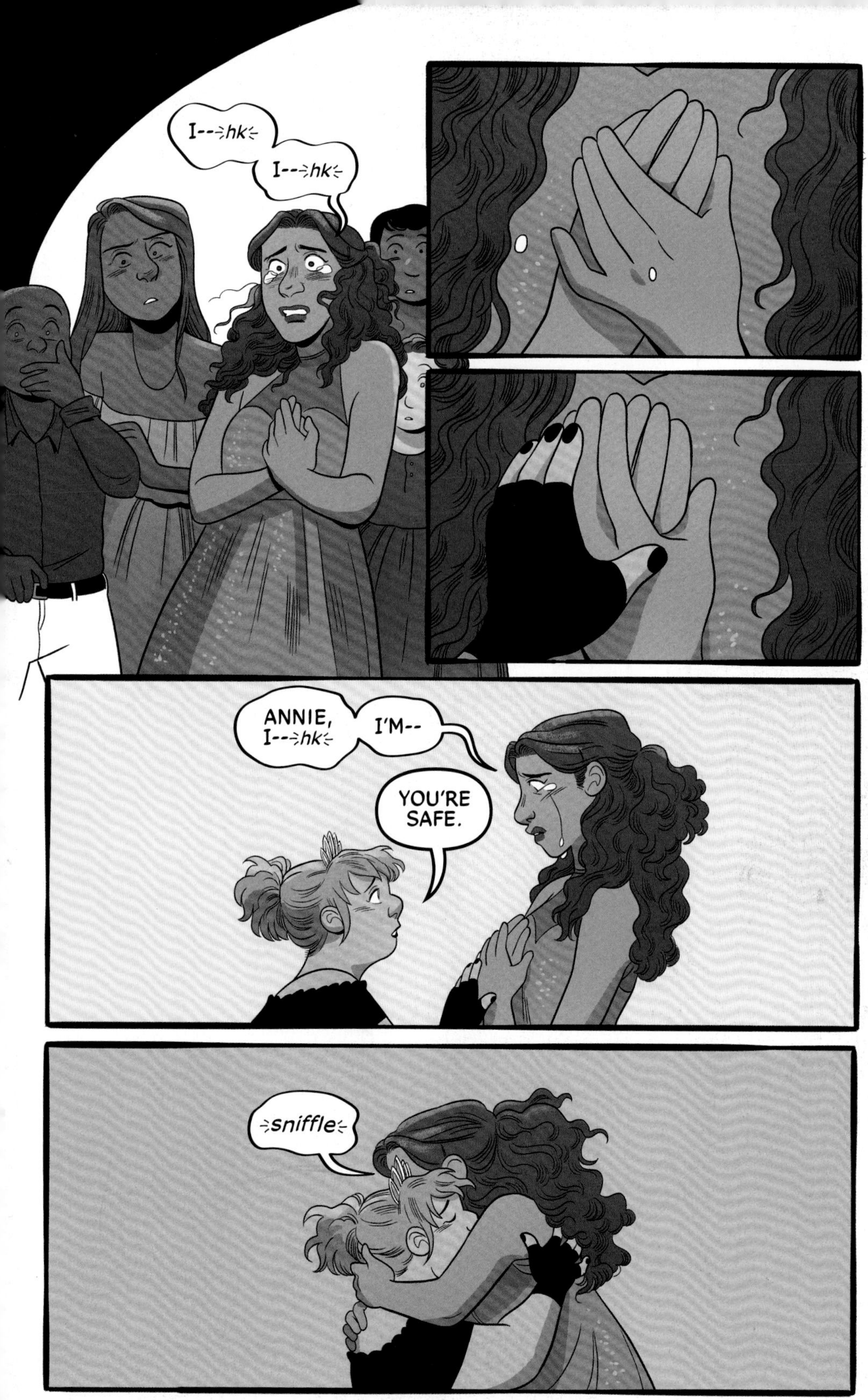
I--⫶hk⫶
I--⫶hk⫶
ANNIE, I--⫶hk⫶
I'M--
YOU'RE SAFE.
⫶sniffle⫶

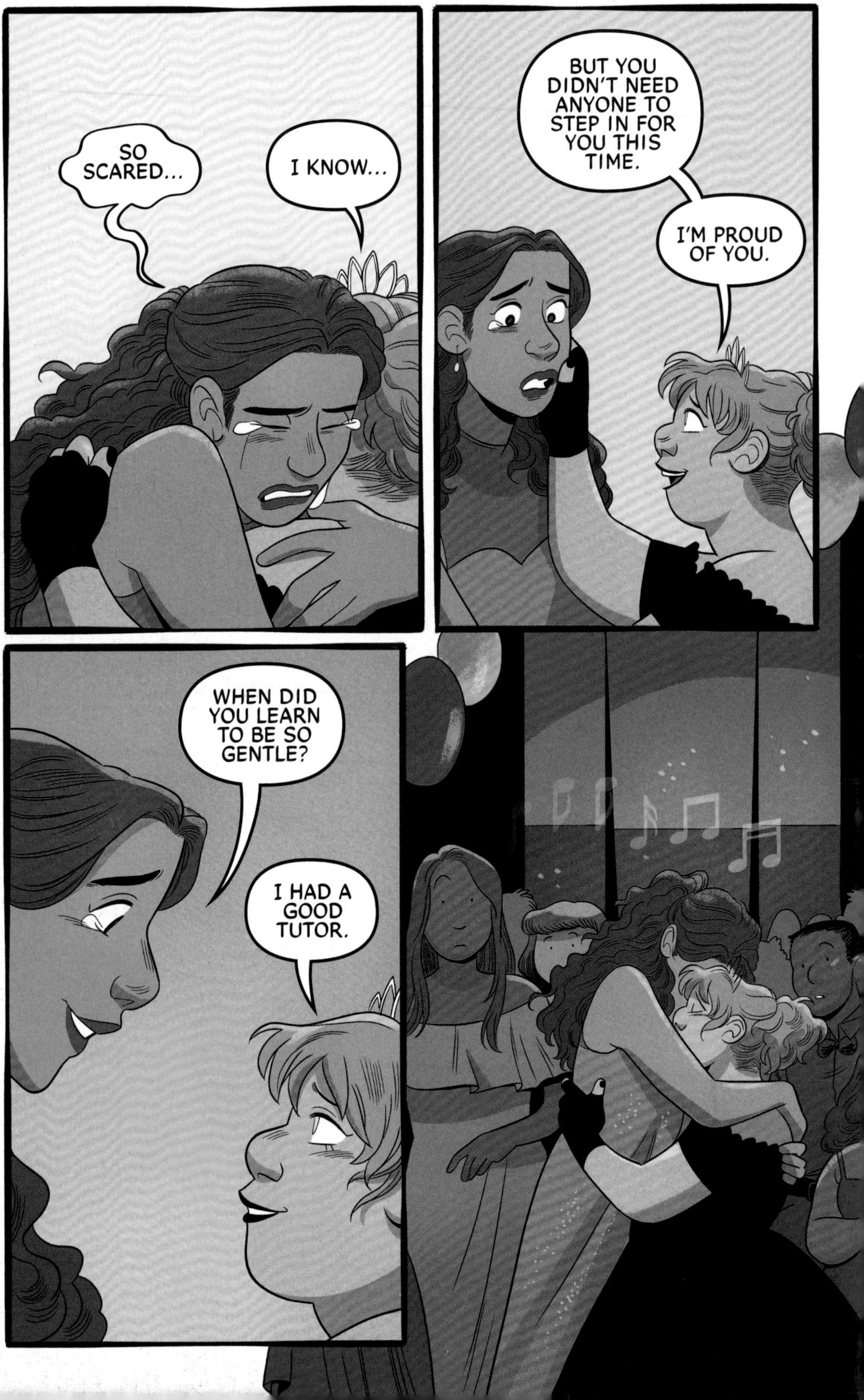
SO SCARED...
I KNOW...
BUT YOU DIDN'T NEED ANYONE TO STEP IN FOR YOU THIS TIME.
I'M PROUD OF YOU.
WHEN DID YOU LEARN TO BE SO GENTLE?
I HAD A GOOD TUTOR.

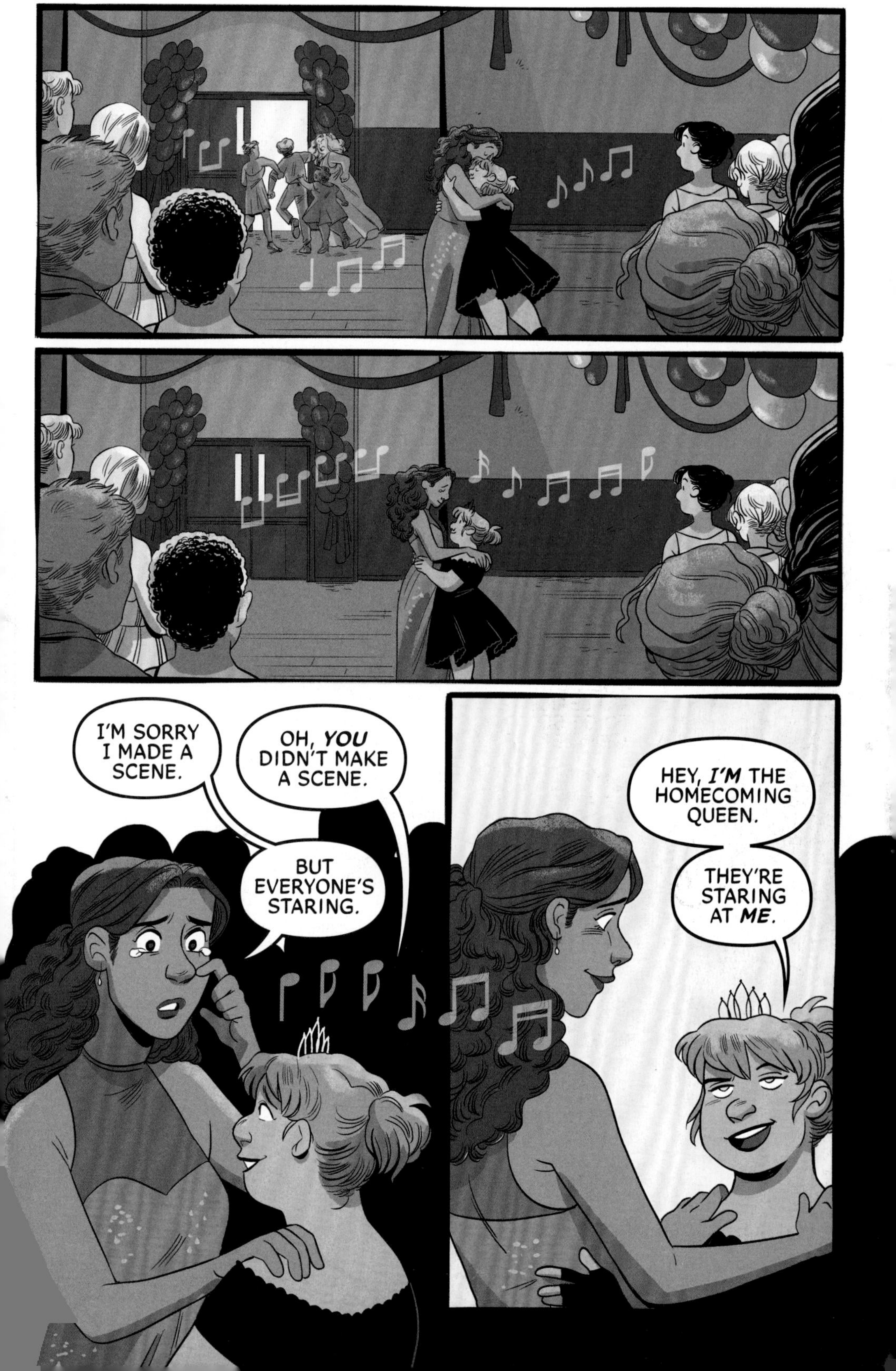
I'M SORRY I MADE A SCENE.
OH, *YOU* DIDN'T MAKE A SCENE.
BUT EVERYONE'S STARING.
HEY, *I'M* THE HOMECOMING QUEEN.
THEY'RE STARING AT *ME*.

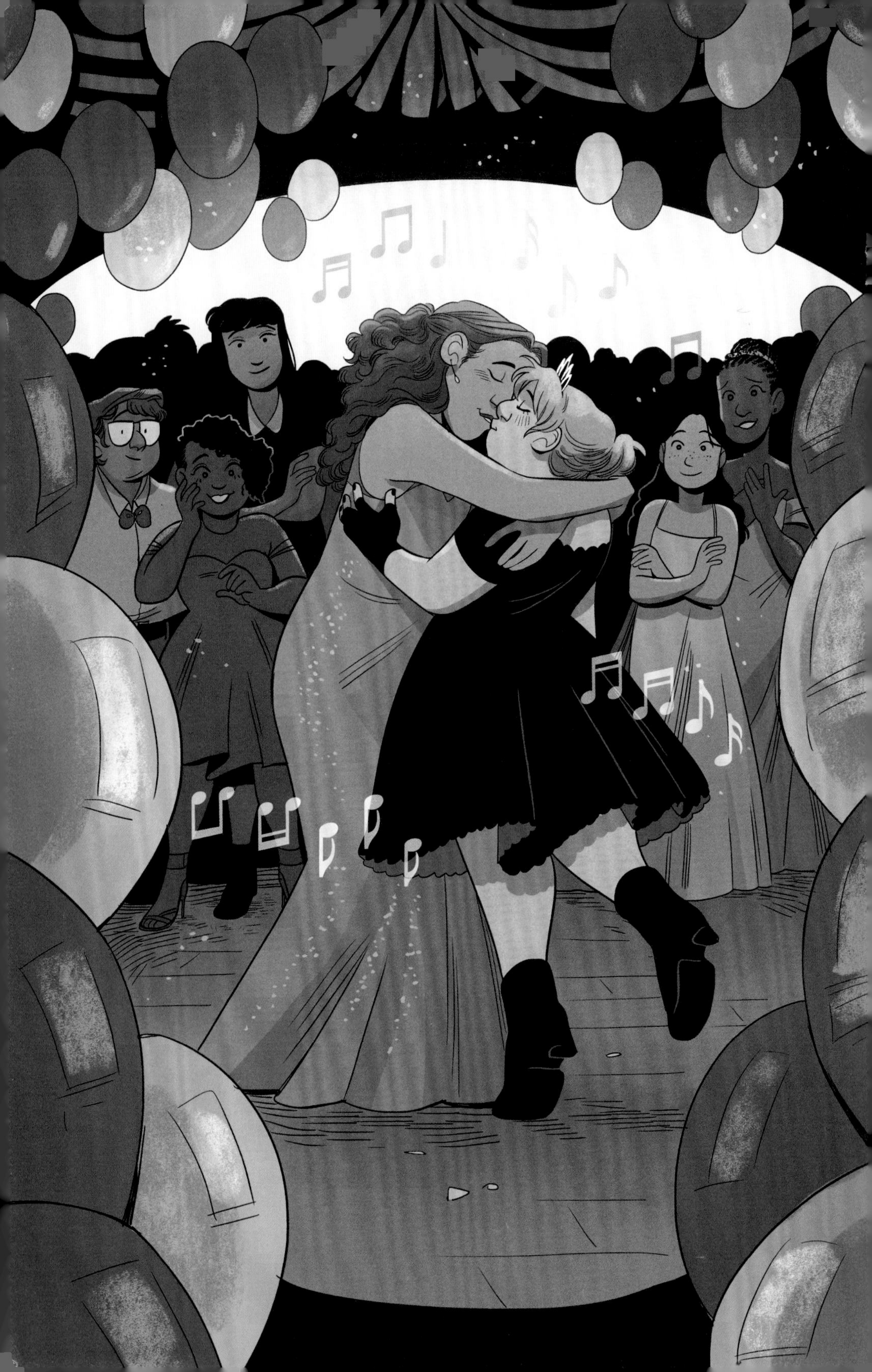

The End

RECIPES!

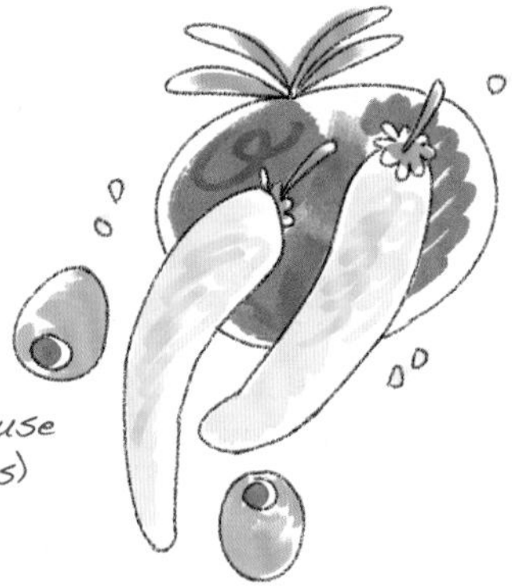

ABUELA'S ROPA VIEJA

INGREDIENTS

2 tbsp vegetable oil
2-3 pounds chuck roast
~~1 tsp~~ salt *(use 2 tsp?)*
2 large yellow onions, chopped
4 cloves garlic, chopped ← *(Dad says use 8. I say 4 is fine because I like having friends)*
1 red pepper, seeded and chopped
2 banana peppers, seeded and chopped *(maybe an Anaheim pepper instead?)*
4 cups water
1 cup brown beer *(if dad says it's okay)*
2 tbsp tomato paste
½ cup sour orange juice ← *(use ¼ cup orange juice and ¼ cup lime juice if the store is out)*
½ cup olive brine
1 tbsp cumin
1 tsp black pepper
2 bay leaves
1 cup Spanish olives, halved
½ cup raisins

Trim the fat from the roast and cut it into 1-inch cubes. Quickly brown the beef in hot oil over high heat in 3-4 batches. Pull out all the beef with tongs and pour in the chopped onions, garlic, and salt, and use them to scrub the little brown bits off the bottom of the pan. Cook 3-5 minutes until the onions are translucent. Add water, orange juice, beer, tomato paste, olive brine, cumin, peppers, and bay leaves.

Reduce to low heat and simmer for at least an hour. *Two or three is better.*

Smash the beef into little shreds with your cooking spoon. Add the olives and raisins and simmer for another half hour. *Dad likes to add cubed potatoes and frozen corn now, too, but Abuela never did that.*

Serve over yellow rice or arepas.

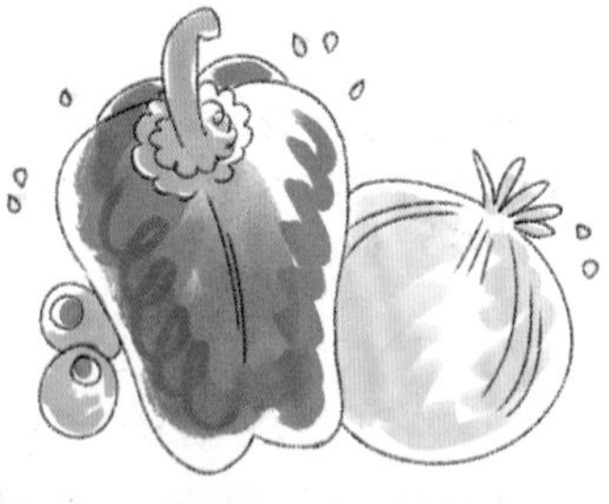

STRAWBERRY SHORTCAKE

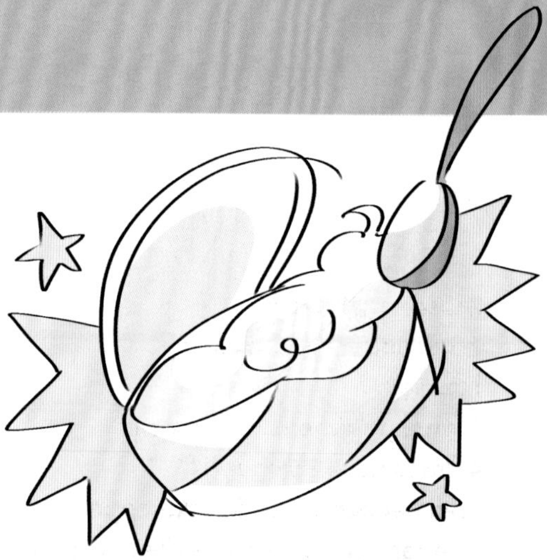

FOR STRAWBERRIES:

1 banana *(gotta get your potassium)*
1 pound strawberries, sliced thin
2 tablespoons sugar
Pinch of salt

FOR CAKE:

3 cups flour *(AP works good)*
¾ cup sugar *(or ½ if you're not a baby)*
2 tablespoons baking powder
1 teaspoon salt
1 cup butter *(cut into little cubes; put in freezer for like 20 minutes)*
1 cup milk
1 teaspoon apple cider vinegar *(I wanna try balsamic vinegar, but that stuff's expensive!)*

For strawberries: Toss the strawberries in sugar (and banana). Seal in a bowl and leave in the refrigerator for at least an hour. Add a pinch of salt and let rest another half hour. You wanna get nuts? Add a half teaspoon of black pepper to your strawberries, but no banana. You're welcome.

For shortcake: These are basically sweet biscuits. Preheat oven to 425. Combine the dry ingredients in a large bowl. Add butter and mash together with a pastry cutter or forks until it's lots of tiny butter chunks covered in flour. Add milk and vinegar and knead together just enough to bring it together. Roll it to half an inch thick.

OR BETTER WAY: Freeze half your butter as a stick instead of chopping it. Grate it in a cheese grater. Cut in the cubed butter and mix in milk. Roll it out gently. Sprinkle on half your grated butter. Fold it over twice. Roll it thin again, sprinkle on the rest of butter, fold it over twice again. Roll it out to a half inch.

Cut biscuits (Use a drinking glass). Arrange side-by-side on a baking sheet. Bake for 15 minutes or until golden brown. *FIRST: brush down with a little more milk and sprinkle with some extra sugar. Because, sugar.*

Once your biscuits are done, put it all together. Cut open a biscuit, add your strawberries and bananas, top the biscuit, add more fruit. Spray on plenty of whipped cream. Get some whipped cream, or make it yourself if you're someone's gramma.

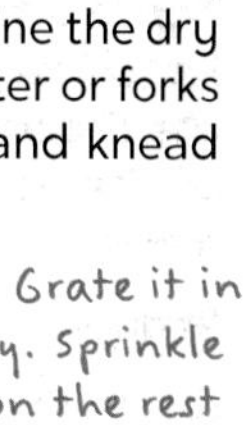

CRYSTAL FRASIER

Crystal Frasier is a girl from small-town Florida who now has twenty years' experience writing for comics, fiction, and games. She has contributed to major brands like Pathfinder and Dungeons & Dragons, as well as small-press projects and anthologies, but she got her start self-publishing transgender-focused webcomics. Today, Crystal is the proud mama of two energetic corgis, Calamity and Adamant.

VAL WISE

Val Wise is a cartoonist originally from Clearwater Beach, Florida. He's contributed to a handful of anthologies, including *Dates!* and *Wayward Kindred*, as well as projects like *Rolled & Told*. He currently lives in the Southern U.S. with his husband, two best friends, and two talkative cats named Biscotti and Ciabatta.